SANDRA EPISCOPO KENDALL was born in Rome of Italian parents. While still a baby, the family moved to India. She was educated in Bombay and Geneva. After school, she was employed by the Italian diplomatic service at the Consulate General in Bombay. In 1960 she moved to Rome and worked in the film business for producer Carlo Ponti, among others. While on a short visit to Bombay she met and married her husband, a Scottish businessman, and ex-Japanese prisoner-of-war. Her two sons were born in Bombay, and the family moved to England in 1968. For twenty-five years she worked at three different Cambridge Colleges, Kings, Corpus Christi and Pembroke. Following her husband's death, she moved to Bristol. She enrolled in two residential Arvon Foundation courses at Lumb Bank where her tutor, the author, David Almond, encouraged her to keep writing. She has travelled widely between India, Italy, Switzerland, Spain, UK, and South Africa. She now lives in the Cotswolds.

Peacocks in the Mist

Sandra Episcopo Kendall

Published in 2019 by SilverWood Books

SilverWood Books Ltd
14 Small Street, Bristol, BS1 1DE, United Kingdom
www.silverwoodbooks.co.uk

Copyright © Sandra Episcopo Kendall 2019

The right of Sandra Episcopo Kendall to be identified as the author of this work has been asserted in accordance with the Copyright, Designs and Patents Act 1988 Sections 77 and 78.

All rights reserved. No part of this publication may be reproduced,
stored in a retrieval system, or transmitted in any form or by any means,
electronic, mechanical, photocopying, recording or otherwise,
without prior permission of the copyright holder.

This is a work of fiction. Names, characters, places and incidents either are products of the author's imagination or are used fictitiously. Any resemblance to actual events or locales or persons, living or dead, is entirely coincidental.

ISBN 978-1-78132-842-2 (paperback)
ISBN 978-1-78132-907-8 (ebook)

British Library Cataloguing in Publication Data
A CIP catalogue record for this book is available from
the British Library

Page design and typesetting by SilverWood Books
Printed on responsibly sourced paper

For Nicholas and Anthony
for Bianca and Bruce
for Stef, Joanne and Katy
and for FDT

Book One

1

Rome, 1994

Sister Clotilda was having her driving lesson, practising three-point turns in the long dusty driveway of the Convento Santa Teresa that stood in ten fertile acres on the outskirts of Rome. Sister Agatha, another learner, was relegated to the back seat, in accordance with the convent rule that sisters must always travel in pairs. Even during driving lessons.

Minnie Dubash watched them from the shaded balcony of her first-floor room in the residents' section of the convent. The dark blue Fiat Uno 1.6, with a grey scrape mark on the front offside bumper, was Minnie's pride and joy until the day some five years earlier when she found herself driving the wrong way up a one-way street. Summoned to court, she was fined two hundred and fifty thousand lire, and was banned from driving for six months. The *magistrato*, in a kind but firm tone, advised her that at the age of seventy-four she needed an eye test and medical certificate before her licence could be considered for renewal.

Minnie was contrite and apologetic, but inwardly she quaked. At the time of the incident her Italian licence showed her age as seventy-four. However, years earlier she had contrived to drop a cup of coffee on her previous licence, after which the replacement showed the year of her birth to be 1914 instead of 1904. If the *magistrato* had discovered that she was eighty-four who knows how high the fine might have been.

In the end, fear and common sense prevailed. Swallowing her pride, she decided during the six-month ban that the time had come to hang up her car keys. She gifted her beloved baby to the convent. Her generosity came with a proviso. The nuns were to drive her once a week to her appointment with Filippo, the hairdresser, and afterwards for a spot of shopping. On these occasions she would, of course, occupy the front passenger seat.

Minnie watched with interest as Sister Clotilda made a hash of it. The car stuttered down the cypress-lined drive towards the small shrine to the Virgin Mary a few metres inside the wrought-iron entrance gates. The nun made an uncertain three-point turn, sending showers of gravel on to the grass. Up the drive the car travelled, jerking to a stop short of the steps leading to the front door and depositing a further scattering of dusty pebbles on the smooth granite treads. In the back seat, Sister Agatha clutched the broom used for sweeping the steps clean at the end of the lesson. She waved to Minnie from the rear window as the car reversed, turned and made its way once more towards the shrine.

Each week Minnie observed their performance, and dispensed advice, commiseration and chocolates when they came to her later for a progress report. The two nuns were Indian. They had the added disadvantage of not understanding the harassed Italian instructor.

Over the years, the convent's function had evolved from convalescent to residential home for the elderly. The change took place at the time when Minnie's great friend, Sister Serafina, was its Mother Superior, and proved most successful in commercial terms. At seventy-five Mother Serafina retired and returned to the rank of Sister and was put in charge of the organic vegetable garden.

The convent had become Minnie's home, her sanctuary, her security. It was where she felt protected and safe. It had been a long journey getting there.

By six o'clock Minnie had finished the customary preparations for expected and unexpected visitors. She checked the small dresser next to her armchair to see all was in place. A silver tray with four glasses, a bottle of Gordon's gin, one red vermouth – Sister Serafina's favourite tipple – an ashtray and a twelve-year-old Glenlivet for when the convent's doctor dropped in after his fortnightly health visit to the nuns. Father Mario too, following his weekly session at the confessional, appreciated the malt. Exhausted from her inspection, she sank into her armchair, put on her distance specs, and switched on the TV for the evening news. Within five minutes she had nodded off, her glasses sliding from her nose on to her lap.

At a quarter to seven, a rapping on the door awoke Minnie from her doze. She reached for her spectacles, adjusted her hearing aid and greeted Sister Serafina, who entered firing a rapid, *'Buona sera*, Minnie.' She waddled to the window next to Minnie's seat and stretched on tiptoe to push open the shutters. A soft mauve light flooded the room. She paused to take in the glorious shades of the late May sky and together she and Minnie gazed at the wide garden with an air of satisfaction.

The design was formal with geometric beds bursting with fresh young colours: irises, peonies, roses, the first hydrangeas, and azaleas. Ancient lemon trees in huge terracotta pots drew the eye towards the vegetable plots at the far end. Weeds abounded in the borders and the gravel. Close to the building a wisteria-covered pergola formed an area of shade to sit in. A thicket of pink bougainvillea half concealed an artificial grotto, home to a small blue and white statue of the Madonna. Pencil-slim cypress trees flanking a gravel walkway poked straight and black into the pale evening sky. The scent of a jasmine below the window filled the room. Beyond the vegetable plots lay the convent's long fields of pale green wheat and corn, bounded by a line of Mediterranean pines like a row of fat paintbrushes. The sun dipped behind a rise of hills thickly painted with the white and ochre of recent housing developments. A rosy glow floated like a veil over the landscape.

'Ah, *carissima* Minnie, each evening our good Lord gives us this miracle of beauty.' Sister Serafina spoke fast in a high, clear voice, the words tumbling as if chased out of her mouth. She turned to Minnie with a look of resignation. 'I fear it may be harder for him to perform a miracle for Sister Clotilda to pass her driving test. Just think, she has had forty-five lessons, poor girl, and still she will not venture beyond the gates of this convent!' She sighed, settled her plump rear on an upright armchair, her feet barely touching the floor, and leaned back, placing her hands under the tabard of her grey habit.

Minnie cleared her throat. 'There's no doubt Clotilda is better at cooking than she is at driving. Now, Serafina, may I offer you a drink?' She fluttered a slim hand in the direction of the silver tray.

'Just a small vermouth and ice perhaps, if you insist – it has been so warm today. Don't you move, dearest Minnie, I will pour it. May I get you a gin and tonic?'

'Too kind. I think I will tonight, thank you,' replied Minnie, who with her arthritic joints had no intention of making a move, fully expecting to be waited on. 'You're right, it is not usual to be as humid as this for May.'

Minnie watched Sister Serafina with affection as she prepared the drinks. *What energy she has still,* she thought. *What would I have done without her friendship and loyalty? When I think back to the time we first met – was it as long ago as 1928? – she was dancing the tarantella, her skirts and rosary and veil flying around like mad things!*

'You have a big smile on your face, Minnie. What wicked thoughts are you thinking?' Serafina asked, placing the G and T on a side table.

Minnie laughed. 'I was just picturing you as you danced the tarantella. Wouldn't surprise me if you were still able to do it.'

Serafina chuckled. 'Not as fast as I did once, but I could still teach the younger ones a step or two.'

They looked at each other with fondness, two old friends with a lot of history between them. They raised their glasses, sipped the drinks, and with the usual proprieties out of the way, Minnie felt able to get down to brass tacks. After all, she had waited all week to learn about the arrangements for her ninetieth birthday celebration the coming weekend.

'Serafina, is everything in order for tomorrow and Saturday? Did my granddaughter phone you?'

'Don't worry, it's all been taken care of. Francesca is a clever, organised girl. I didn't have to arrange a thing – she has it all in hand,' Sister Serafina rattled on without pausing for breath. 'She plans to go straight from the airport to the TV studios in Piazza Mazzini to pick up some equipment for the interview. What with traffic and one thing and another, I doubt you will see her here until after five o'clock tomorrow.'

'What about her room?' Minnie broke in while Serafina took a breather. 'Oh, and did she say if she was coming alone? And who will take me to the hairdresser tomorrow?' Minnie's agitation penetrated her outward composure.

'*Cara* Minnie.' A reassuring smile creased Serafina's dumpling face. 'It is all arranged. Sister Agnes will drive you to the hairdresser tomorrow for your comb-out. Francesca is bringing a cameraman from London, Dominic something or other. I don't know if he is the boyfriend or not. These days one no longer understands the language – boyfriend, friend, partner, it's all the same,' she puffed. 'I've put Francesca in a room along the corridor from you. As for Dominic, I found him a nice room next to Signora Melotti.'

Minnie coughed behind her hand to disguise a giggle. Signora Melotti was as plain as dough and stone deaf, and her room on the third floor at the back of the building was just about as far as it was possible to be from Francesca's room. *Serafina is still incredibly prim and unsubtle,* Minnie thought. *As if distance is going to stop Francesca and Dominic sharing a bed if they want to. Distance never stopped me, for sure.*

'Serafina, you are a wonder, you think of everything, thank you. But what about Saturday, what are the arrangements for the interview?' Anxiety crept back into Minnie's voice. 'I must confess I am nervous. I wish I had never agreed to being interviewed.'

'I understand,' the nun replied with a kind smile. 'Do you remember what you had to face when the scandal broke all those years ago in Bombay? This will be nothing in comparison. Besides you're doing it for Francesca. She's a wonderful journalist; sensitive and tactful, not like some.' Serafina paused to take another mouthful of her drink. 'I can scarcely believe I was at her christening in India in nineteen sixty-something – when was it?'

Minnie recalled it well. 'March 1964, and a sweltering day it was. I remember the tea party in the garden under the banyan tree. Poor mite never stopped howling because of her prickly heat. Claudia had to take off her lovely christening dress. Most of the photos show her stark naked, as if her parents couldn't afford a decent robe.'

When a half-hour was up Sister Serafina heaved herself out of the chair, her black rosary beads jangling against the bunch of keys at her waist.

'Your meal will be here any minute. Father Mario may be in to see you later.' She bent to plant a kiss on Minnie's cheek. 'I'll say a special prayer for you, but don't worry about the interview. Our good Lord will protect you.'

After Minnie finished her meal, a knock on the door announced the arrival of Father Mario, her favourite among the priests who attended the convent. Minnie was always happy in his company. He was young and good-looking. She was sure women had made passes at him and wondered if he'd ever been tempted. She was so grateful that he didn't talk about religion all the time, as the other boring old chap had done.

She knew Father Mario was a keen runner and couldn't help admiring his athletic build, which the black soutane could not hide. After greeting her, he helped himself to the Glenlivet and settled into a chair. They exchanged news and mild gossip. 'Do you know what Francesca has planned for your birthday?' he asked.

'I don't. Francesca is keeping things from me, as if I were a child. I think she has asked the kitchens to prepare something special for tomorrow night, but I'm not supposed to know about it. Serafina won't tell me a thing.' Minnie sounded exasperated; she always wanted to be the first to know what was going on. 'In any case, I shall be too exhausted to enjoy myself. I'm having my hair done in the morning and Francesca arrives in the afternoon, so there will be no time for my siesta.'

'Oh, come now, I'm sure you'll manage,' Father Mario chuckled with the familiarity of one used to Minnie's peppery outbursts. 'What else has she organised?'

'Francesca has already told me. We're going to lunch at Il Casale. She's invited a couple of my friends too.'

'What about your daughter and your son?'

'Claudia lives in Geneva and Roberto in Cambridge, but they will come with their families in the summer for a delayed celebration.' She reached for an olive from the dish on the side table. 'Anyway, I'm looking forward to lunch on Saturday. I haven't been to Il Casale for years. Perhaps you'd care to join us, Father?'

'I'd be delighted. I'm extremely fond of the place.' He drained his glass and got up. 'Before I go, do you wish to make your confession this week?' he asked, as he always did.

Minnie giggled, delighted at his persistence, part of the game they played. 'Not this week, Father. What sins do you think I can get up to at my age? Forty years ago, I could have burnt your ears with sins of the flesh. But now,' she shrugged, 'I can't give you even the smallest sin of greed since I've no appetite these days. Still, be sure to ask me again next week. I have a feeling you may be in luck then.'

'Really?' Father Mario's interest was aroused. 'What are you up to? Have you got some naughty plan afoot?' he teased.

'No, nothing planned, but...' she hesitated. 'I don't know, it's just a feeling a skeleton or two may pop up at the feast.'

Lying in bed that night waiting for sleep, Minnie wondered why she had mentioned skeletons. An aberration, a Freudian slip, perhaps? Skeletons hadn't been on her mind in recent times. More like ghosts, if truth were told. Ever since her bout of bronchitis last winter she saw them from time to time. Of course, she told no one, because she knew it could not be. Of course not. Absolutely not...and yet, she had seen Edoardo only a little while ago. She sighed. There was no question about it: he was sitting at the end of her bed. What a surprise. It was fifteen years since she'd last seen him. He asked after the children and grandchildren and seemed delighted at their achievements. Thank goodness their divorce had been amicable and Edoardo had always maintained good relations with Claudia and Bobby.

She had also seen Franco two or three times, the favourite of all her four brothers. He looked fit, his emphysema quite disappeared. She asked about Clara, his wife, but apparently, she was still mad at Franco for his infidelities and refused to talk to him. Only last week Minnie saw dearest Dolly, her best friend. It was at a distance and they didn't speak. And of course, she had seen her beloved Paolo, but that didn't count because they often spoke.

Minnie sighed again and turned over in bed trying to find a comfortable position. The pain was always worse at night. *Oh dear! What a jumble*, she thought. *Best not mention any of this to anyone. They'll think I'm losing my marbles.* Drowsiness settled as she reflected on her ghosts. *I don't mind seeing them. They don't frighten me.* She switched off the bedside light.

But please God, the one I don't want to see is Darius.

2

Late the next afternoon, Minnie took up her position on the balcony. Seated in a cane armchair she came well prepared for a long wait with her knitting and a small pair of binoculars on a table next to her. From this position she had a clear view of the front steps and the long driveway leading to the entrance gates. She was dressed in black linen trousers and a silk top. She liked dark colours – navy, grey, chocolate – but black was her favourite. She knew how well the colour suited her, set off by her olive skin and silver hair, cut and styled that morning. This time she had chosen to complete the outfit with a cherry silk over-shirt. When Francesca drove in from the entrance gate, she would not be able to miss the splash of bright colour against the faded ochre building.

The heat of the day had warmed the smooth wall behind Minnie's seat. To keep herself busy she was knitting a grey scarf for one of the nuns. She rubbed the callus on her right forefinger formed by years of wrapping wool round it. Her hands used to be much admired. She examined them as she worked. They were all knobbly knuckles now and painful. She dropped a stitch and frowned while picking it up. She tried to remember how many jumpers she had made for the grandchildren when they were little. Now of course they didn't think it was trendy to have hand-knitted stuff. The soft wool slipped through her fingers.

She lifted her head to listen, her hearing aid turned to full volume. She could just about hear the drone of the convent's tractor in the field behind Serafina's vegetable plots and smell the diesel. She picked up the binoculars and focussed briefly on two nuns doing their stint of hoeing between the rows of zucchini. With spectacles pushed up on her head she continued to knit, but from time to time settled them on to her nose to peer in the direction of the entrance gate. Nothing. A dog barked. Somewhere a radio was playing a Neapolitan song by Roberto Murolo – a real oldie. The sweet scent from the potted oleanders below the balcony drifted upwards, and a distant buzzing grew louder as a small twin-engine plane passed overhead. A couple of cars arrived at the front steps, churning up small clouds of dust. Francesca was not in either of them.

Minnie was about to go inside to make a cup of lemon tea when she heard a car scrunching up the drive, toot-tooting the horn. She leant forward to watch it approaching. A bare arm stuck out of the driver's window and waved. Minnie smiled and waved back. At last. The car skidded to a halt in front of the steps, the door opened and a pair of long legs in dark blue jeans swung out of the driver's side. Francesca stood up, smoothed one hand over windblown blonde hair and raised the other in greeting.

'Ciao, Nonna, here I am at last,' she shouted. 'Bet you thought we'd never make it tonight.' She pointed towards the passenger door. 'This is Dominic. You'll meet him later. I'll drop my bags inside. See you in a few minutes.'

Minnie gathered up the knitting and went inside, ready to greet Francesca.

'Nonnina, my darling, how are you?' Francesca rushed into the room laden with flowers. 'Shall I put these in the bathroom? I can arrange them later.' She deposited the flowers before kissing Minnie on both cheeks. Minnie inhaled the lemony scent of her perfume, young and crisp.

'Thanks for the flowers, sweetheart. Anemones, my favourites. So sweet of you to remember.' She gave Francesca a tight hug. 'It is lovely to see you at last, darling. I do believe you've lost a bit of weight.'

'I wish it were true,' Francesca said, settling on a footstool at Minnie's feet. 'You're looking wonderful, Nonna. Elegant as always. Just look at you – nobody would imagine you're ninety.' She squeezed Minnie's hand. 'You look so young with your marvellous skin, not like mine, full of pimples.' She pulled a face, pointing at an imperceptible spot on her forehead. 'Now, tell me the latest gossip around here. What's been happening? Is the handyman, what's his name, still in love with you? Poor chap, you shouldn't encourage him. I bet you never let him win at cards!'

'Shush, Francesca, stop teasing, naughty girl,' Minnie scolded, delighted with the cheekiness of her pretty granddaughter. Her English was good, though heavily accented and somewhat rusty from lack of practice. 'You're just a big flatterer, and you've no respect for my age. In any case it's not true – I let him win last week. Besides, he likes coming to see me, it keeps him young. Let's talk about you. How long are you staying?'

'I'll stay here at the convent for two nights in order to do the interview. Then I'll have a night or two at Mum's flat in town before flying back to London. Now let me tell you what I've arranged for tonight and tomorrow.'

Minnie was eager to hear the plans.

'I know you get tired in the evenings, so we'll eat in tonight. Dominic will join us – you'll like him. I've arranged to have your favourite *penne alla Calabrese* and cassata ice cream for dessert.' Francesca poured herself a glass of mineral water. 'As for tomorrow, I've booked a table for lunch at one o'clock at Il Casale. Your friends the Rossis and the Donatis will meet us there. Afterwards you can come back here for a nap before we start the first part of the interview at, say, six o'clock. Will that suit you?'

Minnie was thrilled. She smiled and squeezed Francesca's hand. 'Darling, what a wonderful surprise. I haven't been to Il Casale for years – it used to be my favourite place. You are sweet to remember. I hope you don't mind, but I asked Father Mario to join us.' Minnie fumbled with her hearing aid, adjusting the sound level. She picked up the knitting, stuck the needles through the ball of grey wool and placed it in the floral bag hooked over the arm of her chair. 'Listen, Francesca dear, about the interview. I'm nervous. I don't know if it's the right thing to do. Raking over the past, I mean.'

Francesca patted her knee. 'Nonna, you know I'll be discreet. If you're too troubled or uncomfortable with any question, I'll stop. In any case, we can edit things out later.'

'Okay. I've said I'll do it, so of course I will go ahead. Meanwhile there is something I want to show you. Pull out the top drawer in the dresser.'

'The one with all the photos on it?'

'That's it. There's a key in a small tin behind one of the frames. Open the drawer and bring me the carved wooden box inside.'

Francesca examined the photos on the dresser. 'You've got a proper rogues gallery of the family here, Nonna! I haven't seen my christening pictures for years. Black and white photos look rather stylish, don't you think? That's me with Mum and Dad and Andrew. Why have I got no clothes on? It must have been very hot.' She picked up another frame. 'And here we've got Uncle Bobby and his family. Where was that taken?'

'I think it was in Cambridge. Roberto had just been posted there.' It was clear that Francesca enjoyed looking at the photos. 'If you want, darling, we can go through my old albums tomorrow.'

'Sure, if there's time.' Francesca turned to face Minnie. 'Tell me, why are there no pictures of you with Grandpa Edoardo, or with Darius?'

Minnie looked vague – a device she tended to use in order to avoid awkward questions.

'Well, *tesoro mio*, you know, I wasn't lucky with my husbands. I want to have happy memories around me. I want my visitors to see my family. They get to know them, they ask questions: how is she doing, what is he doing, is this one married? – which is the question they always ask about you.' She looked Francesca squarely in the eyes.

'Oh, come on, Nonna, not you too!'

'What have I said? All I'm telling you is what other people ask.'

'Well, you can tell them that people don't have to get married these days. We have careers, we have relationships. Ceremonies and pieces of paper don't mean anything. They don't make people happy. Marriage didn't bring you happiness, did it?'

'That's a hard thing to say, dear.' Minnie turned her head to look out of the window. 'Of course, you're right, it didn't bring me great happiness.' She paused, choosing her next words with care. 'You know, it may sound strange, but marriage gave me freedom. It took me away from an unhappy background, and best of all it gave me my children. They were my greatest joy. In those days it was impossible – quite unacceptable, I'd say – to have children outside marriage. It's quite a different matter today. Now bring me that box, please,' she said firmly, changing the subject.

Francesca opened the drawer and picked up the large box. In doing so she dislodged a small photo frame lying on its lid. It showed a black and white photograph of a young man of film-star good looks, with a thin face, deep-set dark eyes and a half-smile under a narrow black moustache. Written across the bottom, in faded ink, were a few words: *To my own Minnie, with love always and for ever.* The signature was half hidden by the frame.

'Nonna, isn't this Darius? I've not seen one of him as young as this,' Francesca asked as she brought the box to Minnie and settled herself on the stool once more.

Minnie became flustered. She hadn't meant for Francesca to see that picture. 'Yes, that's Darius, taken at the time he was courting me. I forget you never met him.'

Francesca stared at it. 'Wow! He was gorgeous. No wonder you fell for him!' She seemed fascinated with his image. 'The ones I've seen during my research don't look a bit like this. They were taken later of course, when he was much heavier, and with long grey hair.'

Minnie looked at the photo in silence. She swallowed hard. Francesca handed her the box.

'Yes, he changed a lot after his…his illness.' Minnie sighed. 'I want you to take this box when you go. There are almost two hundred letters Darius wrote to me, most of them before we were married, but some during the time he was ill.' She rubbed an aching knuckle. 'I want them burned after my death. I've left instructions in my last testament. Your mother knows about this, she is a…how do you say? An executor of my will.'

'It rather feels as if I'd be intruding into something too private.'

Minnie smiled. 'Of all my family you have always been the most curious about my life, forever trying to drag things out of me about what it was like when I was growing up.' She shrugged. 'Well, I didn't like talking about my unhappy childhood, so I only told you about the strange or amusing happenings.'

Francesca laughed. 'Yes, I remember some of the funny stories you told, like when your brother hid hard-boiled eggs under the sideboard because he hated eating them.'

Minnie nodded, and held out the box. 'Well, that's why I want you to have these. To tell you the truth, it was your mother who suggested they might be useful to you as background for the interview. You should read them. But you must promise that no one else will see them.'

Francesca stroked the tissue-thin skin of Minnie's hand. 'Darling Nonna, I don't know what to say. I feel privileged that you should put this trust in me. They'll be a great help I'm sure and I promise not to show them to anyone.'

They sat in comfortable silence, each with their thoughts. Minnie had always felt a particularly close bond with this granddaughter.

'Has my mother seen the letters?'

Minnie shook her head. 'No. Of course she knows they exist, but I never let her read them.'

'Why me, then?' Francesca looked surprised.

Minnie shrugged. 'I think it's because of the generational difference. She was present while I went through that time. I don't think she'd have enough objectivity. It seems right that you should be the one. Dearly as I love Claudia, I feel more at ease with you than I do with her.'

'Isn't it strange? I feel the same way about you.' Francesca smiled. She slipped the photo frame into the box and placed it by her handbag. She touched Minnie's knee. 'Now, would you like me to explain how we plan the programme and the interview routine?'

Minnie had been waiting for this. Francesca explained how, over the next three years, the BBC was planning a series of programmes on India leading up to the fiftieth anniversary celebrations of Indian Independence in 1997. She had been asked to make a documentary on Darius Dubash, on his poetry, his posthumous award of the Emily Dickinson Prize and his rise to cult figure many years after his tragic death, following the issue, several years later, of several unpublished works, anonymously donated.

Francesca said she would begin by talking about Darius's body of work, how it fitted into modern Indian literature and would introduce his estranged widow, whose existence the public had quite forgotten.

When Francesca came to fetch her to take her out for lunch the next day, Minnie was looking her best, and her best even at her age was quite impressive. A touch of lipstick and blusher, a spray of Diorissimo, her aquamarine earrings and matching dress ring, and a thick gold necklace completed her chocolate silk trouser suit.

Francesca managed to find a parking spot close to the arched entrance of the converted farmhouse. In the early sixties Il Casale had been one of the most fashionable weekend eating places, a rural restaurant famous for its distinctive rustic meals. Both it and the nearby convent were favoured country retreats. In the intervening years, the city had spread its tentacles until now both restaurant and convent stood as little oases of greenery in the heart of a sprawling suburban conglomeration.

The place was buzzing as usual, with the kind of chaotic din found in popular Roman *trattorie*, where people come not to be seen, but to enjoy, admire and loudly praise the food and wine. Minnie was guided through the noisy crowd to their table in a corner of the shaded terrace where not only friends and Father Mario were already waiting but, to her delighted surprise, also Claudia with Hamish, and Roberto with his family.

It was a lovely atmosphere, everyone making a big fuss of Minnie, drinking toast after toast while the guitarist sang his special songs from Rome's Trastevere neighbourhood and a stream of mouth-watering dishes kept coming until they were fit to burst. By the time coffee appeared at the end of the meal, Minnie was ready to go back to the convent for a rest, tired but happy, her cheeks flushed with pleasure.

Francesca helped her to the room. 'Why don't we postpone the interview until tomorrow? We're both tired. Besides, I haven't had a chance to go through Darius's letters. I'd like to take my time over them.'

'That suits me. Thank you, my darling, for the most super time,' Minnie said, blowing a kiss. 'It has been the happiest of days.'

She settled on her bed and Francesca pulled a shawl over her feet. 'I'll see you tomorrow, *carissima*,' Minnie murmured drowsily.

*

The next day Francesca arrived at Minnie's room at ten.

'You're early, sweetie.'

'I hope you don't mind. When I was going through the letters last night, I found a few things that needed clarifying.'

'How can I help?'

'Darius writes beautifully. I can imagine falling in love with someone like that through his letters alone.'

Minnie smiled. 'He was most eloquent.'

'They seem to be sorted in batches, starting from 1940.' Francesca referred to a notepad. 'The tone in these letters is wonderfully lyrical, and some have little poems attached. But weren't you still married to Grandpa Edoardo then?'

'Edoardo and I had already separated at the time.'

Francesca looked at her notes again. 'A long gap follows and when the writing starts again the expression has changed. There is an undertone of anger throughout. I'd say a hint of remorse, perhaps?' Francesca looked at Minnie enquiringly.

Minnie stared into the middle distance. 'A lot was going wrong and Darius was going through a troubling time.'

'I won't ask now because I'm sure you'll talk about it in the interview. The last batch of letters dates between 1958 and 1962. A more peaceful quality emerges in these and he mentions poems attached to the letters, but I didn't find any. Didn't he send them?'

Minnie frowned. 'It was such a long time ago—' There was a sharp rap on the door and Dominic entered the room carrying a load of equipment.

'D'you mind, I've come to set up the camera and the lighting.'

'Carry on, Dom,' Francesca replied. 'I'll put some make-up on Nonna in the meantime.'

A few moments later Dominic said he was all set to go. Francesca made a final adjustment to Minnie's hair for the benefit of the camera and they were ready to start in earnest.

'There's one more thing before we begin.' Francesca gathered her notes and settled herself within range of the camera. 'For the purposes of the interview, may I address you as Minnie?'

Minnie nodded in agreement.

'Very well, Minnie it is.' Francesca turned around and waved a finger in the air. 'Okay, Dominic, let's go.'

Francesca stood to face the camera and began her preamble.

'This is Francesca Stuart in Rome for the BBC 'Arts Revival' programme. Today we shall be reviewing the works of Darius Dubash, the Indian poet, who died in tragic circumstances in 1964. Many reasons have been attributed to the motivation – the primary materials – so to say, for Darius Dubash's poetry. For instance, his commitment to protecting wildlife at a time when this was not considered to be a serious environmental issue as it is today. The fire with which he championed the protection of tribal peoples. Indeed, his frequent sexual passions, his excesses. There was, however, a darker side to this complex and gifted man. Not least the experiences of his breakdown, requiring him as it did to undergo years of treatment. Subsequently there came his slow climb out of the pits of darkness to the fragile plateau of equilibrium he found in his last years. Many people have spoken about their memories of this charming, talented man in his glory days. Few of them were around during his years of illness. No one knew him better than his wife throughout their marriage and even after their divorce. Nothing has been heard of her for almost thirty years and she has been forgotten. Most people assume she is dead. In fact, she is hale and hearty. Now in her ninetieth year she is about to break her long silence and has agreed to be interviewed. I am delighted to introduce her. She is my dear grandmother, Minnie Dubash.'

Francesca sat down and turned to Minnie as the camera panned in for a close-up.

'Minnie, you married Darius in 1942, is that correct?'

'That's right.'

'How long did the marriage last before you divorced?'

'We were married for seven years, after which we parted. But we were never divorced.'

Francesca was taken aback. 'Really? I naturally thought…'

'People assumed we were because we had been legally separated for a long time. I had often asked for a divorce, but he would never consent. He finally agreed to one after many years but died before the legal proceedings began.'

'Shall we come back to that later? For now, let's start at the beginning. Where and when did you first meet him?'

'I first met him in India briefly in 1929, and then again, almost by accident, shortly after the war broke out eleven years later.'

'You were born and brought up in Italy, in a strict, traditional way. What took you to India? Would it not have been extraordinary for a young single girl of your background to travel to the East in those days?'

'Oh absolutely. It was unheard of in my circles.'

'So, tell me, what were the circumstances that brought about this unusual and courageous decision?'

Minnie paused before replying. 'I suppose it began when I was eighteen – things happened to make me realise there would be great changes in my life.'

3

Rome, 1922

Maria Erminia Marapodi, eighteen years old and known to all as Minnie, lives with her parents and four brothers at the family home in Viale Regina Margherita, situated on the outer edge of a respectable middle-class residential area.

Minnie's tiny room in the Marapodi's first-floor apartment overlooks the cramped alleyway separating it from the next building. A narrow window and a door give on to a small balcony festooned with washing lines. It was originally intended as a maid's room, but the family cannot afford a live-in maid, and make do with a cleaning girl three mornings a week. In fact, Minnie often wonders how they could afford the apartment at all. Compared to their previous home in the small Calabrian town of Locri in South Italy, it is roomy and luxurious and a source of great pride to her iron-willed mother, Donna Rachele.

The spacious drawing room is furnished with rarely used, gleaming mahogany furniture covered in dustsheets that are removed only when visitors come. Two large windows looking on to the street are permanently shuttered ('so as not to fade the furniture,' Mamma decreed). Crystal chandeliers hang from the ceiling, an ornate Murano mirror dominates the mantelpiece flanked by two oil paintings, both the work of Donna Rachele's father, while the unused marble fireplace houses an empty brass planter. Although the room is spotless, it still manages to smell musty and stuffy.

A gleaming upright piano – Minnie's most hated piece of furniture – stands against one wall. Though no one else in the family plays an instrument, as a child she was forced to take detested music lessons, so she might entertain the infrequent guests when they did come. When her father, Don Peppino – a minor government official – was transferred from Locri to the Tax and Revenue Ministry in Rome, the shiny instrument, to Minnie's dismay, followed the family like a faithful dog.

The uncomfortable sofas and armchairs, upholstered in green plush, look as pristine under their dustcovers as the day they were purchased. As children Minnie and her brothers were never allowed to sit on them, for fear of wearing out the material. But on the occasions when she was locked in the room for an hour of piano practice, Minnie never missed the opportunity to bounce up and down on each one to try them out.

Minnie's eldest brother, Benedetto, known as Neddy, thirty years old, has a bedroom all to himself. When the family lived in the south, he shared a room – and often a bed – with his three brothers, Aldo, twenty-eight, Franco, twenty-six, and Salvatore, twenty. But after they left Calabria for good, Donna Rachele wangled things so that Neddy – always her favourite – got a separate room, while second brother, Aldo, was given the maid's cubicle.

Minnie's parents occupy the largest bedroom, sparsely furnished with a double bed, a chest of drawers and a bedside table. The walls are bare, except for a carved mother-of-pearl crucifix over the bedhead. Minnie often wonders why her mother keeps the cross, as she rarely attends church services except for funerals. In a corner farthest from the bed a curtained-off area hides a narrow divan, a chest of drawers and a bedside commode. Until a year ago, it was here that Minnie slept, in her parents' room, as she had done ever since childhood. Only when Aldo, the second oldest and her favourite of the four brothers at the time, was thrown out of the family home following a furious row with Donna Rachele had Minnie inherited his room.

The heart of the apartment is the dining room, next to the kitchen, where the family gathers to eat, sew, do homework, talk and read.

Minnie is in the dining room one evening helping her mother embroider a tablecloth.

She is fully aware that for years bringing up five children on Don Peppino's small salary required all Donna Rachele's ingenuity and talent to make ends meet. She is an excellent needlewoman – and has passed on her skill to Minnie. After the family moved to Rome, Donna Rachele began taking in piecework on payment and secured a steady supply of commissions from Fontana's, a couture house in the ultra-fashionable Via Condotti. She decided to specialise in wedding dresses and elaborate table linen, which brought in the most money, and got Minnie to help.

In due course Donna Rachele accumulated a small amount of capital and branched out into moneylending as a sideline. To Minnie's shame, her mother is known locally as *La Strozzina* – the loanshark – a slang word commonly used to describe all moneylenders. At the same time, she is aware that her mother's clients treat her with grudging respect for being firm but fair. It was the success she achieved in this field that allowed the family to better themselves and has brought them to their present home.

Minnie, who is as skilled a seamstress as her mother, is made to persevere with the needlework commissions. Although she resents the long hours she is made to sew daily after school, she appreciates the tiny weekly allowance she receives for her efforts, which she saves with great care.

'Listen, my girl,' Donna Rachele says while both work on a delicate tablecloth, 'we need to make certain decisions.'

Minnie as a rule is not consulted on decisions, and wonders with dread what her mother has in mind.

'What about, Mamma?' she asks, keeping her eyes on her work.

'About your future and what we are going to do with you after you leave school. I don't suppose you've given it any thought.'

'Actually, I had thought—'

'Well,' Donna Rachele interrupts, 'I've spoken to your father. We think you should work full-time at Fontana's workshop.' She pauses to snip the silk thread with tiny scissors. 'At least until we find you a husband.'

Minnie's heart sinks. She finds the intricate work a strain on her eyes. Besides, she does not want to be stuck away in the backroom of an atelier, and she does not want a husband – at least not one chosen by her mother. She must think quickly of some plausible alternative.

'After all, you're nearly nineteen. Most girls are engaged by now, if not married,' Donna Rachele continues. 'Besides, my girl, you are not blessed with good looks. Your features are all wrong. Lips too thick. Mouth too wide. You slouch, you never smile and your hair is a wild mess.'

Minnie remains silent. Donna Rachele's words no longer have the power to hurt much for having been repeated so often. Nevertheless, they drain the small reserves of self-confidence Minnie has tried hard to build up. Her mother's voice drones on. 'My friend, Captain Bianchi, has taken a fancy to you…friends in high places…party member…ambitious…only forty…excellent match…has met Il Duce, would you believe… Minnie, are you listening to what I say?' she asks sharply.

'But of course, Mamma,' Minnie murmurs automatically.

'So you must agree that this is the best solution,' her mother continues. 'The sooner we resolve the matter the better. Well, what do you say to that, dear?'

Her mother calling her dear is always a prelude for making Minnie do something she doesn't want to do. She lays down her needlework, takes a deep breath and turns to her mother with an air of thoughtfulness, careful not to show any trace of alarm.

'While you were talking, it struck me that Captain Bianchi must be ambitious enough to expect promotion. He would no doubt want a wife with money.' She reaches for the scissors. 'Failing that, at least one with certain qualities that will be a credit to him when he is promoted. Don't you think so, Mamma?' She hardly ever speaks to her mother at such length and catches the surprised look Donna Rachele gives her.

'You may be right, it's a sensible notion, but at the same time it's most important that he has a dutiful wife.'

'Well, there won't be any money with me. My only quality is that I am good at embroidery. Not much of a catch.'

'Let's not exaggerate. You have other qualities that will come out in time, I'm sure. For instance, you have beautiful handwriting. Besides, I can teach you to become an excellent cook, and that is most important. A man likes his food, you know.'

'Yes, of course.' Minnie is determined not to let this happen. She picks up her sewing and snips off a loose thread. 'You know, recently I heard my friend Annamaria's father say that nowadays there is a great demand for girls with book-keeping and accountancy skills. With proper qualifications, they can earn good money in banks and law offices – and they get pension rights too. Don't you think it would be more appropriate for Captain Bianchi to find someone with that kind of professional qualification?'

'What are you saying?' Donna Rachele inquires. Minnie knows her mother is not in the habit of listening to suggestions from her daughter, though she is always eager to discover new ways of anyone in the family earning money.

From somewhere inspiration strikes Minnie. 'Perhaps if I were able to apply to the Collegio Colonna, I could get a proper diploma in accountancy, maybe even in typing. I'm told there's a lot of demand for typing as well.'

'Indeed, my girl,' Donna Rachele puffs. 'And how much would all that cost, and who is to pay for it?'

Minnie stops stitching and looks at her mother in surprise. 'I thought that since Papa paid for Neddy and Franco…'

'But that's different. Neddy and Franco are men; they need a professional qualification to get good jobs. They will have families to support one day.'

Desperate to pursue her case, Minnie makes a further suggestion.

'I've saved a bit of money from the sewing. It might be enough to pay for part of the course.'

'How long is the course?'

'I think it's three years.'

'Three years! Heavens above, child, you must be crazy. Why that long?'

'Annamaria's dad says a diploma from that college counts for more than others. His bank always takes students who have completed the course there.'

'What sort of wages do they get?'

'I'm not sure, but you can ask Mr Rossi. But it is a lot more than Fontana pay us.' She knows Donna Rachele respects Mr Rossi only because he is assistant manager at the local Banca di Roma.

'He might know also if the bank offers a competition for a bursary.' Minnie casually throws in this remark while sifting through her bunch of coloured threads. It is a wild guess on her part, and she hopes it works. From time to time as they sew, she glances at her mother to gauge her reaction.

Donna Rachele is silent for quite a while. At length she puts down her embroidery and rises to her feet. 'I don't know, I'm sure. I'll talk it over with your father.' She puts away her needles and threads. 'Maybe I'll have a chat with Mr Rossi to find out more about this accountancy business for girls.'

Minnie squeezes shut her eyes with relief. She feels she has won some breathing space.

Later, in the summer of 1922, when Minnie finally left the convent school not only did she apply to the Collegio Colonna but she also won a bursary to the course, much to her parents' astonishment.

Although she was not particularly interested in the subjects she chose to study, she loved attending the college as she had loved going to school, since it got her away from the oppressive atmosphere at home. After the first year, however, she made sure that her initial burst of cleverness, which had allowed her to win the bursary, did not surface too readily during her coursework and exams. In this way, by deliberately failing selected subjects, she managed to stretch out the three years' reprieve by an extra year.

4

Rome, 1926

At five forty-five in the morning on 8 April 1926, the first tram of the day rumbled to a stop outside the Marapodis' apartment block. Its screeching brakes acted as a kind of alarm clock, signalling that it was time to get up. Minnie listened to the tram rattling away to the next stop. She stretched and rolled over in bed for another few minutes. This was the moment she loved best of all, enjoying the luxury of privacy in her own room. Here she belonged to herself alone and could dream of things she dared not even think about at other times.

Moments later Minnie jumped out of bed and slipped into the bathroom, shivering. Although it was the beginning of April and no doubt would warm up during the day, the early mornings still felt nippy in the unheated apartment.

She followed the same routine every day before setting off for college. Ablutions first, then into the kitchen to stoke up the range, place coffee bowls and plates on the table for the family's breakfast, fill the battered *napoletano* machine with coffee ready to place on the stove, then back to her room to get dressed. By the time she returned to the kitchen Donna Rachele was bustling about heating the iron on the range so as to give a last-minute press to Don Peppino's shirt.

'Minnie, take the newspaper stuffing out of Neddy's shoes. Then get yourself quickly to the shop and fetch two litres of milk,' she ordered. 'And I want two large loaves. Look in at the greengrocer and see what's come in fresh today. Tell him that the last lot of artichokes he sold me were not even fit for his goat. And be quick, my girl, no daydreaming; the boys will be wanting their breakfast.'

On her return Minnie prepared the coffee, heated the milk and cut the bread into thick chunks. The smell of the fresh brew brought the menfolk to the table.

Minnie was always struck by how alike they looked. Slightly built, none of them was much over five foot six inches in height. Don Peppino was starting to show a paunch. He wore round, rimless spectacles, had a greying, square-cut moustache and a full head of crinkly hair. Each son had inherited from him a high forehead and prominent hooked nose, giving them an almost Levantine profile.

Franco and Salvatore had their father's jet-black wiry hair, brown eyes and olive skin. In order to achieve the fashionable Rudolph Valentino look, Franco slicked down his hair with copious amounts of pomade and resorted to wearing one of his mother's hairnets at night in order to flatten the tight curls. Neddy, the oldest, had inherited their mother's blue eyes and fair skin. The brothers were handsome in a brooding, intense way, though Neddy appeared less favoured, having no neck and a large head out of proportion to his slight frame. However, he had brains and cunning, qualities that Donna Rachele rated highly.

'Good morning, Papa,' Minnie said, placing a bowl of milky coffee and a chunk of bread in front of her father.

'Good morning, dear,' he murmured, pinching her cheek between thumb and forefinger and stroking her curly black hair. This was one of the few gestures of tenderness Minnie received from any member of the family and she smiled with pleasure. Her mother was always austere and undemonstrative, never showing outward signs of affection to any of her children except Neddy, and Minnie couldn't remember the last time Donna Rachele had kissed or hugged her.

While her mother fussed around with Neddy's shoes, and sewed a button on Franco's cuff, Minnie brought coffee and bread to the table for her brothers, then sat down next to her father with her cup.

Donna Rachele was issuing a stream of instructions even as she sat with bent head, a strand of blonde hair falling over the sewing.

'Don Peppino' – she often used this formal way of addressing her husband – 'you will make sure you won't do any overtime today, won't you? I want you to be here before eight o'clock. We have to eat before Captain Bianchi comes.' She shot him a look with her sharp blue eyes to make sure he understood her.

Minnie's heart sank. Captain Bianchi was the latest in a long line of would-be suitors dragged in by her mother ever since she was fifteen. On these occasions, Minnie always contrived to make herself look as gauche and unattractive as possible and so far was successful in making them lose interest in her. But this tactic had not worked with Captain Bianchi. Minnie loathed him and his groping hands more than she had disliked any of the others, perhaps because he was the most persistent. However, now at her age of twenty-two and being neither married nor even engaged, she knew that prevailing standards would tag her as a *zitella* – an old maid. In their circles this was a derogatory term and reflected badly on her family, so she well understood her mother's desire to marry her off.

Donna Rachele's voice pierced her gloom. 'Salvatore,' she called to her youngest son. 'I've told you before not to make pellets with the bread. Stop it at once. Franco, here's your shirt – next time don't leave it to the last minute to tell me about missing buttons. And listen, my boy' – she shook a finger at him – 'make sure you bring your sister back straight after classes. Minnie, for heaven's sake, do something with your hair – tie it back.' She sighed, raising her eyes to the ceiling. 'What am I to do with this gawky girl?' She turned to Neddy who was on his second bowl of coffee. 'Tell me, dear, have you got a busy day ahead? Any important cases? Will you be home tonight to meet Captain Bianchi?'

'Not tonight I'm afraid, Mamma. I have a late meeting with a client. But give my best greetings to the Captain.'

'Oh, what a pity. But if you must see a client, of course that is much more important.'

Minnie peered at her brother over the rim of her cup, not believing a word he had said. After years of study, Neddy at last had obtained a law degree, the only graduate in the family. She knew Donna Rachele could not restrain herself from boasting to the neighbours about her brilliant son and his position at a renowned law firm in the city.

Donna Rachele left the room and took her husband's jacket and hat from the hall cupboard to give them a brushing down.

'Don Peppino,' she called, 'it's time to go. Salvatore,' she shouted, 'why haven't you brought the coal for the stove, you silly boy? Hurry down to the cellar and bring it up straight away.'

Minnie cleared the table quickly and followed her father into the hall.

'He's always dreaming, that boy.' Don Peppino addressed his wife, slipping into the jacket she held out for him. 'Have patience, Rachele, my dear, don't be too hard on him.'

Donna Rachele stood a head taller than her husband, an erect, imposing figure. 'You're too soft, Peppino, that's your trouble,' she answered sharply. 'He won't learn if there's no discipline. Where would we all be if I had your attitude? Back in Calabria living on a pittance, that's where. Here's your hat. Now don't forget, tell the office first thing, no overtime tonight. Is that clear?'

Minnie was inwardly offended at this slight to her father, but Don Peppino merely nodded without saying a word and put on his hat. Neddy appeared carrying his jacket. He took his mother's hand, bowed and raised it halfway to his lips, murmuring '*bacio la mano*' – 'I kiss the hand' – in the formal gesture of respect to older women that was traditional in the south, before hurrying to catch up with his father on the stairs.

The creep, thought Minnie, as she went to her room to fetch her books.

Back in the hall waiting for Franco, she felt her mother's critical eyes looking her up and down. Her clothes were neat but worn: grey skirt, her mother's blue jacket, and black lace-up shoes on their third re-soling. Her bunched hair was tied back with a navy-blue bow and she carried her books in a worn cloth bag. She hunched her shoulders to try and hide her full breasts and put on her spectacles to give herself a studious air.

Donna Rachele sighed and pursed her lips. 'Heavens above, child, how will you ever get a husband looking like that?'

Minnie lowered her eyes. It wasn't the first time she had heard these comments and had long ago learnt not to show outward anger or answer back.

Donna Rachele turned her attention to Franco as he reached for his jacket. 'You get your wages today, don't you?' she asked.

'Yes, Mamma,' he replied.

'You didn't pay me the full amount last week.' Donna Rachele extracted an amount weekly for board and lodging from each of her wage-earning sons. 'So remember, this week you owe me the full amount, plus what you owe from last week. You'll have to add fifty cents more as interest for late payment.'

'Okay, okay,' Franco sounded peeved. 'As if you'd let me forget.'

'Don't be so cheeky, my lad, I'm just reminding you of your responsibilities,' came the sharp reply.

Franco was the only one who sometimes defied his mother, especially of late. 'But I had to buy new shoes,' he protested.

'Oh yes, and where are they, may one ask? More likely you were buying cigarettes, as if I don't know you smoke on the sly.'

'I'm paying the shoemaker a little bit each week in advance and the rest when the shoes are ready.'

'Indeed. So, made-to-order shoes, is it? Is that what you want to waste your money on? Ready-made are not good enough for our young sir!'

'For heaven's sake! Come on, Minnie, let's go before I start shouting.'

Franco stormed on to the landing with Minnie following.

'Mee-nee,' her mother's voice boomed down the stairwell. 'Don't forget, Captain Bianchi is coming this evening, I want you to look presentable, is that clear?'

'Of course, Mamma.' Minnie escaped into the street, groaning at the prospect. She shook her head. She wasn't going to think about the captain now, and she had the whole day to conjure up yet another scheme to put him off her.

Minnie and Franco walked briskly to the tram stop in silence, knowing their mother was watching from the front balcony. Minnie was not allowed to take the tram by herself, so every day Franco had to accompany her to the *collegio* and fetch her again after classes to take her back home. This task used to be performed by Aldo, her favourite brother at that time, who protected her whenever he could against their mother's harshness. Minnie was bereft when he left home, but although Franco did not have the same caring nature as Aldo, he was fun, and Minnie was surprised at how well they got on.

As soon as Minnie and Franco boarded the tram, they became different people. He lit a cigarette and eyed the young girls. She took off her spectacles and untied the bow from her hair. The black curls sprang loose to her shoulders in a soft cloud. She drew out a long pink chiffon scarf from the cloth bag and tied it loosely round her neck in the latest fashion seen on dummies in shop windows.

'Franco, is it true about the shoes? What are they like?' She nudged him in the ribs.

'Of course it's not true.' He knew Minnie would not tell their mother, just as she knew he never told his mother the true amount of his wages. His weekly payslip showed only three-quarters of the amount he got paid. The remaining quarter was in cash.

'So, what did you spend the money on? Not on gambling?' she whispered.

'Not this time.' He seemed reluctant to say more. 'I've needed to get things…'

'What things?'

'Just things. You know. Things for ladies.'

Minnie was puzzled. Whatever did he mean, things for ladies? She blushed. 'Franco, you don't mean those loose women, you know…the ones hanging around the station?'

'Of course not, you silly girl. I don't *buy* anything for them. I just pay them.'

'Well, what then? Tell me.'

Franco sighed irritably but kept silent. Minnie nudged him again.

'If I tell you,' Franco said reluctantly, 'you have to promise faithfully not to let on to Mamma and Papa.'

'You know I've never told them anything about you,' Minnie said, 'not even about your gambling.'

'Understood.' Franco cast a sheepish look at Minnie. 'Well, I bought a present for someone, a young lady I've been seeing.'

'What a dark horse you are, Franco!' Minnie exclaimed. 'Who is she? Is it serious? Do I know her? What's her name?'

'I don't know how serious, but I am pretty keen on her. She's not like any of my previous flirtations. Her name is Clara. You don't know her, but I'd like you both to meet sometime. And her sister, too.'

Minnie's eyes sparkled with pleasure. 'I'd like that. What's the sister called? Tell me more about them.'

'Her name is Dolly. I met them at work a few months ago. They've been coming to Giolitti's nearly every day for coffee or ice cream.' He got out a handkerchief and wiped the back of his neck. The tram was beginning to fill up and become stuffy. 'You might possibly have seen them at some time. They stay at the *pensione* opposite the *collegio*.'

Minnie shrugged. How could she tell? A lot of people went in and out of the *pensione* and she didn't spend all her time looking out of the classroom window even though her desk was closest to it. She knew the porters by sight, and some of the maids, but they all wore uniforms. Sometimes guests in the first-floor rooms would give her a little wave when she leaned out of the window to open or shut the wooden shutters. Thinking about it, Minnie often waved back at two young ladies, long-term occupants of the middle room, who almost daily leaned over the balcony railings to watch the comings and goings in the street.

'I wonder if they are the ones who wave to me sometimes from their balcony. If they live in the *pensione* they must be visitors to Rome. What are they doing here?'

'They're on a one-year course in Art History, they told me. I think they might be American.'

Minnie's eyes widened with excitement. 'Americans! When can I meet them?'

Franco got up to offer his seat to a lady. 'I'll see what I can arrange.'

Minnie had to be content with this, but she felt a thrill that she would be meeting foreigners, something she knew her mother would never approve of and all the more reason to keep Franco's secret.

The carriage was full now, with people standing in the aisle hanging on to overhead straps. Minnie gazed out of the window as the tram trundled through the early-morning traffic.

In less than three months she would sit her final exams. She knew this time she couldn't push her luck by failing them yet again. Riccardo – Captain Bianchi insisted she call him by his first name – loomed like a black raincloud on the horizon. She did not like him a jot more now than she had four years earlier. The prospect that both he and her mother would soon pressurise her to accept a proposal of marriage filled her with dread.

She felt she had just about run out of delaying tactics and was starting to panic.

5

Minnie and Franco got off the tram at Piazza Venezia, crossed the main road, and walked towards the Collegio Colonna, making their way through the narrow side streets that formed the heart of the old city. A series of small shops and workshops were starting to open for business. Some '*buon giornos*' were exchanged with Franco, while eyes followed Minnie. On the steps of the Monte dei Paschi, the pawnbrokers, a few people were gathered waiting for the doors to open, avoiding the looks of the passers-by. Outside the entrance of a small haberdashery, an old man dressed in black sat impassively on a stool while inside the shop his wife stood behind the counter waiting for the first customer. As Minnie passed him, he followed her with his eyes and, without so much as moving his head or his lips, murmured just loud enough for her ears: 'Ah here come those lovely breasts, how I would like to suck them like sweet melons. Give me a taste, my lovely.'

'Shut up, you dirty old man,' she replied, quite used to this daily smut. 'Do you want me to tell your wife what you're saying?'

They reached Via dei Burrò, a cobbled street not wide enough for pavements, threading its way between Renaissance palazzi, from La Borsa – the Stock Exchange – to Piazza Colonna at the far end. Halfway down, an arched doorway led to the college's courtyard where Minnie and Franco parted company.

'I'll pick you up at one thirty,' he said, and continued towards Piazza Colonna. He had a good job as manager and bookkeeper at Giolitti's, Rome's best-known ice-cream-parlour-cum-café, a couple of streets away.

Across the street from the Collegio building, the porter from the Pensione della Borsa was sweeping the front entrance. The *pensione* was a modest but genteel establishment, popular with foreign visitors, particularly ladies. Minnie's classroom on the first floor overlooked its five geranium-laden balconies. From her desk next to the middle window she could see into the rooms when the balcony doors were left open. This morning she peered out of the window hoping to get a glimpse of what she guessed were the two sisters Franco had spoken of. But their balcony door was shut.

Minnie's class was well into its last lesson of the morning when a newsvendor's voice bellowed in the street below, distracting the whole class. The teacher stopped talking to listen to the shouting: 'Sensational! Special edition! Read all about it! Assassination attempt on Il Duce! Mussolini's miraculous escape! Four shots fired by mad Irish woman. Read all about it in *Il Corriere*!'

The words reverberated through the narrow street. The girls in the class gathered at the three windows to see what was happening, and watched people rushing out of buildings on to the cobbles to buy a paper. Crowds swarmed into the street. Groups bunched at the entrances to shops and bars, talking animatedly and peering at newspapers. Janitors left their cubicles in entrance halls and stood protectively in the half-open doorways to their buildings. Windows were flung open and neighbours shouted across the street.

'Did you hear, Il Duce is dead.'
'Rubbish, he's not dead, he's been rushed to hospital.'
'I heard he was shot in the head.'
'That's not true, it was the stomach.'
'Who did it?'
'Who do you think? A communist, of course.'
'What nonsense – it was a monarchist.'
'Hey, you down there. What's the latest?'
'They killed two *carabinieri* as well.'

Rumour zigzagged its way down the street, gathering flimsy reports like a candy-floss stick, first from the bakery wafting its aroma of newly baked bread, then from the laundry with its odour of damp steam pressing. It paused for liquid and verbal reinforcement at the bar. It darted across to the greengrocer, depositing its message on top of smooth tomatoes and peppers to be carried home with the morning shopping. At the end of the street it turned, heavier now, and hastened back the way it had come, bouncing up to an open window, down to an ice-cream parlour, over to the cobbler, halting to gather snippets from the *pensione* receptionist, before returning to its origin at the newsvendor.

Minnie longed to find out what had happened, but the lesson dragged on.

At last the bell rang and she scooted down the stairs to buy the paper. She stood by the newsvendor deeply immersed in reading the article when she heard

Franco hailing her. He was coming up the street together with two smartly dressed young girls about her age. As they got closer, she recognised them for the two sisters from the *pensione*. She gave a shy smile and folded the newspaper.

'Have you heard the news, Franco? I've got the paper if you want to read about it.'

'I heard,' Franco replied. 'Minnie, I want you to meet my friend Clara.' He turned to the shorter of the two girls. 'Clara, this is my sister, Maria Erminia.'

Clara held out her hand. 'Well, we haven't met formally, but we know each other by sight,' she said, her wide smile showing perfectly even teeth.

Minnie shook hands. 'I'm pleased to meet you. You sometimes wave to me from the *pensione*, don't you? But I almost didn't recognise you, you look so different, wearing hats and all.'

The taller one spoke now. She had greenish eyes and black hair cut in a short bob.

'We had an appointment with our lawyer this morning. You know what it's like. One has to make a good impression.' Her smile revealed slightly buckteeth. 'My name is Dolly Pestonji and—'

Clara interrupted her sternly. 'It's Preston, not Pestonji,' she hissed. 'For heaven's sake, Dolly, please remember that in future. It's Preston.' She pushed Dolly aside. 'Dolly is my younger sister, and we're both so glad to meet you at long last, Maria Erminia.'

Minnie shook hands with Dolly. She was surprised at how well they both spoke Italian. 'Please, do call me Minnie. Most people do. And I'm so glad to meet you at last.' She didn't mention that she had only heard of them that very day for the first time. 'Have you known Franco for long?'

Clara glanced at Franco with a smile. 'We met your charming brother a couple of months ago at Giolitti's when we went there for their famous ice creams. He was most kind and ever so helpful. We've been going back there as often as we can.'

'Yes, indeed,' Dolly added. 'He's shown us around a few places, told us which shops to go to, what sights to see, and helped us in – well – in other matters. He found us the lawyer we've seen today.'

Minnie was amazed. Franco had never mentioned any of this to her. She hoped the lawyer he had found them was not their brother Neddy.

Clara put her hand on Franco's arm. 'Why don't you and Minnie come and have a drink with us now? There's a nice little courtyard in the *pensione*.'

'We have to get back home,' Franco said, but relented when he saw the pleading look in Minnie's eyes. 'Well, just for half an hour, then.'

They settled around a small cast-iron table in the tiny flower-filled courtyard and ordered drinks. Franco and Clara seemed to have eyes only for each other.

'Come on, Clara, enough of the cooing and billing,' Dolly said tersely. 'There is another guest here, remember?'

Reluctantly, and with a dreamy look, Clara turned her attention to the others. By the time the drinks arrived, the topic of conversation had turned to the attempted assassination.

An Irish woman resident in Rome had fired a pistol at Il Duce. If she had been a better shot, he would be lying dead. As it was, the bullet only grazed his nose. There was a lot of speculation about the nature of the crime – was the Irish woman one of his many lovers, discarded and seeking revenge, or was she a fanatic sent by some enemy government to try and get rid of him?

At first Minnie listened to their theories without comment. She felt she didn't know enough about current affairs to offer an opinion. Besides she liked listening to the two sisters speaking Italian, their accent only adding a further intriguing note to the faint air of mystery they exuded.

Franco lit a cigarette and offered one to Clara.

'Do you smoke?' Minnie sounded surprised.

'I do indeed,' Clara replied, inserting a cigarette into a long black holder. 'Dolly doesn't, though,' she mocked. 'Says it's not ladylike, but it's all the rage in England these days, don't you know? Will you try one? Franco, offer her one, won't you?'

'I've never smoked, but I'd like to try.' Minnie reached out her hand.

'Absolutely not,' Franco said firmly, putting the packet in his pocket. 'Italian girls don't smoke.' The implication that *nice* Italian girls didn't smoke drifted over the table to be hastily dispersed by Dolly.

'Clara, leave her alone, poor girl,' she said, touching Clara's arm.

'Sorry.' Clara pouted and blew a puff of smoke upwards. She took up her glass. 'In that case let us drink to Minnie Marapodi, our new friend! Cheers!'

They raised their glasses and Minnie giggled. She was enjoying this. Soon the effects of the Campari soda she'd ordered dissolved the polite reserve she had maintained until now.

'Clara, I know you are not Italian, but what country do you come from?'

'We come from India.'

'India! Really, how exotic,' Minnie said in admiration. 'I thought you were English or American. You don't look at all Indian.'

The others laughed. 'What do you think Indians look like, Minnie?' Dolly teased.

Minnie felt she had blundered. 'I thought they'd wear Indian dress, how do you call them – saris. And a dot on their forehead, like you see in the cinema.' She hesitated. 'And I thought, excuse me for saying, I imagined Indians had dark skin. You know, like Ethiopians.'

She looked across at Franco, but he was laughing with the girls.

'Not all Indians are dark,' Clara explained. 'Actually, we are Parsi, which is a different community. Originally they came from Persia.'

Minnie still seemed puzzled. 'What brought you to Italy? Have you been here long?'

Clara and Dolly exchanged a look. Dolly lowered her eyes and let Clara do the talking. They were studying Italian and doing a course in History of Art. They had been in Rome about six months and before that had a year between London and Paris.

'How exciting. Did you like Paris? I'd love to go there!'

'It was absolutely wonderful, and we had a marvellous time. We went to all the art galleries, and the theatre – we saw lots of shows. It's a most beautiful city.'

'Are your parents here with you?' Minnie enquired.

The two sisters exchanged another glance. Clara leaned across the table and picked at an olive from a small dish. Dolly fumbled for a hanky in her pocket and dabbed her nose.

'Actually, we have a guardian,' Clara said, removing the olive stone from her mouth. 'Our Uncle Harry – he's looked after us since, well, there was a tragedy in the family when we were about ten. We've been in his care ever since.'

Dolly broke in. 'Uncle Harry's been absolutely wonderful. He thought we should live abroad for a couple of years. Broaden our horizons. Get some culture. That's why we're doing the History of Art course. He phones us once a week.'

Minnie was impressed – it sounded terribly exotic and exciting. A tragedy. A guardian. Travel. Overseas telephone calls. Heavens – at home there wasn't even a telephone! They had to use the neighbour's phone upstairs if they needed to make a call. She wanted to ask what the tragedy had been, but felt it was too personal a question at this first encounter.

It was agreed all four would meet again in two days.

During the journey home on the tram, Minnie bombarded Franco with questions about the two sisters. She was curious about them being Indian. They could so easily have passed for European.

'Did you know they were Indian, Franco?'

'Sure I did, but I told you they were American because I thought you wouldn't have wanted to meet them if they sounded too exotic.'

'I think they're great. I suppose they must be rich, don't you think?' she asked, tying back her hair. 'You know, so much travelling and living for months on end at the *pensione*. And you can see their clothes are really good quality and must have cost a bit.'

'They're not poor, I'm sure,' Franco replied, 'but I don't think they're all that rich.'

'Do you think not? I thought they were bound to be related to a rich nabob or something.'

'Silly girl, you read too many romantic novels. If they were, you can bet they'd be living in a better place than that *pensione*.'

I wonder what India is like, Minnie thought, gazing into space. *One thing is sure. Mamma will not tolerate this friendship at all. Foreigners. Travel. Family tragedies. Most unsuitable! She would have a fit if she got to know.*

Minnie pursed her lips. Mamma had better not find out about it.

6

The next few months were amongst the happiest that Minnie had known, as her friendship with Clara and Dolly deepened. She liked them both equally, although as sisters they had different personalities. Clara was the older by a couple of years and was by nature a chatterbox with quite fixed opinions. A bit of a flibbertigibbet, she was not afraid of putting her foot in her mouth. Minnie soon noticed that Clara was always more prepared to take risks than her sister. Though both wore elegant, expensive clothes, Clara tended to dress more flamboyantly; she liked to be noticed, and she liked to shock people – particularly her sister.

Dolly, on the other hand, was altogether more serious and discreet. She was rather shy compared to her more extrovert sister. She didn't have much sense of humour and in some ways Minnie thought this made her slightly vulnerable. But she became quickly aware that Dolly was the more disciplined of the two. Although she deferred to Clara in most things, she would be the one to turn to in a crisis, able to keep a cool head and make sensible decisions.

Minnie found association with them to be liberating. Her views broadened and she was eager to absorb new ways of thinking. As the weeks went by and she became more relaxed with them, she did wonder why they seemed so keen to be in her company. As sisters she thought they would have been enough for each other. But in fact, they actively sought her out, and Minnie felt that perhaps her presence served to help reduce an underlying tension between the two girls. There was a core insensitivity and hardness about Clara, who tended to bully Dolly; it was almost as if she said and did things on purpose to make Dolly uncomfortable.

On her part, Minnie was perfectly happy to be drawn into their circle. She had never had a deep friendship with any girls and experienced a sisterly affection from them which she lacked within her family. It was true that of the two girls she felt more empathy towards Dolly with her kinder and more thoughtful personality. Still, Minnie questioned the ease with which they had drawn her so wholeheartedly into their orbit.

She spoke to Franco about it when they were on the small balcony outside Minnie's room, where Franco was smoking a sneaky cigarette.

'You know, I don't understand it really, Franco,' she said, leaning on the balustrade. 'I can't see what I have to offer them. My life so far has been rather dull compared to all the exciting things they have seen and done.'

'Perhaps they are tired of exciting things and simply want a bit of normality,' Franco murmured.

'Maybe so, but it is almost as if they didn't have any other friends here. Surely they must know more people in Rome?'

Franco took a deep drag and exhaled slowly. 'Dolly said something briefly once. I think they find it difficult. She said they had one or two connections that they contacted when they first arrived, but after being invited a couple of times, they didn't hear any more from them.'

'How awful. Why ever not?'

'I didn't press it further. But you know what it's like. As long as you conform to what society expects of you, everything is fine and one is accepted. But anything out of the ordinary makes people feel uncomfortable.'

'I suppose they are out of the ordinary,' Minnie said.

'I'll say. Two young girls on their own, foreigners, no chaperone, no family, studying a subject that smacks of a bohemian lifestyle. What do you expect?' The cigarette end was getting close to his fingers. 'They live in a respectable but inexpensive *pensione*. They are not wealthy enough to entertain and return the invitations,' he went on. 'The people they contacted will think of them as being rather loose women, out to have a good time. They are bound to feel a bit isolated, so to have someone of their own age as a friend really means a lot to them.'

Minnie felt herself blushing with pleasure. 'Do you really think I mean a lot to them?'

Franco flicked the cigarette over the railing into the street below. He pinched her cheek and smiled. 'They are extremely fond of you, I know it.'

Minnie hugged this knowledge to herself. But in order to deflect any curiosity at home about her newfound contentedness, she tried to please her mother as much as possible. At the same time she began to establish small acts of independence. She went to the cinema with her friend Annamaria occasionally; she would often not come home straight after classes; at weekends, she stopped preparing coffee in the mornings for her brothers. She went so far as to be relatively cordial – or rather, less ungracious – with the dreaded Riccardo, in the hope that Donna Rachele would be lulled into a sense of false security about a prospective commitment.

'Minnie, remind me when you take your final exams?' Donna Rachele asked one evening over their sewing.

'In three weeks.'

Donna Rachele put down her work and looked hard at her daughter. 'I trust this time you will pass all the papers.' There was the tiniest hint of menace in her tone. Minnie pursed her lips. She could sense her mother leading up to an unaccustomed heart-to-heart.

'I will do my best.'

'I've noticed lately you've been staying back at college to do extra studying. I am sure it will pay off.' She paused to thread another needle. 'I see you seem to be getting on better with Riccardo recently. Am I right?'

'I try to find things to talk about with him.'

'I knew you would find him interesting once you got to know him,' Donna Rachele replied, satisfied. 'Of course, after the exams you will be able to see more of him. Perhaps go to the theatre with him? Or to the Caracalla for the opera.'

'Mamma, I know nothing about opera,' Minnie muttered.

Donna Rachele tightened her lips. 'It's time you learnt, my girl; you know how musical Riccardo is.'

Minnie confided her fears to Clara and Dolly. They were sitting in the sisters' bedroom with the balcony door open, letting in a light breeze.

'I don't know what to do. I know I'll pass the exams – I've done them enough times,' she laughed. 'But I don't want to spend the summer having Riccardo courting me.'

'You could always get a job,' Dolly suggested.

'Mr Rossi isn't recruiting until October.'

'What about a temporary summer job?'

'Like a shop assistant?'

'No, not necessarily.' Clara frowned. 'It's a pity you don't dance.'

'Dance?' Minnie was incredulous. 'What *are* you suggesting?'

'Dancing in a chorus line, on stage,' Clara said, screwing a cigarette into a long ebony holder. Lighting it, she shook the match and slowly exhaled a stream of smoke. 'It pays ever so well.'

'Clara! As if I'd do such a thing.'

'Oh, don't sound so stuffy,' Clara puffed. 'I've done it,' she murmured.

'You've never! I don't believe it.'

'She did, you know,' Dolly said. 'In Paris. For six months.'

Minnie was dumbfounded. 'What sort of place?'

'I was in the chorus line at the Folies Bergères,' Clara said, relishing the moment.

'Oh my God, the Folies Bergères! Aren't all the dancers there completely naked?'

'We chorus line girls weren't naked, though we didn't have a lot on, I must admit.'

'Why did you do it?'

Clara shrugged her shoulders. 'We were in financial difficulties. There had been some mix-up about the money from Uncle Harry. Isn't that so, Dolly?'

There was a pause. 'That's right.' Dolly examined her fingernails closely.

'Did you also join the chorus line, Dolly?' Minnie asked.

'No fear. I didn't have the nerve. But I fetched her after the shows. For respectability's sake we had to be seen coming back to our apartment together.'

Curiosity got the better of Minnie. 'What was it like, Clara? Did you have any adventures? Did men chase you? Did you drink champagne? Do tell.'

'Some other time, darling. We've got to think about a job for you.'

A thought struck Minnie. 'Does Franco know?'

'No indeed he does not!' Clara glared at Minnie.

She asked them if Uncle Harry knew.

Clara and Dolly exchanged a guilty look. 'Of course not!' they chorused.

'What's he like, your uncle Harry? You talk about him so often,' Minnie said.

'He's quite the kindest person I've ever known.' Clara blew a cloud of smoke towards the ceiling.

'And the most interesting,' Dolly added. 'He's a judge, you know, the youngest in India.'

'His full name is Sir Hirji Dadabhai Pestonji, Bt – he inherited the title on his father's death,' Dolly started. 'He's known to be extremely kind and generous, and totally honest and fair in all his dealings.'

'What Dolly means is that he can't be bribed – quite a rare thing in the business community in Bombay,' Clara added. 'And he's absolutely passionate about two things: the law and horse racing.'

'He's been incredibly good to us and we love him to bits,' Dolly said.

'Tell me more about him and the family,' Minnie asked eagerly.

Clara, obviously relieved the subject had steered away from her dancing past, took it in turns with Dolly to describe him with such affection that it gave Minnie a pang of envy.

He was a real pillar of the Parsi community and a familiar sight in all Bombay circles. At the High Court, when in session, he could be seen in his judge's robes and wig. At the Royal Bombay Turf Club on Sunday afternoons one could spot him in his box next to the governor's, or in the owners' enclosure, wearing his signature white shantung suit, a brown trilby and a pair of binoculars slung over his shoulder. Later in the evening he could be found at the Willingdon Club at his regular table playing a fiendish game of bridge. And once a week, when not in court, his erect figure in the white suit – appearing taller than he was – and his clear, precise speech captured the attention of university law students crowding the hall to attend his lectures in Jurisprudence.

'He really is extremely well liked,' Dolly went on fondly. 'He is trusted and respected equally by all communities – the British, Hindu and Muslim. Of course, this puts him in a unique position of influence. And in spite of his British education, he is a keen supporter of the Indian Independence movement.'

Clara took over and proudly explained that a starred First in Law from Trinity College, Cambridge, followed by a pupillage at Lincoln's Inn – as well as his even-handed perspective and impartial views – ensured that he was a valued confidant and advisor to Sir John Hardinge, the governor, and officers of the British administration in Bombay. As such, he became the youngest Indian to be appointed to the bench.

Minnie sighed. She wished she had someone in her family like Uncle Harry: someone she could look up to with pride; someone who could show her the sort of affection he had for his nieces.

At home Minnie reflected on her friends' suggestion. She had never thought of getting temporary employment. The promised job at the bank starting in the autumn was a heaven-sent deliverance, but the prospect of a long hot summer at home filled her with dread. The more she mulled over Clara's suggestion, the more she liked it. She realised with growing concern that somehow she must extricate herself from the stranglehold her mother exerted on her.

What could she do, she wondered? What opportunities were there available to her? She'd never have the nerve to do what Clara had done at the Folies Bergères. She remembered with a shudder the times in her childhood when Donna Rachele had forced her to play the piano or made her recite lengthy melodramatic poetry for the entertainment of so-called important guests.

She felt that her shyness would prevent her from being an effective *commessa* in a shop dealing with rich clients. She knew her talents were slight: she embroidered well; she had beautiful copperplate handwriting, though what possible use could that be? Admittedly, she had a good head for figures, although she had been careful to conceal this from her mother.

'What else could I do?' she wailed to Clara and Dolly, the next time she saw them, flopping on to a bed in their room. 'Come on, suggest something practical, but not anything like dancing on a stage.'

'You could be a nanny,' Dolly suggested.

Minnie pulled a face. 'You mean looking after children? My dear Dolly, Mamma would never hear of it. She'd say it's no better than being a servant. No, I've got to think of something plausible that she couldn't object to.'

Clara had been seated at the dressing table applying lipstick in a perfect bow. Now she jumped up and grabbed Minnie by the arm.

'I have an idea, Minnie. Something Franco mentioned the other day. Stand up and turn around.' She dragged Minnie off the bed to the balcony door and turned her this way and that.

'What you need, darling, is a bit of colour in your face. And we've got to do something with your hair.'

'Clara, what are you up to? You know I can't go home wearing make-up.'

'Don't worry, we'll have it all off before you go. Trust me, but we have to hurry and be out of here in twenty minutes. Come on, Dolly, help me with her hair.'

Twenty minutes later Minnie stood in front of the full-length mirror. She hardly recognised herself. Her cheeks were tinted a dusky pink, and her full lips were a luscious cherry red. Her hair was slicked back into a French pleat. Tucked under her arm was a suede clutch bag to go with Dolly's borrowed brown and white spotted silk dress. A long necklace of amber beads and Clara's gold clip earrings completed the transformation. She looked sleek and voluptuous.

Clara dashed down to the lobby ahead of them to make a phone call. By the time Minnie and Dolly joined her she was ready to leave.

'But where are we going?' enquired Minnie and Dolly.

'To Giolitti's,' Clara announced. 'I've just spoken to Franco and he's expecting us.'

'But why did I need to get all made up just for Giolitti's?' Minnie exclaimed, as they hurried down the narrow street. 'I've often been there.'

'Yes, but this time it's going to be different, trust me.' Clara would say no more as they hurried down the cobbled street.

Franco was standing outside Giolitti's smoking a cigarette.

'My goodness, Minnie,' he exclaimed, 'if you weren't my sister, I'd want to ask you out for a date.' Minnie smiled and blushed, delighted with the backhanded compliment.

Clara shot him a cold look. Franco took her hand and raised it to his lips. 'No need to be jealous, my darling, you know that I only have eyes for you.'

'And on me is where you'd better keep them, unless you want one of them blackened.' Clara smiled sweetly, but her tone was sharp.

Franco looked at her through half-closed eyes and took a long, slow drag on the cigarette. 'What a woman! You are a real tigress when you're jealous,' he murmured in his most seductive voice.

'Cut it out, Franco, you can do all that canoodling later,' Dolly interrupted, fed up with their constant flirtation. 'We've come here for a reason. Now tell us what it's about.'

'Of course,' he replied, stepping back into his managerial role. 'Come along, Minnie, Signor Giolitti is waiting for you.'

'What for? Will someone please tell me what's going on?'

Franco explained. Signor Giolitti's cashier was going on maternity leave at the end of the month. He was looking to replace her with somebody reliable, steady and good with figures. Franco had approached him, suggesting his younger sister, who was about to get her diploma in accountancy from the Collegio Colonna.

'What did he say?' Minnie's face lit up with joy.

'Calm yourself, Minnie,' Franco said, straightening his tie and jacket. 'He said he's happy to see you. Let's go.'

That evening, Franco's explanation to his mother and father about a summer job for Minnie was a masterpiece of subtlety and diplomatic manoeuvring. Without overdoing it, he played on his mother's desire to strengthen their connections with the Giolitti family. He told her how Signor Giolitti was anxious to have Donna Rachele's approval about the job, and that he would treat her daughter like a member of the family. It was obvious that Franco himself would also be keeping an eye on Minnie, allaying Donna Rachele's fears of her daughter mixing with undesirable people. His trump card was the matter of a weekly pay packet. As with his own wages, the figure he disclosed to his parents was rather less than the true amount, but both Donna Rachele and Don Peppino were quite satisfied with the salary. They agreed that Minnie could accept the job offer.

'Provided, of course,' Donna Rachele added sternly, turning to Minnie, 'that you pass your exams this time and get your diploma!'

Behind a calm exterior, Minnie was beside herself with excitement. She stayed awake that night worrying if she'd be up to the job, and imagining what it would be like to meet new people. She knew that a great many famous personalities – actors, journalists, such as Aldo Palazzeschi, artists and politicians – often dropped in for a coffee.

In the following weeks she put all her efforts into serious preparation for the forthcoming exams. There was no question of failing this time. The stakes were too high. This was her chance and she had to make the most of it. The various strands of emotions aroused in her since meeting Clara and Dolly were being funnelled towards definite aims. At least now she was sure about what she did *not* want: she did not want to marry Riccardo and she no longer had any desire to take the bank job.

She was asked to start work at Giolitti's at the end of June.

'Now remember,' Clara said, up in their rooms discussing what Minnie should wear. 'You must put on make-up. You're going to be near the back of the café and the light isn't as strong there, so you don't want to look washed out.'

'Anyway, darling,' Dolly said, 'we'll be coming around every day as usual – except of course Thursdays. That's when—'

'Not now, Dolly,' Clara interrupted with a warning look.

'Yes, what about Thursdays?' Minnie enquired. 'I often wonder what you do then. Do you have extra tuition in your language class or something?'

The two sisters looked at each other. Dolly sighed and twisted a ring round and round on her finger; she avoided looking at Minnie.

Clara lit a cigarette and exhaled slowly. 'No. It's not the classes. It's such a bore, really.' She took another puff. 'We have to go to our lawyer. It's to do with the money that Uncle Harry sends for our tuition—'

'—and we take him the *pensione* bills for payment,' Dolly cut in. 'Isn't that so, Clara?'

'That's right,' Clara agreed, looking relieved.

Minnie thought their unconvincing exchange a bit odd. There was something they weren't telling her, but for the present she wouldn't press it. In due course she would find out.

7

Before leaving the house on her first day at work, Minnie went to the kitchen where her mother was rolling out pasta. 'I'm ready to go, Mamma.'

Donna Rachele looked up to see her daughter in the doorway and wiped her floury hands on a towel. 'Come closer, let's have a look at you in a good light,' she said, pointing to the kitchen balcony.

Minnie had chosen to have a new dress made by the local dressmaker and not by her mother. She hoped Donna Rachele would not find fault with it.

'Turn around, I want to see if the hem is even.' Minnie could feel Donna Rachele's critical eye on her.

'Personally, I find it a little too modern,' said Donna Rachele. 'For a start the skirt is too short. Still, this is what young women are wearing these days.' She eyed the dress up and down, turning Minnie this way and that. The broad white sailor collar, the long-knotted tie beneath it, the bodice falling straight to the hips over a pleated skirt.

'Luckily the style makes your breasts look smaller.'

Minnie looked at her mother enquiringly. 'Do you like it?'

'You look all right. The dressmaker hasn't made too bad a job of it. Thank goodness you've done something with your hair. It's a pity about your face; your skin is so pasty, and you always look ill. Are you ready? Do you need to take anything with you?'

'I bought a small handbag.' She showed her mother a blue straw bag. 'I have a comb and a mirror and a hanky and some change. That's all I need, I think.'

'Just a minute. You can't use one of your father's old hankies at a smart place like Giolitti's. Here you are, I made you this.' From her pocket she extracted a tiny packet wrapped in tissue. Minnie opened it to reveal a dainty, crisply folded handkerchief. It was made of the finest bleached linen edged with a border of exquisite lace. One corner bore an elaborately embroidered M.

'Oh, Mamma, it is so beautiful,' she whispered, staring at her mother. She had never received such a personal gift from her before. On birthdays she usually got two pairs of cotton stockings.

'Stop gaping, child,' Donna Rachele said brusquely, accompanying her to the front door. 'Remember your manners, and don't do stupid things. Pay attention to Signor Giolitti. Don't let us down.'

Franco was waiting for Minnie at the tram stop. When they were seated, he handed her the items she had asked him to keep for her: a lipstick, a tiny pot of rouge and a powder compact. At the next stop she quickly applied the make-up and turned to Franco, breathless with excitement. 'How do I look?'

He looked at her for a long moment, smiling. 'You look perfectly lovely. Quite glamorous, in fact.'

'Oh, get away with you, Franco,' she said, looking out of the window, but she couldn't stop smiling.

Minnie knocked on Clara and Dolly's bedroom door early one afternoon. 'It's me, Minnie,' she called.

'Come in, sweetie,' Dolly replied. 'The door's open.'

Dolly sat in her pink petticoat at the dressing table slowly waving a straw fan to dry the sweat trickling down her neck. Minnie kissed the top of her head. In the mirror she could see Clara dozing on the bed in her eau-de-Nil bra and silk cami-knickers, an open book on her bare stomach. The shutters were half drawn; the room was heavy and subdued in the breathless heat of the July afternoon.

'Have a seat, Minnie,' Dolly said, glancing at the bedside clock. 'We have to go out in an hour, and I need to cool down.' Reaching for a bottle of cologne, she splashed some under her arms. The scent of lavender freshened the room. Minnie drew up a chair next to Dolly and they spoke in whispers. In the corridor a door banged. Clara stirred. The book slid off her stomach on to the floor with a plop.

'Clara, are you awake?' Dolly called. 'We need to talk.'

A sleepy groan came from the bed followed by a slurred, 'What about?'

Dolly sighed and turned to face her sister. 'You know perfectly well what about, sweetie. It's got to be done.'

Minnie was all ears wondering what was going to come next. Should she stay, or offer to go if they wanted to talk in private? She decided to stay. Clara pushed herself off the bed and slipped on a silk kimono. Picking up a paper fan from the bedside table, she slumped into the armchair next to the open balcony door.

'Hello, Minnie, have you finished for the day?'

'No, I'm doing another session at four.'

Clara fanned herself. 'God, you can't breathe in this heat. Why can't they have ceiling fans in this country?' she moaned.

Dolly looked at her crossly. 'I suppose the next thing you'll be saying is why can't they have punkah-wallahs here,' she snapped. She wasn't good at sarcasm, but it was hot, and she sounded out of sorts.

'Oh, tut-tut, dear, we are being tetchy today,' Clara drawled. 'Honestly, you've been as sour as a lemon since yesterday. If you've got a gripe, out with it.' Clara fanned herself vigorously. 'But for heaven's sake, stop being so cranky. What's got into you, Dolly?'

'Oh, Clara, you're such a bully!' Dolly's face flushed. 'Sometimes you're quite insensitive. You've no feelings for anyone except your precious Franco.' Her voice quavered. 'That's another thing I want to talk about. What on earth is going on between you two? Are you just leading him on like you always do?'

Minnie looked up in surprise, wondering if Franco was serious about Clara.

'What's between Franco and me is my business,' Clara replied spitefully. 'And you, madam, keep your blooming nose out of it, do you hear?'

'It's not entirely your business. Besides, you shouldn't speak to me like that,' Dolly's voice rose and she burst into tears. 'You know our situation and the problems we have. I'm only trying to get things straight and your high and mighty attitude is no help at all.' Tears were coming thick and fast. She wiped them away with the back of her hand.

'Oh, Dolly, not again!' Clara sighed wearily. She got up and circled Dolly's heaving shoulders.

Minnie was astonished at the tension between the two sisters. Something was troubling them, and she couldn't guess what it was. She knew that Dolly wasn't as tough as Clara and felt sorry for her.

'Are you in trouble, Clara?' Minnie asked. 'Is there anything I can do to help?'

'No, darling, it's a rather private thing. I'll tell you about it sometime, but later.'

Clara opened a drawer and fished out a handkerchief. 'Here you are, give a good blow,' she said, handing it to her sister. 'Come on, sweetie pie, tell me what's bothering you.' She used her most cajoling tones while stroking Dolly's hair.

Dolly sniffed. 'I'm sorry, Clara. I've got my period and I'm feeling ratty. Besides I hate these Thursday meetings. I get so worked up beforehand. Frightened, actually.'

'Whatever for?' Clara sounded genuinely puzzled.

Dolly shrugged. 'I can't explain it. I always feel dreadfully low afterwards.'

'If that's the way you feel, darling,' Clara replied, 'you don't need to come this time. I can go on my own for once. I'll say you're not well.'

'No, Clara, I can't let you down like that. I feel better now. I just wish I had a stronger character, like yours.'

Clara laughed. 'It's a good thing you haven't – we'd be forever fighting like cats and dogs.'

Minnie had followed this exchange with mounting curiosity. 'Why is visiting your lawyer upsetting Dolly so much? Has your allowance been cut?' she asked.

Dolly dabbed her eyes. 'Clara, don't you think we could tell Minnie about—'

'Not now, Dolly,' Clara snapped, glaring at her sister. 'Some other time. I'm sure Minnie doesn't want to know about dreary legal stuff.'

The firmness of Clara's tone surprised Minnie. It sounded like a warning to Dolly.

'Of course, you're quite right,' Dolly sniffed. 'But are you going to tell us the truth about you and Franco? I know you're always falling in love, but this time it is *more* than the usual flirtation, isn't it?'

Clara didn't reply. She sat in front of the mirror, picked up a brush and stroked it through her hair.

'Yes, I guess it is.' She turned to face the two girls, heaving a sigh. 'It started off like a simple flirtation. But it's become something more serious and I want to introduce him to Uncle Harry when he comes here.'

Minnie perked up. 'When are you expecting him?'

'Possibly next month,' Clara said, squirting perfume behind her ears. 'You'll enjoy meeting him. We've written all about you.'

Minnie flushed with pleasure. She glanced at the photo on the dressing table. It showed a handsome older man with shiny black hair over a high forehead. A firm wide mouth took the edge off an austere appearance. A direct and penetrating gaze from dark eyes gave him an air of quiet authority. She was thrilled at the prospect of meeting him. It made her feel closer to her two friends, as if they wanted her to be part of their life.

Clara looked at her watch, jumped up and opened the wardrobe. 'Good heavens, Dolly,' she said in alarm. 'Look at the time! Stop yapping. We'll miss the tram to Trastevere if we don't hurry. Sorry, Minnie dear, but we shall have to rush.'

Something about Clara's abrupt ending of the conversation puzzled Minnie as she hurried to meet Franco at the café. It was odd that the sisters should be going to one of the poorest parts of town. Most legal firms had premises in Via Flaminia. Trastevere was on the wrong side of the river. It was not an area for respectable law chambers.

8

Soon after Minnie started at her new job, Signor Giolitti announced that the café would shut for the Ferragosto bank holiday in mid-August. He himself would not return until early September and during his absence Franco was to be in charge.

A couple of days later Minnie stopped by to see the sisters at the *pensione* before starting her afternoon shift.

Dolly embraced her warmly. 'Clara is out having her hair done,' she said. 'I'm so glad I've got you to myself for a change.'

Minnie returned the hug. 'I know what you mean. Clara does tend to take over. How long before she's back?'

'I guess about an hour.' Dolly took out two bottles of nail varnish and a manicure set from the dressing table. 'I was going to do my nails,' she said. 'Why don't I do yours too? Would you like to try this colour? It's the latest from Max Factor.'

Minnie sat down and held out her hands. She was proud of her long shapely fingers, and colour on nails was the 'in' thing at present. 'It's so lovely to be pampered,' she said.

Dolly took her hand, cleaned the nails with acetone and began applying the cherry-red polish. 'Hardly pampering, darling,' she said. 'I'm just glad of your company. You don't know what it means to me – and to Clara of course – to have a lovely friend like you.'

'What a sweet thing to say,' Minnie replied, almost embarrassed. She'd always thought she was the lucky one to have their friendship. 'But you must have plenty of other friends.'

Dolly dipped the brush into the varnish pot and applied a second coat. 'Actually, we haven't any good friends in Italy; one or two acquaintances, but that's all.'

'Why do you say that?' Minnie was astounded. With their background she thought they would have been out to dinner several nights a week. But according to Franco, they led a rather quiet social life.

Dolly looked up from her task. 'We're never in one place for long. Ladies we've had introductions to tend to be rather snobby about us. They feel we are out to catch a rich husband, so they keep their distance. As for the men, invariably they think we are good-time girls because we are here without a chaperone. You know what I mean. Whereas you've never judged us or thought us odd. We felt rather isolated until we met your brother. You and Franco have been so warm and friendly. You can't imagine what a difference it has made.'

'Oh, Dolly, it's the same with me,' Minnie said. 'I've never had a really close friend, and you and Clara have been wonderful with me.' She sighed. 'You know, my home life is quite…restricted.' She gave Dolly her left hand. 'My parents are extremely conservative, certainly as far as I am concerned, especially my mother. She can be pretty oppressive at times.' Minnie felt disloyal talking about her mother, but words simply spilled out of her. 'She chased away my brother Aldo from home after a fearful quarrel. We were close and I miss him terribly.'

'What was the quarrel about?' Dolly sounded surprised.

'Aldo had different political views to my mother. She said she couldn't tolerate a socialist under her roof. I've hardly seen him for two years, and then only in secret. You can imagine that to have you and Clara as friends has opened up a whole new world for me.'

'As long as we two unchaperoned ladies don't lead you on the road to ruin,' Dolly laughed. 'There, I've finished. Wave your hands about; it helps to dry the polish quicker. I'll do mine now.'

'Are you going somewhere special tonight?' Minnie asked.

'Franco's taking Clara to an open-air dance in the Villa Borghese gardens. He's asked a friend of his, Edoardo Farinelli, to be my escort. I've only met him a couple of times, but I suppose it's better than staying here on my own.'

Minnie blew on her nails and wondered why Franco had not introduced him to her. 'Well, there you are, you've got a boyfriend.'

Dolly flushed and reached for the bottle of varnish. 'He's not my type at all. He's shy, rather hard up and a bit boring – too intellectual for me, really. Besides, I have one in Bombay. At least, I had.'

'Dolly, you never said! Tell me about him!'

'There's nothing much to tell. I've known him almost all my life. He's a distant cousin. We had a sort of understanding before I left India. But I've been away nearly two years and we don't write as often as we used to.' She concentrated on painting her nails.

Minnie could see Dolly didn't want to pursue the subject of boyfriends. She picked up a bottle of cologne and dabbed some on her wrists.

'Do you think we might all go somewhere together over Ferragosto?' she suggested, changing the subject. 'Wouldn't it be nice if we went to the Frascati hills for the day to get away from the heat?'

Dolly looked slightly embarrassed. 'I'm afraid Clara and I will not be able to do that.'

Disappointment slipped over Minnie's face as she met Dolly's gaze in the mirror.

'You see, Uncle Harry will be here soon,' Dolly continued hastily.

Minnie perked up, thrilled at the prospect. The sisters spoke so often about Uncle Harry, Minnie felt she knew him already.

Dolly said Uncle Harry was presently in England on business and outlined his proposed itinerary. Minnie had never heard of half the places Dolly mentioned – Ascot, Epsom, Goodwood – but thought how wonderful it must be to travel like that. She couldn't help noticing how fondly Dolly spoke of her uncle, and how eager she appeared at the prospect of seeing him soon.

'You're ever so lucky, Dolly, to have Uncle Harry,' Minnie said. 'He's been like a real father to you and Clara since your own father died.'

Dolly spun round from the dressing table holding the nail varnish brush. She looked startled. 'Who told you my father was dead?' she asked sharply.

'I– I just assumed… Clara sort of mentioned…well, from what she said I gathered he had died…' Minnie's voice trailed off.

Dolly jumped up and paced the room. She seemed highly agitated.

'That Clara! She gets me mad sometimes. She makes up stuff to suit herself and then ends up believing it. If it's anything unpleasant she pretends it hasn't happened!'

'What do you mean?' Minnie asked.

'What I mean is…' Dolly heaved a great sigh. 'What I mean is, Father isn't dead!' she blurted out.

Minnie straightened up as if stung. 'Sorry, I had no idea.' She couldn't understand why Clara would have led her to believe something like that. 'Is he in England, too?' she ventured.

'No, he's not.'

Minnie waited for more, but her friend seemed unwilling to say anything further. 'Where is he?'

Dolly's mouth tightened. 'Actually, he's here,' she muttered at last.

'What, somewhere in Italy?'

'No, I mean here, in Rome.'

'In Rome! But how...?' Minnie hesitated. 'Why doesn't he come to see you?'

'He can't.' Dolly's reply was terse.

Minnie was baffled. 'Why not, if I may ask?'

'Because we go to see him.'

'I see.' Minnie pretended to be satisfied, as if this reply explained it all, but curiosity got the better of her. 'What do you mean? Is he ill in hospital?' That had to be the explanation, she thought.

'No, he's not ill.'

Minnie was more puzzled than ever. 'Then why doesn't he come here to see you?'

'He can't, because...because he's in prison!' Dolly gasped, bursting into tears.

Minnie's arm circled the weeping Dolly's shoulder when shortly after Clara entered the room.

'Good heavens! Whatever is up?' she asked in alarm. 'Dolly, are you all right, darling? Minnie, what's going on?'

Minnie looked up without replying. She was shocked and embarrassed by Dolly's confession but hadn't the heart to ask the reason for their father's imprisonment. She felt aggrieved that the sisters hadn't seen fit to tell her of their predicament earlier. After all, they were supposed to be such good friends. Whatever could their father have done? Was it a crime of passion? Or, Heaven forbid, was he involved with the Mafia?

She stroked Dolly's head. 'Come now, Dolly, do stop crying,' she murmured.

She had no idea if it was going to be all right or not.

'For God's sake, Minnie, what *has* been going on?' Clara barked.

'Don't snap at her, Clara. I had to tell her about Daddy,' Dolly croaked through her tears.

'Oh Lord!' Clara groaned and slumped into an armchair. 'Dolly, I can't leave you for five minutes... Well, I suppose it had to come out sooner or later.' She sighed with weariness and rubbed her face. 'Minnie my dear, now you know our secret.'

Minnie tried to find the right words, torn between diplomacy and overwhelming curiosity.

'I'm sorry to hear this. I really had no idea; I assumed he had died long ago. Does Franco know?'

'I told him a few days ago. He'd sort of guessed because someone he knew had seen us getting off the number ninety-four tram at Trastevere.'

Minnie nodded. The number ninety-four was well known for being the tram that took visitors to Regina Coeli prison. 'I don't mean to upset you or pry, but may I ask, what's he in prison for and for how long?'

'He was sentenced to eighteen months, last October.' Minnie waited for the important part of her question to be answered.

Clara looked at Dolly, who nodded. 'Go on, tell her the truth.'

Clara tried to brazen it out. 'Well, darling, if you must know, he was imprisoned for bigamy.' The phrase was tossed into the air as lightly as a shuttlecock.

'Oh really. Bigamy. I see.' Minnie looked impassive, trying to cover her astonishment. She cleared her throat, aware that Clara and Dolly were watching her in silence.

'Do you know what bigamy means, Minnie?' Clara asked.

'Well, I don't think it happens much here in Italy. Isn't it something to do with a man having more than one wife?'

Clara let out a hoot of laughter. 'It means a man marrying another woman while he is still married to someone else.'

'But I thought that was allowed in India.'

'Only amongst Muslims,' Clara said. 'And it's definitely not allowed in Europe.'

'How did it happen?'

Clara lit a cigarette and took a deep drag. 'We lived in Paris when we were quite young – Daddy had a business there, but Mother fell seriously ill. She needed lots of treatment for a long time. After she died Daddy went to pieces and so did his business.'

'It must have been dreadful for you,' Minnie said, her arm still round Dolly. 'How old were you?'

Dolly blew her nose. 'Clara was eleven and I was nine.'

'What happened?'

'We were sent back to India to live with Uncle Harry,' Dolly said.

'Didn't your father go back with you?'

'No,' Clara said, taking another puff. 'He needed to sort out the failing business. And then several months later he married Karen. She was the nurse who looked after Mother throughout her illness.'

'We were glad, actually,' Dolly added, 'because we liked her a lot. But Uncle Harry felt we had had too many disruptions to our education. He realised Daddy couldn't look after us properly, so he became our guardian.'

'What happened next?'

Clara put out her cigarette and took up the rest of the story. She told how Karen and their father continued to live in Paris, but after five turbulent, roller-coaster years of marriage they separated, although remained on friendly terms.

'However, Daddy never actually got around to proceeding with a divorce,' Clara continued, getting up to pour a glass of water. 'For nearly ten years Daddy led a pretty rootless life, taking up one business after another, and failing.' She shook her head.

She went on to describe how a couple of years ago, while their father was trying to set up a business partnership in Italy, he had met Cristina, the thirty-year-old only daughter of his wealthy partner. His belated *coup de foudre* blinded him to the fact that he was still a married man, a detail he neglected to reveal to Cristina before they married. Six months later, Cristina learnt quite by accident that she was not the sole Mrs Pestonji. Indeed, the legitimate Mrs Pestonji, far from being dead (their father having passed himself off as a sorrowful, childless widower), was hale and hearty and living in Paris. Cristina's livid father spared no expense in taking his so-called son-in-law to court on a charge of bigamy.

'Well, there you are, that's the whole story,' Clara concluded.

Minnie had listened to the unfolding of this drama in mesmerised silence. She tried to suppress a smile. It sounded like the script for a penny romantic novel. At the same time, she couldn't help admiring the effrontery of this colourful figure, so different from her own meek father.

'When will he leave prison?'

'We hope early in the New Year. I expect we'll take him to Paris. Karen has already said she is willing to have him back, and then that will leave us free to return home. It's what Uncle Harry is coming to discuss with us.'

Minnie's heart began pounding, leaving her breathless. She had never considered the possibility of her friends returning to India.

9

Minnie was busy at the till at Giolitti's one afternoon, chatting with one of the regulars as he settled his bill, when she became aware of someone standing in the open doorway. Thinking it was Clara or Dolly, who were expected any minute, she peered at the figure against the light and gasped, feeling her heart lurch.

It was Donna Rachele. Wearing a grey linen dress and a long gold chain over her generous bosom, her blonde hair twisted into a soft chignon, she looked every inch the prosperous Roman matron. Minnie knew that her mother's sharp eyes would have taken in the scene of her daughter in a seemingly intimate conversation with a man. Minnie licked her dry lips.

'Mamma, what a lovely surprise!' she said, stepping down from the till. 'What brings you down to these parts? Is Papa with you? Let me offer you something on the house. The speciality – a *tartufo* ice cream, perhaps?' she chattered nervously while ushering her mother to a table by the window.

Donna Rachele settled herself and looked around the room. 'I had to deliver some work to the Fontana sisters and I decided to stop by and see how you were getting on. Yes, a *tartufo* ice cream would be nice.' She turned her piercing eyes on Minnie. 'Now, tell me, who was that man? You were much too familiar with him. A nice girl doesn't act like that. Who is he anyway?'

Minnie said the first thing that popped into her head. 'That's Signor Giolitti's cousin.' She lowered her voice and leaned closer to her mother. 'He's a partner in the business. He likes to chat. We all have to be nice to him – you understand, don't you?'

Donna Rachele's face softened. 'Well, if he's a proprietor that's a different matter. I'm glad to see you're showing some judgement. But I hope you're not as familiar with the staff.'

Looking over her mother's shoulder, Minnie saw Franco descending the stairs. He hadn't seen Donna Rachele. His eyes were fixed on the tables outside. A customer came up to pay and Minnie went behind the till to deal with him.

She looked at Donna Rachele spooning her ice cream, glanced at the door and saw Clara and Dolly entering, smiling and waving to her. They looked in a buoyant mood.

'Ciao, Minnie! Ciao, Franco!' they exclaimed cheerfully.

Franco had started eagerly towards Clara when Minnie called out: 'Franco, look who's here! Mamma has come all this way to pay us a surprise visit!'

Franco stopped in his tracks and spun round. He hurried to where his mother sat, covering his confusion by kissing her on both cheeks. 'Mamma, we are honoured,' he said in a breezy voice. 'To what do we owe this pleasure?'

Meanwhile Minnie exchanged warning looks with Dolly and Clara and put a finger to her lips. They nodded and returned to their table on the cobbles.

Minnie heard Donna Rachele telling Franco the reason for her coming.

'By the way, who were those two young girls who just greeted you both? Are they Signor Giolitti's daughters?' she asked.

Franco nodded with a tight smile, grasping at this straw with relief. 'I believe they're expecting to meet friends, otherwise I would introduce you. Will you excuse me – I should take their order if they're staying.'

'Of course, my boy.' Donna Rachele seemed only too pleased that Franco should be on sociable terms with Signor Giolitti's daughters. 'Those are the sort of friends you should have,' she remarked to Minnie, who had come to sit with her.

By the time Donna Rachele left the café she was in good cheer. Minnie accompanied her to the door and noticed that Clara and Dolly were no longer there.

'Signor Giolitti's daughters have gone.' Donna Rachele sounded disappointed as she left. 'It's a pity I couldn't meet them. Perhaps another time.'

Minnie collared Franco in his office. 'What did Clara and Dolly want?'

'Only to say Uncle Harry arrived yesterday and they want us to meet him.'

A day or two later, Minnie and Franco were invited to meet Uncle Harry for lunch at the Hotel Bernini.

'I'm told he speaks reasonable Italian,' Franco said as they waited for a cab, 'so you needn't worry about talking to him.'

'But what should I talk about?' Minnie asked anxiously.

'How should I know?' Franco snapped. 'Anything you like. Try talking about horse racing – that's his passion. Or snuff boxes – he has a huge collection apparently. And by the way, don't call him Uncle Harry straight off unless he tells you – be a bit respectful.'

Minnie pulled a face. *What do I know about horse racing? Or snuff boxes, for that matter?* Her stomach churned.

They entered the sumptuous hotel foyer, all white and gold, gleam and sparkle. Marble stairs led up to the dining room with French doors opening on to a wide cane-furnished terrace. Uncle Harry sat at a table between Clara and Dolly and rose as they approached. He shook hands with Franco and turned to Minnie.

'At last we meet, my dear Minnie. My two darlings have told me so much about their wonderful friend.' He spoke gravely, taking her hand in both his. 'And I see that you are just as beautiful as they have described.' A slow smile softened his face. 'Now come and sit next to me and tell me all about yourself.'

Minnie felt herself blushing – she'd never been called beautiful before, and he was still hanging on to her hand. At first, she simply answered his questions. Although he spoke slowly, his Italian was good. She listened attentively to the conversation and bit by bit her shyness melted. By the end of the meal she was chatting with ease. He had a disturbingly direct gaze, but there was a kindness in his eyes, and something more – as if he would be able to find the solution to any difficulty.

'Franco told me that you are interested in horse racing,' she said over the dessert.

'That's quite right,' he replied.

'Have you been to Siena to see the Palio? That is our most famous horse race,' she said, pleased to be making a remark that was surely appropriate to his interest.

To her astonishment the others laughed loudly, and her cheeks reddened with embarrassment. What had she said wrong?

But Uncle Harry didn't laugh. 'No, I haven't seen the Palio, but of course I have heard of it. Unfortunately, in India our races are not quite so spectacular, nor are they as daring and dangerous as the Palio.' He dabbed his mouth with a napkin. 'The races I attend are run on the flat and are mostly about speed and stamina. In fact, when I return in October, I could take you to the first race meeting at Vallelunga. How would you like that?'

'Oh yes, I'd love it.' She looked around at the others, smiling, her embarrassment fading. 'I didn't know you were coming back in October.'

'My ship leaves Naples at the end of October, but I want to see Clara and Dolly settled into their new apartment before my departure.'

Minnie was stunned and turned to Dolly. 'What new apartment?'

'Uncle has rented a place for us until we go back to India. We went to see it yesterday. It's ever so spacious – three bedrooms, a big drawing room and a terrace and the cutest kitchen.' She laughed. 'I suppose we shall have to learn to cook. It's just off Piazza Bologna.'

Minnie's heart sank. *Heavens above,* she thought, *it's miles away, near the university. How will I manage to see them?* 'Sounds nice,' she murmured, forcing a smile.

But it was the phrase Dolly had uttered casually – 'until we go back to India' – that disturbed her more. A small balloon of sadness floated overhead, momentarily spoiling her enjoyment of the lunch.

10

Clara and Dolly moved into their rented apartment a few days before Uncle Harry's departure. While they were busy settling in, he took Minnie out to lunch at Rosati's near the Piazza del Popolo. Minnie's pleasure knew no bounds, partly because of the choice of one of Rome's best restaurants, which she'd never been to before, and partly because the invitation itself made her feel important and special.

Her shyness towards Harry melted as he ordered an aperitif before the meal, and she found talking to him without the presence of Clara and Dolly surprisingly easy. While waiting for their order, Harry gave Minnie a potted history of the family background. Minnie listened agog, marvelling at the exotic and colourful life he described.

After dessert Harry sat back, lit his pipe, and ordered coffee from the waiter. 'Minnie, my dear,' he said, puffing briefly to get the pipe going, 'there's something I wanted you to know, and that is how grateful I am – and relieved – that you are such a good friend to my darling Clara and Dolly.'

Minnie blushed. 'It is they who have been so good to me, Harry.'

'I'm sure it is a mutual thing but having met you I am certain that the friendship that has developed means more than you can realise.'

Minnie didn't know how to react, but simply listened to what he had to say.

'You know they have been through an unsettling time and your presence has helped them come through this bad patch. I can see exactly why they have become so fond of you.' He patted her hand. 'Do send me your news from time to time when I'm back home. I would be delighted to hear from you.'

Minnie beamed with pleasure. 'I will, certainly, Harry.'

Minnie's fears that she would see less of her two friends after Harry's departure proved to be unfounded. Having settled comfortably into their new flat, the sisters came into town daily to attend their classes and afterwards paid their regular visit to the café. Minnie was enjoying her life, now well established in her job, having convinced her parents that she earned more than the bank position offered, and was a firm favourite both with clients and staff.

Just after Easter, Franco was put in charge of the café while Signor Giolitti lay in hospital with a broken hip. On Clara's birthday he and Minnie organised a small celebration for her. Minnie carried a fancy cake to their table by the window and Franco brought out a bottle of champagne.

'Happy birthday, Clara,' Minnie wished her.

'Let us toast the most beautiful girl in Rome,' Franco said, embracing her.

They were on their second glass of champagne when Minnie happened to see a familiar figure crossing the cobbled square and heading in their direction.

'Franco,' she hissed, nudging him, 'Mamma is on her way here. I'm making myself scarce.' She plonked her glass on the table and scurried behind the till, from where she watched anxiously as her mother approached.

'Franco, I want a word with you,' Donna Rachele said, surveying the café with a pleased expression. 'Excuse me, ladies,' she addressed Clara and Dolly with a gracious smile. 'I won't keep him long, but I need to discuss something with him and my daughter.' She nodded in Minnie's direction. Minnie's heart was racing but she forced herself to return the smile.

Donna Rachele took Franco to one side, then hesitated, and on impulse turned back to speak to the girls.

'Signorine, although we have not been introduced, let me say how sorry I am to hear about your father and his unfortunate accident. I gather he will be in hospital for some weeks. When you next visit Signor Giolitti please be sure to give him my good wishes for a speedy recovery.'

Horrified at what she overheard, Minnie searched urgently for Franco, but he had quickly escaped to the office upstairs. She could see Clara completely at a loss for words, her mouth gaping in embarrassment.

Dolly rose to her feet. 'Signora, there is some misunderstanding,' she said with a sweet smile. 'My sister and I are not members of the Giolitti family.'

Donna Rachele looked taken aback. 'Oh, pardon me, I'm so sorry,' she stammered, 'but I was under the impression…that is to say…I've seen you here before…I thought— Well, I don't understand.'

'Our name is Preston, Clara and Dolly Preston.' Dolly used the anglicised version of their surname. 'We're good friends of Franco and Minnie.'

Minnie watched petrified as her mother's face slowly reddened, her smile vanished and her back stiffened. 'I see, just acquaintances, then,' she said abruptly.

'Forgive the error. I knew nothing of this friendship.'

Minnie cringed at her mother's rudeness. She approached their table. 'Dolly, Clara,' she started to say, but her mother interrupted, throwing her a frosty look.

'I'd better go,' Donna Rachele said, frowning and glancing at her watch. 'Tell Franco I want a word with you both as soon as you get home.' She gave a stiff nod to the two sisters, turned and stalked out of the café.

11

On the way home in the bus, Minnie managed to have a word with Franco.

'What'll we tell her?' Minnie whispered. Her face was drained of colour and her hands trembled as she gripped her handbag. 'I dread what she is going to say or do.'

'Let me do the talking,' Franco said, giving her hands a squeeze. His expression was grim.

They were summoned to the dining room where Don Peppino sat looking at the floor, nervously drumming his fingers on the table. Donna Rachele stood next to him, unsmiling, a slight tremor at the corners of her mouth.

'Sit down,' she ordered. 'You two have some explaining to do.' She paused. 'I was made to look foolish today. Who were those two women you seem to be so friendly with?'

Her voice was controlled, the words clipped, anger crouching like a tiger with tail twitching, ready to leap out. 'Minnie, how do you know them?' she demanded. 'Why haven't you mentioned them before?'

Franco spoke up. 'Mamma, I'll tell you about them…'

'Keep quiet,' she snapped, her tone rising. 'I'm asking your sister. Well, my girl, how long have you known them?'

'Just a few weeks, Mamma,' Minnie lied.

'Don't take me for a fool, young lady. They wouldn't be so familiar with you on just a few weeks' acquaintance!'

'I haven't counted the weeks; maybe it's a couple of months,' Minnie replied with a sudden spurt of courage. She looked to Franco for help.

Donna Rachele raised her voice, threatening. 'Don't you take that tone with me, if you know what's good for you. Why did you tell me they were Signor Giolitti's daughters? Do you know how embarrassing it was to find out they weren't? Why did you lie to me?'

Franco got up and grabbed his mother's arm. 'Mamma be quiet a minute and listen to me. Stop badgering the poor girl!' he yelled.

Don Peppino's fingers stopped drumming the table, his head snapped up and he looked at his son in astonishment.

Donna Rachele's eyes blazed, but Franco continued in a calmer voice. 'If you want to know anything about my friends – yes, that's right, *my* friends – I'll tell you. You assumed they were Signor Giolitti's daughters when you saw them at the café. We just let you think they were.'

'But why? Did you want to make a fool of me?'

'Of course not. It was simply to avoid the very fuss you are making now. In fact, I didn't think you'd ever meet. At least, not yet.'

'So, I was right, you were deceiving me! Anyway, I want to know who they are. They sound foreign.'

'Yes, they are.'

'Aha, I thought as much. American, I suppose?'

Franco took a deep breath. 'No. They're part Indian. From India.'

'India!' the word shrilled from her lips. 'Peppino, did you hear that?' Donna Rachele glared at her husband. 'This gets better and better. So now you are associating with cheap little half-castes!'

'Mamma!' Franco shouted, his temper flaring. 'I will not have you speak like that. They come from a good family. I've known them a long time and they are well brought up, cultured young ladies.'

Instead of his words placating her, they seemed to arouse Donna Rachele to further anger. 'Don't you shout at me!' she thundered. 'Now it comes out. You've been carrying on behind my back for months. And pray what are they doing all this time in Rome? As if I couldn't guess! And what does their father do?'

Minnie watched her mother and brother facing each other like two fighting cocks. She shut her eyes. *This is it, this is the end*, she thought, wishing she could sink through the floor into oblivion.

'Their parents are both dead,' Franco said.

Minnie's eyes popped open in amazement.

'They have a guardian,' Franco continued, 'but they are here on their own, studying History of Art.'

'Oh indeed, on their own, are they? Well, that speaks for itself. These foreign women who travel around, unchaperoned, are here for one thing and one thing only,' she ranted on, her voice shrill and denouncing. 'They're just loose women, trollops, sluts, nothing more!'

Minnie couldn't stand this tirade any longer. 'How can you say such things!'

she burst out hotly. 'You don't know them at all. They are the kindest of friends, and extremely respectable, just like any of us.'

Donna Rachele shook her head. 'You've betrayed me, both of you. I can't forgive it. Meeting these women in secret indeed! They can't be all that respectable if you didn't want to introduce them to us.'

Franco snorted. 'Oh really, Mamma, and what would you have done if I'd asked you to meet them? Given me short shrift, I shouldn't wonder. You have always been against any foreigners. In your eyes, someone from Milano is an outsider, let alone anyone from abroad!'

'Don't speak to me like that, young man, show some respect.'

Franco sighed. 'For heaven's sake! It's my business who I see and don't see. I'm fed up with always having to do what you want. Of you ordering us about. Of having to hide things from you for fear of the inevitable scene you'll make if it doesn't meet with your approval. We're grown up now, Mamma, and the sooner you get used to it the better.'

Donna Rachele grasped the back of a chair. 'I can't believe that a son of mine can talk to me in this disgraceful way. After all I have done for this family, working my fingers to the bone. If it hadn't been for me, where would you be? Not in this nice apartment, I can tell you. We'd be in the backwaters of Calabria, in some dreadful little provincial town living on the pittance your father made.'

Minnie jumped to her feet. 'Mamma, that's too unkind to Papa.'

Don Peppino looked crestfallen. 'Rachele, we know how much the family owes to your efforts, but all the same—'

'Ah, keep quiet, Peppino. What would you be if I hadn't scrimped and saved, if I hadn't known how to make the right contacts, if I hadn't pushed and shoved and clawed our way out of there? You'd have remained a small pen-pusher in a council office, not making enough money to feed the family for a fortnight. We'd be stuck in some godforsaken town like Grotteria or Mammola, up to our necks in debt. Or worse. The boys could have been involved with the local 'Ndrángheta or the Sicilian Mafia and heaven alone knows how that would have ended. So, if I have an opinion about these two girls, maybe it's because I have more judgement than the rest of you.'

Having vented her righteous indignation, she stopped for breath. She pulled out the chair and slumped on to it. Franco and Minnie made eyes at each other. This was a familiar refrain that she often waved over the family, like a wand of guilt.

'Mamma, we all know how much you've done for us,' Minnie said, trying to mollify her, 'but honestly, Clara and Dolly are not what you think.'

'She's right, Mamma,' Franco added, 'and I'm glad this has come out, because I *do* want you and Papa to meet them – officially, I mean.'

Donna Rachele bristled. 'What do you mean, officially?'

Franco paused before replying quietly, 'Because I want to marry Clara.'

Minnie gasped. Don Peppino straightened as if he'd been stuck with a pin. Donna Rachele looked thunderstruck.

'Marry?' she squeaked. She cleared her throat, then roared, 'Marry! You must be mad. Never, never, never. What, bring a woman like that into our family? I absolutely forbid it!'

Franco's face drained of colour and his eyes glittered. 'How do you propose to stop me, Mother?' he asked coldly. 'I *will* marry her, you can be sure of that.'

Mother and son glared at each other. 'Franco, this is too sudden. I'm telling you, if you intend marrying that woman, you can leave this house. I will not have her under my roof.' She stood up as if to emphasise her words. 'I mean it, you go tonight, unless you reconsider.'

Franco shrugged his shoulders in disgust. 'You are being completely unreasonable.' His face grew dark with anger. 'Very well, I shall leave tonight, but you'll be sorry after I'm gone.'

Minnie was panic-stricken. *Oh, dear God, he can't go, he's got to stay.* 'Mamma, please listen to him,' she pleaded in alarm. 'He really loves her, and she loves him—'

'Quiet,' Donna Rachele barked, turning on her daughter. 'As for you, I forbid you to see them again. They've been a bad influence on you. You can forget about your job at Giolitti's – you're not going back there, that's for sure!'

The shock was too great for Minnie. Without thinking, she blurted out, 'I will not leave Giolitti's! I love the job. You can't make me leave it.'

'Oh, can't I? I'll lock you in your room, madam, until you see sense. You will stay here, and you can work for the Fontanas like before, until you get married to Riccardo.'

'No, no!' Minnie shouted in desperation, banging her fist on the table. 'I will not marry Riccardo. Never – not if he were the last man on earth. Don't you understand, I can't bear him!'

'But you are promised to him – he's expecting to marry you!' Donna Rachele sounded astonished.

'Maybe that's what *you* arranged with him, but I have never said I would marry him – and I never will.' She was trembling with emotion but faced her mother defiantly.

Donna Rachele lashed out and slapped Minnie across the face with a force that sent her stumbling into Franco. As she raised her arm again, Don Peppino stood up and grabbed it.

'Rachele, *basta*!' his voice thundered. 'That's enough. You will not touch her again, do you understand? I won't have it. She is not a child any more. You cannot treat her in this fashion.'

Three pairs of eyes looked at him in astonishment. He had never reacted before with such authority and forcefulness.

'For once you will listen to me,' he continued. 'You have always done things your way. But you are too unbending, too unreasonable. It achieves nothing. All you are doing is chasing them away from home, one by one. First Aldo, now Franco – who next?'

'I'll tell you who next, Papa,' Franco spoke up. 'Minnie, that's who.' He turned to his sister. 'Minnie, I'm not leaving you here. Will you come with me?'

Minnie felt overwhelmed. Her eyes smarted with tears, red fingerprints bright against her left cheek. Bewildered, she looked at her father. He gave a brief nod of assent. '*Sì*, it's for the best,' he said.

She turned to Franco. 'Yes, I'll come with you.'

12

Franco asked the taxi driver to stop at a bar while he made a phone call. On his return he directed him to the Pensione Doria in Piazza Bologna.

Both sisters were waiting outside the *pensione* when the cab drew up. They listened, appalled, to Franco's account of Donna Rachele's ultimatum.

'Don't worry, Clara and I have talked it over,' Dolly said, taking charge. 'We didn't book you into the *pensione* as you asked. You will stay with us – there's room enough in our new apartment for the time being. Come, I expect you've had nothing to eat since lunchtime. You'll feel better after a nice meal. There's a good pizzeria around the corner. Wipe your tears and let's go.' She held out a tissue, tucked her hand under Minnie's arm and led the way.

Minnie lay awake most of that night crying and miserable, fearful of waking Dolly, whose room she was sharing. Towards dawn she fell into a deep sleep. It was past nine o'clock when she woke with a start. She jumped out of bed knowing she was late for work and rushed to the bathroom. She hardly recognised the person that stared back at her from the mirror with puffy, swollen features and eyes still red from crying. *A real mess*, she thought as she soaked a towel in cold water and pressed it to her face.

She got dressed quickly and went into the kitchen. Dolly was seated at the table with a cup of steaming coffee in one hand and a recipe book in the other.

'Hello, sweetie, did you sleep alright?' she asked.

'I couldn't sleep much. I was too upset,' Minnie sniffed. 'Then I overslept and now I'm late for work.' Minnie leaned on the table. 'Where's Franco?'

Dolly put down her cup and book. 'Franco's gone to work. He said he would tell them you had a doctor's appointment and would be in for the afternoon shift. Here, let me pour you some coffee.' She made a fresh cup of *café latte* and pushed it across the table.

Minnie downed the hot drink gratefully. 'Glad I don't have to go in just yet. I feel wrung out. Is Clara about?'

'She's gone food shopping. I was looking up recipes – we thought of making meat loaf this evening. To tell you the truth, she and I barely know how to cook. Eggs – boiled, fried and scrambled – are about the limit of our range. Hope you know how, sweetie.'

Minnie smiled. 'It is one of my few accomplishments, besides embroidery and neat handwriting. I shall be delighted to make dinner tonight and I'd be happy to teach you, if you want.'

Sitting around the kitchen table after the evening meal, the four discussed a plan of action regarding the accommodation arrangements.

Franco drained the last of the wine. 'However much I enjoy the company of you three lovely young ladies, I've decided to move out as soon as I can arrange it.'

'Shall I come with you, Franco?' Minnie asked.

'Not at all,' he said. 'Is it okay with you, Clara and Dolly, for her to stay on here? It would mean she wouldn't have to share Dolly's room.'

The sisters agreed only too happily.

Clara laid a hand on Franco's arm. 'But where will you go?'

'Not too far away, actually. My friend Edoardo Farinelli – you remember him, don't you? – has suggested we can share rooms at his lodgings.'

'You all seem to know this Edoardo except me,' Minnie said, feeling slightly put out.

Franco got up and patted Minnie on the head. 'You'll meet him soon enough. He'll be coming in to Giolitti's from time to time. Thanks for the dinner, *cara*, you excelled yourself.'

Despite the shock of being turned out of her home in such a peremptory manner, Minnie adapted to her new surroundings with surprising ease. She still felt moments of sadness and twinges of guilt, but as weeks and months went by also a great sense of freedom. Her new life was altogether more pleasant and less stressful, not least because she had more opportunities to encounter other people.

She was hanging up her jacket behind the cashier's desk one afternoon when Franco called out, 'Minnie, there's someone here who wants to meet you.'

A thin young man with a studious expression followed him and stood awkwardly in front of the till. Coming around from behind her desk, Minnie thought he looked shy and ill at ease and seemed to have outgrown his suit. Black hair slicked back above a high forehead emphasised a sallow complexion.

Deep blue eyes behind round spectacles peered myopically at her, giving him a preoccupied air. *He looks like a professor*, she thought, giving a tentative smile.

'This is my friend Edoardo Farinelli – I've told you about him, the one I'm sharing rooms with,' Franco said. 'He's at the Polytechnic, you know, and he's been pestering me for an introduction.'

'Oh, shut up, Franco,' Edoardo muttered in embarrassment, but Franco was off to attend to other customers. 'Signorina Minnie, I am delighted to make your acquaintance,' he said in a slightly nasal voice, shaking her hand vigorously.

'Pleasure to meet you,' Minnie murmured, retrieving her hand. 'Are you a professor at the Poly?'

'Alas, no, I am merely a struggling student, Signorina,' he replied with a shy smile.

'What are you studying?'

'Civil engineering.'

'Oh?' She looked blank.

'You know, constructing buildings, bridges, dams, that sort of thing.'

'Of course. How interesting,' she said out of politeness rather than interest. Not knowing what more to say she asked if he cared to have a coffee or an ice cream.

'Franco said it is on the house,' she said with a smile, noticing his hesitation.

'That's very kind, Signorina Minnie. I would certainly enjoy a cappuccino with cream.'

They conversed for a few minutes, as the café was quiet.

'How did you get to know Franco?' she asked.

'It is your other brother, Aldo, I knew well. We used to attend the same meetings. I met Franco through him.'

Minnie viewed him with new interest. *He must be another socialist, like Aldo*, she thought.

'Have you seen Aldo recently?' She hoped he'd be able to give her news of her estranged brother. Now that she wasn't living at home it would be quite in order to see him again.

'Not for months,' Edoardo said. 'He seems to have gone to ground. Besides I don't have time to go to those meetings any more. Too much studying to do.'

'What brings you to these parts, then? It's a fair distance from the Poly.'

Edoardo finished his cappuccino, fishing out the last of the cream with a spoon. 'I give private maths coaching to a couple of students in Piazza del Pantheon. Giolitti's is on my way.'

'In that case I'm sure we'll meet again soon. But now I must leave you and get back to my desk.'

From then on Edoardo became a regular visitor to the café. One day he asked her if they could go for a walk in the park sometime? Or take a tram ride out to the Gianicolo gardens? Minnie had never been out alone with a man before but agreed to a walk in the Villa Borghese gardens that were not so far away.

As she got to know him better, Edoardo began to call for her at home on Sundays. It was soon apparent that as a student he had little money, so their dates were confined to long walks in parks, getting an ice cream or a coffee, sometimes a tram trip, but mostly doing things that didn't cost much. They watched puppet shows in public gardens, went to local street fairs, to St Peter's Basilica and the Sistine Chapel – anywhere where entrance was free.

At first Minnie had found Edoardo a bit boring and rather too serious. He was knowledgeable, had read a lot, and always talked of things she knew nothing about or that didn't particularly interest her. Gradually she found herself reading more newspapers, magazines, even books from the library, in order not to appear too ignorant.

He was passionate about cycling and his ambition was to ride the entire length of Italy. He was saving to buy a newer bicycle than the ancient one he rode at present, which had seen better days. The private maths coaching to high school students was his means of earning the necessary money towards this goal. Minnie hadn't been much interested in cycling, but his enthusiasm was so infectious that she soon wanted to have a go herself. Edoardo was only too pleased to teach her, and they were able to hire a bike at little cost for an afternoon. She learnt quickly and loved it. The freedom. The exhilaration. The speediness. Best of all was the thrill of danger that speed brought with it. But as winter approached and Edoardo couldn't afford an overcoat, their outdoor jaunts were limited. However, on Sunday afternoons the friends all met at Franco's lodgings where his landlord and wife held musical soirées followed by card games. Although Minnie's singing voice was poor, she discovered to her amazement that she was an astute and lucky card player, and the thrill she got from speed was replaced by the dangers of playing poker.

She was happy. Her only sadness was her mother's refusal to speak to her or Franco, having made no contact since their hurried departure, despite Minnie's efforts to get in touch. But she often met with her father, who would come to see her at Giolitti's, not far from his work, and once he even came to the flat to meet Clara and Dolly.

Minnie walked down the stairs with him to the ground floor to see him out.

'They are not what I expected,' Don Peppino said as they stood at the entrance. 'From your mother's description of them, I thought they would be bad company for you. Instead I find them rather charming, polite and well-mannered.' He looked at Minnie with a half-smile and pinched her cheek gently. 'Their outlook is very modern, of course…but I think that is not a bad thing for you, *carissima*. The world is changing; you need to flap your wings. One day your mother will understand.'

13

The church bells for the ten o'clock mass on New Year's Day 1928 woke Minnie from a deep sleep. Her head throbbed, and her eyes felt heavy. She pulled the blankets to her chin and waited for the ringing to stop. She liked the sound and if she listened hard, she could hear what seemed like an echo coming from the church in the next district. Resisting the urge to spring out of bed and get dressed, she let her mind drift back to the previous evening.

It was her first exciting New Year's Eve celebration. Franco had booked a table for twelve at a popular *trattoria*. After a substantial meal accompanied by lots of wine, laughter, paper hats, crackers and throwing of streamers, they proceeded at ten thirty to a New Year's Eve ball at the sailing club on the banks of the Tiber. Minnie was glad Clara had taught her to dance a little and managed reasonably well during the evening – better than Edoardo, who trod on her toes a lot. Midnight signalled the moment to let down one's hair, with lots of cheering and hugs and kisses between one and all.

The party broke up just after two o'clock. There was no public transport or cabs at that time. The roads were made hazardous by the tradition for households to throw out their cracked pots and glassware on to the street and make an auspicious start to the New Year with newly acquired replacements. Dodging the sharper bits and avoiding being hit by crockery chucked out of an upper window turned the narrow cobbled streets into an obstacle course and it took the girls and their companions over an hour to reach home.

Minnie listened to signs of life from the kitchen, guessing that Dolly must be up and about. Slipping out of bed, she pulled on a heavy cardigan over her nightdress and thanked the good Lord for the apartment's central heating and the bliss of constant hot water. How different to the perishing cold rooms at home.

Dolly had coffee percolating on the stove when Minnie entered the kitchen.

'Good morning, darling, and a happy New Year.'

'And to you too.'

'How did you sleep?' Dolly asked.

'Like a log! Though not long enough!'

Dolly eyed her friend. 'Now tell me all about you and Edoardo. What happened after we came upstairs? He was being quite romantic with you when we were walking back.'

Minnie blushed. 'Yes, he was. By the time we got here, my hands were freezing, but he warmed them up and then he…well we…he kissed me.'

'But he's kissed you before, hasn't he?'

'Not like this time. It was different. I could hardly breathe. He made me feel tingly all over. Every time he touched me, it was like an electric shock going through me, and he kissed so hard I thought my teeth would crack.'

Dolly put her hand over her mouth and giggled. 'Oh, Minnie, I hope you behaved yourself!'

Minnie feigned shock. 'But of course I did, what do you think I am?'

'Just be careful, darling, and control yourself.' Dolly poured the coffee and milk into small bowls into which they dunked sliced panettone left over from Christmas. 'So what do you think of Edoardo?' she asked. 'He seems quite smitten with you. Are you in love with him?'

What could she say to Dolly's question? 'It's too soon to tell, I suppose,' she said thoughtfully. 'We haven't known each other that long. But I am fond of him.'

Still weary from the exertions of the previous night, they sipped their coffee in silence, each retreating into their own little world.

Minnie wondered about her feelings as she bit into the softened panettone. At first, she hadn't given Edoardo much thought, but he had grown on her. It was not only the physical thrill she got from his touch. Although this awakened sensations of intense pleasure and desire she had not experienced until now, there was an emotional aspect to her feelings towards him she had not expected.

She knew that Edoardo came from a modest family and had struggled against all odds to go on to higher education that his father could not afford to fund. He was not a hands-on, practical person like his brother Emilio, whose aptitude for mechanics had earned him an apprenticeship with a motorcycle works. In fact, Edoardo was rather clumsy as a young man but had a talent for understanding abstract issues. His great strength lay in mathematical concepts and from his mid-teens he had earned money through coaching his weaker schoolmates and preparing them for examinations. In his final examinations he received the highest results his school had ever achieved and had been awarded a scholarship to study civil engineering at the Polytechnic.

What Minnie admired was that Edoardo was not shallow or a show-off, but a man of some depth, more so than Franco or her other brothers. He had an encyclopaedic knowledge of diverse subjects ranging from dinosaurs and fossils, volcanic eruptions, architecture, archaeology, and railways, his particular favourite. She found his shyness and modesty endearing and it brought out in her an almost maternal tenderness for him. No one had ever shown her so much affection and consideration, and she soon realised just how much she needed this attention.

The sound of the toilet flushing brought her back to the present.

'That'll be Clara, at last.' Dolly rose to fetch another cup. 'Clara, do you want milk in your coffee?' she called.

There was a muffled response followed by a sound of scuffling. Minnie looked up from her bowl. Clara stood in the doorway in her dressing gown, her face rosy and glowing, all smiles, hand in hand with a sheepish Franco, bleary-eyed, slightly dishevelled and unshaven. He was wearing the evening suit from the previous night, minus the jacket, with collar and cuffs unbuttoned and a silly grin spread on his face.

'Franco!' Minnie gasped. 'What are you doing here at this time? Why are you still wearing your dinner suit?'

'Minnie don't be so dumb,' said Franco. 'Isn't it obvious?'

'Why do you think?' Clara murmured shyly.

Minnie blushed, feeling foolish.

'We have something to tell you,' Franco announced, putting his arm around Clara. 'Clara and I are engaged!'

The next few weeks passed in a dizzying round of activity, with preparations for the wedding marred only by Clara announcing one day that their father was to be released from prison at the end of February. The dilemma they faced was what to do with him. Uncle Harry had told the girls that they were to return to India after Russi's release, possibly with him, but their father was 'on no account' to be left to his own devices.

Clara wanted to get married as soon as possible and, of course, take Franco with her to India. But what were they to do with her father?

The three girls were in the kitchen preparing the evening pasta.

'Honestly, Dolly, it couldn't have happened at a worse time,' Clara said, slamming the colander into the sink.

'Why do you say that, Clara?' Dolly asked, perplexed. 'After all, he'll be able to attend the wedding.'

'That's just it – I don't want him at the wedding.'

'Oh, Clara, how can you say such a thing? Your own father?' Dolly was clearly shocked. She stopped grating the Parmesan.

Minnie continued chopping the garlic and parsley and listened to the sisters. She wanted to keep well out of this argument.

'Dolly, for heaven's sake, grow up! You know what he's like. He'll bumble around interfering in all our affairs, making unwanted arrangements that he can't pay for. I get angry at his endless grand gestures!'

'I know, Clara, but he means well,' Dolly said soothingly. 'Maybe he's changed after all this time.'

Clara snorted. 'Don't count on it. No, enough is enough. How many times do we have to continue being nursemaid to him? We did it in Paris and in London, always there ready to pull his chestnuts out of the fire.' She drew a strand of pasta out of the pot and bit it. 'It's too *al dente*, needs another two minutes. Honestly, Dolly, we've been here for the past year and more pretending everything is okay when it's not. Inventing a fictitious business that takes our dad all over Europe. Going to classes we don't really want to attend, just to create a respectable cover for ourselves. After all, we can't very well tell people our dad has been in prison for the last eighteen months.' She began laying the table. 'Dolly dear, do finish grating the cheese.'

'Sorry. No, of course we can't say that.'

'I should think not. And I certainly don't want him travelling out with us on the ship. Can't you just see him, using his famous charm, his lavish ways, beguiling the other passengers, and then conning them? Oh no, I'm not having that.'

'But surely Daddy will have to stay with us here after his release?'

'Not if I can help it.'

'Clara dear, you are too hard. I'm sure he wouldn't be a nuisance. Haven't you noticed how much more sensible he seems on our recent visits?'

Clara sighed. 'Dolly, my dear girl, you're *so* gullible.' She tested the pasta again, took the pot off the hob and drained it in the sink. 'Oh, let's hope this time he's learnt his lesson and won't try the bigamy game again. He's much better at embezzlement. But bigamy?' Clara rolled her eyes upwards. 'In a Catholic country? I ask you. Really, he needs his head examined!'

The three girls burst out laughing, but in the following days Minnie couldn't help being bewildered as she was swept along in the wake of her two friends' excitement. Franco had applied for a passport and was checking on medical requirements. All the talk was about the wedding in six weeks and their departure a month after that.

In a way that she couldn't pinpoint, Minnie felt herself becoming more detached from the preparations. It was all happening to them, not to her. She felt left out and became increasingly anxious about her own future. What was she to do after they left?

As the time for Russi's release drew nearer, Minnie noticed that Clara was unwavering in her determination that he was not going to ruin the happy run-up to her wedding, and she was adamant that he would not travel back to India on the same ship with them. Minnie had been thinking about their dilemma and although she felt it was not her place to interfere in this family matter, she could see a solution to the problem.

'I've had an idea about what to do with your father after his release,' she said over dinner one evening.

The two sisters stopped eating and looked at her in surprise.

'You mean something we haven't thought of ourselves?' Clara said sarcastically.

'Shut up, Clara; at this stage any suggestion is welcome,' Dolly said. 'Fire away, Minnie.'

Minnie put down her fork. 'I imagine that you will want him to be at your wedding. If you are going to invite Karen too, why not get Karen to take him back to Paris with her after the wedding?' she said quietly. 'You told me she was willing to have him back and they're still on good terms. It seems to me she knows how to keep him in check.'

There was a pause as Clara and Dolly exchanged looks. 'Oh my God! Why didn't I think of that?' Clara said. 'I'll book a phone call to Karen straight away.'

The nearer it got to the date fixed for Clara's wedding in mid-March, the more worried Minnie became about where she was to live after their departure. In the kitchen one evening, she found Clara and Dolly huddled together reading a letter from Uncle Harry. They spoke in English, which they often did when discussing family matters.

She flopped despondently on to a chair.

'Hey, Minnie,' said Clara, 'what are you looking down in the dumps for?'

Minnie shrugged without answering.

'Come on, sweetie, what's up?'

'Nothing's up,' she replied scratchily. 'Oh! I don't know. I feel…sort of nervous, you know – well I'm sad that you're all going away and I'll—' and covering her face with her hands she burst into tears.

Dolly pushed her chair closer to Minnie. 'We should have spoken to her before,' she murmured to Clara. She drew Minnie's hands away from her face.

'And you thought you'd be left here all by yourself?'

Minnie nodded, too choked to speak.

'With nowhere to live – perhaps thinking you'd have to go back home?'

Minnie nodded again, sniffing.

'And you really thought we'd let that happen to you?' Clara butted in.

Minnie stopped sniffing. She squinted up at Clara through her tears, nodding.

Clara's smile grew wider. 'As if we'd do that! You're like a sister to us. No, my sweetie pie, you're coming with us. And here's the letter to confirm it!' she cried, handing Minnie an envelope with her name on it.

Minnie slit open the envelope and drew out the letter it contained. It was from Uncle Harry, and it invited her to come to India with Clara and Dolly, as his guest, for as long as she liked, but for at least a year. 'You cannot imagine how much your friendship has helped my darling girls through a difficult period in their lives,' he wrote. 'You mean a great deal to each of them in different ways. With Dolly you are gentle and patient and sensitive, where Clara would be impatient and aggressive with her. She has always played second fiddle to Clara's more exuberant personality, but you make Dolly feel she is important to you. As for Clara, she appreciates the way you can calm her down or bring her down to earth when she is too impulsive and how you can soften her often-untactful remarks. Your presence in Bombay would help them settle back into life that for them has undergone considerable interruptions and uncertainties in the last few years.'

Minnie sat in a daze, her despair turning to euphoria.

'Well, darling, what do you say?'

'Unless, of course, you want to stay because of Edoardo?'

'No, no, no,' the words tumbled from her mouth, Edoardo forgotten for the moment. ' I definitely want to go. How wonderful. I can't believe it. For a year? Does Uncle Harry really mean it? I haven't a passport. Is there time?'

'Of course he means it. There's just time, but we'll have to step on it. You'll need vaccinations, and photographs, and you'll have to get measured for clothes and give notice to Giolitti's, and confirm the tickets and…'

*

Before falling asleep that night, Minnie tried to put some order into the jumble whirling around in her mind. She could hardly believe her luck. Tears pricked her eyes as she thought of the extraordinary kindness of Uncle Harry. She had never encountered such fairy-tale generosity. Her heart beat faster as she tried to imagine what India would be like. Would wild animals wander in the streets? Would people ride on elephants? Would houses be equipped with running water and toilets? Would there be apartment buildings or only houses? *What foolishness*, she said to herself. *No doubt there will be modern amenities. After all, Clara and Dolly and Uncle Harry are amongst the most modern, forward-looking people I've ever met.*

She thought of Edoardo and how this trip might affect their relationship. Her emotions were torn between whether to stay in order to secure their growing feelings, or to take a once-in-a-lifetime opportunity of seeing a new world. She knew she would never get this chance again. And if Edoardo's feelings for her were genuine, as he often stated, they would surely stand the test of separation.

She sighed and turned out the bedside light.

Franco and Clara were married in a civil ceremony at the Town Hall on 17 March. Neddy and Edoardo acted as witnesses for Franco, while Dolly and Minnie stood for Clara. Don Peppino and Donna Rachele did not come, but Salvatore attended, as did several friends from Giolitti's, as did Russi and Karen. Afterwards they repaired to Osteria dell'Orso, where Neddy had laid on a wedding luncheon. Copious amounts of *spumante* were consumed, and the guests became a little tipsy and in the late afternoon accompanied the wedding couple to the railway station. There, at one platform the happy couple caught the train to Naples for their four-day honeymoon in Capri, while from another platform Karen and Russi boarded the wagons-lits to Paris.

A month later, Mr and Mrs Franco Marapodi, Dolly and Minnie arrived at Naples harbour to board Lloyd Triestino's liner, the MV *Galileo*, bound for Bombay. A pale spring sun shone without warmth on the clusters of visitors gathered for their farewells at the quayside. Edoardo had accompanied Minnie on the train from Rome. Minnie hadn't been able to say goodbye to her parents, Donna Rachele having refused to speak to her. She had to content herself with a farewell letter to them, giving her postal address in India should they decide to communicate with her.

To Minnie's astonishment, Don Peppino turned up with Neddy and Salvatore.

He hugged her silently and they spent a quiet half-hour together in the ship's lounge. When he rose to let her be alone with Edoardo, he handed her an envelope.

'This is for your expenses during the voyage. When you reach India, I will send you what I can from time to time.' Then he pressed a small package into her hand. 'Open it later,' he said, his voice thick with emotion, 'when you are alone. Think of me when you use it, as I shall think of you always, my beautiful daughter.' Close to tears he held her in a tight embrace before releasing her. 'Now, let me go and find Franco and Clara.'

Too choked for words and with eyes streaming, Minnie clutched the package and hugged him tightly as if she couldn't let go, and then together they went up to join the others on deck. Edoardo drew her aside out of earshot of her family and told her once again how much she meant to him. 'Don't forget to write to me as often as you can. We must not lose touch,' he said. Out of view of curious eyes, they exchanged a lingering kiss. Before walking back to the gangway, he took both her hands in his and kissed them. Gazing deeply into her moist eyes, he whispered: 'Don't forget me, *carissima. Buon viaggio* and God bless you.'

'I'll never forget you, *carissimo* Edoardo,' she replied, stroking his cheek, 'and remember, a year will pass quickly.'

The apprehension that weighed like a stone in the pit of her stomach was lifted by the knowledge that Edoardo would be the strand that kept her linked to the country she was leaving behind.

With the visitors ashore, the ship slowly edged away from the quayside. Minnie stood at the rails with Franco, Clara and Dolly, waving to the members of her small world. She continued waving and wiping her eyes even when the tiny figures had been reduced to shapeless blobs blurred by her tears. A shiver of fear went through her. Was she doing the right thing? It was too late to turn back now.

As she swayed with the roll of the ship, she wondered sombrely what the future held for her.

Book Two

14

At dinner on the first night out Minnie, Dolly, Clara and Franco were placed at the first officer's table. Their dinner companions were a young couple from Turin whose family owned a well-known chain of hotels in India called Faletti's, and an older couple, a doctor and his wife from Florence returning to his practice in India after a long leave. The first officer was a pleasant young man, about thirty years old, called Paolo Della Croce. This was his third tour of duty to India on the *Galileo*, his previous tours having been on the South America route. He informed his table guests that the ship was to make an unscheduled stop the next day at Messina to pick up a group of missionaries who had been unable to get to Naples in time for the departure.

'How long will the ship stay in port?' Franco asked.

'Only about six hours,' the first officer said.

'That gives us plenty of time to go ashore,' Franco said enthusiastically. 'I haven't been back since we lived there as children.'

Minnie looked astonished. 'I don't remember living there at all.'

'You will when you see it, little sister.'

Walking ashore next morning they made for the tree-lined esplanade about fifteen minutes away from the port. Minnie looked around her to see if she could remember any landmarks, but nothing seemed familiar. The orange blossom was out; spring was more advanced than in Rome. There were a few beautiful buildings, but a lot were badly neglected and dilapidated. The streets were dirty and there was a general air of seediness about, as if the whole area had seen better days. Now it just looked poor and miserable, with smelly drainage too. Clara and Dolly left them at the promenade to go and explore the local shops. Minnie and Franco strolled along the walkway, which was pleasant enough, curving round a splendid stretch of beach with a long row of white cabins at one end. They were quite big, with small chimney pipes at the back; they looked vaguely familiar.

'Where have I seen those beach huts?' Minnie asked, frowning.

Franco stopped in his tracks. 'They're called *baracche*. Don't you remember them?'

'Not really. Should I?'

'Well, we lived in one of them for several months when you were about four or five.'

'I've no memory of that at all. It must have been uncomfortable. Tell me about it.'

They found a bench shaded by oleanders and sat down.

'Papa was working at the City Council,' Franco said, lighting a cigarette. 'Salvatore was born here in the summer of 1908.'

'Wasn't that the year of the huge earthquake?'

'It certainly was, just after Christmas.' Franco went on to tell how the family managed to flee from their apartment before the building partially collapsed. People from nearby streets ran towards the safety of the beach and they followed the crowd.

As he spoke, flashes of memory came to Minnie: being carried on her father's shoulders clutching his thick curly hair. Franco confirmed this and told how their mother carried the baby and shooed the three older boys in front of her, each carrying bundles of clothing, blankets and cooking vessels, while Concettina, the family's maid, carried the precious pasta pan on her head and screamed all the way to the beach.

'I had quite forgotten Concettina,' Minnie murmured, smiling. 'She burnt her long braid while roasting chestnuts for me, and Mamma had to cut her hair short.'

As Franco continued telling what happened, more memories came to Minnie. She recalled feeling unbelievably cold and being frightened all the time; that they all slept on a couple of mattresses on the floor of a *baracca*, which was assigned to them; that baby Salvatore slept in a wooden fruit crate; and that she was constantly hungry.

Franco described how he, Neddy and Aldo went out in the mornings to scavenge for wood or coal for the stove. He told of the long walk along the beach to the toilets and washrooms, which were always full of people, and of Concettina forever being sent out to get buckets of water at the communal taps. She was a distant relative, a poor cousin who helped their mother to look after Minnie and Salvatore. Minnie remembered the girl giving her a hot chestnut, which she didn't eat but held tightly to warm her hands.

Minnie became lost in thought. She had learnt that more than a hundred thousand people had lost their homes in the earthquake. She didn't know how long the family had lived in the *baracca* and couldn't recall her parents ever speaking about it when she was growing up. When she questioned Franco as to why, he seemed unwilling to talk.

'It was never spoken of in front of you because of the tragedy, which obviously you don't recollect,' he said hesitantly. 'The doctor told Mamma that since you were so young you were likely to forget all about it in time, but that the family should never say anything to remind you of the unpleasant incident.'

'What happened, Franco? If it concerns me, I should be told now, at least.'

Franco sighed and glanced at his watch. 'We should be getting back.'

'Not before you tell me,' Minnie insisted.

He sighed again and took a deep draw on his cigarette. 'Late one afternoon, as Mamma was preparing the evening meal, she scolded Concettina for not having fetched enough water earlier in the day. Concettina was playing with you and didn't want to go out but Mamma forced her. Since you were clinging to her skirts she asked if she could take you with her. Mamma was only too pleased to get you out from under her feet in that cramped space...' He paused.

'Go on, Franco,' Minnie urged, seeing how reluctant he was to continue.

Franco stubbed out his cigarette. 'When you and she hadn't returned more than an hour later, Mamma and Papa became worried and together with a bunch of neighbours they started searching for you. It was a long time before you were found – nearly midnight – way down the farthest end of the beach, well beyond the town lights where there were no *baracche*. You were huddled next to Concettina, who was stretched out on the sand, wordlessly shaking her, trying to wake her up.'

'What happened?'

Franco drew in a deep breath. 'Concettina had been raped and strangled. You didn't utter a single word for weeks, months even. But for a long, long time Mamma and Papa never left you on your own for a minute.'

Minnie put her hands to her face, utterly shocked. Tears welled up in her eyes and she wept, not knowing why because even now she had no memory of the tragedy.

Franco put his arm round her shoulders. She shuddered. Perhaps, subconsciously, her unreasonable fear of the dark since early childhood was due to this dreadful incident.

*

Two days after leaving Messina, Minnie started the first letter to Edoardo.

On board the MV Galileo
22 March 1928

Carissimo Edoardo,

Here is the first of my letters/chronicles, as promised, describing my impressions of this extraordinary adventure.

We are approaching Port Said and I am sitting in the shade on the promenade deck. It is hot, although still early in the morning. I hardly know where to begin – so much has happened even in this short time.

As the ship left the quay at Naples, I watched you and the others waving and becoming smaller and smaller. Even from a distance I recognised you waving that ridiculous yellow hat and I watched until you were only five centimetres high and then I am afraid that tears blurred my vision.

I was happy that Papa came with Neddy and Salvatore to say goodbye, although disappointed that Mamma was not with him, but I know she is still angry with me. I was dreadfully upset to think I was leaving for such a distant place with bad blood still between us, so it was a great relief to see Papa. He gave me a present, a leather-bound Italian–English dictionary, small enough to keep in my pocket always. He wrote some sweet words in it that made me cry. Thanks to all of you for giving us the most wonderful send-off. It wasn't until the ship turned around and I could no longer see the docks and the coastline that I realised the enormity of the adventure I have embarked upon.

I share a cabin on B deck with Dolly, while Franco and Clara have one a few doors down. It is most comfortable and has every comfort, including a shower. The first night out, before docking at Messina, we were not expected to wear formal dress for dinner, which was just as well, since we were all tired and hadn't properly unpacked. The tables are set for eight in the sumptuous dining room. The décor is stunning, with modern chrome fittings and glass screens etched with mermaids and Neptune designs. We have been placed at the first officer's table. His name is Paolo Della Croce. The meals are simply delicious and if I go on eating the food set before me, I shall become as fat as a cow. Thank goodness there is a swimming pool (tiny though it is) and lots of active deck games. Also, we all do a dozen laps of the deck daily in order to keep fit.

We are about to berth, so I will send this letter off with the ship's mail. I shall go ashore soon with the others and will tell you all about it in my next letter. I wish you were sharing these exciting experiences with me.

With my fondest love,
Minnie

On board MV Galileo
24 March 1928

Here I am once again, carissimo Edoardo, on the promenade deck. After spending a whole day and night in Port Said, we left for Port Tewfik early this morning. Ships must travel through the Suez Canal by day only, at slow speed and in convoy, and it may take as much as sixteen hours to reach our destination. Clara insists that I wear dark glasses when on deck and I have also on my head a strange hat called a topee that she bought for me in Port Said. It's a military-looking pith hat, and not at all elegant, but it does cut the glare. It is extremely hot now and I have stopped wearing stockings. In fact, I dress in trousers for comfort. Does that shock you? It is quite the thing and all the younger women wear them. They are baggy and cool, especially practical for playing deck games. I bought them in Port Said at an amazing shop called Simon Artz.

I must tell you about Port Said. We arrived in the morning, but before we could go on shore after lunch, a score of small boats came alongside to sell us things. We found out later that they charge twice the price for the same thing sold in shops. But it was entertaining and colourful to watch and of course lots of people bought things. To attract the attention of a passenger, it is the custom for the boatmen to address women passengers as 'Signora Mussolini', and the men as 'Signor Duce'. It was most amusing. They throw up a rope to anyone who shows an interest, the passenger then shouts out which item he wants to look at, and it is put in a basket at the end of the rope and hauled up for inspection. A lot of haggling goes on until a final price is agreed.

To get ashore we walked across pontoons stretching from the quayside to the ship because the water was too shallow for large vessels to dock at the quay. I was a little frightened on land at first by the sheer mass of people. We fought our way through crowds of young boys, some only about ten years old. I didn't like it when they grabbed our sleeves and jostled us while trying to sell all kinds of odd things; most were quite shocking, dirty postcards and so on. You wouldn't believe it, but one chap wanted to sell Franco his sister: 'Very young and pretty – only sixteen – first time – you want try – special price!' Few women were around. Those that one did see were covered from head to toe in a sort of billowing black tent with a small patch of netting in front of their eyes that allowed them to see where they were going. They all looked the same shape, and you couldn't tell if underneath was a slim young girl or a plump matron.

Most of the streets were smelly. A lot of men were drinking coffee at little bars, and smoking. There were many food stalls cooking the strangest things, with the most appetising smells. I wanted to have a taste, but Clara warned against it. She said it was asking for stomach trouble. And the clamour! You cannot believe how noisy it was, worse than Naples, with motorcars tooting and hawkers shouting out at the top of their voices. It was all hustle and bustle and chaos. We bought several souvenirs at Simon Artz, but it was hot and dusty and it was a relief to get back to our cabin for a cool shower.

Today we started our journey through the Canal before breakfast. Because it is an extremely narrow waterway, the ship travelled almost at walking pace – that's to say camel walking pace! We reached the Great Bitter Lakes, which is a wide resting place where ships travelling from opposite directions can pass. We waited there six hours. The heat was unbelievable. There was not a breath of air in the cabins, and we were better off on deck. The intense glare bleached out all colours. Out there on the sands it was a black and white world. Even the few date palms looked black. I was glad of the breeze when we continued the journey and we will shortly be arriving in Port Tewfik.

I forgot to mention that I met those missionaries we picked up in Messina. They are travelling in second class, and I have become friends with one of the nuns. Her name is Sister Maria Serafina, and would you believe it, but she lived in the same little town in Calabria where I was born and knew my late grandmother. She comes from one of the local aristocratic families, is only about twenty, and has not yet taken her final vows. She is teaching us to dance the tarantella. I am sorry she is not posted to Bombay but to a small town with an unpronounceable name in South India.

I am being called for lunch and will finish this later.

At lunch Minnie noticed her place had been changed and she was now seated on the first officer's right, and Dolly on his left. At one point she noticed that Paolo Della Croce was paying her more attention than he was Dolly. This pleased her, although it made her a little flustered. She became acutely conscious of his closeness to her, aware of his faint body scent, a mixture of pine, tobacco and starch. His tanned left hand bore no ring, she noticed. When he leaned towards her to pour water into her glass, the mere brush of his arm on hers sent little pulses of heat through her. She felt her cheeks flushing. *Good heavens, whatever would Edoardo think*, she thought guiltily, and turned to talk to her other neighbour.

At the end of the meal Paolo asked if she and the others would like to have a conducted tour of the ship to those areas usually off limits to passengers. They accepted eagerly and spent the next hour clambering up and down steep gangways, squeezing into narrow corridors, descending further into the bowels of the ship. The often slippery and steep surfaces caused Paolo to take Minnie's hand with a firm and lingering hold to guide her over tricky spots. By the time they were escorted back to the lounge, an unspoken rapport had grown between them and she agreed to his suggestion of taking a stroll on deck the following night when he would teach her the names of the stars.

Two evenings later she and Dolly were dressing to go to the captain's cocktail party. Minnie spent a long time struggling with her unruly hair, brushing and combing until she was satisfied that it looked sleek enough. She applied lipstick carefully to her full lips, while Dolly looked on.

'Have you written to Edoardo today?' Dolly asked.

'Uh-huh.'

'I don't suppose you've mentioned that the first officer is flirting with you?'

Minnie's hand jerked, leaving a crimson streak above the lip line. 'Oh, Dolly, look what you've made me do, saying silly things like that. I'll have to start all over again.'

'But it's true, isn't it? Anyone can see how he is attracted to you. And what went on last night when he was supposedly teaching you the names of the stars?' Dolly said mischievously.

'Don't be silly, Dolly, nothing at all happened,' Minnie replied primly. But she was rather pleased. 'He's only being kind to a first-time traveller,' she added dismissively.

'In that case why are you taking so much trouble about how you look if you don't think he's interested?'

'Dolleee,' Minnie groaned, turning to her friend. 'You know it's not true!'

'Be careful, Minnie darling,' Dolly warned.

'Careful of what?'

'Of shipboard romances, sweetie. They never last.'

'I'm not having a shipboard romance,' Minnie snapped.

Dolly ignored her remark. 'I know I'm only a year older than you, but I feel almost more sisterly towards you than to Clara. I've seen more of life than you have, darling. And I've had a shipboard romance myself once, so I know what I'm talking about. Anyway, come along, Minnie, we don't want to be late for the captain.'

Later that night, Minnie reread the letter she had left unfinished, but her thoughts kept returning to Paolo Della Croce and his interest in her. He was good-looking and amusing. There was a quality of stillness about him she found disturbing. His manners were polished. He was attentive yet reserved. He had thick blonde hair. A deeply tanned face showed up the fine white crow's feet around the eyes, which were the colour of the sea. Sitting next to him at the dinner table that evening, she had to suppress a sudden urge to touch his hand.

No, she would certainly not write to Edoardo about Paolo Della Croce!

She ended her letter with:

Once again, I wish you were here with me to share this incredible trip. Only three weeks ago, I could never have imagined anything like this. It is such a different world to the one you and I know, but I assure you, carissimo, even you could become accustomed to it quickly, as indeed has Franco, who acts as if he were born to it. My next letter will be posted from Bombay. I will tell you about our arrival and give you my impressions of the Red Sea, which we are traversing at present.

I can't imagine why it is called that? It is not red at all, but the deepest blue.

With all my love and affection, as ever,
Your Minnie

15

Bombay, 1928

A piercing shriek woke Minnie from the deep sleep that enveloped her after hours of tossing and turning in a new bed on her first night in Bombay.

It was dark. She reached for the bedside light switch, but her hand met an unfamiliar resistance. It took her a moment or two to realise it was the taut mosquito net tucked around the bed like a cocoon. The thin sheet was tossed aside, and her body was sticky with perspiration. A thread of grey showed through the tops of the louvred shutters, but otherwise the huge room was filled with velvet darkness. The oil lamp next to the bathroom door had gone out. Lying motionless, she willed herself not to panic. She listened for sounds she might identify within the stillness of this strange room, afraid to untuck the mosquito net and stretch an arm into an alien darkness to search for the light switch.

Her eardrums flickered with the effort of listening. Had she dreamt the shriek? It had sounded like a baby in pain. But all was still now. She recognised a slight whirring noise as the slowly rotating blades of the ceiling fan. The distant whoosh-whoosh came from the surf breaking on rocks at the end of the grounds. The occasional sibilant drones she heard belonged to the mosquitoes that failed to reach her damp flesh.

The silence was broken by three thumps on the wooden floor of the veranda outside the bedroom, followed by a soft cough and throat clearing. Goose pimples of fear peppered her arms until she remembered Uncle Harry telling her about the night watchman's hourly rounds. This was his way of reassuring the family that he was on the job as he passed the bedrooms. She turned over, comforted by the thought.

A while later the scream woke her again. More shrieks followed, rising to a crescendo then stopping abruptly. There was no mistake. This was a child in agony. Faint light filtered into the room through the shutters, allowing her to make out the shapes of the furniture. She tugged at the netting, untangled herself and scrambled out of bed. Slipping on a kimono over her cambric nightdress, she padded to the louvred door and stepped on to the veranda. There was silence. The air was filled with the heavy scent of champa flowers from a tree growing close by. Grey dawn mist shrouded the grounds and trees beyond. She leaned over the dew-moist railings to see if anybody was about. Surely the others must have heard the dreadful sound? Why were they not doing anything about it?

Another piercing shriek tore the air, this time much nearer. She froze. A slight movement to the left caught her eye. Biting her lip, she watched as first one, then another long, low shape strutted majestically out of the thinning vapour. The creatures circled each other, shrieking and dragging their long train of plumes behind them. Raising them above their backs, they spread their tails like gigantic fans. With dazzling feathers trembling, blue-green, iridescent, gold-shimmering, the two peacocks slowly circled their way out of the lifting mist towards the first glints of sun.

Minnie soon found herself faced with a multitude of unfamiliar sights and customs – almost too many to assimilate – not least the change of food and eating habits. Her best policy was to look and learn and say little. If she needed explanations, Harry was the best one to approach. He was gentle and considerate and never made her feel foolish or inadequate, as a few of the new acquaintances did. She was determined to make the most of this experience.

It looked increasingly as if she might have to do it on her own. Clara and Franco were wrapped up in each other. They had rented an apartment by the seafront in Mafatlal Park, an ultra-modern complex of six buildings with a communal swimming pool, one of the first of its kind in Bombay. It was only a short distance away from Uncle Harry's rambling house on Malabar Hill where she and Dolly were staying. She didn't see them as much as she expected, but as Dolly pointed out, once they got over the honeymoon phase, they would become more sociable. In any case, Franco was working full time, having been offered a job as assistant manager at Faletti's Hotel through the couple they had met on the boat.

Dolly, too, was not as available as she had been in Rome. It was soon apparent that Harry's nephew, Jimmy Dubash, and she were romantically involved, the same young man Dolly had been reluctant to talk about to Minnie at the *pensione* in Rome. As a result, Minnie frequently found excuses to stay at home while they went out.

She entered the drawing room where Uncle Harry was listening to a record of classical music on the gramophone.

'My dear Minnie, have I the pleasure of your company again this evening?'

Harry always addressed her in English. He had arranged for her to have conversation coaching five days a week. She was hugely thankful she had chosen English as one of her options at the *collegio*, as already her spoken language was reasonable. The deal with Harry was that if she was fluent by Christmas, he would teach her to drive a car.

'Yes, it's just you and me for dinner tonight.'

'In that case, we shall dine at the Willingdon Club. I want to introduce you to some young English friends of mine. It'll be good to practise your English with them.'

Minnie enjoyed these evenings, where she could learn new things all the time. With the amount of entertaining that Harry and the girls did, she soon picked up the names of the bewildering variety of drinks that were served on these occasions. Whisky soda or dry martinis were offered in the evenings only. Gin and tonic at any time, and pink gin only at Sunday curry lunches. Her own favourites were gimlet and shandy.

The monsoon season, when it broke in June, was an experience. Minnie had never encountered such lashings of rain. She associated heavy rain with cold weather, but here it was warm, even if one got soaked. Little charcoal burners called *sigris* were placed daily in front of open wardrobe doors. If not, the humidity caused clothes, shoes and bags to grow a thick layer of green mould overnight. She now understood the meaning of clothes having the 'monsoon smell'. She learnt to cope with frequent electricity cuts, and always to have oil lamps ready for use. She became used to looking carefully at the veranda before venturing out, as it was often possible to find snakes traversing it in search of drier hideouts. She soon learnt the Hindi word for snake and to call the watchman or gardener if she saw one.

'Minnie dear, you must remember to lock the drinks cupboard,' Dolly, who oversaw the day-to-day running of the household, remarked primly.

'Did I leave it open? I'm sorry.'

'It must be kept locked at all times – no matter how trustworthy the servants are, there is always pilfering. The same goes for the kitchen storeroom. It's a temptation for them. They can sell a bottle of Scotch down in the bazaar for more than they earn in six months.'

Minnie learnt how to address servants: never too familiarly. She noticed that others hardly ever bothered to say please or thank you to them, but she continued to do so. *Always remember to let them do everything for you*, she had been told. *They won't thank you if you make your own bed or wash your own undies. Be firm but fair, and don't be a soft touch or show favouritism – it'll only cause dissatisfaction in the servants' quarters.*

She found most things unfamiliar, but perhaps the strangest aspect was the change in Dolly. In Rome, she had been soft and mild, always underplaying to Clara's vivacity and daring. But here, in her own element, she was firm and decisive; she managed an orderly household, and knew how to deal with the servants, of whom there were a great many. *Far too many for a household of only three or four people*, Minnie thought, when she was taken on a tour of the house and introduced to them. There was a cook and his assistant (called the matey), both Christians from Goa, Dolly explained, since religious rules precluded Hindu or Muslim cooks to handle the various meats or pork. Then there was the head bearer or butler who attended principally to Uncle Harry, preparing his bath, his clothes and shoes. His duties also entailed waiting at table, serving drinks in the evenings and generally controlling the other servants. He was the only one allowed to take Dolly's keys to the various store cupboards. Below him were the number-two bearer and a house cleaner and all three of them were Hindus.

A woman from the Harijan or untouchable caste, who wasn't allowed in the house and did not live on the premises, came to clean all the bathrooms daily. It had puzzled Minnie at first why each bathroom had a back door as well as the internal one until she learned about the caste system. Finally, there was the ayah, the only female servant, who attended to Dolly, and now to Minnie as well, washing and ironing their clothes and generally looking after them. The gardens and grounds were tended by a head gardener – the *mali* – and his assistant and, in Harry's case at least, there was also a syce at the stables who looked after Harry's and the girls' horses. Lastly, Harry's chauffeur, Abdul Aziz, was the only Muslim, whose quarters, because of his wife's purdah, were slightly apart from all the others, and his little wife only joined the other women when there were no menfolk around. Dolly knew all the family members by name, except for the new babies born during her stay in Italy.

'It is like a small village,' Minnie remarked as she was shown around and introduced to the wives. 'Do they live here permanently?'

'Our servants do. But in most of the other households, they only let each family in turn come down from their village to stay for a month each year. And then once a year each servant goes back to his village for a month's holiday. Or for the death of a family member. You'll find that all servants seem to have about six grandmothers.'

Minnie raised her eyebrows seeing the wide grin on Dolly's face.

'And believe it or not they all die around harvest time!'

Minnie laughed. 'But why do you let them stay here all the year round?'

'I suppose it's because Uncle has a more enlightened policy than most. He thinks it is hard on the men to be separated from their families for long periods. They know that if their wife or any of the children are ill, they'll get proper medical care here.'

'With so many kids each, I imagine it could be quite expensive for them.'

Dolly laughed. 'Oh, they don't pay for it. Uncle pays. The family's company doctor comes down once a month to check them out. They get properly inoculated for various things; you know, cholera, small pox, typhoid, that sort of thing. And she tries to teach them about hygiene and family planning too, but I fear in that sphere she's not been too successful.'

Minnie didn't know what to say. Words seemed inadequate in front of such benevolence. It was an action she could only equate with the works of the church in Italy. Her admiration for Harry's kindness and generosity grew immeasurably on discovering that he not only supplied medical care for the dependants of his employees, but also saw that all their children of school age were admitted to the company's school.

'But if he's a judge,' she asked Dolly, 'how can he have a company?'

'He's related to the Dubashes. Pestonji & Dubash is their company, and he's a director.'

Minnie had realised only recently just what an important industrial conglomerate the Dubashes owned. Their core businesses were shipping and construction, but they also owned all kinds of smaller businesses: factories that made fine muslin for men's dhotis, a biscuit factory, interests in jute mills in Calcutta, and a pineapple farm at Chembur, amongst others.

As outdoor activities were somewhat limited during the rainy season, this was a time for ladies' coffee mornings, cocktail and dinner parties, and weekly dinner dances at some of the clubs. One or two grand balls were held each year at the Taj Mahal Hotel – the 14 July celebrations by the French community and a charity ball held by the British Women's Association in aid of local charities were the top social events. The attendance at these, though mixed, was predominantly British, and soon Minnie began recognising people she'd met at different events, which made her realise that for all its vast population, Bombay society was rather small and restricted.

These social engagements required a constant renewal of wardrobe, and frequently Minnie found herself being measured for new outfits. The situation made her feel uncomfortable because when she protested, saying she could not afford so many new clothes, her protests were gently but firmly overruled. She became increasingly worried.

'I feel most embarrassed,' she confided to Dolly. 'No one lets me pay for anything, and I am quite unable to reciprocate in any way. I am not used to this level of largesse. I simply can't go on accepting so many gifts.'

'Don't worry about that, darling, Uncle Harry's got plenty of money, and you *are* his guest, after all.'

'Yes, but guests don't get their hosts to buy them all their clothes! Please try and understand, Dolly. I feel like I'm a charity case. I need to pay my way somehow – get a job or something. I need to find a way to repay this generosity.'

Dolly touched Minnie's arm. 'But you are not a charity case, darling. I'm so sorry, I never realised how awkward it might be for you. Leave it to me. I'll have a word with Uncle – I'm sure he'll find a solution.'

Dolly was out when Harry spoke to Minnie a couple of days later. Lighting his pipe after dinner, he leaned back in the armchair, puffed a few times to get it going and blew a stream of aromatic smoke towards the ceiling, which the circulating fan quickly dispersed. Minnie sat across from him close to the reading light on the small table separating them, intent on a piece of embroidery. The rains had eased and a light breeze coming off the sea spread the scent of joss sticks burning in the darker corners of the room to keep mosquitoes at bay.

'Dolly says I am making you feel embarrassed,' he said between puffs.

Minnie reddened, putting down her work. 'Not you, but by all you are doing for me. It is too much. I feel— I feel…'

'You feel like a kept woman, I suppose you're trying to tell me,' he teased.

She laughed. 'Well, not exactly, but…'

'My dear Minnie, I do understand. I wish you didn't feel that way. You know it is no hardship for me. It is no more than I would do for Clara and Dolly. Besides,' he continued in his quiet, deep voice, trying to ease her qualms, 'I am much in your debt for having been such a good friend to them. As I've told you before, they went through a difficult time in Rome. Your friendship meant a great deal to them.'

Minnie protested. 'No no, *their* friendship meant much more to *me*. Without them I would still be in Rome – and not nearly as happy as I am now.'

'Very well, let's say we are quits on that score at least. But you are quite right, and I have a suggestion.'

Minnie looked up, waiting for him to continue.

'I need a social secretary, someone to keep my private engagements straight. I don't like to entrust that kind of thing to my secretary in chambers. I've done it myself until now, but lately I've got into a few muddles. The last two trials have been complicated and my mind has been too preoccupied with them. I need to be properly organised.'

'What about Dolly, wouldn't she be more suitable?'

'Dolly has quite enough to do running the household now that Clara is married. Besides' – he gave a soft chuckle – 'haven't you noticed she has other things to think about? She is quite preoccupied these days with Jimmy. My guess is another wedding celebration won't be too far away!'

He leaned back, looking at Minnie through half-closed eyes. Minnie was silent. Of course, she knew that Dolly was all a-dither about Jimmy, although according to her, he had not actually popped the question yet.

But what neither Dolly nor Harry knew – and Minnie would never dream of telling them – was that Jimmy was always finding excuses to be alone with her.

'Minnie, a penny for your thoughts,' Harry's voice cut into her musing.

'Sorry, Harry, I was just thinking what a lovely idea, but will there be enough to do? I mean, it hardly seems difficult.'

'Don't you worry about that, my dear, you'll find yourself pretty busy. I shall want you to do typing as well as other office work and to answer phone calls. It's not just writing a few dates down in a diary, you know. I will pay you a regular salary, the same as I paid my previous secretary. I will expect you to work at my chambers Mondays to Thursdays from nine until three. Is that agreed?'

'Oh, Harry, I'd be delighted.' She got up and kissed his cheek. 'You've been unbelievably kind to me, just like a father,' she said.

Later that night in front of her dressing table mirror, she listened to the rain drumming against the canvas monsoon screens erected along the length of the veranda. As she applied vanishing cream to her face, she pondered what Harry had said about Dolly and Jimmy.

She recalled the first time she had met Jimmy. He had accompanied Harry to meet the ship as it docked at Ballard Pier. Jimmy did not stay long and only managed to grab a few moments alone with Dolly before hurrying back for an office meeting. Her first impression in that short time was of a tall, slim, handsome young man with a surprisingly pale complexion, lively black eyes and a hawk-like nose. His mobile face was animated, and his smile lent him an air of mischief. He had the confident look of someone at ease with himself and those around him and was brimming with barely controlled energy. It wasn't until a couple of months later that their friendship really started.

Minnie had cooked a traditional Italian meal for a few friends one evening. Jimmy, who rather liked his food, was most impressed with her efforts and could hardly believe she had prepared it all herself.

'What we have here,' he teased, 'is not just a pretty face, but a clever cook too. What other talents are you hiding?'

'That's for you to discover, not for me to say,' she answered. Later in the evening, over a game of poker, Jimmy was condescending towards her, but quickly changed his mind when she called his bluff and won the biggest pot of the evening. After that occasion, Jimmy always seemed to enjoy her company.

The night watchman's cough from the veranda announced the start of his night duty. Minnie frowned at her reflection in the mirror, gently massaging in the face cream. She couldn't help having doubts about the seriousness of Jimmy's intentions towards Dolly. Now that she knew him better, she could see how attractive he was to women. A sharp intellect was matched with an easy but sincere charm, a witty tongue, and a considerable knowledge of home and world politics. He was widely travelled, forward thinking and daring. He had firm opinions yet was diplomatic in all ways. He was also a flirt, with a wandering eye for the female shape and – when given the slightest chance – wandering hands. Minnie herself had been the recipient of an unsolicited grope or two and she wondered to what extent Jimmy's hands had wandered over Dolly, who was coy and rather a prude in her attitude towards men.

She sighed, taking up a tissue to wipe the cream from her face. It was none of her business. But though Jimmy's surreptitious advances were harmless enough and ended with them still being friends, she wished Edoardo were with her, as his presence would protect her from the many inappropriate attentions she received from others, both bachelors and married men.

Shortly after the monsoon ended, Jimmy invited a large group of friends and family to a dinner dance at the Taj Mahal Hotel to celebrate his engagement to Dolly.

'You'll be seated next to Jimmy's brother, Darius. He's a bit young, but I hope you don't mind.' Dolly was driving them to the dressmaker for a fitting.

'I knew Jimmy had a sister, Roshan. I've met her a couple of times.' Minnie had not liked her much. 'I didn't know he had a brother.'

'Actually, they were adopted by Jimmy's parents.'

'That's something else I didn't know,' Minnie said with surprise.

'They are distantly related to Jimmy's dad. Their mother and father were killed in a car accident when Darius was only six. Roshan was older and virtually brought him up from then on. He used to have terrible tantrums after his mother's death, and Roshan was the only one able to cope with him.' Dolly parked the car and they made for the entrance to Pompadour's, the dressmaker. 'As head of the family, Jimmy's father became their guardian and eventually adopted them. The three kids were brought up together. You'll see though that Roshan and Darius are extremely close. She's terribly possessive with him, practically smothers him, I feel. That's one reason we've seated him next to you at the dinner.' Dolly laughed. 'Give the poor chap a chance of getting away from her!'

Minnie was happy to be seated next to Darius. She found him easy to talk to. He was nineteen, he told her, and was shortly to leave India, to take up a place at King's College, Cambridge. It amused Minnie to see how grown up he was trying to act, smoking and drinking rather to excess. Most of the guests at the table knew him well and tended to put him down, treating him like a naïve teenager. Minnie didn't. She saw something vulnerable in him and was happy to listen seriously to what he had to say and persuaded him on to the dance floor. He was thin and gangly, all arms and legs; he had a finely chiselled nose, high cheekbones and deep-set velvety brown eyes. *Give him a few years from now, and he'll have the most amazing film star looks*, she thought.

'I hear you are Dolly and Clara's great friend from Italy. Clara's married to your brother, yes? Is that him?' Darius pointed to Franco at the far end of the table, engaged in conversation with Roshan while Clara was on the dance floor.

'That's right,' Minnie nodded.

'How did you all meet? In Rome, was it? Such a beautiful city, and what a lovely country.'

'Do you know Italy?' Minnie asked, pleasantly surprised.

'No, unfortunately not, but one knows of its beauty, its art, its marvellous ancient ruins. And, of course, its poets, Dante, Petrarch, D'Annunzio… Marvellous, marvellous stuff.'

'I'm impressed someone as young as you knows the poetry of my country so well. Have you learnt many of their works? Which are your favourites?'

Darius descended rapidly from his lofty enthusiasm. 'Well, actually not much, a few translations we studied at school, but naturally one has heard a great deal about them and would like to learn more.'

Minnie smiled. 'Yes, of course, though I confess that I do not have the same passion for them as you do.'

'I cannot believe that. They are amongst the greats. How can you not like Dante or D'Annunzio?'

'You know, when you are forced to do something you don't want to do, you soon grow to dislike it.' She recounted how her mother had forced her, as a child, to declaim poetry or play the piano for their visitors, despite her painful shyness, and that was why to this day she felt no great love for Dante, D'Annunzio or the piano.

As the evening's dancing ended, she found herself once again in Darius's company. They talked about his school, how glad he was to have left it. He told her he had received a car for his birthday and was due to retake his driving test the following week, having failed it the first time round.

'Uncle Harry has told me that he will teach me to drive just after Christmas and I look forward to that,' Minnie remarked.

'He'd better teach you properly – women don't usually make good drivers.'

Minnie's eyes flashed. 'First let's see if you pass your test this time and I pass mine, before I accept such a rash statement.'

They laughed and then Minnie asked what he proposed to study at Cambridge.

'My family wants me to read Law or Economics,' he replied, shrugging his shoulders.

'You don't sound enthusiastic at the prospect. Is that what you really want to study?'

'No, decidedly not, but I shall have to do what they want.'

'Why?'

'Because they expect me to go into the family business at some stage.'

'I see. I suppose they have a point; it's only natural to want sons to continue in the business. But are you interested in it?'

Darius pulled a wry face. 'Not at all, unfortunately.'

'I suppose it could grow on you. What would you *really* like to do, if you had the choice?'

He glanced at Minnie sheepishly. 'Promise you won't laugh? Or tell anyone?'

Minnie kept a straight face. 'I won't laugh, you can rely on it.'

'I'd like to read English Lit. What I really want is to write poetry. I want to live in London or Paris, and mix with other artists and write, and listen to music.'

Minnie suppressed a smile. 'Poetry alone may not earn you a living.'

'Oh, I don't care about the money.'

She smiled. *These are words from one who has enough wealth not to be concerned by the lack of it*, she thought wryly. 'If that is truly what you want then you should do it,' Minnie said. 'Don't be forced to study something you have no feeling for. Well, that's just my opinion. And good luck at Cambridge.'

She felt a sort of tenderness for this young man in many ways so like Edoardo in his enthusiasm and idealism of life. She was sure Edoardo and he would get on well if they ever met. She noticed Jimmy beckoning her. 'Sorry, Darius, I've got to go now, Jimmy's signalling it is time to leave.'

Darius grasped her hand and kissed it in a theatrical way. 'What a shame – but bossy brothers have to be obeyed. Minnie, I'm delighted to have met you; you have filled me with confidence. Yes, English Lit is what I shall read. One day when I am famous, I shall come back and marry you!'

Minnie laughed, tugging her hand away from his grasp.

'If that's the case, don't make it too long – I may not wait for you.'

16

By Christmas Minnie's English conversation had improved to such an extent that Uncle Harry kept his promise and began giving her driving lessons early in the new year. To her astonishment, she took to it with great ease and by the start of the hot season in February, was able to pass her driving test at the first attempt.

Minnie was ensconced in the shade of the veranda one Sunday afternoon reading the latest letter from Edoardo.

Rome, 1 March 1929

My darling girl, I am thrilled to hear that you have not only learnt to drive a motor car but have passed your test and are the proud possessor of a full driving licence. Well done! I will certainly let Neddy know when I next see him.

Your letters give me so much pleasure, it seems as if I hear your voice and I almost forget you are not here with me. It is almost a year since you left and one would have thought that such a long absence would dim the recollection of your sweet face, lessen the fervour swelling in my heart for you.

Instead, the memory of your bewitching eyes, your lovely mouth that I long to kiss again, your perfect silky skin, the smell of your hair – all these are before me as fresh and as vibrant as the day we parted (perhaps helped by the beautiful photo you sent me). As for my ardour, it burns as fiercely as ever, fuelled no doubt by your loving letters.

The wonderful descriptions you give of the exciting things you see and do make me quite enthusiastic about that colourful country. But I am so pleased that your head and heart have not been turned by the events you recount and that your feelings for me have not changed.

My news is that, as you know, I graduated last week with a 'laurea con lode' and the best thing is that I have been offered a six-month placement with Balletti & Bandini, the engineering firm. It is only temporary at present (though it could well turn into a permanent position), but still will mean good practical training for me. The experience would stand me in good stead should I decide to seek better job opportunities in India, as Franco strongly encourages me to do.

With this thought in view, I am taking English lessons twice a week at the British Council. My tutor says that I am making good progress and I hope to be proficient by the time we meet again. When and where do you think that might be? Here in Rome, or in Bombay, perhaps!?

I miss you so much and long to hold you in my arms again…

Minnie gazed into the middle distance. Although she missed Edoardo and wished he could be with her, she was in no hurry to go back to Italy just yet. Harry had assured her that she was welcome to stay for as long as she liked and so it would be much better, she thought, if Edoardo were able to come out to see her here. At least that way they could decide if they had a future in India. Besides, he was right in thinking there would be more work opportunities for him here than back home.

Minnie got out her writing case and pen to reply to his letter before Harry's guests arrived for the weekly game of poker.

By the time the game ended that evening, the overall winner was Jimmy and he left the table feeling satisfied.

'You see, Minnie, you aren't always the clever one,' he said as the guests prepared to leave.

'When the cards are against me, I don't push my luck,' she replied tartly.

'Not like your brother – he was dreadful tonight,' Jimmy murmured.

Minnie raised her eyebrows. Everyone knew that Franco could be a pretty rash player and often ended up losing quite a lot of money. She took Jimmy's arm and pulled him aside.

'I need your advice about something, Jimmy,' she said in a low voice. 'Could we have a word in private some time? But I don't want the others to know.'

Jimmy stopped his bantering tone. 'Of course, sweetie. I'm busy in the evening this week but come and have lunch with me tomorrow at my office. Say, one o'clock. It's on the fourth floor.'

*

The small dining room adjacent to Jimmy's office was airy and bright with tall windows overlooking the Gymkhana Club cricket grounds. A butler dressed in white tunic and black trousers stood ready to serve them from dishes placed on a heated trolley.

'What have we got today, Peter?' Jimmy asked.

'Consommé to start, sir, followed by grilled pomfret with green masala sauce and rice, mixed salad, and for dessert fruit macédoine with cream.'

'Very nice. Hope that suits you, Minnie.' He gestured to Peter to start serving. 'Now, Minnie, what did you want to ask me?'

Minnie sipped a couple of spoons of soup before replying. 'Dolly must have mentioned that I am in regular correspondence with a friend in Rome.'

'You mean your secret boyfriend?'

Minnie felt herself bristling. 'His name is Edoardo Farinelli. He's a bit more than just a boyfriend.'

'Sounds serious.' Jimmy grinned. 'Is he the reason you ever so nicely rebuffed me?'

'Stop teasing, Jimmy.' Minnie felt embarrassed. 'That, and because Dolly's my friend, you know.'

'I know, sweetie. It's good you have principles, especially in a place like this.' He reached over and patted her hand. 'I'm glad we two are friends. Tell me about Edoardo.'

The butler cleared away the dishes and brought on the fish course.

'He's intelligent. He graduated last week with top honours in Civil Engineering and he's been offered a temporary placement for six months with a well-known engineering firm, Balletti & Bandini. But he's thinking about the future.' She stopped.

'And? Go on…' Jimmy said while filleting the pomfret.

'Do you think that as an Italian there would be good work opportunities for someone like him in this country?'

'More than likely, I'd say. One day India will get independence. When that happens, huge expansions will take place. Engineers and technicians will be in great demand and I don't mean just British ones. France, Germany and Scandinavia will send people out. All countries with established track records in engineering and construction.'

They finished the main course in silence, during which Jimmy seemed to have forgotten Minnie's presence. When the dessert was served he turned to her.

'I tell you what. One of our directors, Homi Kapadia, is going to Milan on business in June. Let Edoardo meet up with him there for a talk. Our company has a couple of industrial building projects in the pipeline. If Homi thinks Edoardo is a suitable prospect, we can get him to come out here for a trial after his placement.'

Minnie's face lit up with delight. 'Oh, Jimmy, that would be wonderful. I can't thank you enough. I'll write to him tonight.'

'But listen, darling,' Jimmy said with a smile, 'make sure he makes an honest woman out of you!'

17

'Roshan has invited the three of us for lunch today at the Willingdon Club,' Dolly announced one day. They were driving to Pompadour, the dressmaker, for a fitting.

Minnie showed little enthusiasm.

'What is it, darling? You don't seem at all keen. Has she upset you?'

'No, of course not. It's just that – she intimidates me.'

Dolly laughed. 'That's just her manner. She's terribly bossy but you mustn't take any notice.'

'I'm sure she doesn't like me.'

'You do talk nonsense, Minnie. I'm sure she likes you. She made a point of telling me she'd like to get to know you better.'

Minnie raised her eyebrows in disbelief as Dolly prattled on.

'It's true that she isn't exactly a warm personality, but then not everyone is.'

About as warm as a lizard, Minnie thought. Why could she not take to Roshan?

Roshan shared the same good looks as her brothers, but whereas Jimmy and Darius were quite tall and well built, Roshan was petite and pencil-slim. Her narrow face, sharp cheekbones, thin lips and heavy eyelids together with a wiry body made her look more athletic than feminine. Minnie had observed that Roshan's manner was aloof, prickly and controlled. She could be appallingly rude to people, and only became gentle and animated when with her brothers. She tolerated the outrageous teasing she got from Jimmy with good humour and was protective and schoolmarmish with Darius. Minnie understood that growing up with boys had given Roshan an easy confidence in the presence of men. She was ten years older than Darius and exerted a huge influence over him.

Of course, Minnie remembered meeting Darius at the dinner dance the previous year, shortly before he left to study overseas.

'Didn't Roshan accompany Darius to Cambridge to see him settled in?' Minnie asked.

That's right,' Dolly replied. 'And on her return home, she moped around the house for weeks as forlorn and desolate as any mother who sees her favourite chick leave the nest. Since their parents were killed in a car crash when Darius was six, she's always looked after him. That is why they are so close.'

'I remember Uncle Harry telling me something about it,' Minnie said. 'He said Roshan was about nine years older than Darius, and the only one who could control his tantrums.'

Dolly parked the car in front of Pompadour's. 'That's right. They were taken in by Jimmy's father who became their guardian and eventually adopted them. The three children were brought up together.'

'Why is she still unmarried at the age of twenty-nine?' Minnie asked. 'She doesn't appear to lack suitors.'

'No indeed,' Dolly said. 'Lots of eligible young men – and in fact some much older ones – have tried courting her. They'd be only too happy to marry into the powerful Dubash family.' But the fact was, Dolly went on, until now those who dreamt of proposing were sent on their way with a cold rebuff, whereas others whom Roshan might have wished to attract kept well away, frightened off by her strong and domineering character.

Her relationship with other women was ambiguous, as Minnie knew only too well. None of them knew when they were in favour with her or not. She had a small handful of friends who shared her passion for stray dogs and cats and together they had set up a home for sick animals. In general, however, she did not take to any woman she perceived as being a threat where her brothers were concerned. Dolly was an exception and Roshan had always encouraged her relationship with Jimmy to develop.

Minnie couldn't understand Roshan's sudden overtures of friendliness. Ever since the dance at the Taj Mahal Hotel at which she had struck up conversation with young Darius, Minnie had sensed hostility from Roshan. Now she wondered if she had misjudged her.

The lunch at the club was particularly pleasant, with Roshan showing an unsuspected sense of humour. Clara had been her usual ebullient self, and even Dolly had let her hair down for once, joining in the light-hearted gossip. Minnie found herself alone with Roshan after the meal as Dolly and Clara went to book a round of golf.

'What do you do with yourself all day, Minnie?' Roshan asked, handing her a cup of coffee.

Minnie described her secretarial work for Harry and mentioned the English lessons she was taking.

'Work for Harry doesn't take up the whole day. You must have a bit of time on your hands. I wonder if you would be interested in taking on something else?'

Minnie was interested, but did not want to appear too eager. 'What had you in mind?'

'A great friend of mine, Sir Farouk Batliwalla, is keen to have Italian conversation lessons. He is already learning French. He has a charming personal assistant, Suzanne, who acts as his language coach, and I know he'd like to brush up his Italian. What do you say?'

'It sounds like a good idea,' Minnie said with enthusiasm. 'What business is Sir Farouk in?'

'He isn't in business, my dear,' Roshan drawled in amusement. 'He doesn't need to do anything. He is immensely rich.'

Minnie flushed. 'I'll let you know, Roshan. I shall have to consult Harry.'

Roshan reached for her coffee cup. 'No, don't tell Harry for the moment. Let me clear it first with Farouk.'

'If you say so.'

'Listen, I have an idea. Farouk and Hilla – that's his wife – have invited me to their place on Thursday evening. Quite informal – just a few friends. I'll take you along and that way you can meet him and see what you think.'

Minnie was amazed at Roshan's warmth. She even felt guilty for having misjudged her.

'That sounds marvellous, Roshan, thank you.'

'That's settled then. By the way, best not to mention this to Dolly or Clara. It's a bit embarrassing because they haven't been invited. We'll just say you are coming to me for dinner.'

'Very well, I won't say a thing.'

Roshan's driver came around to fetch Minnie on Thursday and then drove back to pick up Roshan at her house before setting off.

Batliwalla Hall at the far end of Cuffe Parade, a good twenty minutes' drive, was a gloomy pile of red brick plonked at the far end of a long Italianate garden bordered by gravel drives. Gas lamps surrounded three sides of the rectangle and shed a bluish light on a couple of dozen white marble statues standing in square beds surrounded by low box hedging. Most were female figures in varying stages of undress, wearing expressions of coy seductiveness. Minnie made a comment about the quantity of statuary in such a limited space, like an outdoor museum.

'Oh yes indeed, Farouk is very much a member of the "cheaper by the dozen" school,' Roshan said. 'He's a great collector, though his taste is often questionable. Probably the best of the lot are his books. His private library is one of the finest in India. He specialises in…certain collections, if you know what I mean,' she said with a knowing smile.

Minnie hadn't any idea what she meant but nodded distractedly. She was too taken with the extraordinary ugliness of the building they were approaching, which more than anything resembled a railway hotel.

Several cars were parked in front of the sweeping granite steps leading to the front entrance. Inside the cavernous hall, a doorman in white and green livery ushered them up another flight of stairs to the first floor. He led them down a wide corridor flanked on both sides with marble busts of British politicians past and present, and – in pride of place – one of Shakespeare. He tapped softly at the heavy door at the end, and stood aside to let the two ladies in.

Minnie followed Roshan into a badly lit chamber the size of a ballroom with several Persian rugs spread on the parquet floor. Four electric ceiling fans whirred at varying speeds. At the end nearest to the door was a sitting area with a group of sofas, chairs and tables, where about twenty guests were already seated and talking in low tones. Introductions were made, Roshan and Minnie found seats and were handed drinks by Lady Hilla, who returned to her place on a throne-like armchair.

Minnie felt uncomfortable. The atmosphere was decidedly odd. Perhaps it had been a mistake to come. She knew none of the others, a few of whom were Europeans but mainly they were Indian.

She wondered why it was necessary to sit with such poor lighting. There was a somewhat brighter area further down the room, which was screened off with a curtain. The dining area, no doubt, she thought.

'We're all here now,' Lady Hilla announced in an unnecessarily loud voice. She pressed a button on the wall near her. A brighter light illuminated the far end of the room, immediately rendering the curtain transparent.

To her astonishment Minnie saw a raised area in the centre of which stood an enormous bed. In the middle of the bed, pointing straight at Minnie, so it seemed, was a pair of large brown feet. Minnie blinked in disbelief, squinting her eyes to get a clearer view. Straddling an area beyond the feet were two smooth, moon-white globes the size of melons slowly gyrating below a slim waist, and a smooth pale back topped by a mass of bouncing golden curls. A deep gasping voice from beyond the gyrating globes called out.

'Has Roshan arrived at last with her beautiful Italian friend? So glad to meet you, my dear. Ohhhhh! Arghhhhh! I'll be with you shortly – bit busy just now.'

'Farouk *chéri*, shut up,' said a heavily accented voice rising from the midst of the golden curls. '*Dépêche-toi, je n'en peux plus, j'y suis presque.*'

Minnie's jaw dropped. She stared, mesmerised, watching the gyrations become more rapid, rocking back and forth, up and down, the moon globes clenching and releasing, faster still until a shudder rippled down the white back that heaved upwards as a voice groaned, 'Ahhhh, Suzaaaanne!' The brown feet twitched and jerked, the white back arched, then fell forward, the golden hair muffling the growling voice.

Minnie felt a rush of fire to her face, her cheeks and ears tingling with heat. Embarrassment and anger overwhelmed her. She turned to Roshan who was watching her with a triumphant look and glittering eyes mocking her.

'Italian conversation indeed!' she hissed at Roshan. Words in English simply failed her. '*Quanto mi fai schifo, brutta strega!*' she spat. She looked around. This was a nest of vipers – she had to get out. She rose abruptly, sending her glass crashing to the floor, tripped over outstretched feet and stumbled from the room. Her shaking legs carried her into the corridor, past Shakespeare and the politicians' heads whose cold eyes seemed to be following her, jeering at her prudishness. Outside she found Roshan's driver and ordered him to take her home.

'But what about Roshan memsahib…' he protested.

The look on her face stopped him and they drove off. Tears of fury and humiliation rolled down her cheeks, her breath nearly choking her.

'Wait, driver, don't go home,' she called. 'Take me to Clara memsahib's house.'

Franco was furious when he learnt what had occurred, storming up and down the sitting room, offended for his sister's mortification.

Clara spoke with controlled anger.

'Just wait until I get my hands on that bitch.' There was no love lost between her and Roshan. 'But, Minnie, sweetie, you should never have gone out with that woman. Unless you know how to handle her she can be terribly unpredictable and nasty.'

'How was I to know that?'

'You should have told Harry – he would have warned you.'

'But she told me not to tell him.'

'There you are. That just proves what a scheming bitch she is.'

'Can I stay the night, Clara? I really don't feel up to facing Harry and Dolly.'

'Certainly you can, my darling. Here, take this, you need it.' She handed Minnie a stiff brandy and soda. 'How could she have taken you to Farouk Batliwalla – he's known to be a depraved shit. And they call Suzanne his personal assistant. That's just a polite term for whore.' She poured herself a drink and one for Franco. 'Do you know what he makes Hilla do if he's annoyed with her? He obliges her to watch while he makes love to her older sister.'

'Good heavens. Why does she let her sister into the house?'

'She has no choice, darling.'

'Why doesn't Hilla leave him, in that case?'

Clara shrugged. 'Social position. She doesn't want to give up being Lady Batliwalla. The title means a lot to her, and what goes with it. When in Britain, they get invited to the Royal Box at Ascot no less, or they go shooting with the king at Balmoral. She's willing to pay the price for those privileges.'

Franco spoke up. 'I need to speak to Jimmy about this – I can't let it rest.'

'I agree, darling. Roshan's obviously got it in for Minnie and he's the only one she will pay any attention to.'

'Why should Roshan have it in for me?' Minnie asked.

'She doesn't need a reason. She doesn't like any woman she thinks is a threat.'

'But how could I possibly be a threat to her? I hardly know her!'

'True, but you spent a lot of time with Darius at that dance before he left for England.'

'Darius? You must be joking! He's little more than a schoolboy, for heaven's sake.'

'Maybe so, but you must understand how possessive she is about him. She obviously did not like him enjoying your company so much. I'm told he couldn't stop talking about you. She might have thought you were trying to cradle-snatch. She's probably jealous.'

'Well, she has no cause to be jealous, I can assure you.'

Minnie slept badly that night. Images like a jerky cine reel kept crossing her vision: a pearly bottom, long brown legs, a muscular arm, large hands gripping soft white flesh, lifting and pushing down, an arched back. Minnie's breathing quickened.

Italian conversation indeed!

The next afternoon, the bearer knocked at the door of her room and announced that Roshan memsahib was asking for her. Nervously, Minnie went to see her in the drawing room. She kept reminding herself of Clara's advice to stand up to her.

'What can I do for you, Roshan?' she asked coldly.

'Hello, Minnie,' Roshan replied as if nothing had happened. 'I came around to drop off some curtain material Dolly asked me to get.'

'Dolly's not here.'

'I know.' Without asking, she settled herself comfortably on the sofa. 'Ring for the bearer and ask him to bring us tea, will you?'

Reluctantly, Minnie rang the bell. Her hackles rose. *The cheek of the bloody woman, acting as if she owns the place.* 'Please bring tea for Roshan memsahib,' she said when the bearer appeared.

'Aren't you having any?'

'No, I've already had mine.'

'Suit yourself.' Roshan patted the sofa. 'Come and sit here, I have something to say to you.'

'I don't think we have anything more to talk about.' Minnie kept her voice low and controlled. She turned a desk chair around and sat down. The chair was slightly higher than the sofa, which made her feel more in control. She wanted to keep her distance from Roshan's glittering eyes.

'But I think we do,' came the firm reply.

The bearer returned with a silver tea tray, placed it on a low table in front of the sofa, poured a cup and handed it to Roshan. She sipped the tea while observing Minnie over the rim of the cup.

Minnie lit a cigarette and inhaled slowly. *She wants me to say something, but I'm not going to play her game.* She waited.

Roshan finished drinking and put down the cup.

'You're annoyed with me, Minnie, because of what happened at Farouk's place.'

Minnie said nothing, her face impassive.

Roshan drawled on. 'It's such a ridiculous attitude to take, isn't it – most immature. It was only a bit of fun, after all.'

'Fun for you, perhaps.'

'Oh, don't sound so pious and moral. It doesn't suit you. After all, we all know why you've come to India.'

'What do you mean, Roshan? Explain yourself.'

'You know how it is. British girls do it all the time. They are called "the fishing fleet".'

'The fishing fleet?'

'That's right. Fishing for a husband. They come out here for six months or a year – girls from perfectly good families, mind you – to find a husband. They nearly all go back engaged. It's well known.'

Minnie bristled. 'How can you imply that about me? I'm not doing that.'

'Oh, I'm just saying that is what the British girls do. You wouldn't stand a chance with the Brits here. You don't have the proper background, and you certainly don't have any money.'

Minnie's face reddened as Roshan went on. 'One can only assume you are a bit of an adventuress, looking for a rich Indian husband or lover.'

Minnie stubbed out the cigarette with shaking fingers. She seethed with indignation. But it was essential to keep outwardly calm. She kept her eyes fixed on the teapot. *Concentrate,* she told herself, *don't say a word; there is more to come.*

Roshan took her silence for acquiescence.

'I'm going to be frank with you, Minnie, for your own good. It's obvious what you're up to, but it is not going to work.'

'What is not going to work, Roshan?' Minnie forced herself to sound reasonable.

'Catching a rich Indian husband. You don't have any wealth, you don't have family connections to speak of and your educational background – well, you are hardly privately educated, are you? No offence, of course. All you have is a pretty face. That's why I took you to Farouk's place.'

'I don't follow your reasoning.'

'Farouk is interested in you. I know that. You could do worse than become his personal assistant. You'd get well paid, live in the lap of luxury; you'd travel all over with him, even abroad. Besides, he is a most generous man. You really couldn't hope to do better.'

Minnie slowly raised her eyes to look at the woman whose words hissed like whiplashes.

'And in return, my duties would be…like Suzanne's?' she asked with quiet control.

Roshan looked at her with malice gleaming in her eyes. 'It goes with the job. I suppose it's no different to the duties you perform for Harry. Everybody knows why you are here.'

Minnie shot to her feet and stood over Roshan. 'How dare you suggest such a thing!' she blazed with fury.

'My, my, losing our temper, are we?' Roshan said with a thin smile. But she was startled and leaned further back into the sofa.

'You are a disgrace, Roshan. It's hard to believe that someone as evil and nasty as you can come from the same blood as Harry and Jimmy.'

Roshan sat up straight. The smile vanished. 'You leave Jimmy out of this,' she spluttered. 'I know what you're scheming at. You think that Jimmy is a better bet than Harry. Well, you stick to Harry, my girl, if you wish, but leave Jimmy alone. He's spoken for – you'll never get him. And don't even *think* about Darius. Darius is mine – I practically brought him up, he'll do what I say. Don't you dare get any ideas about him.'

Minnie looked aghast. 'Roshan, you are quite mad. I don't know what you are talking about. What has Darius got to do with anything?'

'Don't pretend. I saw how you bewitched him at that dance. He could talk of nothing else for days after.'

Minnie pushed her hands through her hair. 'For heaven's sake! He's a child, a schoolboy I only met once.' She paused, narrowing her eyes. 'It seems to me you sound jealous, Roshan. What's going on?'

Roshan blustered. 'I'll tell you what's going on. You flirted with him to make Jimmy jealous. It won't work, though. Jimmy's going to marry Dolly, so stop chasing him.'

'You know nothing. What makes you think I'm interested in Jimmy? More like the other way around.'

'Don't flatter yourself, Minnie. There's only one thing Jimmy may want from you – what Harry is getting, that's what Jimmy wants.'

Minnie's hands were shaking. She shoved them into her pockets. Rage was rising uncontrollably. *If she says another word, I'll tear the bitch's hair out.* 'Harry is the kindest man I've ever met. He is like a father to me. If you make one more remark about him, I shall tell him what lies you are spreading. Oh yes, don't deny it – you spread rumours all the time. You have a nasty mind, Roshan, and an evil tongue. You are spiteful and malicious. It's no wonder not one decent man wants to marry you.'

Roshan sprang to her feet, furious. 'You little tramp, how dare you speak to me like that!'

'Oh, I suppose you can speak to *me* any way you please, but I can't do the same to you, is that it?'

Roshan opened her mouth to retort, but Minnie got in first.

'Shut up, Roshan, I've had enough of you.'

She walked to the door. Roshan's words followed her.

'Just as long as you understand to keep your grasping hands off Jimmy and Darius.'

Minnie stopped and looked over her shoulder at Roshan's twisted face.

'You stupid woman. You understand nothing. I'm not interested. I don't want either of your precious brothers.' She paused. 'Why should I? I'm already engaged to be married.'

Of course, this wasn't quite true – not yet anyway – but it gave her great satisfaction to see Roshan's jaw drop.

'Get out, Roshan,' Minnie said sharply. 'I want you to leave right now. The bearer will show you out.'

She turned her back and walked out of the room.

18

The monsoon that year was particularly heavy and overseas mail took longer than usual to arrive, so it wasn't until the end of August that Minnie received Edoardo's latest letter. *A quick note this time,* it read.

> *I have received such good news I don't know where to begin.*
>
> *You remember I wrote to you about my meeting in Milano with Mr Kapadia, and that we had an interesting talk (with the aid of a translator, of course!) but that I had heard nothing further.*
>
> *However, a month later I received a communication from Pestonji & Dubash's London office: subject to meeting certain requirements at the end of my present placement, the company have offered me the position of assistant to the chief engineer on a project to build a paper-producing plant in Poona with a projected start date in ten months' time!*
>
> *You cannot imagine how happy I am not only to be reunited with you again at long last, but also at the prospect of embarking on such an exciting project. My mother burst into tears on hearing the news, fearing that a tiger might eat me in that faraway wild land, but my father was pleased – although the first question he asked was how much I would be earning!*
>
> *I will write again soon. Now I am too keyed up to get my thoughts in order.*

Minnie put down the letter. Tears of happiness filled her eyes. She took out her writing pad and penned a note.

Dear Jimmy,

I have just heard from Edoardo about the result of his meeting in June with Mr Kapadia. Thank you, my dear, dear friend. You have made two people extremely happy.

Minnie

September marked the end of the wet weather – to everyone's relief. In Harry's household there was a flurry of activity to get rid of the musty smell of damp the extended period of rain had imparted to almost everything in the house. Cushions, sofas, mattresses, pillows, bedding, clothes and shoes were spread over the lawns or hung on lines for a few days in succession to thoroughly dry out in the hot sun.

'This is the sort of thing we do in spring at home,' Minnie said to Dolly, who was discussing with a man the job of repairing the bamboo blinds battered by the wind and rain.

'Here we do this right after the rainy season. Tomorrow I've arranged for painters to come and varnish the window frames and the veranda railings and next week we whitewash the servants' quarters. The household has got to be ready in time for Diwali.'

Minnie remembered the Diwali celebrations from the previous year. She had wondered why Harry's household observed this Hindu Festival of Light when they were not themselves Hindu, but became aware that nearly all households – British, European and others – marked the occasion.

This year Diwali turned out to be an even more magical event with tiny clay oil lamps outlining the house, the driveway and the garden paths. In the servants' quarters the tiny lights surrounded each dwelling, and all windows and doors were left wide open.

Minnie asked about the open windows while helping Dolly to hand out sweets to the little children who crowded round them.

'It's to guide the goddess of wealth, Lakshmi, into people's homes,' Dolly explained.

Harry had thrown a small dinner party for a few friends and family. After the meal the guests repaired to the garden for a traditional firework display and all the servants with their families were called and sat on the grass to watch. Afterwards, in accordance with tradition, Dolly presented each of the servants with a new uniform, each of the wives with a new sari, and new shorts and dresses for the children.

Minnie took the opportunity of having a word with Franco.

'Have you heard from Edoardo?'

'I have just had a letter,' Franco said, putting an arm round his sister's shoulders. 'Is it true that you two are secretly engaged? Why didn't you say anything?'

Minnie blushed. 'Well, he asked Papa, but Papa isn't here, so he wanted to tell you as…sort of *in loco parentis*.'

'I understand, *cara*, and I'm delighted to hear it. He's a good chap. He said he will be coming out here next year?'

Minnie nodded excitedly. 'It's true. Jimmy's firm has offered him a job, but he doesn't want to talk too much about it until the contract is signed. He thinks it might be unlucky.'

'Will you get married out here?'

'We haven't decided yet, but I think we will probably marry in Rome. Papa would be upset not to be at my wedding, and Mamma too I think, and there's no chance they would both come out here.'

'I'm sure that's for the best, *carissima*.'

After most of the guests left, Harry asked Jimmy, Clara and Franco to stay on for a nightcap on the veranda. A sickle moon and countless brilliant stars seemed to be stitched on to the black velvet sky. The Diwali lamps shed a soft glow so there was no need for extra lighting that would only attract mosquitoes. Harry's pipe smoke battled with the powerful scent from nearby jasmine bushes. Jimmy took hold of Dolly's hand.

'There are a couple of things I wanted to tell you all but didn't want to say in front of the other guests,' Jimmy said. 'Dolly and I have set a date for our wedding.'

'Not before time,' Harry murmured. 'So, when is it?'

'February third next year.'

'Wonderful, that gives us plenty of time to prepare,' Clara said, jumping up to give her sister a kiss.

'Before I forget, there's another thing,' Jimmy went on. 'I had lunch with Binky yesterday. He's invited us up to his place for ten days at Christmas. It will be a big house party and he's arranging a *shikar*.'

Dolly and Clara became animated. 'Is Binky staying in town? Why hasn't he come to see us?'

'Flying visit, I'm afraid,' Jimmy said.

'It will be wonderful to go up to his place,' Clara said to Franco. 'You'll absolutely love it. Beautiful countryside, and quite cold I should think at Christmas.'

Minnie looked puzzled. 'Have I met Binky before? Who is he?'

'He's the maharajah of Chhota Chembur,' Jimmy said. 'Good friend of mine. We were together at school in England.'

Minnie's eyes widened. 'You know a real maharajah?'

The others laughed. 'Ah, Minnie, that's what I like about you,' Jimmy said gently, 'you're so unpretentious. I know several "real" maharajahs.'

Minnie wasn't sure that she liked being considered unpretentious. It made her sound provincial and clumsy. She longed to be sophisticated, worldly – even glamorous. She would have to do something about that. Paint her nails bright red and take up smoking with a long cigarette holder, ebony and silver, just like the woman in evening dress in the adverts for De Reszke cigarettes. Oh yes, and get her hair bobbed and pluck her eyebrows into thin curves like Clara Bow. She'd practise that sultry air, too, with head lowered and eyes looking upwards. She sighed.

'Minnie, you are daydreaming again.' Harry's voice brought her back to the present. 'You haven't heard what Jimmy's been saying.'

'Sorry, I was miles away. But, Jimmy, if he has invited you, surely you can't just bring other people along with you? He doesn't even know me.'

Jimmy laughed. 'This is India, Minnie; extra guests are no problem. Besides, he will love having such attractive young ladies as guests.' He stood up. 'It's time I went home, I've got an early golf game tomorrow. Dolly, do you fancy a walk down to the sea wall before I go?'

The next morning at breakfast Minnie asked Dolly the meaning of the word *shikar*.

'I guess you mean what Binky Chhota Chembur has arranged. It's a tiger shoot.'

Minnie gasped, clapping her cheeks. 'A tiger shoot? Oh my God. Isn't it terribly dangerous?'

'Yes, quite. But it's well organised, with experienced guides. They're all good shots, especially Binky. You go riding out on elephants to reach the *machan* in the shoot area – that's the hide set up in a tree, where you have to keep utterly still and as quiet as a mouse until the tiger comes.'

'Are you going to be in the *machan*?'

'No fear!' Dolly exclaimed. 'I went on one once. I was terrified, and I got such bad cramp I thought I would fall out of the tree. No, you're going to have to do it without me.'

Minnie's mouth went dry. 'You mean I'll ride on an elephant, and sit in a *machan*?'

'Only if you're not scared to do it. But it really is the experience of a lifetime. You won't be alone; Jimmy or Binky will be with you.'

'How close does the tiger come?'

'About ten, fifteen metres.'

Minnie began to laugh with excitement. 'Oh my God. That's really scary.' She shook her head in amazement. 'I can't believe all this is happening to me.'

19

Ramniwas Palace
Chhota Chembur
Christmas 1929

My dearest Edoardo,

Firstly, I have told Franco and Clara and Uncle Harry about our plans to get married and they are delighted. Jimmy and Dolly already knew, of course, and immediately offered to have the wedding at their house, but I think it best to marry in Rome.

In answer to your question, of course I am happy. I love you dearly and think of you constantly – only I find it hard to put such emotional words on paper. I'm glad you've told Neddy and that he says you should go around to meet Mamma and Papa. Be careful – Mamma is not an easy person and will give you a good grilling. I have written to tell them but have not yet had a reply.

Now let me tell you what I've been up to. This is the first chance I have had to write since we left Bombay last Monday for our journey to Chhota Chembur. I can't tell you what a commotion it was. The main station is called Victoria Terminus – it seems to me that all important buildings in this city are named either after Queen Victoria or the Prince of Wales! Anyway, the station is immense and built in an elaborate architectural style – it looks like a palace for the King of England – and is at least four times bigger than our Stazione Tiburtina in Rome. It also seems to be a roosting place for every pigeon in the city! We had loads of luggage because we needed to take our own bedding as well as plates and cups and saucers, iceboxes and drinking water, as it is not safe to drink water on the train or at the stations.

The carriages here are much wider than those in Italy and each one is separate with no interconnecting corridors. We booked two carriages for our party. Both had four berths and private bathrooms. Dolly, Clara and I and a friend of theirs shared one, while Franco and the other men had the second one. During the day we met up in each other's compartments. Needless to say, the men got a poker game going and Clara and I got roped in.

Dolly's ayah and Lalji, the bearer, travelled with us though their berths were in the third-class section. During the day it was extraordinarily hot, and we had the ceiling fan on the whole time. At all the big railway stations, Lalji saw to it that the ice-wallah filled our icebox to keep the water and drinks cool, and that the water reservoir for the bathroom was replenished. He arranged for our pre-ordered meals to be brought to us in tiffin-carriers at the meal stops and generally saw to it that we were not unduly bothered by beggars. At night he and the ayah prepared the berths and laid out our bedding rolls.

The journey lasted three days and two nights. It was a good thing we had our own bathroom, as we all got grimy faces from the soot drifting in through the open windows. We read and played games to while away the time, especially crossing the Deccan plateau, an arid and monotonous countryside.

Whenever we reached a major railway station where there was an hour's stopover, we took advantage to step out on to the platform and stretch our legs. The platforms were incredibly crowded with all kinds of people, passengers, hawkers, baggage coolies (very colourful in red tunics and turbans), food vendors, beggars. You cannot imagine the noise and bustle, the colours and the strange smells. Everywhere were swarms of little kids begging for money or wanting to polish your shoes or sell you a paper, or simply wanting you to watch them sing or dance or perform magic tricks. You would have loved it, and I have taken lots of photos for you with Uncle Harry's Rolleiflex camera.

We changed trains twice, the first time at Delhi and then again at Pathankot before Calcutta. From there we only had a three-hour journey to Chhota Chembur, but it was rather slow. The carriages were much smaller because of the narrower gauge track, almost like a toy train, and it was uphill all the way. The scenery became lusher, the temperature more bearable and the views spectacular as the train twisted slowly up the gradient. The hills were covered in dense green jungle, and we caught glimpses of all kinds of wildlife: monkeys and parrots and hoopoe birds. At times we travelled so slowly that village children ran alongside. Now and then when the train stopped to catch its breath like an old lady, and to fill up with water and wood to stoke the engine, the children would appear selling the most exotic flowers I've ever seen.

We arrived at Chhota Chembur at four p.m. The maharajah, Binky, had *sent three canvas-topped Lancia Lambdas to meet us. We drove to Ramniwas Palace about twenty minutes away just as the sun was lowering its fat golden belly behind the blue hilltops. The palace is an enormous building of pinkish sandstone. I can't describe what style it is – it seemed to me a hodgepodge, but you will see for yourself from the photos. It's a pity you can't make out the colours, especially at sunset, when the light makes it look like a pink fairy cake with white icing and candles as it has at least a dozen turrets. I'm told it has one hundred and ten rooms – can you imagine? – with twenty-five guest suites, all with bathrooms attached (although not all with running water), and I don't know how many drawing rooms there are, each furnished in a different style.*

We were shown to our suites by a gaggle of servants. Mine is next door to Dolly's on the first floor, and we share a bathroom and a balcony that overlooks the gardens of the zenana – that is the women's quarters where men are not allowed – with a beautiful white marble fountain in a lotus pool. Tea was brought to our rooms, our suitcases unpacked, dresses taken to be ironed, dirty clothes whisked away to the laundry. Fires were lit in both rooms because we are quite high up and it had become rather cold, and buckets of hot water brought from I don't know where to fill our baths. I couldn't lift a finger to do anything for myself.

As it was our first evening, we were not required to be formally dressed for dinner. I wore a plain navy-blue dress with a lacy pale blue mohair cardigan I had knitted (copied from a Fontana pattern), fastened at the neck with a single diamante button. We met Binky for cocktails at six thirty in the Ivory Room. There were twenty-five houseguests, including Jimmy, who had arrived the previous day from Calcutta. It was a comfort to see a familiar face. Binky was charming when I was introduced to him; he is tall and dashing, with a wide moustache and spectacular white teeth. His wife, Maharani Devika, is beautiful, tiny and delicate, but I think with a strong personality. Apparently, they both hold progressive views that are frowned on by the more traditional princely families. They are shocked by Rani Devika's refusal to observe purdah like the women in the zenana who are not allowed to be seen by, or have contact with, any male outsiders.

Dinner followed at eight in the aptly named Long Dining Room. It had the longest dining table I have ever seen – quite large enough for us to have danced on – laid with the loveliest Sèvres dinner service which Binky brought back from his last trip to France. All the plates had his crest and a different bird motif painted in a central medallion. Baccarat glasses sparkled like diamonds from the light thrown from two huge Bohemia crystal chandeliers. Turbaned servants stood at attention on both sides of the room ready in an instant to replenish empty glasses or remove plates before the next course. It quite made my head whirl. After dinner, those who still had energy left joined Binky in the card room to play bridge. Although Jimmy tried to persuade us to play, Dolly and I were too tired, and we excused ourselves and went to bed.

The following day, yesterday – Thursday, I think, though I seem to have lost track of time – we were given the grand tour of the palace and grounds. You can't imagine the richness of the furniture, the precious objects, the paintings. It is my opinion, though, that good taste does not always prevail, submerged as it is by the huge quantity of objects on display in all nooks and crannies. In one room, I noticed that an exquisite green jade horse carving was displayed next to a tacky china figurine of two plump women bathers holding a banner with 'Souvenir of Brighton' written across it. And all the side tables were adorned with brown Bakelite ashtrays, like those in station waiting rooms.

I think what impressed me the most were the stables. Binky showed these to us personally. He has forty horses, some for racing, others for playing polo, and still others for hunting – pig sticking, mainly. But the most amazing were those for his elephants – yes, elephants! Somehow, I never imagined elephants to be in stables. He has ten at present, and they are used for various ceremonies as well as for tiger and wild boar hunts. He has told me that before we go on the shikar, he will take me for a ride on one so that I can get used to the swaying motion. Binky talks exactly like an Englishman in his expressions and pronunciation. One of the guests is Sir Rowley Poole, here with his wife, Lady Rosamund. He is something high up in government. Sir Rowley talks in such a manner, without moving his lips and with such an 'aw, aw, aw' accent, that I can hardly understand what he says. So, I just smile sweetly and make assenting noises. He and Binky sound just the same when they're together, which is not surprising since they were both at Eton. That is the smartest school in England, where only the aristocracy send their sons.

Lady Rosamund only talks to Rani Devika or the other English guests, and hardly at all to our little group. Today, however, at lunch she discovered that Franco and I are Italian and said how much she loves our country. Apparently, when they go home on leave every three years, she always goes ahead of Sir Rowley and spends the month of May in Florence – 'for the music, you know,' she said. Then she rattled on about Rome and all the people she knew there and asked me, 'Of course, you must know my dear friend, the Principessa Colonna.' As if! By this time, I was thoroughly irritated with her name dropping and answered as quick as a flash: 'Not personally, but my family is close friends with her cousin, the Contessa Flavia Pincopallino.' At which she beamed at me and replied, 'Ah the Contessa Flavia, indeed, I expect to make _her_ acquaintance the next time I'm in Rome.' Franco heard this exchange and almost choked while Clara and Dolly had a job trying to suppress their laughter. I saw Jimmy nudge Dolly and heard him ask in a whisper who was this contessa, and Dolly replied sotto voce, 'She's non-existent – "pincopallino" simply means thingammybob!' Jimmy winked at me while Dolly hastily changed the subject.

In the afternoon, Binky showed us his trophy room. All the guests were oohing and aahing about the animals he, his father before him and his brothers had shot. Twelve tiger skins with heads stared at us from the walls with their glassy orange eyes. There were panther heads, wild boar, water buffalo, sambar deer, and goodness knows what else. The only thing missing was an elephant's head, though he had several pairs of tusks. It made me rather sick and has quite put me off the idea of going on the shikar. Later, he showed us a pair of his hunting cheetahs, with their Muslim trainer. Apparently, only Muslims can be trainers; I suppose because they must handle meat to feed the animals, which the Hindus can't do. We were told it is an ancient princely tradition to use trained cheetahs for hunting blackbuck. This pair was so beautiful that I couldn't bear the idea of other handsome beasts such as leopards and tigers being regularly shot for sport. I don't want to take part in the shikar except to photograph the animals. I noticed that even Jimmy was bothered by his visit to the trophy room. If we are to be in the machan – the hide – together, he must promise me not to shoot anything.

I shall send this letter tomorrow as all mail is being taken to the post office in town in the morning. Did you know that most of the princely states can issue their own postage stamps? Binky has let me have many attractive ones, which I know you will love to add to your collection. Now, I must go to put more logs on the fire as it has turned rather chilly. We are at high altitude here, and although it is warm during the day, at night it is perishing cold and we are glad of fires in the rooms – and a hot water bottle in the bed!

I send you my dearest love and many hugs and kisses.
Your loving Minnie

Ramniwas Palace
Chhota Chembur
New Year's Day 1930

My dearest Edoardo,

This is to send you my best wishes and love for a happy and successful New Year. As promised, I thought of you at midnight last night, while the celebrations to see in the New Year were taking place in the ballroom. I thought back to the first New Year's Eve we spent together in Rome just two years ago. Do you remember the long walk back home after the dance, picking our way carefully through the broken glass and china lying in the streets? It was bitterly cold, and I remember you blowing on my frozen fingers and rubbing my hands to warm them. What a lot of events have happened since then.

The New Year's Eve we celebrated here last night was very different indeed. First, although it was cold, there was no broken glass in the streets. We didn't see the streets at all, because there was a dance here at the palace.

Let me start with Christmas, though. More guests arrived, among them a high-up British government official and his wife. In their honour, Binky and Devika – we are on first name terms, they are most informal – tried to make it as English a Christmas as possible. For lunch, they laid on a typical festive meal and, for those who wanted it, there was roast turkey, baked ham, bread sauce, stuffing, redcurrant jelly, roast potatoes and spiced cabbage, followed by a huge flaming plum pudding with brandy sauce. It all seemed much too heavy for my liking and I stuck to the vegetarian meal, but I did taste the plum pudding, which was delicious.

At each guest's place at table was a gift box wrapped in red paper. The men received a silver matchbox inscribed with the royal crest and the words 'Chhota Chembur, Christmas 1929'. The ladies received a silver powder compact, the lid encircled by a row of turquoises, with the same inscription. I am thrilled with mine.

In the evening, we were invited to a performance of Indian music and dances, held in the Durbar Room (that's like a council chamber, a huge hall with lots of chandeliers). I can't say I enjoyed the music much – it was quite different to Western music, and the sounds grated on my ear, especially the singing, which was not at all operatic or even romantic like Neapolitan songs. It sounded more like a nasal wail, but then you know I don't have much of a musical ear. Many of the guests didn't seem to care for it much either and only gave lukewarm applause. But others obviously appreciated it and clapped as enthusiastically as the Indian guests who all declared it to be first rate. In time I expect I shall get used to these strange sounds and learn to recognise their finer points.

However, the dancing was quite a different matter. I loved it and even enjoyed its accompanying music which consisted of complicated drum beats on instruments called tablas, together with verbal repeats of the rhythm: tha-tha-thuk the-tha the-tha tha-thuk thuk the-tha. The dancers were all young and beautiful with flashing eyes, arching eyebrows and exaggerated facial expressions that were just as much part of the dance as their hand and feet movements. They wore brilliantly coloured swirling skirts or pantaloons and short blouses heavily embroidered with silver and gold thread. They performed barefoot and wore three or four rows of silver anklet bells whose sound synchronised with the drumbeats. It was quite magical!

The day after Christmas (they call it Boxing Day) Binky organised a hunt meeting. We watched the hunters ride off quite early and it was a real picture to see. The horses' coats shimmered like silk in the sunlight, the men wore khaki trousers, red jackets and black hats and two ladies who went with them wore topees with a veil. They told me that in England they hunt foxes in this way.

On another day we watched the men playing polo against a visiting team from Durgapur. I found it tremendously exciting, as it is a fast and dangerous game and a great deal of skill and strength is required of the player to control horse and 'ball' at the same time. I didn't realise that Jimmy played polo, and he acquitted himself well. Dolly was jumping up and down in her seat, hardly able to contain herself with excitement – I've never seen her as animated as that before, she's usually so contained.

Finally, there was the famous tiger hunt. I was in two minds about going: I couldn't bear the idea of them shooting such a beautiful creature. At the same time, I was curious to see one at close quarters. In the end I decided not to go along, partly because it meant the likelihood of spending the night in the machan – in the dark, with no lights, no talking, no smoking. Fear prevailed, and I chose to stay behind with Clara, Dolly and the others.

The men returned next morning with their bag: a beautiful male tiger, quite an old one, with an old injury, the guide said, which was why it hunted close to the jungle villages and needed to be killed. Sir Roley, who had been *given the shot generously by Binky, was proud of his achievement and was photographed in the traditional pose next to Binky, with Lady Rosamund, Jimmy and the guides, with the tiger lying stretched out at their feet. I am sure enlarged copies of the photos will adorn the rooms of Sir Rowley Poole's houses both in India and back home in England in years to come, as will, no doubt, the tiger skin.*

Last evening a grand New Year's Eve ball was held in the Durbar Room, with guests invited from miles around. It was a splendid occasion with everyone dressed in their best. Most of the Indian ladies wore jewellery that you wouldn't believe: precious stones as big as quails' eggs flashed and glittered around necks and fingers and wrists. I danced a lot and enjoyed it tremendously. At one point after a foxtrot with Jimmy, we went out on the veranda for a breath of fresh air, although it was too cold and we didn't stay long.

I thanked him again for offering you work with his organisation and told him you and I would marry in Italy later this year. So, you see, there will be two marriages in the same year, though of course ours will be a more modest affair. We talked about the future and he reckons there will be plenty of work for qualified engineers and architects such as yourself as India becomes more industrialised.

I am certain you will come to love this country as much as I do, and that you will find working here most interesting. There are lots of opportunities to be had, more than there are in Italy. And we will be lucky enough to have the right connections. Altogether it seems to me a happy and encouraging start to the New Year.

I send you a big hug and kiss.
Your loving Minnie

20

Bombay, 1930–1940

Minnie's parents were delighted to welcome her upon her return from India, albeit a little in awe of the sleek and sophisticated young woman she had become. Donna Rachele had made peace with her daughter, happy at the thought of her marrying a respectable young Italian with prospects, instead of a feared foreigner. Minnie and Edoardo's marriage took place at a registry office in Rome in July 1930. Edoardo was not particularly religious and had not wanted to have a church service that would have required a lengthy wait as well as making promises he did not wish to make. They spent their honeymoon cycling around Lake Como and shortly after prepared to sail to India.

They arrived in Bombay just as the worst of the monsoon abated. Soon after settling into the new flat Clara had found for them in a new development, complete with communal swimming pool, Jimmy Dubash signed Edoardo to a five-year contract not only to assist in the building of the paper plant in Poona, but thereafter to design and build an important housing development for factory workers on the outskirts of the city. Minnie was overjoyed at finding herself back in her beloved Bombay with her new husband. Marriage gave her a sense of freedom and security she had not felt previously.

They were happy enough, it seemed to her, over the next five years, although in time Minnie realised that what she felt for Edoardo was not the grand passion she had expected. It was true she loved him, but something was missing.

She thought she had found the missing element after the birth of their daughter, Claudia, in 1936. This gave a sense of fulfilment that surprised her, as she had never believed herself to be particularly maternal, considering her experience with Donna Rachele. She adapted to her new role with relish, determined to be the perfect mother, lavishing all her newfound love and attention on this adorable little bundle of humanity who had changed her world so completely. At the same time, she recognised how lucky she was to have the daily assistance of a capable live-in ayah, not to mention several servants who took over the more tedious tasks of baby care and housework, leaving Minnie free to continue with a full and satisfying social life. She often wondered how she would have coped with the responsibilities of motherhood had she been living in Italy, with less domestic help and her forceful mother dictating how she should look after the newborn.

Minnie was devastated, however, when shortly before Claudia's first birthday, Uncle Harry died suddenly of peritonitis following a ruptured appendix. Her grief was alleviated only when little Roberto was born about six months later. Edoardo, too – despite being wholly immersed in his work and at times being quite absent-minded on the domestic front – turned out to be an affectionate father, happy to bounce the children on his knee and sing them the only nursery rhyme he knew. Minnie realised that his attention span was short, and he quickly grew weary of doing babyish things with them, but he developed a passion for photography and would snap the children at every excuse.

Edoardo also enjoyed their social life; he felt comfortable with Parsi and Italian friends but was rather shy and reserved with the English crowd. However, he felt most at ease with those acquaintances of a more adventurous nature and frequently went with a friend or two exploring some of the wilder parts of the country. He had a great interest in ancient ruins and temples and didn't mind roughing it on camping trips. These of course did not appeal to Minnie at all, and she was much happier socialising in more civilised surroundings.

As time passed, Edoardo grew to love India just as Minnie knew he would. What she had not anticipated was how much Edoardo would grow to love Indian and Anglo-Indian women.

She could not pinpoint any single incident that began the end of their marriage. There was a snail-creep of awareness that things were not right. Although the children brought them closer for a while, nevertheless she recognised signs that Edoardo's eye, and probably his hands, were wandering elsewhere. Veiled innuendoes and warnings from friends fuelled her suspicions. Roberto was only a year old when her eyes were opened to what was going on.

Minnie's good friend Barbara Davidson invited her for a quiet lunch one day. 'Just the two of us, darling,' she said. 'It's so nice to have time to ourselves.'

The conversation eventually got around to the latest gossip about one of their friends whose husband was rumoured to be having an affair.

'The trouble with a lot of the foreign men here is that their heads become easily turned,' Barbara said. 'They get themselves into situations they would not dream of embarking on back at home. There are so many temptations for them out here. You must have heard people talking about "office nookie".'

Minnie giggled. 'Well, I've heard people saying that Percy Rowling was having office nookie. I suppose it means he's being, well, naughty?'

'Yes, but he's only one amongst many,' Barbara replied. 'It's common knowledge he's sleeping with his secretary.'

'Does Maureen know?' Minnie asked.

'If she does, she knows she's better off to keep quiet about it.'

'If I were her I'd kick up a huge fuss,' Minnie blurted out.

'No you wouldn't, dear, not if you knew what was good for you.'

'What do you mean?'

'She'll keep it quiet, of course,' Barbara said. 'As long as he is reasonably discreet, she will ignore it and never admit it in public. The moment she does, she compromises Percy's position and her own. It's just not done.'

'But that's not fair.'

'Of course it's not fair. But think what she'd be giving up if there were a scandal and the company head office got to know about it. They'd probably be sent back to England to a rather dull life in the suburbs.' Barbara rang the bell for the bearer to remove the lunch dishes.

'Let's have coffee in the study where it's cool. I need to talk to you,' she said, rising from the table.

Minnie followed her, looking pensive. She had a sense of foreboding, as if the entire luncheon invitation had been engineered to lead to this moment. What did Barbara have to talk about?

The newly installed air-conditioner in the study made the room feel cool and dry.

'How are things now with you and Edoardo?' Barbara asked at last when they were settled with their coffee.

Minnie glanced up at her friend. Barbara knew about her suspicions regarding Edoardo's little office dalliances, but recently things seemed to have quietened down on that front.

'I think things are all right now. In any case he seems to be too busy. To tell you the truth, he's away an awful lot. I hardly see him.'

'Oh! Where does he go?'

'He's designed that big workers' housing project in Nasik for John Butterworth's new factory.'

Barbara nodded but remained silent.

'Why do you ask?'

'Minnie, I don't know how to say this nicely.'

'Say what?'

'Rumours are flying around about Edoardo and Angela Butterworth.'

'Angela? What about her?'

'That they're having an affair.'

'Oh, Barbara! I don't believe it. I know Edoardo has flirtations with his office staff, but Angela? She's always been charming and sweet with me – she invites us over for dinner all the time. I'd have known.'

'That's her way – always befriending the wife. Besides, you've just said Edoardo's away a lot.'

'Yes, but genuinely for work in Nasik.'

'Nasik is a small place. They've been seen there together. Very often. According to her, he's mad about her.'

Minnie's mind went numb. This could explain why relations with Edoardo had been strained in recent months. She'd put it down to the stress of the workload.

'Does John know?'

'John always knows.'

'You make it sound like a habit.'

'It *is* a habit. Angela gobbles men up like cocktail snacks. Apparently, John isn't too active on the bedroom front. But he has drawn up certain boundary lines, and if she keeps within them, he turns a blind eye to her affairs.'

'Surely it is just gossip?'

'I don't think so, darling, or I wouldn't have brought it up.' Barbara twisted the wedding ring around her finger. 'Actually, I wanted to have a word with you about this. I thought you should know and better coming from me than from someone else.' Barbara could barely meet Minnie's worried look. 'I've heard lately she's told friends that Edoardo wants to marry her.'

Minnie felt the blood drain from her face. 'Marry her? She's mad.'

Barbara poured out two glasses of ice water from a thermos flask.

'If it's any consolation,' she said, 'she'd never marry him. Oh, she's quite capable of encouraging him to leave you with implied promises of marriage. She's done it before. But she'd never marry him.'

'Why wouldn't she?'

'He doesn't have the right background. Or enough money.'

Minnie shook her head. 'I had no idea about any of this. Do many people know?'

'Quite a few, I'm afraid.'

The blood coursed through her veins in a hot tide of humiliation. 'I've just accepted an invitation to their anniversary dinner next month. I shall have to cancel it.'

'I wouldn't give her that satisfaction, if I were you,' Barbara said. 'Besides Henry and I will be there too. But my advice is that next time Edoardo goes up to Nasik, make sure you go with him.'

It took a week for Minnie's towering anger to simmer down. At first, she wanted to follow Edoardo up to Nasik to see if he was carrying on with Angela. No, she might make a fool of herself if she did. She could not concentrate on anything while thoughts of them together filled her mind. She wondered how many people knew. Perhaps Barbara had exaggerated or been misinformed. Surely Minnie would have guessed if her husband were having a serious affair with anyone.

By the time Edoardo returned from Nasik, it took all Minnie's willpower not to show him her anger and resentment.

She didn't want a confrontation. Not yet.

John and Angela's anniversary dinner was to be special. Minnie was determined to dazzle and chose her dress carefully, a simple shift in pale aqua chiffon with a scattering of embroidered sequins. Her wedding ring and a huge aquamarine ring on her left hand were her only jewellery.

Thirty-six guests were seated at six separate tables. Fifteen-minute breaks followed the end of each course while everyone switched seats to different tables, in the manner of musical chairs. Minnie found herself on the opposite side of the room to Edoardo but had a clear view of him. From time to time she observed the way he and Angela, seated at the same table, studiously avoided eye contact, ignoring each other, as couples who are secretly intimate often do when in public.

In the break between the entrée and the main course, Minnie took the opportunity to go to the ladies' room. The guest bathroom being occupied, she wandered down the corridor until she found an en suite to one of the bedrooms. While washing her hands, she glanced at the mirror. A movement caught her eye. The communicating door to the bedroom was slightly ajar. In the mirror's reflection she caught a glimpse of the room. Angela was pressed up against the wall, her head thrown sideways, eyes closed, mouth open and gasping, her blonde curls cascading over her shoulder, while a dark-haired head kissed her exposed neck. Her evening dress was pushed up over her hips, one breast exposed from her décolleté, its pale nipple stiff as a little finger. One long tanned leg was pressed tightly across the man's muscular bottom, his trousers round his ankles. Minnie recognised the check Jockey underpants she had bought for Edoardo as she watched him thrust into the moaning woman, his hands gripping her buttocks closer with each heave.

Minnie crept silently into the corridor, shaking from head to toe, her face flaming. Her vision blurred, there was a roar in her ears, the breath squeezed out of her body in short bursts. 'Are you all right, Minnie?' somebody asked at her table.

'Just feeling the heat a bit,' she replied, taking a fan from her handbag and fanning herself briskly.

She watched Edoardo return to the dining room, slicking back his hair as he took his place at a new table. Angela entered a few moments later, as if coming from the kitchen, her hands smoothing down the silk of her dress, a smile on her pearly glowing face. John Butterworth stared at his wife, who seemed to avoid his look.

Minnie barely touched the interminable main course but managed to keep up a brittle patter of conversation with her table companions while observing Angela. At the next interval before the dessert, while everyone milled around table-hopping again, Minnie lit a cigarette and made towards Angela's table.

'Minnie darling,' Angela's voice gushed loudly, 'do come and sit here. Oh, you're smoking a cigarette again. Darling,' she laughed, 'you know it's such a rude American habit to smoke between courses.'

'Is it?' Minnie drawled just as loudly, standing over her. She took a deep drag and slowly blew the smoke towards Angela. 'Not half as rude, I'd say, as fucking someone else's husband between courses!'

The room fell silent. Nobody moved. Angela's mouth dropped. 'I – I don't know what you mean,' she blustered.

'Oh, I think you do, Angela. You can fuck other women's husbands if they let you get away with it, but you're not going to fuck *my* husband any more, is that clear?'

'Minnie, for heaven's sake, let's not have a scene here.' Angela sounded defiant.

'Why not? We have a good audience,' Minnie replied, dropping her cigarette on Angela's sandalled toes. She stretched across the table and with both hands scooped up a large mound of mango ice cream from a bowl in the centre and squashed it on to Angela's head. Wiping her hands on a napkin, she watched with satisfaction as thick globs of the yellow goo dribbled down Angela's hair, covered her face, slid into her gasping mouth and on to her bare shoulders before slithering into her cleavage.

A gasp followed by a titter ran through the room.

Edoardo shot out of his seat and caught Minnie's elbow, his face red with embarrassment. 'Minnie, what do you think you're doing?'

'Shut up, Edoardo,' she said in Italian, shaking off his hand, her eyes boring into his with cold fury. 'Come on. We're going home.'

Grabbing his arm firmly, she marched him away from the table, through the door, along the hall to the entrance, and down the front steps to their waiting car.

In the week following the Angela incident, the atmosphere at home crackled with accusations, recriminations, promises and tears. Minnie sent the children to stay with Clara and Franco. Edoardo was banished from the marital bedroom to his study at the opposite end of the apartment. As the dust settled, Minnie began to listen to her inner voice again. Pragmatism was required at this stage. She needed breathing space to think and was relieved when Edoardo returned to the building site at Nasik for a week. The scene at the dinner party apparently did not have disastrous consequences for his work. John Butterworth was a practical man and was not about to jeopardise a building project that was close to completion. Besides, Minnie suspected that he was used to Angela's behaviour and managed to keep the business and personal parts of his life in separate airtight compartments.

During Edoardo's absence, Minnie spent a lot of time thinking about what she should do next. She wished she could turn to Harry again for support and guidance. He would have listened and cared and put things into perspective. She missed him terribly: his unfailing kindness, his wisdom, the safety net of his affection for her. She even missed the smell of his pipe. The shock of his death sixteen months earlier ached now as much as it had then, and she felt bereft.

Edoardo's actions had made her furious, though if truth were told her anger was not caused so much by jealousy as by humiliation and hurt pride. The worst aspect was the betrayal of trust that in her heart she knew would be impossible to regain. It had drained the love out of her.

On Edoardo's return, they had long discussions about his affair. With mounting anger, Minnie listened to him admitting to being completely infatuated with Angela. He stood by the picture window in the study looking out on the garden. 'She was like an addiction, a craving I couldn't resist,' he tried to explain over and over. 'I don't expect you to understand.' He gave a short laugh. 'I can see now that I meant nothing to her, just another meaningless conquest. A curiosity, the token Latin lover,' he added bitterly.

Minnie felt almost sorry for her remorseful husband. After all, he had many good points, but he was weak, and she despised him for not being able to keep his flies buttoned. She tried summing up her feelings for him. She was hurt but didn't hate him. She hated Angela. But she knew there had been an irrevocable change. If she didn't hate him, perhaps it was because she could no longer love him enough.

Eventually they agreed to go on living under the same roof, as normally as possible for the sake of the children. But a few months later, Minnie could see no way in which they would become fully reconciled. Too much in their feelings for each other had changed. If there was to be no return to how things were, then it was best to cut the cord. They agreed that an amicable split would be the right course to follow.

In July 1939 Minnie visited the offices of Osborne & Carmichael and filed for divorce on the grounds of incompatibility. It would be a lengthier procedure, but less messy than grounds of adultery. She and Edoardo decided to leave their domestic arrangements unchanged. The apartment had two entrances and was large enough for each to have their privacy. They would lead separate lives but continue going out as a couple when the occasion required.

It seemed a civilised solution, particularly regarding the children.

21

Satara, 1940

Minnie left the chambers of Osborne & Carmichael after a long session with Mr Michael Bentley, the senior partner. Exasperated and hot, she slumped into the car and told the driver to take her to the Taj Mahal Hotel. An iced coffee in the soothing ambience of the Harbour Lounge was what she needed before going home.

Her favourite table by a picture window on the veranda was free. She never tired of the spectacular view overlooking the Gateway of India, crowded as it was even now at midday with scores of people thronging the shade of the huge archway: beggars, hawkers, families, British sailors, gawkers and gazers. As always, little urchins in tattered shorts were diving from the slipway for coins tossed by onlookers into the choppy waters. Sailing boats, dhows and coastal craft with their white sails bobbed up and down on the dark blue waters of the harbour, a few ships steamed in and out of port and on the opposite side of the bay rose the hazy mauve hump of Elephanta Island.

Minnie lit a cigarette, inserted it into a black and silver holder and inhaled deeply. She mulled over the outcome of the meeting as she waited for the iced coffee she had ordered.

As usual, she had found Mr Bentley to be annoyingly phlegmatic, with apparently no sense of urgency for the matter in hand. Not a bad thing on reflection, but irritating nevertheless. Admittedly, his composure offset her anxiety. It made her listen to that inner voice of caution that had so often helped her in the past. *Act calmly*, it said now. *You gain nothing by losing your temper.*

'The proceedings must take their course, Mrs Farinelli,' he had said in that slow, plummy King's English she usually admired, but which now she found annoying.

'But it's taking such a long time. Christmas and New Year have come and gone. We are now at the end of February. It's been more than eight months, Mr Bentley, and we seem to be no further forward.'

'My dear Mrs Farinelli, but look what's happened in the meantime. Britain has declared war with Germany. At the best of times divorce is never a simple matter, but at present things are likely to take much longer. We are still awaiting a document from Rome, and in the current circumstances goodness knows how long that will take.'

'Even so, Mr Bentley, it seems too long drawn out. After all, it is only the decree nisi we are waiting for.'

She hoped he noted her implied criticism. But he merely replied that the decree absolute could take up to five years. Not made any easier, he added, leaning back and tapping his arched fingers together, by the fact that she was still living under the same roof as Mr Farinelli. Of course, he continued, he knew it was for reasons of convenience. Indeed, he understood perfectly that she wanted to maintain good relations for the sake of the children. Quite so. But a judge might see it differently and deem there to be collusion in such a situation.

Collusion? What on earth was collusion? Mr Bentley, Minnie told him when the term was explained, could rest absolutely assured that there was no collusion. Mr Farinelli no longer shared the marital bedroom. Indeed, his room was at the far end of the apartment. They both came and went as they pleased. The shared roof was merely a matter of economics. She hadn't yet the resources to rent another apartment or she would have moved out long since. The mere thought of having caught her husband in flagrante with one of her friends and, adding insult to injury, also with his secretary, made her wild with rage and humiliation. Not to mention the string of suspected flirtations over the past five years.

'Collusion is out, Mr Bentley,' Minnie said, tapping her finger on the desk. 'Please make this absolutely clear in your submission. And kindly let me know how much longer you expect it to be before the case is heard?'

Mr Bentley smiled sympathetically while shrugging his shoulders and advised patience.

He was irritatingly ponderous, but Minnie hoped that after today's meeting, Mr Bentley would speed up obtaining the decree nisi.

Minnie finished her coffee and a second cigarette, beckoned the waiter for her bill, and asked him to call her car. She gazed with unseeing eyes at the ant-like figures below her, their lives carrying on unchanged. She couldn't help smiling to herself at the memory of the incident with the mango ice cream almost a year ago.

She *had* behaved badly.

Terribly un-British, of course. Her smile broadened.

But hugely satisfying.

*

'Minnie, Minnie, come quickly. Read this,' Edoardo called from the dining room early one morning a few months after the visit to the solicitor. Minnie emerged from her bedroom, stood behind him and leaned over to read the headlines in *The Times of India*.

MUSSOLINI DECLARES WAR ON THE ALLIES

Minnie's hands trembled as she clutched the high back of the chair.

> 11 June 1940. Britain and France were formally notified by the Italian Foreign Minister, Count Ciano, that hostilities would begin at midnight.

'Dear God, what's going to happen to us?' she whispered. 'What about Mamma and Papa and Neddy in Rome, and your parents too?'

Ever since reading the news in April that Mussolini had ordered the mobilisation of all Italians over fourteen years old, Minnie had been on edge, worried about the future, about their families in Rome, about Edoardo's work. She had noticed a subtle change in the social atmosphere recently. It was apparent that they were invited less often to predominantly British functions. Occasionally, upon entering a room at a party, she was conscious that conversation hiccupped, then changed gear and carried on in a different direction. Greetings were more reserved than usual. Thank goodness for Dolly and Jimmy and the protection she got from their position in social and financial circles. The children, too, had been sidelined. This year they had not been invited to the annual Easter Egg Hunt held at Government House.

She finished reading the article. 'Can we phone Rome, do you think?'

'I'll try to book a call when I get to the office.'

'Have you spoken to Franco?'

'He rang earlier. Said he would go to the consulate today to find out what the position is. What are your plans for today?'

'Nothing much. I'm supposed to be playing bridge this morning.'

'Good. But don't take any engagements with the English crowd for the next few days.'

'Why ever not?'

'Use your head, *cara mia*. There may be some unpleasantness.'

'Why should they be unpleasant to me? I've known them – you've known them – for years. They are friends.'

'We'll see who our friends are soon enough. This war will change everything. We are the enemy now, you know.'

The enemy. How could she be the enemy? She'd done no harm to anyone. She admired the British and had made a few good friends. They loved coming to her parties – probably for the food she laid on, she suspected.

She couldn't get Edoardo's words out of her head. Did he mean that they would no longer treat her as a friend? If the roles were reversed, she would never drop anyone she liked just because their respective countries were at war. No, the British would never do that to her. Ridiculous to even think it. Absurd. It wouldn't happen. Surely not? And yet – well, could it?

'There's talk of internment camps, like the ones they put up last year for the Germans,' Edoardo said later that evening. Jimmy and Dolly, and Franco and Clara had come over to discuss what to do. They had heard that many in the Italian community had made contingency plans regarding their businesses. The Bernasconi brothers had taken on a Hindu partner at their glass factory. The Valli family too, had appointed their assistant manager, Patel, to run their silk mill should they be interned. Several had been prudent in this way.

Edoardo had not.

'How can you get anyone to manage an architect's office? My ideas are in my head,' he said.

'What about your chief draughtsman, Tony D'Mello?' Jimmy suggested. 'He could keep the office ticking over. It's the only solution. I strongly advise it.'

'Who will be put in the camps?' Minnie asked. 'Only the men, I suppose.'

'No, I believe not,' Jimmy said. 'It applies to wives and children as well.'

'Will I have to go even if we're getting a divorce? Surely not?'

'I'm afraid so, Minnie, the children too.'

They waited. While preparing for a prolonged absence, Minnie kept the household routine running as normal. In the mornings the children, Claudia and Bobby, went to the Montessori school as usual. In the afternoons, their ayah, Mary, took them as always to Breach Candy Gardens playground, a favourite meeting place for English and European children. At five they returned home, had their bath and dinner and waited until Edoardo returned home to play with them, carrying them piggyback or playing horsey-horsey.

One afternoon Mary ayah and the children returned home early. Mary sounded furious as she jabbered in Konkani to the cook.

Minnie wanted to know what it was all about. Mary ayah tried to explain but burst into tears.

'They said we're not allowed to go there any more, Mummy,' Claudia said in a small voice.

'Who said that?'

'Sheila's mummy said it, she told Mary.'

'Is that true, Mary?'

'Yes, memsahib. Jones memsahib said children are not to come any more to the gardens, not allowed.'

Claudia piped up, 'She said Italians are very naughty people because they are fighting with the English.' She sniffled. 'Am I Italian, Mummy? But I didn't fight with any of the children. I just wanted to play.'

Minnie hugged Claudia closely. 'There, there, my pet, I know you didn't, it's all right.'

'Sheila's mummy said I mustn't play with Sheila and we can't go to Breach Candy Gardens any more, because of war. Sheila said Bobby and me will be locked up. I don't want to be locked up.' Claudia shivered and started to cry. 'We didn't *do* anything,' she wailed.

Minnie tightened her arms round Claudia, rocking gently to and fro.

'Don't worry, my darling, we don't have to go back to silly old Breach Candy if they're horrid with you. We can go to the playground at Hanging Gardens, it's much nicer and bigger.'

She felt tears of anger that anyone could be so cruel to her lovely children, to this precious little girl whom she loved with all her heart. She drew Claudia closer, breathing in the smell of little-girl hair as she kissed the top of her head, and they rocked together until Claudia stopped crying.

Edoardo came home early that day. He looked pale and worried.

'I can't play now, children, I have to talk to Mummy.' He called the ayah: 'Mary, please take the children to their room.' He sat heavily on the sofa. 'And tell the bearer to bring me two suitcases from the store room.'

Minnie sat next to him. 'Is it definite?'

He nodded.

'When do we have to go?'

'Tomorrow. But only the men. A bus will come to take us to the station. We've been told not to leave our homes today.'

'Only the men? Not all of us?'

'No, just men for now. Women and children will follow later.'

Minnie took his hand and squeezed it.

He sighed. 'There's one good thing – we've been allocated to Satara Camp.'

'Oh, thank goodness. What a relief.'

It could have been worse, Minnie thought. Satara was quite close, near Poona, and reachable in less than a day. It would be easy for visitors. Most of the camps were a couple of days' train journey away.

After a while they went to play with the children.

'Come and sit on my lap, Claudia,' Edoardo said, picking her up. 'I have something to tell you.'

'Promise you won't tickle me?'

'No, darling, I won't tickle you. Come here, Bobby, you too. Now listen, children, Papa is going away tomorrow.'

'Where are you going, Papa? Will you bring us back a present?'

'No, my pet, I'm going away for a long time.'

'Are you going, too, Mummy?'

'No, darling, I'm staying here with you and Bobby,' Minnie replied.

Claudia looked at Edoardo. 'Are you going to jail, Papa, like Sheila said?'

'No, it's not a jail. It's a camp, near Poona, not far. I'm going by train.'

'Oh, how lovely. Does it have tents? Can we come too? I love going in trains.'

'It's not that kind of a camp. No tents. It has little bungalows. I will go up first and choose one. When I've made it all nice with curtains and beds and things, then Mummy and you two will come and stay with me.'

Monsoon rain lashed down from a black sky next morning when a coach arrived to pick up Edoardo. Sheltering in the entrance to the apartment block, Minnie recognised all the men in it.

She lifted Claudia in her arms. 'Look, darling, there's Uncle Franco – give him a wave. And there's Marianna's papa.'

'Are they going to the same place, Mummy?'

'Yes, darling.'

'Will Marianna be there as well?'

'Later, but not just now.'

'Oh good, then we can play together.'

'Of course, darling, there will be lots of other children. Now come and say goodbye to Uncle Franco.'

Franco came down from the bus and put his arms round Minnie. 'I've asked Clara to keep an eye on you,' he said. 'She's not going to be joining us at the camp.'

Minnie looked at him curiously. 'Why not?'

'She kept her British Indian nationality, so she is exempt even though we are married. But, she will come and see us as often as she can. I'm told family can visit once a month. Now I'd better get back on the bus.'

Franco gave her a kiss and hugged the two children. 'Be good, you two,' he said, 'and, Claudia, you look after Mummy. And don't forget to eat your carrots; they'll make you see in the dark. Bye bye now, sweetie, see you soon.'

Claudia pulled a face. 'Uncle, you know I hate carrots.'

Edoardo made his farewells, starting with the servants. He picked up Bobby and hugged him tightly. *'Ciao, ciao, Bobbino mio, stai buono* – be a good boy.' He kissed him and handed him to the ayah.

Then he gathered Claudia in his arms and she clung to him, her chin quivering. 'I don't want you to go, Papa, even for a little while.'

'It won't be long, sweetie. As soon as I find a house there, I'll send for Mummy and you and Bobby, and then we'll all be together again.'

'How soon, Papa? Before Christmas?'

'Oh, soon, soon, sweetheart, long before Christmas.'

He kissed her, put her down and turned to Minnie. They moved away from the others.

'You know you can stay in the apartment until the end of the month. I can't keep it on after that. But if you want to go to Jimmy and Dolly's earlier, they insisted you should. Tony D'Mello will oversee the office; he's got instructions to bring you a cheque weekly. Look after yourself, and the children. I'll write and tell you what I need you to bring.'

'How long before we join you, do you think?'

'A few weeks, not more.' He paused. 'Minnie *carissima*, I'm sorry. For everything. You know what I mean. The divorce – goodness knows what will happen there. I'm truly sorry for you. It's going to be awkward up at Satara, isn't it?'

'I know, my dear. It can't be helped – the war isn't your fault. We shall simply have to wait and make the best of it. Look after yourself. Let me know how you are as soon as you can.' Tears filled her eyes.

He kissed her cheeks and held her close for a moment. Taking out his hanky, he cleaned the lenses of his glasses, wiped away Minnie's tears, then blew his nose hard. He looked at Minnie once more, stroked her face gently, turned and climbed into the waiting bus.

22

At the beginning of hostilities, several camps were set up throughout India, most to accommodate German and Italian prisoners of war, usually in separate sections of the camps. A few were established to contain German and Italian civilians, many of whom had lived in India for years. The nearest civilian camp to Bombay was at Satara, near Poona and considered to be a reasonable place, being an ex-army barracks close to the town. Conditions for the internees at Satara were more relaxed and they were allowed limited freedom that was not permitted at the Prisoner of War camps. People were able to go for short walks outside the precincts of the camp, and on occasion were allowed supervised visits into the town. The main drawback of civilian camps was boredom, particularly among the men, who were unable to conduct the business or continue the employment they had left behind in Bombay or other cities.

Prior to the menfolk being interned, the Italian consul general in Bombay had prepared the Italian families for the conditions and regulations that would await them as internees. The men would be taken first and established in the camp, after which the women and children would follow.

Minnie, therefore, knew what to expect, but her worry was the fact of being thrown together with Edoardo in the middle of their divorce proceedings. Would the divorce go through as expected? Would there be a long delay? How would her situation be affected if it came through while in the camp? How would the other Italian women treat her once they knew about her impending divorce? Already she knew that her local priest strongly disapproved and had refused to give her communion.

She spoke of her worries to Dolly and Clara. Dolly assured her that Jimmy would use his considerable influence to try and get her an exemption, but that it could take several months to achieve, if at all. Minnie contented herself with this hope and prepared for the transfer to Satara.

*

Early in September Minnie and the children arrived at Poona station together with other Italian families. After a quick lunch and a cup of tea, they were bundled into buses for the two-hour drive to Satara Camp. They rattled and jolted along the dusty, potholed road. The seats were hard and uncomfortable. Hand luggage crammed the aisle and projected from overhead parcel shelves. The children became fractious. Everyone felt the heat and humidity and wondered whether cool drinks and washing facilities would be available at their destination.

By the time they reached Satara they were covered in a film of red dust. Minnie leaned forward and spoke to her friend Peppina, Marianna's mother, seated in front of her.

'I think we've arrived,' she whispered, squeezing Peppina's shoulder. *Thank goodness for Peppina,* she thought, *here with six-year-old Marianna and four months pregnant with her second child.* She was a teacher, pragmatic, cheery and physically tough; a good person to have around in difficult situations.

The bus stopped in front of a wooden sentry hut flanking the barriered main gate. Two guards armed with rifles emerged, spoke to the driver and examined his papers. After a quick check and head count, they raised the barrier and waved him on. Minnie had imagined the camp to be grim and forbidding, unconsciously fearing that the inmates would be subjected to physical cruelty, even torture. But at first glance she found it was not as bad as she had anticipated. It consisted of a huge compound surrounded by fencing posts sparsely linked by strands of barbed wire. Hardly a defensive enclosure. White painted stones marked the edges of a tarmacked road leading to the administrative buildings.

The passengers got off the bus and formed a queue in front of the reception office. Minnie peered beyond the building at what she supposed were the living quarters. Grouped in rows or semi-circles of six were wooden barracks and bungalows to house the hundreds of internees. Nearby a larger building surmounted by a bell and a cross was recognisably the church. A long low hut had a tin roof on which was painted a faded red cross and the words 'Satara Hospital'.

Bobby made a beeline for one of the large white stones edging the paths of packed red earth leading to the bungalows, several of which displayed a semblance of vegetable garden at the rear.

'Claudia, bring Bobby back and hold his hand,' Minnie said. 'I don't want him disappearing while I'm in the office.'

She and Peppina moved up the line of women waiting to enter the office. It was fiercely hot and sticky, with not a breath of air. Wiping the perspiration from her neck, Minnie scanned the depressing surroundings with mounting gloom.

Peepul and neem trees grew randomly throughout offering much-needed patches of shade and greenery to the arid landscape. Here and there attempts had been made to plant a few straggly bougainvillea against the huts, their purple bracts adding a touch of colour to an otherwise stark veranda.

Outside the camp, fronting the main entrance, a series of small bungalows for civilian personnel surrounded a rudimentary playground. A couple of slides in need of a coat of paint and four unexciting-looking swings stood forlornly in the heat, while two stray dogs lay panting in the shade of a straggly lantana bush.

'Mummy, can I have a go on the slide?' Claudia asked.

'No, darling, I don't think we're allowed out yet.'

Claudia stood with finger in mouth looking longingly at the slide beyond the fence.

'I'll ask if we can go later. How's that?' Minnie said, retying the bow on Claudia's braid. The cawing of crows and squeal of monkeys rose from a thick stand of mango trees growing behind the civilian lines. In the distance, behind the camp, rocky outcrops, barren except for a few thorn trees, stood like sentinels at attention.

After registration in the main office, each passenger was issued with a ration card and a roll of marking tape to identify belongings. With formalities completed the new arrivals joined the group of men and women waiting outside to greet them.

Edoardo waved and called out to Claudia.

'Go on, darling, say hello to Papa,' Minnie said, giving her suddenly bashful daughter a little push. She picked up Bobby, hitched him firmly on her hip and pulled his thumb out of his mouth. She gathered the ration books and tape and went to the waiting men.

'It's good to see you,' Edoardo said, kissing Minnie on both cheeks. He hugged Claudia, tickled Bobby's cheek, and led them towards their bungalow. 'Was the journey all right? I'll come back for the cases later. You look hot. I've managed to get one of the better bungalows.' He pointed to a group of housing near a large banyan tree. 'We are sharing with Franco, but that's okay – at least we all have our own rooms. There's not a bad bunch near us, people you know. Dr and Mrs Baumgartner are on one side and the Vogels are just across the way.' He pointed them out to Minnie as they reached their bungalow. 'And I think that Peppina and Lionello are housed next door, so Claudia will have Marianna to play with.'

Thank God for that, Minnie thought, setting Bobby down. They would be in good hands. Baumgartner had been her dentist. Half the doctors and dentists in Bombay were German and many were interned here. At least it promised to be a healthy camp.

Looking around at the clusters of housing, little flashes of recognition stirred her memory, just out of reach, elusive as fireflies. The sand-coloured bungalows with their white veranda rails and red corrugated tin roofs reminded her of something from long ago. A word popped unbidden into her mind: *baracche*. Rows and rows of them, all identical, painted white. She shivered.

'Minnie, are you listening? You seem miles away.' Edoardo's voice jerked her back to reality.

'I'm here – go on, what were you saying?'

She listened as he explained the rules of the camp and showed her the living accommodation: three bedrooms, a sitting room, a kitchen and bathroom. She wrinkled her nose at the sparse utilitarian cane furniture in the sitting room and wondered if they would be allowed to have more comfortable pieces sent from home.

She called out to Claudia who was dashing up and down on the veranda running a stick against the wooden posts of the railings 'Stop that racket, darling, you'll give Mummy a headache,' she said, gritting her teeth. The noise stopped and presently Minnie felt a tugging at her skirt.

'Mummy, Mummy! Look what Bobby's doing,' Claudia whispered urgently. 'Look quickly!'

Minnie stepped on to the veranda and peered over the railing. Bobby was sitting on the dusty red path tugging at one of the edging stones.

'Bobby, stop that at once!' Minnie cried, exasperated.

The little boy let go of the stone and looked at his mother, his eyes wide and mouth open. Minnie gazed in horror as he wiped filthy hands on the front of his new rompers. He rose unsteadily to his feet. Red smears covered his face and the front of his blue outfit, and a damp red patch marked his seat. Pink dust covered his arms and legs. A trickle of perspiration inched down one leg, leaving a rusty furrow like a snail's trail.

'Oh, Bobby, what have you done?' Minnie wailed. 'Just look at you! Edoardo, where's the bathroom? I shall have to wash him completely. Get me a towel and look for his case please.'

'I have to warn you,' Edoardo said, leading the way to the bathroom, 'there's a water shortage, and we are rationed.'

'What do you mean?' Minnie's voice rose in alarm.

'I didn't have time to tell you. We only have running water twice a day – two hours in the morning and two hours in the evening. We fill buckets and use the water from them between times.'

Minnie shut her eyes and took a deep breath. She supposed it could be worse. Dear God! What else was in store?

She entered the Indian-style bathroom. In one corner stood an old-fashioned thunderbox with a wooden surround and lid, and a tin jug on the floor nearby.

She groaned. 'How often does that get emptied?'

Edoardo peered at it. 'I think the sweeper woman comes in four times a day.'

There was no bathtub. A teak washstand on rickety legs, one propped up with a brick, leaned against a wall. Set into its wooden surround was a chipped white enamelled basin with a matching ewer next to it and a soap dish. A square mirror in a green Bakelite frame hung from a nail in the wall. A corner shelf supported a petromax oil lamp, while from the ceiling a single bulb dangled at the end of a twisted cord. *I suppose there is bound to be electricity rationing as well.* 'Where's the water?' she asked.

Edoardo pointed to several large enamel jugs and a bucket near the door to the yard and to a tap sticking out of the wall. Under it lay an oval tin tub full of brownish water. Minnie twisted the tap. The pipe juddered as spurts of pale red liquid hiccupped and splashed into the tub then stopped. She turned it off and looked around for another source of water. A grey metal pipe fastened to the middle of one of the tiled walls sprouted a galvanised showerhead like a spent sunflower but dispensed only a trickle of cold water. There was a wide drain hole in the centre of the tiled shower floor covered by a metal basin.

'What's that for?' Minnie asked. 'Is it to prevent the smell?'

'No,' Edoardo said a little nervously. 'It is to prevent snakes getting in.'

'Snakes? Oh my God!' Minnie shrieked. 'That's all I need, bloody snakes coming up the drain hole!'

'Minnie, *carissima*, you're tired, you'll soon get used to things. It's not so bad. Come into the kitchen, I've made you a cup of coffee.'

Still carrying Bobby, she followed him into the tiny kitchen. Their entrance sent a small tribe of geckos scampering up the walls, leaving behind the unwary flies that were to have been their prey. Minnie screamed and rushed into the sitting room.

'Edoardo, kill them. Where is the Flit pump?'

'No, you mustn't kill them. They keep the flies down.'

'But I hate lizards, and snakes and cockroaches.' She glanced at his sheepish face as he followed her. 'Don't tell me. We have cockroaches here as well?'

'I'm afraid so. Big fat ones, but only at night.'

'Is that supposed to make me feel better, only at night?' she snapped. 'I shan't be able to sleep.' She bit her lip to stop it trembling. 'What else should I be aware of? You might as well tell me all the bad news now.'

'Not much else, really,' Edoardo called from the kitchen where he had carried the Flit pump. He took a deep breath. 'The mosquitoes, of course, but I've managed to get nets for the beds. There are hairy caterpillars too, mostly on the veranda. Don't touch them, they give a nasty rash.' He came into the sitting room handed her a cup of coffee, picked up Bobby, gave him a biscuit and led them to the sofa. 'Oh yes, centipedes and scorpions. There are plenty of those both in and out of the house. They like to hide inside shoes, so don't put your feet in your shoes without first tipping them upside down. Better still, keep them under the mosquito net at night.' He placed his cup on the table. 'Tell the children to be careful, especially outdoors. They must never lift up any big rocks in the gardens – that's where scorpions like to hide to get away from the heat.' He looked to see how Minnie was taking it all in. 'Oh, and do warn them about the monkeys. They can be quite vicious, and they carry rabies.'

Shocked by this last warning, Minnie burst into tears. Would she ever get used to these ghastly creatures, she wondered, unable to stop weeping. Silently, Edoardo handed her a hanky and patted her shoulder. She wiped her eyes, blew her nose and tucked the hanky into the top of her bra. Shaking her head, she rose and picked out some clean clothes for Bobby from a suitcase.

'Come on, darling, let's clean you up,' she sighed, lifting the little boy on to her hip. 'Claudia, go next door and ask Signora Peppina to come to the bathroom if she's free.'

Minnie was glad to have Peppina as a close neighbour. They knew each other quite well and Peppina's husband, Lionello, was one of the first ones to be interned, and she had learned from him much about the workings of the camp.

Peppina entered a few minutes later. Lighting a cigarette, she pulled down the lid of the thunderbox and sat on it while Minnie took off Bobby's clothes, stood him on the washstand, scooped water out of a bucket with a dipper and poured it over him. Claudia came in to watch.

'How are you feeling, Peppina?' Minnie asked, while stopping Bobby from licking the water from his arm.

'I'm okay. A bit tired, and my ankles have swollen, but not too bad considering.'

'I'll massage your legs for you later, if you like.'

'Oh wonderful, thanks.' Peppina leaned back and exhaled. 'I've found out the basics from my husband. First, there's a KP store where we can get our rations. Each of us is only allowed half a pound each of tea and coffee per week, and a quarter pound of sugar. There's a long list. I've written it all down and you can copy it.' She inhaled deeply. 'But one packet of butter has to last the whole family for a week. Still, I expect we'll get by.'

'Claudia, pass me the towel, you can help me dry Bobby.' Bobby grabbed the soap and squeezed it, shooting it across the room. He and Claudia giggled as Minnie stood him up.

'What about bread and pasta, and eggs and meat?' she asked, turning her attention again to Peppina.

'We can buy fresh bread every day. As for pasta, Lionello says that one of the men will arrange to make fettuccine or tagliatelle if people will give him their flour rations. It's the best they can do. No imported stuff. I think you'd better get used to eating rice. We have to buy the meat – mainly mutton – and eggs and vegetables, and live chickens.'

'Oh my God, I don't believe it! I can't possibly kill a chicken.'

'Signora Peppina, are we going to kill a chicken?' Claudia asked.

'Somebody will have to, my dear. I'm going vegetarian. Your papa can kill it.'

'You must be joking!' Minnie said. 'Edoardo can hardly shave without cutting himself.'

Peppina laughed, lifted the toilet lid, dropped the cigarette butt in the pan and sat down again. 'Your brother Franco will find a volunteer to do that job, I'm sure. He knows how to get things done, my husband says. In any case, we shall have to eat lunch in the canteen. There are two sittings. A notice in the clubhouse – that's what they call the communal hall – will show us our times. We can cook the evening meal at home, if we want. Just as well since there is a nine o'clock curfew.'

Minnie set Bobby on the floor, patting his bottom. 'Off you go with Claudia and find Papa – mind you don't play in the dust again.' She took off her blouse, splashed water on her face, neck and under her arms to cool off. 'I suppose we'll get used to the routine in time. It's difficult to know how many days the rations are meant to last. Did you find out anything else? What about laundry facilities?'

'Lionello was pretty good at finding things out. Oh yes, the laundry. Well, the camp washer-men, the dhobis, come once a week to take away the sheets and towels and bring clean ones. I hope you've brought enough with you. If not, you can write to Clara and ask her to bring more when she comes to visit Franco. Incidentally, all the mail is censored.'

'Is it really? I'll have to be careful what I write. I think I brought enough linen, two changes each.'

'You might need more. People sweat a lot with no air-conditioning. You'll have to sew the bungalow number tapes on all items. Otherwise they will just disappear.'

'I'll do that. Pass me the towel, would you?' She caught the tossed towel and dabbed under her arms. 'What about laundering our clothes?'

'You can wash the smalls yourself. There's a hanging place outside the bathroom. But for the bigger clothes, the dhobi-wallah's wife will come and wash them here. Many of the women have made that arrangement and it works well. You must pay for it, of course. Here, splash some cologne.' Peppina reached up to a shelf for a bottle of lavender water.

'Heavens, Peppina, you have been busy. I don't know how you managed it in such a short time.'

'I asked Mrs Baumgartner. Another thing to remember. All drinking water *must* be boiled and cooled before use. There's a special earthenware pitcher in the kitchen for storing it. That's the only water to use for drinking, for making tea or coffee, and for cleaning your teeth and even for washing the vegetables with. In fact, all vegetables and fruit need to be soaked in potassium permanganate before eating. What the servants at home called pinky water – it's essential if you want to avoid dysentery. Each kitchen is issued a tin of crystals – you'll find it in the cupboard.'

That evening they had a supper of roast chicken and vegetables prepared for them by another friend, Signora Valli, from two houses away.

By curfew time, they were all tired and ready for bed. When the electricity went off at nine, hurricane lamps were lit in each room. Claudia and Bobby had gone to sleep earlier. Minnie found herself with Edoardo in the room next to the children. She was relieved to see that they had single beds and she dragged hers further away from Edoardo's.

'Don't go getting ideas into your head, Edoardo,' she said, observing his crestfallen expression. 'We may be together under one roof and *force majeure* obliges us to share the same bedroom, but please remember that the divorce proceedings are still going ahead.'

'But goodness knows how long that will take. In the meantime—'

'In the meantime, nothing,' Minnie said sharply, cutting short his protests. 'Don't even think of it. You are the one who provoked the situation. You can't have your cake and eat it, *caro mio.*'

*

Minnie and the children soon settled into camp routine, which wasn't as bad as she had expected. Franco and another hotelier were appointed to help run the camp canteen, while Edoardo and other engineers were called on when required to supervise any building or construction works.

Although the adults were permitted to take short walks in the countryside, the main drawbacks were the rather cramped conditions in the bungalows, boredom and the tensions brought on by the enforced company of a disparate group of people. Visitors were allowed once a month, and the men had the use of workshops for making odd pieces of furniture and helping to extend the community hall. A few bungalows developed flourishing vegetable plots while other families raised chickens to supplement the rations.

A month after their arrival, Dolly and Clara, now six months pregnant, visited the camp, bringing with them a large hamper of goodies, extra linen and few toys for the children. At Minnie's request they also brought some of Clara's outgrown maternity clothes for Peppina.

'How are you feeling, darling?' Minnie asked Clara.

'Fine on the whole. No more morning sickness, thank goodness.' Clara lit a cigarette.

'I'm making sure she takes things easy, aren't I?' said Dolly.

'Dolly's been wonderful,' Clara said. 'People are being so helpful. But I'm quite a tough cookie, you know.'

'Minnie, what about you?' Dolly reached for the jug of water on the side table and poured herself a glass. 'How is it going with you and Edoardo? I've brought your documents from the solicitor.'

'It's a strain, but we're managing. But let's not talk about that just now. What's your news? How are the twins?'

After seven years of marriage and several miscarriages, Dolly had finally produced twins: a boy, Homi, and a girl, Nina, now three years old. It had been a difficult birth and she had had to spend nearly six months in bed. She was advised not to have any more children. The result was that she was overprotective and anxious about their welfare. The least little snuffle was excuse enough to call in a specialist. She lovingly recounted their progress, what they ate or didn't eat, their naughtiness; she described in detail their colds, fevers, stomach upsets, bowel movements, their cute lisping speech.

'What you're saying is, they're absolutely fine, aren't they?' Minnie asked, getting up and making her way to the kitchen. 'I'll make us all some tea.'

'Yes, they are fine, thank God,' Dolly called out. 'Listen, Minnie, I may have some good news for you.'

'I could do with some. What is it?'

'Jimmy has had several meetings with Sir Roger Lumley at Government House. He's told him about you. It seems Sir Roger has agreed that you and the children will be allowed to leave Satara, on the condition that you come and live with us.'

'Oh, Dolly, how wonderful!' Minnie called from the kitchen. 'Who is Sir Roger Lumley?' she asked a few moments later, bringing in a tray with cups and a teapot.

'The new governor of Bombay.'

'I didn't know that Jimmy had such influence with the governor.' Minnie poured out three cups and handed them round.

'This governor is quite an enlightened man. He knows that India will get independence one day soon.'

'What's that got to do with Jimmy?' Minnie asked.

Dolly smoothed the folds of her sari and smiled a little primly. 'He's quite aware of how important the Dubash Shipping Corporation is to the war effort. He realises the significance of keeping good relations with those Indians who will be powerful businessmen after we get independence. And Jimmy's one of them, it seems.' She lowered her eyes and took a sip of tea. 'There's no doubt he'll be able to get you out of here.'

'What about Edoardo? Or Franco, for that matter?'

'Not them, I'm afraid. The men can't get dispensation. They will have to sit it out until the war ends. Let's hope that won't be too long.'

Minnie reached over and squeezed her friend's hand. *Dear Dolly, always wanting to help, always loyal to her friends.* 'What other news? Any gossip from Bombay, Clara? You are always the one to know what's going on.'

'Well, many of the British families have already left. Loads of troop ships are coming in. Nearly all the young British bachelors have joined up. Oh yes, I nearly forgot.' Clara handed her cup to Minnie for a refill. 'The funniest thing. You know that many ladies have joined the Red Cross or are working as nurses at St George's Hospital. In fact, I shall be going back to St George's as soon as I can after the baby is born. We are all doing our bit, and Roshan decided she was not going to get left out. Wanted to do *her* bit for the war effort and so on. She kitted herself out with a nurse's uniform – starched cap, badges and all. She looked like a proper matron.' Dolly giggled. 'She turned up at the hospital and told them she was going to be in charge.'

Dolly was aghast. 'At St George's? Bloody woman! What cheek!'

'Not St George's,' Clara roared with laughter. 'At the dog's hospital in Bandra!'

23

Life in the camp became duller after Dolly and Clara left a couple of days later. They had been a breath of fresh air. Minnie was despondent for weeks after. Tensions between her and Edoardo grew, until Minnie decided to move in with the children in their room.

Jimmy's efforts to get Minnie and the children released from the camp were taking longer than expected. Over the next few months, Claudia attended school and Bobby went to a kindergarten where Minnie helped in the mornings. Teachers who lived outside the camp taught the children in English and Peppina taught them in Italian. In the evenings families visited each other, and regular card games were held in the community hall until curfew time.

Quarrels broke out between some of the German and Italian families. The Germans were organised, correct, methodical and formal. They were polite but not effusive, disapproving, mostly humourless but respectful of authority. They were always first in line for the rations and arrived on the dot for the midday meal. They were never late for church services and invariably bagged the front rows at any community meeting.

The Italians were noisy, informal, chaotic, bad timekeepers, and showed a consistent disregard for camp rules and authority.

'These irritating buon giorno Italians, they are always so cheerful. They are completely irresponsible and do not take their situation seriously,' was one of the complaints the Germans made to the camp adjutant. 'Also, they are never on time for roll-call and meals, and they do not discipline their children who have no manners.'

'These pompous guten tag Germans are always telling us what to do,' complained the Italians. 'They grab all the best places everywhere. Even in the KP they buy up anything in sight before we have a chance. They are not considerate of others, and they scold our children over nothing at all.'

March and April brought the steaming hot weather and its accompanying discomforts. Children and adults alike were to be seen with face and body daubed with the chalky pink streaks of calamine lotion used for prickly heat rash. Silence and quiet prevailed in the afternoons as people stayed indoors to escape the stifling heat. People longed for the monsoon to break, to feel the cooler, wet weather, even if it meant clothes smelling of mildew and the earth turning into a quagmire of red mud.

The monsoon didn't break in its usual way, all at once. Instead there were a few heavy showers followed by periods of leaden skies and intense humidity. Minnie suffered badly from mosquito bites and sent Edoardo to the KP for a bottle of neem tree oil, an effective measure against the maddening insects. A bite behind the knee bothered her particularly. Although it didn't itch much, it became swollen and angry-looking.

One morning she could hardly get out of bed. Tiredness overwhelmed her, she ached all over and had no energy. She spent the day lying in an armchair doing little. The following morning, she woke with a throbbing headache behind the eyes. The pounding and aching intensified throughout the day. Dr Vogel came to see her, diagnosed flu and gave her some aspirins. 'You must drink plenty,' he instructed.

The headache worsened; she couldn't open her eyes and her head felt as if it would burst. Edoardo took the children to stay with a neighbour and made barley water for Minnie to drink. She developed a slight fever, but a few hours later the fever rose dramatically. She began sweating profusely and complained of fearful pain deep in her calves and back, painful enough to make her moan and cry; bouts of profuse sweating were followed by intense shivering. Dr Vogel was sent for again.

'This looks bad, Edoardo,' the doctor pronounced, 'but it's not malaria. Let me know if she comes out in a rash. Meanwhile, keep the fever down with cold cloths and an ice bag on her head. I will look in first thing tomorrow.'

By next morning Minnie had developed a strange pink rash. It didn't hurt or bleed or itch, but spread rapidly, covering her chest, her belly and her back.

'Into hospital with her straight away,' Dr Vogel said when he came around. 'I am pretty sure she has dengue fever. If that is the case, you will need to spray the whole house, most particularly the area outside the bathroom. Get rid of any pot plants. Any place where there is standing water must be sprayed. You can buy the spray at the dispensary.'

Dr Vogel's diagnosis proved correct. Minnie had contracted the dreaded dengue fever. In the next few days her temperature stayed exceptionally high, she suffered severe nausea and vomiting, blinding headaches and excruciating pain in the muscles and joints. The rash spread to her face, arms and legs. The symptoms lessened somewhat after a day or two, only to return with redoubled intensity.

'Dengue is also known as "break bone fever",' the attending English doctor told Edoardo. 'It causes agonising pain in the bones and joints. Usually it subsides after the second crisis, but I warn you that she will be extremely unwell for several weeks after the fever goes. It will affect her legs mainly. She won't regain full muscle use for several months.'

For two weeks Minnie lay in the hospital bed periodically sliding between lucidity and incoherence. She sweated profusely, and her nightdress was changed two or three times a day. One morning she woke and was not drenched in perspiration. She felt hungry and asked for a banana. In a few days she was out of danger and ready to return to the bungalow. Edoardo came to fetch her. She had lost weight and was too weak to walk, so the ambulance brought her the short distance to the bungalow. Edoardo carried her into the sitting room and set her down on the sofa.

'Hello, darling,' a familiar voice greeted her from across the room.

Minnie turned to see a smiling Dolly by the window.

'Dolly, whatever are you doing here?' Minnie gasped weakly.

'I've come to fetch you.'

'Fetch me? I don't understand.'

'I've got permission for you and the children to leave the camp. You are coming to live with Jimmy and me in Bombay.'

Minnie listened to Dolly and the camp doctor discussing travel arrangements. One option was to drive all the way.

'Minnie is too weak for such a long car journey,' the doctor said.

'What about the train from Poona?' Dolly asked.

'Not a good idea,' he pronounced. 'Too crowded and unhygienic. She would be exposed to infection. A relapse would be a serious matter and could lead to complications. I would prefer her to wait until the monsoon is properly over.'

'But that is almost two months more.' Dolly's anxiety was plain.

The doctor tapped a pencil on the table, looking thoughtful. 'There is another way, but it's a bit of a tall order.'

'What is it?'

'She could be flown down – it really would be the quickest way. Would you be up for that, Minnie?'

Minnie nodded.

The doctor turned to Dolly. 'I believe you have the connections. There's an airstrip at Satara, you know. Not much in use at present except in emergencies.'

Dolly's face lit up. 'Of course, it's the ideal solution. Leave it with me, Doctor,' she said. 'I'll speak to my husband. I'm sure he'll be able to arrange something.'

'As soon as possible, I'd suggest.'

After several phone calls arrangements were made and permissions obtained. More importantly, precious fuel was procured. Four days later, during a sustained break in the rains, a de Havilland Leopard Moth landed at the Satara air strip; borrowed from the Bombay Flying Club under goodness knew what excuse, it was piloted by Jimmy himself. A nurse was on hand to assist Minnie on the flight.

Farewells were said all round. Minnie lay on her bed waiting for the ambulance to take her to the plane. Dolly busied herself with packing a suitcase for Minnie and a separate one for the children. Franco helped, but Edoardo, despondent and near to tears, was pretty useless. He hovered between the bed and the children whom he hugged closely as if to imprint their faces on his heart, their kisses on his cheeks. Claudia clung to him but was excited at the thought of flying. Bobby seemed unconcerned about all the fuss, playing happily in a corner of the room.

'No, darling, you're not coming in the plane with me,' Minnie whispered in a thread of voice in response to Claudia's insistent questions.

'Why not?' came the disappointed wail.

'There's only room for Uncle Jimmy and the nurse in the front seats and a place for me to lie down in the back.'

'But I could sit on your lap, or on the nurse's lap.'

'That's not allowed in aeroplanes, my love. It's not like a car.'

'But, Mummy, please, I'll sit on the floor.'

'No, my pet, you can't. But I tell you what – you and Bobby can come to see the plane and wave as we take off. And then you'll drive to Poona with Aunty Dolly and take the train to Bombay. And we'll have a race to see who gets home first. How about that?'

'Oooh yes, I'd like that. Shall I go and get my doll ready?'

'You do that. Where's Bobby?'

Bobby was busy trying to stuff a gecko into the pocket of his shorts.

'Edoardo, do something!' Minnie croaked. 'Get that dreadful creature out of his hands.'

The liberated lizard streaked up the wall and out of sight while Bobby set up a roar of outrage at this separation and burst into tears.

'Dolly, please wash his hands and put his case in the car.'

'Come along, Bobby. You too, Claudia, come with me,' Dolly said, leading them off for Minnie and Edoardo to have a few moments alone.

'Take care of yourself, *carissima*,' Edoardo said, kissing her on both cheeks. 'You are in good hands with Dolly and Jimmy. I shall miss you and the children.'

Minnie looked at his pinched face and squeezed his hand. 'Yes, I know. And they will miss you. Promise you will write to them.'

'I promise. And you too, *carissima*. Let me know how things proceed, won't you? Please keep an eye on the office for me when you are better. D'Mello has written updating me, but I'd like you to check on him.'

He sat on the edge of the bed.

'Regarding the final divorce papers, do whatever you need to speed things up. I'll sign the documents as soon as I get them – I won't delay things.' He sighed. 'I'm truly sorry, Minnie, that things have turned out like this. I never wanted to hurt you. It was just – oh, I don't know, I can't even explain.'

'Let's not go over it again, Edoardo. It's done. I want to maintain harmony, for the children's sake.'

'Of course.' He stroked her hair. 'I still love you, you know.'

'I know, my dear.' She gave him a tiny smile.

He smiled back. 'Perhaps we'll get on better divorced than we did married.'

'More than likely.'

'Will you visit when you've recovered? With the children?'

'Yes, I will, *caro mio*. I'll never keep the children from you. You know that I will always be your friend, Edoardo, despite our differences. You can count on it.'

He kissed her as Dolly and Franco entered the room with the children.

'The ambulance is here,' Dolly said gently. 'We must get going. Jimmy wants the plane to take off before noon while the weather holds. Now, children, say goodbye to Papa and get into the car.'

Minnie embraced Franco. '*Ciao, caro*. Keep an eye on Edoardo. He's bound to feel low after we leave.'

Minnie was carried into the open-sided ambulance.

'Come along, children,' Dolly said. 'It's our turn next.'

With Claudia clutching her doll, Bobby gripping a forbidden stone in the pocket of his shorts, they climbed into the back of the waiting car. As it followed the ambulance to the exit, Minnie raised herself on the stretcher to watch the children standing on the back seat of Dolly's car blowing kisses and waving to their father from the rear window until he was out of view, and both ambulance and car passed through the camp gates.

24

At Stonehill House, Dolly made her way down a flight of steps to the open corridor, shielded by monsoon attap screens made from woven palm fronds which connected hers and Jimmy's quarters to the separate guest suites of their sprawling split-level home. Despite the screens, the tiled floor was slippery with seeping rainwater, and she picked her way carefully to the steps leading to Minnie's set of rooms.

The large room, separated into a sleeping area at the rear and a small sitting room in front, was dark with monsoon gloom. She switched on a couple of table lights and tiptoed to the bed. Minnie was lying quietly, her pale face framed by the dark curls spread on the pillow. Dolly drew up a wicker armchair, settled down and waited for Minnie to wake up.

Rain drummed steadily against the wooden window louvres. From the roof came the sound of water as it glugged and gurgled into the gutters and cascaded on to the thick growth of sansevieria and canna leaves in the waterlogged flower beds below, splashing red mud on to the whitewashed walls. In the room, the charcoal sigris had not yet been lit and a faint smell of mildew hung in the air.

The ceiling fan creaked as its blades undulated sluggishly, creating an illusion of freshness. Thin spirals of smoke rose like grey string from citronella sticks burning on a table in the corner, keeping the mosquitoes at bay.

Minnie stirred and opened her eyes.

Dolly leaned forward. 'Are you feeling any better?'

'Much better, headache's gone.' Sleep slurred Minnie's words. 'How long have I slept?'

'More than two hours. It's almost four o'clock.'

'Goodness, you should have woken me earlier. Where are the children?'

'In the nursery learning new songs with Zella. She'll send them along in a minute.'

Zella was Fraülein Linzella Meyer, a Swiss governess whom Dolly had employed to look after her twins, Homi and Nina, and now also Claudia and Bobby. She was a qualified teacher (geography her special subject), spoke fluent French as well as German and English and played the piano. She was a treasure and the children adored her.

'Good, I'll get dressed and freshen up.'

Minnie got to her feet shakily, went into the bathroom and turned on the tap in the washbasin.

'Are you up to having visitors this evening?' Dolly called out.

Minnie popped her head round the door, patting her face dry with a towel. 'It depends. Who did you have in mind?'

'Darius actually. He rang earlier to say he'd like to come over to see you. He'd heard you'd been ill, of course. I said I'd let him know.' Dolly came to the bathroom door and watched as Minnie applied powder to her face.

'That's sweet of him. Goodness me, it must be ten years at least since we met – more perhaps. It will be nice to see him again.'

'That's fine, I'll ring him to confirm,' Dolly said. 'We'll meet at six thirty on the veranda,' she added before leaving the room.

Minnie looked at her pale face reflected in the mirror. Dipping a finger into a pot of rouge, she put two dabs on her cheeks and gently smoothed the colour into her skin. She touched her lashes with mascara and passed a rose-pink lipstick over her lips. Her hair hung too heavily against her face. She pushed it back with a silk Alice band and splashed cologne over her neck.

She had barely finished dressing when the children rushed in and threw themselves at her, clasping her around the knees and waist, then flung themselves on the bed, bouncing up and down.

'I've learnt a new song,' Claudia boasted. 'It's called "Here We Go Round the Mumbly Bush".'

'Me too,' lisped Bobby.

'No, you haven't,' cried Claudia. 'You can't say the words. I've learnt to count to a hundred, too.'

'Me too.'

'No, you haven't, Bobby! Mummy, it's not true, he can only count up to ten.'

'But I can say it in Hindi as well.'

'That's easy-peasy. So can I,' Claudia said, poking her tongue out at him.

'You're both so clever, my cherubs. I'm glad you are learning new things. Tell me more while we go and have tea with Zella.'

*

At six thirty Minnie was seated comfortably on Dolly's veranda reading an old edition of *The Saturday Evening Post*. Dolly was on the phone in the adjoining drawing room. Eventually she joined Minnie and sat down, just as the sound of wheels splashing through puddles signalled the arrival of a car. From their vantage point on the top level of the house they saw a flash of shiny blue enter the portico at the front entrance followed by a car door slamming.

'I see Darius is using his new Chrysler,' Dolly remarked. 'Heaven knows where he gets petrol for it.'

Presently the bearer tapped on the French door.

'Darius sahib downstairs. Also, there is phone call for Dolly memsahib.'

'I'll take the call. Show Darius sahib here, and bring the drinks,' Dolly said, going to the telephone extension in the sitting room.

Minnie heard footsteps on the stairs. She put down the magazine as Darius stepped on to the veranda. She caught her breath. *Surely this can't be Darius?* She remembered him as a gawky, skinny youth. Before her stood the most handsome man she had ever seen, tall and slim, with an intense, brooding expression. He had film-star looks, a cross between Rudolph Valentino and Errol Flynn, with velvety brown eyes and a generous mouth under a pencil-thin moustache. A slow smile lit his face, his eyes crinkling at the corners, sparkling, magnetic.

'Minnie, my dear, what a pleasure it is to see you after all these years.' Darius came forward, took her hand and bent to kiss her lightly on both cheeks. She noticed with surprise a shallow dimple in his chin. He drew up an easy chair.

Minnie's breathing returned to normal. 'Darius, I can hardly believe it is you. You have changed so much!'

'Ah, but you haven't, dear Minnie, except that you are more beautiful than ever.'

Minnie smiled, blushing slightly. 'Darius! Ever the sweet talker, aren't you? It's nice to see you, of course. I'm told you did get to write poetry after all, is that right?'

'Indeed, it is. I've had a slim volume published.' He laughed. 'A positively skinny volume, actually.'

'Well, congratulations. Do tell me, why on earth did you come back to Bombay? I thought you would have stayed in England for ever.'

'But my dear Minnie, it is obvious.' His tone was bantering as he swiftly dropped on one knee and took her hand. 'I came back to marry you!'

Minnie threw back her head laughing. It felt like a release, and all the tension of the last few months fell away. She had not laughed as light-heartedly as this since before she was interned in Satara.

'Well, Darius, I'm sorry to say you are too late. I am already married.'

He rose to his feet. Drawing a silver case from his pocket, he offered her a cigarette, took one himself, tapped it on the back of the case and struck a match. His eyes held hers as he lit both cigarettes. Slowly he blew out the flame.

'Nothing that can't be remedied,' he murmured, with an intensity that made her heart jump.

'Hallo, Darius dear!' Dolly exclaimed jovially, bustling in from the sitting room. 'I thought you were bringing your friend with you.' She turned to Minnie. 'He has a houseguest, you know, Albert something or other. A Jewish refugee from Poland. Met him in England, or was it Paris? Tell her about him, Darius, I don't remember the details of his story…'

She fussed around Minnie's armchair, slipping another cushion at the back. 'Minnie, this young man collects bohemians like we would collect stray dogs. What would you like to drink, Darius? A whisky soda? I'll call the bearer. And you, Minnie, some lime juice?' Dolly hardly paused for breath, but her chattering broke the electric tension.

Darius laughed. 'Whoa, Dolly, you are gabbling like a mother goose. Do sit down, old girl. Whisky soda would be fine, thanks.'

'What's the story regarding Albert?' Minnie asked.

'I met Albie Kuczynski in Paris, in thirty-six, I think. I thought Paris would be nice for a while after my time at Cambridge and London. Met him in a café called Les Deux Magots – a bohemian place, full of artists and writers. In fact, I thought that was his home, because there wasn't a time of day when I didn't see him there. We called him *le Professeur* because he was always expounding one theory or another about modern art. He'd left Poland in thirty-three. Felt uneasy about being a Jew.'

'Was he a real professor?' Minnie asked.

'To this day, I can't tell you exactly what he is.'

'He's a professional sponger, that's what he is!' Dolly exploded.

'Now, now, Dolly, he pays his way.'

Dolly snorted. 'With the odd favour or two. Meanwhile he's lived free of charge with you and Roshan for more than a year.'

The mention of Roshan's name put Minnie on the defensive. 'Do you live with Roshan?' she asked.

'Yes. We're very close since my mother died. We lead our own lives, of course, but she runs things – it's a large house. You must come over when you're better.'

Minnie smiled. *Not if I can help it*, she thought, but said nothing. She observed

Darius as he continued talking, noticing his outstretched feet. Slim. Like those on a Roman statue. He wore cowhide chappals, the open-backed sandals used by peasants, that on him looked elegant and fashionable. Like the rest of him. His hand movements were graceful. His fingers were long, squared, with manicured nails, a signet ring on the little finger of the left hand. A cream silk shirt, the sleeves casually rolled up his smooth light-brown arms, unbuttoned at the neck, revealed a barely perceptible Adam's apple, and a slight hollow above the collarbones. She found this intensely erotic. Heat surged through her body.

The bearer appeared carrying a silver tray of drinks that he handed round.

'What's Roshan doing these days?' Dolly asked, picking up her glass. 'She didn't want to join any of my committees.'

Darius took a sip of his whisky soda. 'You know about her animal hospital in Bandra. She's got a big expansion project under way there.'

'So I hear. *Very* useful war effort, I'm sure.'

'Dolly, come on now, somebody has got to do it. She doesn't approve of war, you know that. She leaves all that charity stuff to you, and the nursing to people like Clara.'

'She doesn't like people, is more to the point,' Dolly murmured. Darius frowned at her but remained silent.

Voices from the sitting room drew their attention. Zella, the governess, had brought the children from the nursery. A cheery woman of about forty, she had twinkling blue eyes, bushy blonde hair, freckles and a throaty laugh.

'Allez, dites bon soir à maman,' she said, pushing them forward.

Homi and Nina bounded over to Dolly, each vying to climb on to her lap. Claudia hugged her mother round the neck in a stranglehold, making sure that Bobby waited his turn. Bobby stood to one side with a finger in his mouth, staring tongue-tied at Darius.

'Look who's here, children,' Dolly said. 'Uncle Darius has come to see us. Say hello to him. Thank you, Zella. Come and join us for a drink after they are in bed.'

'Hello, Uncle Darius,' Homi and Nina shouted, jumping off Dolly's lap and rushing to their uncle. 'Have you brought us a present?'

'Hello, Uncle Darius,' Claudia and Bobby repeated.

'Darlings, he is not your uncle,' Minnie corrected. 'You should call him Mr Dubash.'

'That's all right, Minnie,' Darius laughed, his arms full of two wriggling children. 'I'm happy to be their honorary uncle. Come over and tell me your names.'

They came to stand beside him. 'I'm Claudia, and I'm five. He's Bobby, but he's only three.'

'Tell me what you've been doing today.'

The four children started talking at once. 'We went to the Hanging Gardens to play.'

'But it started raining,' Homi said.

'Did it indeed. And was the rain wet?' Darius asked straight-faced.

Shrieks of laughter followed. 'Of course it was wet. And *we* got wet.'

'Really? You're much too big to go wetting yourselves.'

'Noooo!' they screamed. '*We* didn't wet ourselves. The *rain* wet us.'

'Ah, I see, so the rain *was* wet after all.' Darius's dark eyes sparkled while he kept a straight face.

'Of course it was wet, Uncle. Rain is water.'

'I see, that explains it.' He broke into a broad smile. 'I only asked because sometimes it rains cats and dogs, doesn't it?'

The children looked at each other. This was a truly stupid man! Peals of laughter spilled out again.

'That's silly. Rain has *got to* be water. Rain *can't* be cats and dogs.'

'Oh yes it can. It rains cats and dogs in England. And I've lived there.'

'Where's England?'

'Far away.'

'That's where the war is, isn't it, Uncle,' Claudia asked smugly with all the superiority of an eldest child.

'Some of the war.'

'Where's my present?' Homi and Nina chorused.

'Downstairs in the hall. One for each of you.'

The four were off in a flash, Bobby trailing behind crying, 'Wait for me.'

The bearer appeared and murmured that Dolly was wanted on the phone again. The caller was Roshan memsahib. Dolly went into the sitting room to pick up the extension.

Minnie was acutely aware of Darius's presence. She sipped her drink nervously and crossed her legs. 'You seem to be awfully good with children,' she said.

'Only with some children, and only in small doses, I'm afraid. I have a low patience threshold.' Darius picked a couple of cashew nuts from a bowl and nibbled them.

'Tell me about your time at Cambridge,' she said.

Darius sat down next to her on the sofa. 'At first it was a hard adjustment. My family wanted me to read Law, you know, or Economics. Well, I knew right away that Economics was a non-starter. I tried Law, but by the end of the first term, I realised it wasn't for me. I remembered our talk at the dance before I left India and how you had encouraged me. I switched to English. Best thing I ever did. I had the most inspiring tutors. One of them was a writer, E.M. Forster, you might have heard of him?'

'Oh really?' Minnie nodded, none the wiser as to who Forster was. She couldn't remember exactly what she had said to Darius at the ball all those years ago.

'I enjoyed myself immensely; perhaps too much. My director of studies said I wasn't disciplined enough. But I met several extremely interesting people, both undergraduates and tutors, who influenced my ideas. There were quite a few wild parties, too, I can tell you.' He smiled at the memory. 'Unfortunately, I didn't get my degree. I got sent down in my final year.'

'What does that mean?' Minnie asked.

Darius laughed indulgently. 'It means I got kicked out.'

'Whatever for?'

'Well, we won't go into that just now. Not until I know you better.'

'I see. And do you think you will get to know me better?' Minnie was astounded by her coquettish question.

His eyes bored into hers. 'You can bet on it,' came the low reply.

She glanced at him sideways. 'I suppose you were a naughty boy.'

'Oh yes.' Darius's smile made her heart thud. 'I was a very naughty boy,' he drawled.

They laughed, breaking the tension. 'Oh dear, yes.' Darius nodded. 'After that, though, I had a great time in London, working for an unknown literary magazine, now sunk without trace. But, it wasn't until I got to Paris that I took up poetry seriously.' He rose and poured himself another drink from the tray the bearer had left. 'That is a city to inspire one. There was a freedom in Paris – of thought, of behaviour, of expression – which was lacking in England. I found such a fresh approach most appealing. I should love to go back.'

He handed her the bowl of nuts, but she shook her head. Minnie was only half listening, entranced by his gestures: the way he moved his body as he spoke, the intensity of his gaze, the timbre of his voice, the double crease in one cheek when he smiled, the shadow on his clean-shaven jaw. The way he looked at her.

Dolly returned to the veranda with the children now in their pyjamas. 'Say goodnight, children. Zella will read you a story before bed. But first, what do you say to Uncle Darius?'

A chorus of 'Thank you for our presents, Uncle Darius', 'Goodnight, Uncle', and 'Goodnight, Mummy' followed, accompanied by hugs, then a mad dash for the nursery.

'Darius, Roshan was on the phone. She called to find out where you were. She sounded annoyed that you hadn't told her you were coming here. I can't think why.' Dolly finished her drink. 'Anyway, she wants you back at the house for dinner. She says you shouldn't have left Albie all on his own – he is your guest. I don't dare ask you to stay or I really will be in the dog house with her.'

Darius downed his drink and rose to his feet. 'And I suppose I shall be in the dog house myself if I don't obey orders from my dear sergeant major,' he said, pulling a face of mock fear. 'Bye bye, Minnie,' he said, taking her hand and raising it to his lips. 'It was lovely to see you. I shall come to visit again soon. Perhaps you'd enjoy a game of gin rummy – I hear you are a real demon at cards.' He turned around and embraced Dolly. 'Bye, Dolly dear, give my best to Jimmy.'

After he'd gone, Minnie asked Dolly about the brother and sister. 'She sounds possessive, more like a mother with a naughty teenager than a sister.'

'Roshan has always been like that.' Dolly picked at a bowl of nuts. 'In my opinion she's totally obsessive about him,' Dolly sniffed. 'Doesn't like anybody to have an influence over him, unless she approves.'

'She's not that way with Jimmy.'

'No, but he doesn't put up with her nonsense.'

Dolly looked at her watch. 'She smothers Darius. As for girlfriends, she puts a stop to anything she thinks is serious. Her work's cut out though because he's extremely attractive, as you well know.' Dolly looked at Minnie pointedly. She rang for the bearer and asked for dinner to be served in half an hour.

'But he is spoilt, and unpredictably moody, believe me,' she continued after the bearer left. 'Don't get too involved with him, Minnie darling. Oh, come on now,' she added, 'don't give me that innocent look. I saw the way you two were gazing at each other. I'm not as dumb as you may think. I'm warning you, though, be careful of him. But more than that, be especially careful of Roshan.'

The next day a cellophane box arrived for Minnie from the florist at the Taj Mahal Hotel. It was tied with a white satin ribbon. Inside was a single long-stemmed orchid carrying a profusion of pale orange flowers along its stalk. Each perfect, waxy petal glowed like an ember on a bed of white silk. Minnie had never seen such a beautiful bloom. A card lay in the folds of the tissue.

Minnie

Roses are the traditional gift for women, but you are no rose.
You are an orchid: rare, exquisite, dazzling, mysterious, unique.
This Dendrobium Burana Fancy is called 'Heartsflame'.

Darius

She read and reread the card and smiled, her cheeks burning. She put the orchid into a narrow crystal vase on the side table near her armchair. Carefully picking the fullest bloom on the stem, she laid it between two tiny pieces of tissue paper. From her bedside table she took the dictionary given by her father and opened it at the letter D.

She placed the flower and the card on the page and pressed the book shut.

25

1940–1945

Minnie continued to visit Edoardo at the camp once a month, taking the children, who loved the thrill of the train journey.

'I feel sorry for him,' she told Dolly while packing in preparation for a trip to the camp. 'To tell the truth I feel guilty.'

'Why?'

Minnie shrugged. 'I'm free, here with you and the children. He's stuck there with nothing much to do, just stagnating.'

'It can't be helped. He has a lot of friends with him.'

'It's not the same thing at all.' Minnie folded four cotton knickers into her valise. 'I'm having a good social life – perhaps I shouldn't say this, but I'm enjoying myself.'

Dolly laughed. 'I'll say you are! Darius is monopolising you. People are starting to talk, you know.'

Minnie smiled. She loved the attention Darius lavished on her, but knew she should be more circumspect about her behaviour for the time being.

Minnie's divorce became absolute on 16 February 1942, the day after the fall of Singapore.

She sat at her rosewood desk at Stonehill House, holding the document of her decree absolute, folding and unfolding it. Tears smarted her eyes. She ought to be feeling elated that she was finally free. Instead, there was a sense of loss, almost of bereavement, as if the last link with her roots, her country and her family was severed. Where did she belong now? What did the future hold? Darius? Even that was uncertain. She reached for a handkerchief and blew her nose.

There had been a few veiled hints about his unsuitability, from several quarters. There was something in his past she knew nothing of but felt sure he would tell her in due course. His family was ganging up on him because he was unconventional, a free spirit. That's what she liked about him, and the slight aura of danger and unpredictability surrounding him was exciting.

Unlike Edoardo, Darius was a romantic, always giving her surprises: an exquisite silk scarf; chocolate-filled wooden Easter eggs for the children (heavens only knew where he had obtained such luxury in these difficult times); a jade horse following the day he first took her riding; a silver and sapphire cigarette case. Each item was accompanied by a bewitching, sensitive poem.

A tap at the door broke into her musing. She wiped her eyes, took a last look at the divorce document in her hand and locked it in the bottom drawer of the desk.

'Who is it?'

'Karsan bearer, memsahib.'

'Come in.'

The bearer entered carrying a massive bunch of brilliant dahlias and a bottle of Veuve Clicquot champagne.

'Please, memsahib, Darius sahib driver come. He bring letter.'

Minnie opened the envelope and extracted the card. She read the words and smiled.

To my Heartsflame,
Hello to freedom.
Yours forever – D

Minnie avidly followed news of the war with its increasingly dire headlines. For a while after the fall of Singapore, the public thought the Japanese might target Calcutta or Madras next, perhaps even Bombay. But so far it seemed as if Bombay would escape the worst of the troubles. To be sure, more troop ships came in and out of the port, and soldiers disembarking and embarking for different arenas of combat were a common sight. There was a great deal of tension in town, but no fighting, no feeling of real panic, merely a sense of waiting. The city was on the periphery of the action happening elsewhere. Shortages of all goods arose, and a flourishing black market developed. Despite these difficulties, a sense of frantic gaiety prevailed, and social life went on at a rather more hectic pace, as if each party were going to be the last.

The greatest concern for Minnie in the months following her divorce was to find work that would bring in an income enough to keep her and the children. She could not rely on Edoardo's maintenance contribution that was likely to dry up, and she did not want to be more of a burden than necessary on her hosts.

The three friends were at Clara's apartment one evening waiting for the car to take them to dinner at the Willingdon Club.

'You know how grateful I am to you and Jimmy for what you are doing for us,' Minnie said to Dolly. 'But I do feel it is time I got out from under your feet.'

'Nonsense, darling, it is the least Jimmy and I can do. We love you dearly, and the children, too.' Dolly was entirely genuine in her statement. 'You know you can stay as long as you like. I mean it.'

Minnie knew it, but at the same time wanted her financial independence.

'Yes, but there's gossip going round.' Minnie noticed Clara and Dolly exchanging glances. It was true. Rumours were spreading. That she was a sponger on their charity…that she was Jimmy's mistress…that they formed a *ménage à trois*…that she was out to get her hands on the Dubash fortune and was trying to snare Darius to achieve this end.

'We know it's the ghastly Roshan spreading them, don't we?' Clara exploded.

'You can't say that, Clara, we don't know,' Dolly remarked, trying to keep a balanced view.

'Nonsense. Who else could it be? She's a vindictive bitch.'

'But why should Roshan be vindictive with me?' Minnie asked Clara after Dolly went home. 'Why does she dislike me so much?'

'Because, darling,' Clara drawled through a haze of cigarette smoke, 'you are taking her precious Darius away from her.'

'But I'm not,' Minnie protested.

Clara looked at her sideways and smiled. 'Darius is crazy about you. He's never been like this with any other woman. Roshan saw to that. This time he's defying her, which is why she's worried. I bet he's asked you to marry him, hasn't he?'

Minnie made no reply. He had asked her to marry him. She had turned him down at first with the excuse that she was married, but since the divorce her new excuse had been their age difference. She felt uncomfortable being older than him.

She gazed at the view from the picture window, across the gardens to the shoreline with its thick fringe of palm trees. Darius. He was constantly in her thoughts. When she was not with him, her head took over from her heart and she could control her feelings, think pragmatically about their situation. But as soon as she was with him, feeling his cool fingertips on her skin, his warm breath in her ears, she was lost.

'You know you're in love with him even if you won't admit it,' Clara said. 'Just don't rush into anything you may regret.'

Minnie's hackles rose. 'Why does everybody warn me against Darius, even you of all people, Clara? What has he done that is so awful?'

A guarded look came into Clara's eyes and she turned her head. 'He wouldn't make you happy. He's…he is – moody. Unpredictable. Erratic.'

'But naturally, it's his artistic nature. Creative people are like that.'

'He has a filthy temper.'

'I've not noticed it. He's gentle enough with me.'

Clara shrugged, but said nothing more. She rose to go into the nursery with Minnie following. 'I want to feed little Harry before we go out. Pass me his bib, darling.'

Minnie fetched the bib from the chest of drawers and handed it over, tacitly acknowledging Clara's change of subject. She watched her sister-in-law with tenderness as Clara tied the bib around the neck of her year-old second son, Harry, named after Uncle Harry. She smiled as Clara cooed and cuddled him, kissed the top of his head, placed him in a highchair, and reached for a bowl of pureed carrot and rice which the ayah had brought in.

It amused Minnie to see the way Clara behaved with this child and with Joey six years earlier. There was no trace of the insensitive, brittle Clara of old. Here was a warm softie, making goo-goo eyes and speaking fluent baby talk. Minnie smiled. Motherhood suited her friend. She glanced at her watch. They were due at the Willingdon Club monthly dinner dance in half an hour.

'Isn't he a sweetie?' Clara said, holding him out for Minnie to take. 'Let Aunty Minnie give you a goodnight kiss, my poppet,' she added, then handed him to the ayah to take off to bed.

They left the apartment and took the stairs. In these times of austerity Clara insisted on walking down, to save on electricity. 'Helping with the war effort, you know,' she always said. Minnie admired her for doing more 'war effort' than most. For the past six months she had worked with total dedication as an auxiliary nurse at St George's Hospital four days a week, with four night shifts a month.

'Darling, I've snagged my nail. Have you an emery board in your purse?' Clara asked as they climbed into the back of the waiting car.

Minnie opened her evening bag and passed Clara the file.

'I say, what an absolutely gorgeous handbag! Wherever did you manage to buy it?' Clara turned it over and over.

'I didn't buy it. I made it,' Minnie replied.

Clara looked at her in astonishment and examined the bag more closely. 'Darling, I don't believe it! You are a clever girl! It looks like a Paris model. It is the most exquisite beadwork. Do you think you could make me one like that?'

Minnie flushed with pleasure. 'Certainly I could, if you want.'

'I'd pay you for it, naturally.'

'Nonsense, I wouldn't hear of it.'

'Don't be such an idiot, Minnie, of course I'll pay for it. You must be practical. You need the money. The bag is totally professional-looking – why don't you make a few more? I'm certain some of my friends would buy them.'

'Do you think so?'

'I'm sure of it.'

Minnie said nothing further, but the next day she fished out some old embroidery patterns from the Fontana Sisters she had brought with her when she left Rome. Quite a lot of the designs could be adapted to beadwork. She spent time working out the cost of the handbag Clara had admired. Perhaps this was the opening she was looking for. The more she thought about it over the next few weeks, the more possible the idea seemed. She had noticed that even in a time of war women were prepared to spend on luxury items. She sketched new patterns with different colour combinations and then made out a rough business plan. She couldn't possibly do all the sewing herself. She would need to employ workers, and probably rent premises to work from. She approached Jimmy to ask his advice.

'An excellent idea, sweetie. It's difficult getting imports these days. I'm sure ladies will be delighted – after all they could be called genuine Italian creations, couldn't they? I'll be happy to put up the starting capital.'

Minnie flushed with pleasure. This was more than she had expected. 'On the strict understanding that it would be a loan, Jimmy?'

'As you wish, my dear. A loan it is – interest free.'

Minnie smiled and nodded. 'That's too generous.'

Obtaining premises proved to be the big stumbling block. There was little availability at prices she could afford. What was available turned out to be too large, too small, or too expensive. She would have to consider renting an apartment, which was more space than she needed. Besides, she discovered that landlords did not want her as a tenant. Whether this was because she was a foreigner or a woman, or both, she never knew, but certain doors were firmly closed to her.

'No, sweetie,' Clara laughed, 'that's not the reason they won't rent property to you.'

'What is the reason, in that case?'

'It's because you haven't negotiated any *pugree* with them.'

'What on earth is that?'

'*Pugree* money is like a back-hander. Usually a pretty substantial one.'

'But the conditions they ask for are already exorbitant! Three months' rent in advance, plus three months' rent deposit – that's a huge amount, surely that's enough?'

'But *pugree* doesn't appear on the books. It's an under-the-counter payment – and you don't get it back when you leave at the end of the contract.'

'That's outrageous – surely it must be illegal?'

'It is outrageous. But that's how things work here, especially if you want desirable premises.'

Minnie explained all this to Sister Serafina during one of her regular visits to St Theresa's Convent. They had remained firm friends ever since their meeting on the ship that had brought them both to India. Even when Sister Serafina was posted for five years to a convent in South India, they had kept in touch and Minnie made small donations whenever she could. In the last year, Serafina had been transferred back to Bombay to be deputy Mother Superior at St Theresa's Convent situated less than a mile away from Minnie. They were delighted to renew their friendship.

Sister Serafina's loyalty to Minnie and her attitude to Minnie's divorce – though not recognised by the church – was in total contrast to that shown by Father Alfredo Alessi, who had also been on the same ship. He told Minnie – with regret and a certain embarrassment – that following her divorce, he would be unable to give her communion or receive her at services in the church. This did not prevent him, however, from happily accepting Minnie's frequent invitations to lunch, or any financial handouts. Nor did it stop him from asking Minnie to use her influence with Jimmy and persuade him to make substantial donations to Father Alessi's building fund for an orphanage for Catholic boys.

Sister Serafina, always happy to see Minnie, pondered over her friend's problem.

'Maria Erminia' – she always called Minnie by her full name when excited – 'I think I may have the solution. But I must clear it first with Mother Superior.'

'What's the solution, Serafina?'

'The convent has an old garage which is not being used. I suppose "garage" is too grand a word. Besides we do not have any cars to put in it. It used to be the old stables. It has direct access from the road, which is handy. It needs a lot doing to it, but I'm sure Mother Superior would be happy to get a rental for it. What do you think?'

Minnie was thrilled. They went together to inspect it. It needed a lot of work to put it in working order but it would be perfect.

'Perhaps you could employ some of the girls in our hostel,' Sister Serafina suggested. St Theresa's was well known for taking in abandoned teenage girls and teaching them trades, usually dressmaking, embroidery or weaving.

Minnie felt as if most of her difficulties had been solved at a stroke. She employed four of the best embroiderers from among the girls recommended by Sister Serafina. All that she had learnt from her mother came flooding back to her. She remembered how fastidious Donna Rachele had been about Minnie's needlework; how meticulous her mother had been in executing the designs supplied by the Fontana Sisters; how much attention she had paid to detail. Silently she sent a prayer of thanks not only for the lessons she had learnt so long ago, but also for the instinct that had prompted her to bring all the old patterns with her to India – little had she imagined then how useful these would prove to be in her new venture.

And silently, as she did each night, she prayed for the safety of her mother and father in her beloved war-torn country.

Minnie bought an old Singer treadle sewing machine and engaged a full-time durzi: a tailor. She scoured the bazaars for silks and velvets, bought remnant fabrics from the two main department stores, Evans & Fraser and Whiteway Laidlaw. She found suppliers of beads, bugles and sequins. In the Muslim quarter in Mohamedali Road she discovered a small workshop ready to make frames, clasps and chains for the handbags. She pored over back issues of *Vogue* magazine for ideas. She prepared a sample book of patterns. A few months later she had produced forty stunning evening bags ready for sale.

She opened for business in December 1942.

26

Darius carried on an intense courtship of Minnie. She found him to be sensitive, romantic and passionate, but she also saw in him a sense of insecurity.

A pattern emerged over time. She noticed that he was prone to periods of moodiness, just as she had been warned. For weeks their relationship would progress at a normal rate with the usual daily phone calls and meetings. Then, without warning, he would cancel an engagement at the last moment, or simply not turn up at all. The first few times this happened, Minnie was hurt and angry by his cavalier behaviour. She phoned his house only to be told that sahib had gone away. This made her even more annoyed.

'Oh dear, Minnie, it is typical of him,' Dolly commiserated. 'He's probably had a blazing row with Roshan and gone off somewhere to calm down. Albie might know – you remember him, he's their houseguest.'

Albie invited himself to the house for lunch to discuss the matter 'without fear of being overheard. You take my meaning, *n'est-ce pas, ma chère?*' he said to Minnie. The prospect of a free luncheon with what he termed as real food, instead of the cranky vegetarian diet provided by Roshan, proved irresistible.

'Ah, *ma chère* Minnie,' he said, wiping his small goatee beard as they left the table after a satisfying meal of fillet steak. He circled her shoulders with an avuncular arm and steered her towards the sofa in the drawing room, unaware that this familiarity irritated and amused Minnie in equal measure. Settling himself comfortably to await the coffee, he looked around as if missing something.

'I don't suppose Jimmy smokes cigars, *n'est-ce pas?* No, I thought not. No matter, a cigarette will do. Aha! Craven A, my favourite.' Peering through his thick spectacles, he took a cigarette from the flat red tin lying on the coffee table, gave it a couple of taps against the lid, lit it and inhaled deeply.

'*Quel plaisir, ma chère,*' he murmured, closing his eyes and exhaling through his nose. 'Of course, at home Roshan does not allow me to smoke in the drawing room. She says my Gold Flake smells horrible. But they are cheap and all I can afford, so I take myself off to the garden or to my room.' He sighed. 'It is a small room – very hot – near the kitchen.' He put on a pathetic expression, flicked ash into an ashtray and reached for the tin again. '*Ma chère* Minnie, but where are my manners, I ask myself? I forgot that you too smoke.'

He opened the tin, passed it over to her and leaned forward with the Dunhill lighter. 'I wonder, *ma chère*, if I may take the rest of the tin?' he murmured. 'I am sure Jimmy will not miss it. It would give me several hours of pleasure to enjoy such a smooth smoke.'

His cheeks bulged with his most winning smile as he glanced pleadingly at Minnie. She burst out laughing at this play-acting. 'Go on then.'

He slipped the tin smoothly into the breast pocket of his shirt and settled back with a sigh of contentment. Minnie poured him a demitasse of coffee and got up to fetch another tin of cigarettes from a drawer in the sideboard.

'Now, *ma chère*, you want to ask me where Darius has got to, *n'est-ce pas?*'

'You are his friend, and I thought he might have told you. It's not the first time he has missed one of our engagements with no excuse – no phone call, no message, nothing!'

'I'm sorry to hear that, but perhaps he has his reasons.'

'That is exactly what I want to know. What *are* his reasons – do you know?'

'Does he not tell you when he returns?'

'Not at all. He disappears for days on end, then turns up as if nothing had happened – as if we'd met the previous night.'

'I see. What mood is he in when he returns?'

'In an excellent mood – in fact, he's elated, charming and full of good humour. All he tells me is that he needed to be on his own for a bit to think and to write.'

Albie drained his cup and held it out for a refill. 'That's true enough, *ma chère*. You know the creative process. You must understand, those of us of an artistic temperament need our freedom – we need to breathe, not be suffocated. We need the liberty to explore ideas, and every now and then we have to escape from the constraints of convention.'

Minnie pursed her lips in annoyance as he crushed the cigarette in the ashtray. What a nerve he had to associate himself with Darius's 'artistic temperament'. To all intents and purposes, Albie was a jack of all trades, having declared himself at various times to be a lecturer in languages at the Sorbonne, an architect, a manufacturer of roof tiles, a book-binder, a philosopher and a captain in the Polish cavalry.

'Why did you ask me about his mood after these mysterious absences?'

'It is a typical reaction, *n'est-ce pas?*' His flippant tone had gone.

'Reaction to what, Albie? You know more than you are telling me – please don't play games.'

'I assure you, *ma chère*, I am not playing games. I simply don't know how to put things in a way that you would understand – that would not cause you distress, or to have an adverse reaction. He is, after all, my very good friend, and I know that he is much in love with you. At least, as much as he is capable of.'

'I'm glad to hear that, whatever you mean by it. But do go on, please. I promise I won't have an adverse reaction. I just want a logical reason for his behaviour.' She leaned forward and took a cigarette from the new tin.

Albie sighed. 'You know, he often has fearful rows with Roshan – I mean really terrible. She is a strong personality, very…hard.'

'You don't like her, do you?'

Albie permitted himself a smile and another cigarette. 'She is not as *gentille* as you, *ma chère, c'est sur*. I neither like nor dislike her. I try to keep out of her way. However, it is a fact that she dislikes me.' He shrugged his shoulders.

'For all her harshness,' he continued, 'she loves her brother deeply. I think he is the only thing in her life that she truly loves, apart from her dogs, *naturellement*. Unfortunately, she does not want to see that he is a grown man. She acts like a jealous woman at times and would like to control him as if he were still an adolescent.' He crossed his legs. 'This creates great friction between them, of course. They explode, they say cruel things to each other. Quite often Darius smashes things in rage. Then he shuts himself away in his rooms, doesn't appear for meals. However, the next day the storm has passed. It seems he has apologised and made peace with Roshan.'

'Does she ever apologise to him?'

'Never! That is not in her. I don't know how I know, but I am quite convinced it is always Darius who asks pardon. Nobody ever witnesses the apology, but the next day things are back to normal. Except that Darius is quiet and subdued.'

Minnie made no comment, waiting for Albie to continue.

'It is at these times that he goes off for a few days. Occasionally I go with him. He may drive to the beach house at Juhu, or he will go to Powai Lake – somewhere rural to watch the village dances or help the fishermen bring in their catch. But mostly he will go down to Grant Road.'

Minnie gasped, sitting bolt upright. 'Grant Road? But – but that's the red light district! The cages. It's where the prostitutes sit in the windows, so I'm told.'

'Indeed it is – but, believe me, *ma chère*, he doesn't go there for the women. I've gone with him a couple of times, so I know.'

'Then what *does* he go for?'

'He goes to gamble. Yes, he goes to play cards. And to smoke.'

Minnie looked astonished. 'But he can smoke as much as he likes at home.'

'Dear girl, it's not for ordinary cigarettes. He goes to smoke ganja. Or to take bhang.'

'What are those?'

'Narcotics.'

Minnie was horrified. 'You mean like opium – he's a drug addict?'

'No, not like opium. He's not an addict…he just smokes the ganja sometimes – it makes him feel relaxed. Takes away the stress. And bhang is taken in a drink. It's quite mild, actually. I've tried them both myself.'

'But why does he do it?'

'It's a form of escapism, *ma chère*. When life gets too much for him, the ganja and bhang let him forget all his troubles. He is weightless, at peace. He says it allows him to free his mind so he can be creative. And afterwards he is able to face his world again.'

Minnie's face expressed her worry.

'You must understand, dear Minnie,' Albie continued gently, 'that when he comes to you after these episodes, he barely remembers them. For him they are not important – merely a way of clearing his mind. That's why he dismisses your questions. He is a complex character. But bear in mind that he comes to *you* afterwards – not to anyone else – because you make him feel safe.'

'How so?'

'You are not like his previous women. You do not try to manipulate him. You see what is good in him. You believe in his talent and encourage his qualities. Others, including – indeed mainly – his own family, merely see his weaknesses.'

After Albie left, taking with him not only the tin of cigarettes but also the remainder of the coconut pancakes they had eaten for dessert, Minnie had time to reflect on his observations. She didn't know whether to be pleased or alarmed. She was glad to be reassured of Darius's love. Until this moment she had had a lurking feeling that Darius might be susceptible to the flirtatious advances of the many young Parsi girls who itched to marry him. According to current gossip they felt that they alone had the right to be considered as suitable marriage material for him rather than an outsider like herself. She knew that in large part this notion was put about and encouraged by Roshan, so Albie's remark was a boost to her morale.

Although she didn't much care for Albie's opportunistic ways, she was more inclined to believe his judgement of Darius over that of other family members, who seemed prejudiced towards their wayward relative. No, she thought, behind Albie's pomposity and posing, there was a basic honesty about him. The kind often found in the insensitive and self-centred; a sort of honesty by accident rather than intention.

However, she was more fearful of the narcotics aspect than she had initially thought. She knew nothing about drugs, except that opium was 'a very bad thing' to get hooked on. She was vaguely aware that within the Indian community it was considered unexceptional and was widely used in their homes as a sign of hospitality. She wondered why Darius felt it necessary to visit such a dangerous area to indulge this fancy.

'Strangely enough Roshan does not know about his visits to Grant Road,' Albie had said, 'and Darius wants to keep it secret from her at all costs.'

The explanation did not satisfy Minnie, but she had to make the best of it. If Darius wanted his freedom, surely he would recognise that she was not preventing him from it. He, meanwhile, continued to shower her with gifts.

'Here is something I'd like you to try, my love,' he said after one of his absences, holding out a soft, tissue-wrapped parcel.

She opened it to find folds of peacock-blue shot silk.

'It's a sari!' she exclaimed, lifting it out and throwing a curious look at Darius. 'Is it to make an evening dress?'

'No, darling, I want you to start wearing a sari. I think it would suit you perfectly.'

'Do you think so?' she asked in a dubious voice.

'Trust me, you will look fabulous.'

He was right. Minnie looked marvellous in the brilliant blue sari, with its gold and silver woven border. It took a bit of getting used to. She had to learn to pleat it and tuck it correctly into the waistband of her petticoat. The hardest thing was learning how to walk correctly with six yards of material around her legs.

Minnie looked at her reflection in the mirror. She was surprised to see how easily she could pass for an Indian. The first time she dared to wear the sari in public was to accompany Darius to a Hindu wedding reception. She caused a sensation. An Indian film producer at their table promptly offered her a contract for his forthcoming production, and the mother of the bridegroom addressed her in Hindi.

*

Minnie called her new business La Bottega, and within a few months of its opening word had spread, and her order book was beginning to fill. All the weeks of hard work she had put in to set it up were paying off. After breakfasting with the children and seeing them off to school, she drove to her atelier for the daily meeting with the durzi, two of the girls from the convent who did the embroidery work, and Ruby, an older girl from the convent whom Minnie had appointed as supervisor. They would discuss the orders, talk about patterns and decide on colour schemes. Minnie then spent the rest of the morning in her office sketching new designs or experimenting with different techniques of embroidery or beadwork. Once a week Ruby did a stock-take of materials and prepared a list of silks and beads and anything else that needed reordering. She would give the list to Minnie who then took it to her bead supplier in Mohamedali Road. She made a point of spending a couple of hours each afternoon at home with the children before going back to the atelier to lock up.

She enjoyed this special time with the children. Claudia was pretty as a picture and always eager to help Minnie. She loved coming to the atelier and Minnie was happy to let her sort through the various bobbins of thread and arrange them in rows of varying shades of each colour. From an early age she showed an instinct for matching colours or threading beads into pretty necklaces. Bobby was more adventurous. Not for him to be surrounded with pretty materials and coloured threads, he liked nothing better than kicking a ball around, or when he came to the atelier he would soon leave Minnie and Claudia together while he got a game of cricket going in the parking lot with the watchman's children, roping in a neighbour's servant to be wicket keeper.

As the weeks progressed and more orders came in, Minnie realised she would soon have to employ one or two more girls for the intricate beadwork for which she was becoming well known.

Once a routine was well established Minnie decided it was time to have a short break. Darius suggested going away for a long weekend to see the cave sculptures at Ajanta. Darius had spoken admiringly of this extraordinary monument that not many appreciated, and she was infected by his enthusiasm for it.

She was greatly looking forward to the trip, and to the ten-hour train journey in a private compartment alone with him. What bliss to be away from the prying eyes and big ears of relatives, friends, servants. The children were going to stay with their cousins, as Aunty Clara had promised to take them to a circus.

On the Saturday they were due to leave, after a light breakfast she was ready and packed. She was excited as she waited for Darius in the drawing room. He was late. Punctuality was never his strong point, and she worried they would miss their train. Her excitement waned as time passed with no sign of him. By lunchtime she guessed he was not going to turn up. With the last embers of hope, she phoned his house.

'Sahib has gone away,' was the answer. 'No, madam, he did not say where.'

'No, madam, he did not take any luggage.'

'No, madam, he left no message.'

'I don't know when he will come back, madam – maybe Monday, maybe Tuesday.'

'Very good, madam, I will tell him you called. Do you wish to speak to Roshan memsahib?'

'No thanks.' Minnie hung up, furious.

On Sunday evening, having picked up the children earlier than planned, they sat together before dinner and she listened to them describing the exciting weekend with their cousins and to their tales about the circus.

'It was a long drive, Mummy,' Bobby said. 'And ever so hot.'

'And there was this big tent,' Claudia said, 'and it smelled of horse poo.'

'And Aunty Clara took us right up to the front row and...' Bobby looked at Claudia and they both burst out laughing.

'What's so funny?' Minnie asked.

'Aunty Clara brought out a big white sheet and covered the five seats with it, and then she brought out the Flit pump and flitted the seats and all round us and the people behind made a face because of the smell. But she said it was because she didn't want any of us getting fleabites because she said circuses were well known for having fleas and bugs because of the animals and all...'

Claudia was interrupted in mid-flow as the bearer came into the room and spoke to Minnie in a low voice saying that Darius sahib's chauffeur, Jeevan, was downstairs and needed to speak to her urgently.

This was strange, Minnie thought – what could possibly be so urgent?

'Tell him I'll come as soon as the children finish dinner.'

'Please, memsahib, Jeevan say please no wait, please come urgent.'

Jeevan was not merely a chauffeur. The role he played in Darius's life was complex. Minnie realised quickly that their relationship was more than that of master and servant. There was a special bond between them. She knew the story of how Uncle Harry had rescued Jeevan from a life of begging on the streets when he was about fourteen. Harry had been struck by his intelligence and thought the lad could be a minder for the six-year-old Darius, after the loss of both parents, and take the pressure off his teenage sister.

The two had taken to each other right away, and ever since, Jeevan had been Darius's minder, servant, driver, protector and general factotum. Jeevan remained loyal to him no matter how badly Darius treated him. As he grew older, Darius's violent temper was often vented – verbally and physically – on the long-suffering Jeevan.

Darius trusted Jeevan completely, and because he did, so to a certain extent did Minnie. She knew she too could depend on him, particularly in matters that concerned his master. Not everyone felt the same. Dolly, for instance, disapproved of what she termed as Jeevan's over-familiarity towards Darius, and Roshan could not stand him, possibly because she resented anyone other than herself holding her brother's trust, particularly a servant. But Minnie knew that because of Darius, Jeevan's loyalty extended to her too.

She met him downstairs. 'Jeevan, what is it?'

'Memsahib, I must speak. Private, please, memsahib.'

There was urgency in his voice. She took him into the empty drawing room. 'What is it?'

'Is Darius sahib, memsahib. He be in bad trouble. Bad peoples with him.'

Claws of fear grabbed at Minnie's throat.

'What sort of trouble? Where is he?'

'He gone Grant Road, memsahib. He do bad thing. Playing cards with bad peoples. Taking much ganja. No good. After, I don't know exactly. Some Hijra peoples coming in asking baksheesh, very rude. So Darius sahib be very rude also, no want give baksheesh. *Hijra lok bohut bure badmash hain,* mem – Hijra peoples very dangerous. One Hijra take knife and stick my sahib. Much blood. He very bad hurt. Please, memsahib, you come straight away.'

'Didn't you call Roshan memsahib?'

'No, not must to tell Roshan memsahib. I think Darius sahib want you. Better you come, you take him to your Serafina Sister. She calling doctor, no tell police.'

'I'll get some money.'

'Memsahib, please no come in dress like this, please to wear sari. More safe memsahib look like Hindu lady.'

Ten minutes later, dressed in the plainest of her saris, Minnie climbed into the front seat of Darius's car. Jeevan primed her as he drove with only sidelights showing because of the blackout. She had only the vaguest idea what Hijras were but had heard they always roamed around in groups demanding money and could be threatening, violent and sometimes murderous. She felt sick with fear.

Please God, she prayed silently, *don't let him die.*

27

The car crawled, threading its way through the warren of narrow streets behind Crawford Market. An anxious Minnie pressed Jeevan to hurry. But he drove cautiously, not wanting to attract undue attention, trying to avoid bumping into the numerous jaywalkers who were a constant hazard in these crowded bazaar areas. It was not quite eight o'clock but fully dark and stiflingly hot. Throngs of people crowded the streets; a few emaciated cows ambled aimlessly, eager to eat anything offered to them; hurricane lamps hung in still busy shops; street vendors shouted out their wares.

Minnie's nose wrinkled in distaste at the stench drifting through the open car window – a combination of open drains, cow dung, joss sticks, kerosene fumes, frying garlic and ginger, and roasting chickpeas. She drew the border of her sari forward over her head so her face was in half-shadow, in the gesture of modesty Hindu women showed when in public places.

The car braked suddenly. She glanced up. A cow with a crippled rear leg, its ribs and hip bones projecting sharply against a taut brown hide, stood in front of the car gazing curiously at them through the windscreen. A bunch of coriander leaves disappeared into its slow grinding mouth as it blinked its large sad eyes. Jeevan did not honk the horn but thumped the outside of the car door with his right hand, attempting to shoo the animal away. A passer-by took pity on them, slapped the cow on its skinny withers to get it moving and was rewarded with a jet of warm urine splashing on to his sandals. The cow lost interest and hobbled towards a food stall. Jeevan drove on.

Minnie glanced surreptitiously at both sides of the somewhat wider street they were on now. The pavements were choked with people. She was surprised to notice among them numbers of men in British uniforms – both army and naval, who, she thought, would normally frequent the brothels in safer areas of the city, rather than this seedy red-light area. To her furtive eyes, the buildings appeared to be crammed together although not more than two or three storeys high. The ground and first-floor frontages were made up of a series of three or four closely placed windows opening to floor level, all with wooden shutters, many of which were closed. The open ones were fitted with vertical iron bars like an enlarged bird's cage. The interior of each room was lit and clearly visible from the pavement and high-pitched songs crackled from the odd wireless set. Women sat close behind the bars of each window, dressed in brightly coloured saris, calling to passers-by in the road. Some had their hair done in a traditional bun or braid, others left theirs flowing over their shoulders. One would wind and unwind her sari to tempt a client, another would comb out her hair, raising her arms and stretching seductively, while yet another would stand up and press her breasts between the bars of the cage to attract attention.

While the car crept along at walking pace, Minnie observed that once a deal was done, the man entered the building through a side door, handing over payment to a keeper sitting in the entrance, while the chosen woman reached her arms between the bars of her cage to close the shutters.

So, these were the famous 'cages' of Grant Road, Minnie mused. Curiosity, disgust and pity swamped her as the car crept down the street. It was clear that the older and plainer women, past their best, occupied the upper floors. At street level, those displaying their attractions were the pretty, the voluptuous, the bold – and the very young, so young that many appeared to be barely out of childhood.

A few of the houses looked to be in better condition than others, more gaudily lit, the rooms painted the favoured sky blue, the girls nicer looking. Other buildings were more ill kept, their shutters and outer walls streaked with the red stain of betel nut spittle, and the women here were drabber and coarser.

'How far now, Jeevan?' she asked.

'Not far, mem.'

'You do the talking, Jeevan.'

'Very good, memsahib.'

'Find out what happened and come and tell me. I'll pretend to be shy and keep my head down. You can say I am Darius sahib's sister, if they are curious. Do you understand?'

'Okay, mem.'

Jeevan turned the car into a narrow, less crowded lane and came to a stop in front of a poorly lit doorway. He beckoned to the burly Pathan watchman sitting on a stool guarding the entrance. The man sauntered to the car and peered into the window. Minnie was aware of a round face, bushy eyebrows and large fleshy-lobed ears uncomfortably close to her. Her heart beat faster as she pulled the sari border over her head and modestly lowered her eyes. Jeevan got out and the two men spoke in low tones. Minnie noticed a few coins disappearing into the watchman's waistcoat pocket. She felt nervous, her hands clammy.

'Come, memsahib, we go up,' Jeevan whispered through the window. 'This man look after motor. See nobody steal tyre and hubcap. I be telling him, afterwards you give him ten rupees baksheesh, is okay?'

She nodded, got out of the car and followed Jeevan through the doorway. Gathering the skirt of her sari in one hand, she climbed up the dimly lit flight of creaking stairs from which rose an overpowering stink of urine. Scuffling sounds came from the bottom of the stairs. She pulled the sari border across her nose to cut out the stench, clenching the material between her teeth to keep it in place. She shuddered at the thought of using the handrail on the banisters and forced herself not to imagine the sticky filth covering it. The scuffling became more persistent. *Oh please, Holy Mary, Mother of God, don't let the rats get me!*

On the first floor, Minnie stood behind Jeevan while he knocked at a door. It was opened presently by a tall, heavily made-up woman wearing an orange cotton sari with a purple border and blouse. Her face was mask-like, caked with pale powder, her eyes rimmed with kohl, her lips a scarlet slash. She wore silver drop earrings, and her wrists were encased in several inches of jangling glass bangles. The cloying smell of tuberoses wafted from her oiled hair. The palms and back of her hands were traced with an intricate henna tattoo pattern. Her big feet were bare, her voice hoarse and rough.

Jeevan spoke to her in a low voice, after which she stepped back and jerked her head towards the room behind her, beckoning them to enter. With the fold of sari still clenched between her lips, Minnie looked quickly round the large room illuminated by a ceiling light with dim-wattage bulbs behind three dusty glass shades. A rush mat covered most of the floor. In the centre stood a low round table surrounded by six or seven dirty white cushions still bearing the imprint of bottoms that had recently sat on them. Cards and dice lay scattered over the table, and several metal tumblers balanced on the matting below it. An icebox stood in one corner with more beakers on top of it. An open door at one end provided ventilation and led on to a small rear balcony. A birdcage containing two plump canaries hung from the centre of the curtainless window.

Minnie couldn't place the strange sweet smell that pervaded the room. A woman stood near the window dragging on a stinking beedi – those foul-smelling cigarettes made of rolled-up tobacco leaves and smoked only by the poorest. Two others were crouched on the floor next to what looked like a blood-stained mattress, drinking tea from tin mugs. They, too, were heavily made-up, wore garish saris, silver earrings and nose studs.

The woman smoking the beedi stared at Minnie with an unfriendly look. Her face was hard and behind the heavy make-up she seemed older than the others. Minnie lowered her eyes. She could almost touch the tension in the room. A fat black cockroach crawled across the matting towards the table. Minnie's stomach muscles clenched in revulsion at the sight. She nudged Jeevan. He spoke to the woman smoking the beedi. They exchanged a few sentences. The woman seemed angry and spoke loudly, Jeevan's answers appeared more conciliatory.

The first woman who had opened the door to them joined in, moving towards the table and pointing at the cards while talking loudly and gesticulating. The ceiling light fell fully on her face and it seemed to Minnie's startled eyes that beard shadow lined the woman's jaw. Minnie tried not to stare, but doubt crept into her mind that perhaps this woman was not after all a woman. Was she one of those people – what had Jeevan called them? – Heejis, Heeras, no...Hijras, that was it. Hijras. Men who were women. Minnie suppressed a shudder. This one must be a Hijra – that would account for her big feet. What about the others? Surreptitiously, she looked again at the other three. They all had big feet, big hands too, and thick wrists. Bigger than women's. How could she have missed the signs? It was obvious on closer inspection that they didn't really look feminine at all.

Jeevan drew Minnie aside to confer.

'She be say sahib come here two days back,' Jeevan whispered. 'He be playing card with four-five other sahibs – not pukka sahibs. All is drinking plenty bhang and smoking ganj.'

'But what happened exactly? Did these women hurt him?'

'I not understand properly, mem. These peoples talking much rubbish Hindi. I think sahib getting angry because is losing. Hijra peoples coming inside for to get baksheesh. They is do singing, dancing. My sahib no want give baksheesh, say rude things to Hijra womans. She be saying my sahib just like drunk man – too much ganj. Then 'nother sahib is winning game and my sahib saying he be cheat.'

Minnie gasped. 'Then what?'

'Then bad sahib taking out knife from pocket and sticking my sahib.'

'Where?'

'In leg, memsahib, here,' he pointed briefly to his upper thigh. 'Very big cut, too much blood all over. My sahib is fall down. Other sahib want sticking him again, but Hijra womans stop him. Then she see much, much blood, she think my sahib dead. She taking card money, then all other sahibs run quick quick. But Hijra womans stay.'

'Why didn't they leave, too?'

'They be frighten police catching them. Is sure that police saying Hijra womans theyselves doing knife sticking, then put in jail. Jail very bad place for Hijra womans, memsahib. They be very frighten.'

'What did they do?'

'They call one hakim. He is keep quiet.'

'What is a hakim?'

'Is like doctor for Muslim peoples. When I come for to fetch hakim, he say sahib very serious, must to go hospital *ekdum juldi* – quick quick. He putting bandage, but too much blood coming out. Hijra womans telling me same like hakim. When I seeing sahib, he is look like dead man, but I think can't take to General Hospital because them peoples calling police. So I am thinking only you memsahib can to do something with no calling police.'

'Where is he, Jeevan?'

Jeevan turned to ask the women. One rose to her feet and pointed to a closed door at the back of the room. There were more exchanges among the Hijras.

'What are they saying?' she asked Jeevan, keeping her voice low.

'They say want money. They staying here two days and lose much baksheesh money. Also, hakim want money.'

'How much do they want?'

'They ask five hundred rupees.'

'That's too much – tell them I haven't got that much. Say that I am grateful they looked after my brother. I am sorry for the trouble that has happened, and I will give them two hundred and fifty rupees, and fifty rupees for the hakim.'

Jeevan conveyed the message to the women, who all started arguing and waving their arms about.

'They say not enough, they want more, memsahib.'

'Not more than three fifty for them, Jeevan,' she whispered. 'If they don't accept, then I shall have to call in the police. Tell them.'

The women argued a bit more among themselves. At last they waggled their heads in assent. Minnie reached for a small pouch of money that she had pinned to the waistband of her petticoat. She drew out a few notes and handed them to Jeevan to pass on to the first woman they had met, who appeared to be their leader. She tucked the money inside her blouse and opened the door to the next room for Minnie to enter.

The atmosphere inside was stuffy and rancid. Little natural light fell from the small shuttered window. It was sparsely furnished: a rickety chair, a table leaning against the wall. On it stood a metal lamp with a pink torch-shaped glass shade enclosing a forty-watt bulb. The feeble light cast a rosy circle against the wall and the straw matting on the floor, leaving the rest of the room in a depressing gloom. From somewhere came the low hum of an unseen table fan. Beyond the table hung a curtained partition from behind which came the sound of laboured breathing and an occasional groan. Minnie grabbed the lamp, tugged to uncoil the twisted flex and drew the curtain aside.

She didn't know whether to cry with relief or fear at what she saw.

Darius lay on a low divan half propped up by a bolster under his shoulders. His eyes were closed, and even by the pinkish light thrown by the lamp his skin looked grey, drained of colour, his lips thin and dry, his eyelids as pale as wafers. At intervals a tremor shook his body and he groaned. He was half lying on his right hip, with bent knee, the left leg stretched out and raised by a greasy pillow under the buttock and thigh. His trousers had been slit from hem to crotch, and the material lay flopped over either side of his leg, like the wings of a dead crow. A greyish mass of cloth covered the length of his thigh. In the middle of it a dark brown stain stretched from the groin to just above the knee. In spite of the feeble draught from a table fan in the corner, flies hovered and landed on the caked dressing.

Minnie blinked back tears. This was no time for emotion – she needed to keep a clear head. She touched Darius's forehead, which was dry and burning hot, brushing aside strands of black hair plastered to his skin.

She beckoned to Jeevan standing inside the door.

'Tell them to boil some tea with lots of sugar. And bring me cold water from the icebox.'

He brought her the water and said the tea would come in a minute. She would not risk giving Darius unboiled water to drink, but tea would do him good. Minnie lifted the skirt of her sari and tore a strip off her petticoat, which she dipped into the iced water. Wringing out the cloth, she placed the cool material on Darius's forehead. He moaned and opened his eyes, staring without recognition at first, his eyes dull and feverish. 'Minnie, what are you doing here?' he muttered at last.

Minnie put a finger to his parched lips. 'Shhhh, my darling, don't say a word. Time enough for that later. We need to get you out of here. First let me look at your leg.'

Once more she dipped the cloth into water, wrung it and placed it on his hot forehead. He tried to smile, mumbled her name and words of apology, then shut his eyes again. Gently she lifted the wadding off his thigh. He flinched as the cloth stuck in parts to the wound, but she was careful not to pull it off. The cut on his thigh was deep and several inches long, starting near the groin. The flesh around it was red and swollen – she could feel the heat from the inflammation. On closer inspection, it was clear that the wound was still seeping and halfway down it, a finger length of thick yellow pus had formed. His pulse was rapid and he appeared to be dehydrated. The hakim may have managed to staunch the worst of the bleeding, but it was obvious that a serious infection had set in and proper medical attention was a matter of urgency.

Jeevan brought in a cup of tea. He poured some of it into the saucer to cool it down and handed it to Minnie, who held Darius's head up and got him to sip a little of the sweet brew.

'Jeevan, we need to carry sahib down to the car, and we must try not to bend his leg or the wound will start to bleed too much. Ask the women if they can help.'

She heard him talking to the Hijras before returning to the room.

'Them say can to carry sahib in chair. Them be strong strong. And I holding sahib's leg straight, try not move much.'

'Darius, can you hear me?' Minnie shook his shoulder. 'The Hijras are going to carry you downstairs. It will be painful but try to hold on. I'll go ahead to open the car door. We need to get you to a hospital quickly.'

Two of the Hijras helped Jeevan to manoeuvre Darius as gently as they could on to the chair. The movement caused a groan of pain. 'What hospital? Not St George's?' Darius asked through clenched teeth.

'Not St George's. I'm taking you to St Elizabeth's Nursing Home.'

His attempted laugh came out as a gasp. 'But that's a maternity hospital!'

'Yes, it is, but a discreet one. I'm sure your name will not get out.'

Her confident manner belied her inner nervousness. By the time they negotiated the chair down the badly lit staircase to the street and carefully propped him on the back seat of the blue Chrysler, Darius was almost unconscious. *Thank God for large American cars and thank God it is still here in one piece*, thought Minnie as she paid the Pathan watchman the promised ten rupees plus an extra five for looking after it.

Darius's wound had started to bleed again. Now she was desperate to get him into the hands of a doctor. She handed the Hijras an extra ten rupees for their trouble and climbed into the passenger seat next to Jeevan. She needed to make a phone call and told Jeevan to stop at her bead supplier's shop near Mohamedali Road. From there she dialled Sister Serafina's number.

St Elizabeth's Nursing Home – or St Betty's as it was commonly known – was run by an order of Carmelite nuns and was attached to their convent. The Mother Superior, Mary Joseph, and many of the nuns were Irish.

Mother Mary Joseph had wanted to be a missionary in the Congo, but her order had sent her to India instead where eventually she established a small charity hospital in one of the poorer districts of Bombay.

In time, as the reputation of St Betty's grew, she required larger premises, which were donated by a wealthy Hindu friend who had been her fellow medical student at Girton College, Cambridge. It consisted of a large mansion set in spacious, secluded grounds in a good residential area. With it came a substantial endowment and a modest condition that preference be given to difficult maternity cases, and free care to indigent women. In this latter category, her friend Sister Serafina was a constant source of supply. However, it was not uncommon for well-to-do women of all religions to prefer a lying-in at St Betty's, such was its reputation for care and discretion, for which they were happy to pay handsomely.

In emergencies and for special difficulties, Mother Mary Joseph could call on a small number of excellent doctors and surgeons of different nationalities, though mainly Indian, who gave their services free of charge. With the advent of war bringing larger numbers of troops to the city, and the subsequent pressure on existing hospitals, she perceived the necessity to add a small wing of a dozen beds and a few private rooms for men only, and it was to this wing that Minnie brought Darius for treatment.

Jeevan drove into the grounds of the nursing home just after ten p.m. They were expected, Sister Serafina having made the necessary arrangements with Mother Mary Joseph. A trolley whisked Darius through rear corridors, avoiding the wards full of sleeping or feeding mothers, to a private room in the men's section. While Dr Peter Pereira was examining Darius, Minnie sat in the small empty waiting room. She was thankful that at this hour of the night no visitors were around who might have known her and wondered what she was doing there.

After what seemed hours and a lot of hustle and bustle in and out of Darius's room, Dr Pereira, accompanied by Mother Mary Joseph, entered the waiting room to speak to Minnie. His reputation as the soul of discretion was well founded. This stabbing was a matter that ought normally to be reported to the police, but he assured Minnie that there would be no question of police intervention. However, Darius was seriously ill. He would need surgery. The wound had been drained and cleaned up, but the infection had spread and there was danger of septicaemia. Until that was brought under control with sulpha drugs, an operation would have to wait. The patient was sedated, Dr Pereira said; a nurse would be at his bedside throughout the night. There was no point in Minnie waiting; it would be best to go home and rest. Things would look better in the morning.

'I am certain he will pull through this. Please reassure his family,' Mother Mary Joseph said as she accompanied an exhausted Minnie to the waiting car.

'Thank you, Mother, for all you've done. I can't say how much I appreciate your help.'

'It is Sister Serafina you should thank. She is most persuasive and fond of you.'

'Yes, I know.' Minnie's reply was automatic. By now reaction had set in. She felt light-headed with fatigue, her knees trembled, she could barely walk straight and Mother's echoing voice came and went like waves crashing and receding on a sandy shore.

'We shall pray for his safe recovery,' Mother Mary Joseph continued, 'and you too should pray, my child. Not only for him, but for yourself. You look in need of it.'

What did she mean? Minnie wondered. 'Of course, I'll pray for him. I never forget my prayers, Mother,' she said, climbing into the back seat of the waiting car.

'I'm sure you don't, my dear. But now, more than ever, you are the one in need of our dear Lord's guidance. Remember, the power of prayer is strong.' Despite all the years spent abroad, her speech still retained the gentle lilt of her native Ireland. 'What you did tonight required strong nerves, and a lot of courage. You must love him very much. You will need much more of that courage in the future.'

28

Dolly and Jimmy were waiting up for her by the time Minnie returned home. Both showed signs of strain when Minnie entered their sitting room, tense with fatigue and her face drained of colour.

'How is he?' Jimmy asked. 'Tell me everything that's happened.'

'Let me get out of these clothes first and have a shower. I feel filthy.' More than anything else she wanted to get rid of the smell of that dreadful place that seemed to have saturated her hair and clothes.

'Of course, darling,' Dolly said, putting an arm round her. 'The servants have gone to bed. Let me put out your night clothes. Jimmy, prepare her a stiff whisky soda for after and a cheese sandwich. I bet she's had nothing to eat since lunchtime.'

'Dolly, how do I prepare a cheese sandwich? Can't I wake up Lalji to do it?'

'Don't be ridiculous, Jimmy. We don't want any servants around at this time.' Dolly sighed with irritation, then addressed herself to Minnie. 'Can you imagine? This man is head of one of the largest companies in the country, does business all over the world. He can pilot a plane, drive racing cars, set up factories with hundreds of workers – but he can't make a cheese sandwich!'

'Dolleee, I was only asking, sweetie – I've never made one.'

'Well, it's time you learnt. Use your imagination and get on with it. You'll find all you need in the fridge and the pantry.'

'Where's the pantry?'

Dolly whipped around, her irritation boiling over, only to find her husband with a broad grin on his face.

'Just joking, sweetie.'

'Get away with you, you monkey!' she laughed. 'Come on, Minnie, let's go before he drives me to distraction.'

Dolly had a knack for defusing a tense situation by talking about totally trivial or irrelevant subjects. Often it gave the impression she was being shallow, even a bit dim, but Minnie was immensely grateful for it while being whisked away towards the cool, clean white tiles of her bathroom.

Half an hour later, powdered and perfumed, Minnie sat in the sitting room in pyjamas and housecoat, her wet hair wrapped turban-like in a towel, eating a hearty cheese sandwich, with a stiff whisky soda on the table beside her. It was gone midnight by the time she finished telling Jimmy and Dolly about Darius.

'Minnie, you've done splendidly,' Jimmy said. 'I'm truly grateful.' He stood up and paced the room. 'What annoys me is his irresponsibility. It's all very well him being artistic, a free spirit, a poet and all that, but he never stops to think what his reckless actions might do to the family. The firm is in high-level negotiations presently with the government for a contract. You know what sticklers the British are for correctness. Can you imagine our chances if there is a scandal? I wish he could see the consequences of the scrapes he gets into. Of course, this time it's more than a scrape.'

'Jimmy, perhaps if you were to give him a job he could get his teeth into – this new factory of yours, for instance,' Minnie suggested, rising to Darius's defence. 'Put him in charge of it.'

Jimmy shook his head. 'I think not. Besides, I'd be accused of nepotism. I don't want to go down that road. He needs to prove himself, prove he's capable of running something like that. Take an interest.'

'How can he prove himself if you don't give him a chance?'

'Darling, I understand your feelings for him – in fact your influence has done him the world of good. But he treats everything like a game. Look at that job he took at the hospital recently. Swanning in when he felt like it! How long did that last? Two months. I know it was voluntary, but even so he should have taken it seriously.'

Minnie protested. 'You're not being fair, Jimmy. He did take it seriously – he told me so, but he got frustrated when his suggestions were not acted on.'

'My dear, he needs to be more disciplined. He does a good job for two or three weeks, and then suddenly he will take off for days without notifying anyone. That is not acceptable behaviour in business.' Jimmy got up, yawned and stretched. 'We need to address the problem at hand. I shall visit him tomorrow and speak to Dr Pereira. We must come up with a plausible explanation for his injury. Meanwhile I think we can all do with a good night's sleep. See you in the morning.'

Before turning in, Minnie crept into the children's bedroom adjoining hers. It was a warm, sticky night, and the room felt airless despite the open windows.

She turned on the ceiling fan to low and listened to the hum of its three blades as it stirred the thick air into a reluctant breeze. Bobby was lying across his bed, the top sheet kicked off, arms and legs flung wide like the letter X, his head thrown back almost over the edge, with little whistling sounds coming from his wide-open mouth. She turned him right side up, put the pillow under his head and smoothed his sweaty hair. She bent to kiss his head, breathing in his little-boy-after-bath smell of Johnson's talcum and minty toothpaste.

How different these two are in sleep, she thought, turning to Claudia. The child was curled into a pink ball round her favourite doll, her pyjama trousers riding up her legs, and her curly black hair spread in long fronds around her head. Minnie dabbed the sweat from her forehead and pulled the sheet over Claudia's legs.

To see and touch these lovely sweet children dissolved the fear and squalor Minnie had endured in the previous few hours. All of that seemed like a receding dream, almost as if it had happened to someone else, quite unconnected to her. The reality of her world was here, in this room, at this moment. Only now with her sleeping children did she feel restored to herself again.

Jimmy joined Minnie and Dolly at breakfast the next morning. They went over Darius's movements in the last three days, such as they knew them. Jimmy suggested a credible story to justify Darius's injury: he had gone on one of his camping trips up country, as he often did. He lost his footing in the course of a ramble and fell into a steep gully, crashing into a thicket of trees. A branch pierced his thigh and he was knocked unconscious. Many hours later he was found by some villagers, but by the time they got him to the local doctor, infection had set in. The doctor phoned a colleague in Bombay who arranged for him to be admitted to St Elizabeth's.

'That's the story we should stick to, and that's what I shall tell Roshan,' Jimmy announced as he rose from the table. 'If people are curious, just be a bit vague about the details.'

They telephoned St Elizabeth's for news, but Mother Mary Joseph sounded grim. She said Darius had spent a restless night. His high temperature was causing concern and so far he was not responding to treatment. The next twenty-four hours were crucial.

Cold fear swamped Minnie as she walked back to her bedroom on unsteady legs. The palms of her icy hands were sticky with sweat. *He can't die. He can't possibly die. He's part of my life now.* Her breath came in short bursts and she thought she would faint. She sat on the edge of her bed with eyes shut and hands tightly clasped. Silently, her lips moved. *Holy Mother of God, save him. Please don't let him die. I love him.*

Minnie tried to keep herself busy until visiting time, to take her mind off the previous evening's ordeal. She drove to the convent to thank Sister Serafina for organising Darius's admission to St Elizabeth's. Later, she stopped by at her workshop to check on the work in progress, but her heart was not in it. The inside of her head seemed to be filled with cotton wool. She could not concentrate on the work. The hours dragged by. At last, unable to wait any longer, she drove to St Elizabeth's. She had to see Darius.

'Mr Dubash is sleeping,' the nurse told her when she reached his room. 'But you can sit by his bed for a while in case he wakes up.'

She pulled up a chair to his bedside. Darius was muttering and moving restlessly in his sleep. His cheeks were flushed, his face gaunt. His forehead felt hot and dry to her touch. She stroked his hand. An overwhelming wave of tenderness flowed over her as she watched him. Presently the twitching and fitful movements quietened, and his breathing became less shallow.

Minnie had almost dozed off herself when she heard a commotion outside and the door opened. Before she knew it, a hand shook her shoulder roughly and a voice hissed at her.

'What the hell are you doing here? Who do you think you are? Get out and leave us alone! You're not wanted here.'

Minnie turned to find Roshan's face inches away from her, with lips narrowed to a slit of hatred. She pushed Roshan's hand away and stood up.

'Don't be silly, Roshan. Why shouldn't I be here?'

'You've no right, Minnie. Always pushing your way into places you're not wanted.'

'Really! That's too harsh and you know it's not true. Darius needs me.'

'That's what you think. He doesn't need you at all. It's me he needs. He's always needed me.' Roshan smiled in triumph. 'Please leave before I call the doctor,' she added icily. 'Only family members can visit him. I'm his sister. After all's said and done, who are you?'

Minnie took a deep breath.

'I, my dear, am his future wife.'

Roshan gave a gasp of disbelief.

'That's right, Roshan, we *will* be married. You had better get used to the idea.'

29

1943

Minnie and Darius set their wedding date for early April. Jimmy was adamant the reception should be held at Stonehill House, and Dolly and Clara quickly got down to making the necessary arrangements.

Minnie wanted a relatively quiet celebration, whereas the guest list Dolly insisted on preparing grew to three hundred names. In the event, the war proved to be a legitimate reason for limiting the numbers of guests to one hundred, much to Minnie's relief.

A few days before the wedding, Roshan arrived at the house to see the happy couple. Minnie and Darius were playing Monopoly with the children after their tea, when Roshan was dragged into the sitting room by a pair of tall Afghan hounds straining at their leashes. As soon as the dogs began barking, the children dropped their cards and ran to the safety of the nursery. At Roshan's stern command, the animals quietened down.

'They are called Bright and Breezy, and I've trained them myself,' Roshan announced with a proud smile.

Accidentally – or so it appeared – she released Breezy's leash. The beast immediately lolloped over to Minnie, silky hair flopping in all directions, put its paws on her shoulders and licked her face. With huge effort Minnie managed to hide her panic while Darius hastened to get the animal off her. Most friends knew that Minnie was frightened of large dogs.

'For God's sake, Roshan!' Darius exclaimed in irritation. 'Keep the beast under control, can't you? You know Minnie is allergic to dog hair!'

'I had no idea!' Roshan's eyes widened with feigned innocence. 'What a shame. I've brought them as my wedding gift to you.'

Minnie struggled for composure, determined not to let her future sister-in-law gloat over her discomfort. 'You must have given a great deal of thought to choosing such an unusual present.' She caught the triumphant expression on Roshan's face. 'I'm sure Darius especially will enjoy having them. Won't you, darling?'

Darius's jaw tightened. 'Sure, I will, Roshan. Now be a good soul and give them to the bearer for the time being. I'll see to them later.'

By dinnertime a red itchy rash had erupted on Minnie's neck, on her arms and under the armpits, and only copious applications of calamine lotion in the following days brought it under control in time for her wedding.

Minnie and Darius were married in a civil ceremony on a hot, golden day in April. The evening reception was held at Stonehill House, as Jimmy had insisted. It was only when Minnie inspected the buffet laden with drinks and food not seen since the beginning of the war that she fully appreciated how Dolly's and Clara's organisational skills and powers of persuasion had been stretched to their limits to provide for such a large crowd.

The three-tiered wedding cake, baked in the kitchens of the Taj Mahal Hotel, was a masterpiece of icing craft. Dozens of waiters stood ready in their impeccable white uniforms, blue cummerbunds and blue and silver pugrees – the traditional turbans. Tiny coloured lights outlined the gateway, the drive and the steps to the front entrance. More were suspended from trees in the back garden. It looked like fairyland. Three shamianas – rectangular marquees – had been erected in the garden to cover the tables, the bar area, and a small dance floor. The air swelled with music as Goody Servai and his band plunged into a medley of the latest American hits to greet the first guests.

All the children – Minnie's Claudia and Bobby, Dolly's twins Homi and Nina, and Clara's Joey and Harry – had been allowed to stay up and join in the celebrations. Dressed in their best, they stood at the top of the stairs and helped to escort new arrivals to the drawing room where Darius and Minnie greeted them as they entered.

Minnie was aware they made a striking couple, Darius with his Hollywood looks, handsome and elegant in narrow white trousers and a long black high-necked achkan. Minnie felt she was looking her best. She had chosen to wear a deep crimson silk sari with a gold embroidered border and a simple tight low-cut choli blouse. Around her neck she wore Darius's wedding gift: a magnificent necklace of pigeon-blood cabochon rubies to match her engagement ring and ear-clips.

'Minnie you look utterly ravishing,' boomed Binky Chhota Chembur, planting a fat kiss on her cheek. 'The sari suits you beautifully; you look just like one of us now.' He put an arm round her shoulders. 'Your husband has excellent taste, I see. That ruby necklace is quite exquisite. Darius, old boy, you are a lucky devil,' he roared. 'Make sure nobody steals her from you.'

'Minnie, you look splendid. And what stunning jewels!' her good friend Barbara Davidson said, giving her a hug. 'May I wish both of you all happiness.'

'Darius darling,' Barbara said, turning to him, 'you look just like that gorgeous actor, Tyrone Power – too, too divine.'

A haze of happiness and delight surrounded Minnie and throughout the evening she and Darius constantly looked for each other, found each other, touched each other. She glanced at him. He winked at her. She smiled, her heart melting. With her darling man and children near, her contentment was complete.

After dinner the children said their goodnights and left before the speeches and toasts. The glasses were refilled, and the guests applauded Jimmy's speech. Then the happy couple moved to cut the wedding cake.

As they posed to be photographed cutting the cake, Minnie became aware of a scuffle in the background, with raised voices and someone saying, 'Let me go.' Darius was about to take her arm to lead her back to their table, when he was shoved from behind. It was Roshan. A very unsteady Roshan. She rocked back and forth on her heels. She was dressed in a black and silver sari and wore heavy gold jewellery. Her lipstick was smudged, and she waved an empty champagne glass at the waiter trying to restrain her.

'Eh, Darius, what about a toast to me?' Her voice was slurred. 'To you and me. We've been together a long time. Why don't I get a toast? Why should she be toasted? She's only known you for five minutes.'

'Roshan, pull yourself together,' Darius muttered, 'you've had too much to drink.'

'Rubbish! Bearer, fill my glass.' She teetered on her heels. 'Do as I say.'

Darius shook his head at the waiter. Conversation at the nearest tables tailed off. Heads turned to see what was going on. Minnie felt a sharp elbow in her ribs as Roshan pushed past and grabbed Darius by the arm. In doing so she slipped. He held her up to stop the fall. She clung to him.

'You're drunk, Roshan,' he hissed. 'Try and get a grip, old girl, and stop making a scene.'

'I'm telling you, Darius, she'll never be as good as I've been to you,' Roshan whined. 'I've looked after you since Ma and Pa died.' She clutched his arm, her face flushed, eyes glittering. 'And now you're abandoning me? Throwing me out like an old shoe?'

A hush settled on the nearby tables. As if sensing an audience, Roshan raised her voice. 'For her? She's nothing. She's common. She has no breeding, no education. Why, she's just a gold digger—'

There were audible gasps from the tables and one or two smothered giggles.

'Roshan, shut up.' Darius was furious. 'How dare you!'

Minnie, her face ashen, looked around desperately for help, for anyone to take charge of this frenzied woman. She caught Albie's eye close by. With a nod, Albie rose from his table and sidled over.

'Come, Roshan, *ma chère*,' he murmured quietly, taking her arm, 'let me take you back to your table. The party will break up soon and I'll take you home.'

Roshan became more agitated, struggling out of Albie's grasp. 'I want Darius to take me home.'

Minnie stepped forward. 'No, Darius,' she said firmly, putting her hand on his arm. 'Let Albie take her. Remember, this is *our* wedding day!' She turned to Albie. 'Get her away as quick as you can, Albie.'

Roshan ignored Albie. 'Darius, darling, take me home,' she slurred.

Darius hesitated, glancing at Minnie. 'It might be best if I went with her and Albie – just as far as the car,' he suggested.

Minnie withdrew her hand from his arm. 'If you think that's best,' she said, her voice heavy with disappointment.

'I'm sorry about this, my love,' Darius apologised. He kissed her gently on the lips. 'I won't be long.'

They left, supporting a wobbly Roshan under the arms. Minnie made her way back to the top table. She knew Darius would not be back soon. *What a way to start my honeymoon*, she thought. All the happiness she felt moments ago burst, like bubbles swizzled out of a champagne glass.

A sense of unease seized her as she joined Jimmy and Dolly.

30

Darius had chosen the hill station of Simla for their honeymoon, a three-day train journey from Bombay with a day's stopover in Delhi to change to a narrow-gauge train. In spite of their luxurious first-class carriage, the journey was unbearably hot and sticky. Coal dust filtered through the louvred windows. Water for washing from the bathroom tap was never more than tepid and brought little relief. As they travelled north, the heat became drier and easier to bear, but after two days Minnie longed for nothing more than a cool, darkened hotel room and a long cold shower.

Delhi in April was like an oven, with its dry, searing heat. Minnie and Darius spent a morning tramping around the sandstone and marble monuments in temperatures over a hundred degrees Fahrenheit, driving through areas of stinking squalor and filth to reach them. Minnie felt utterly exhausted. She longed to please Darius and share his enthusiasm for the monuments he admired, but she longed even more for the cool hills, and was glad when they took the train the next day for the journey to Kalka where they were to change to a narrow-gauge railway for the last stretch.

What seemed like a toy train soon took them away from the foothills and began climbing and twisting up stomach-churning bends, crossing hundreds of dizzying bridges and passing through more than one hundred tunnels. By early evening they reached the destination altitude of 7000 feet where the cold, thin air of Simla was a welcome relief from the hot plains. Even more welcome was the Cecil Hotel with its polished wooden floors, high ceilings and the comforting aroma of log fires flickering in the grates.

Perhaps it was the journey or the altitude, or a combination of both, but Minnie felt ill and giddy for the first few days. The hotel doctor said she was suffering from heat exhaustion. All she needed was a period of two or three days to rest and she would be as right as rain.

Sitting by the window in her dressing gown in the late afternoon, Minnie gazed out at the majestic view of the snow-covered Himalayas in the distance. A movement on the mountain road far below caught her eye and she called out to Darius.

'There are four men running down there with huge bundles on their back. What on earth can they be carrying?'

Darius slipped his arm round her waist and peered out. 'Oh, them,' he said dismissively, nuzzling her neck. 'They are the runners who bring the ice for the hotels every day.'

'Where do they get the ice from?' Minnie asked, puzzled.

Darius pointed to the crescent of jagged, snowy peaks tinged pink by the setting sun.

'But that's miles away. Poor fellows!'

'It's a day's run, I'm told. But they're used to it and it earns them good money.' He moved away from the window and glanced at his watch.

Minnie continued to look at the tiny figures until they were out of sight, trying to conceal the shock she felt by her husband's callous attitude. She felt only pity for the men and their hard life.

'Darling, when are you going to feel better?' he asked rather petulantly. 'There's so much I want to show you.'

'I'm sorry, Darius, I don't feel up to going out just yet.'

Darius heaved a sigh and began to chew nervously on the nail of his little finger. 'Surely if you have no fever it can't be that bad. Perhaps you could come down for cocktails before dinner?'

She was surprised at his childish reaction to her malaise. 'I'll see how I feel. But why don't you arrange a game of bridge for this evening, darling?'

Darius's face brightened. 'What a good idea. Are you sure you won't mind if I don't stay with you?'

'Of course not.' She smiled tolerantly.

'In that case I'll be off now.' He bent to kiss her lips and hurried out of the room.

After Minnie had recovered, Darius behaved like a small boy, wanting to show her everything. They took rickshaws to the centre of the small town, explored the bazaar, got themselves measured for custom-made walking boots and jodhpurs, and bought two rods for coarse fishing.

'There are some wonderful angling stretches a few miles north of here,' Darius enthused, before changing for dinner after a day in the bazaar. He weighed the balance of the rods in his hand and made a few practice casts. 'I thought you might like to have a go. I've hired a shikari who arranges marvellous fishing. He sets up a pretty good camp. You cannot imagine how beautiful the spring flowers are at this time, and the countryside is so…so unspoilt, pristine, so…' He stopped, noticing Minnie's less than enthusiastic expression. 'What is it, my love?'

Minnie's interpretation of unspoilt, pristine countryside was synonymous with primitive conditions. She tried to choose her words with care.

'It sounds a bit…uncomfortable – I'm not used to camping. I wouldn't know how to cook on an open fire, and…'

'You don't have to worry about a thing, sweetheart.' Darius laughed, elated at the prospect in store. '*You* won't have to cook. The shikari will see to it all – it is part of his job. He will have people go on ahead and set up the tents, the camp cots, get the meals ready, and all that.'

Minnie smiled to herself. She ought to have known better. Darius's idea of the simple life, roughing it, communing with nature, however he described it, was to do so only in great comfort. If those were to be the conditions, she was game for it.

'What about…you know…toilet facilities?'

'Ah, now that *is* a little primitive. One uses the bushes, of course – totally private, nobody around, you see. There will be a tin tub for bathing. Heating up water to wash won't be a problem.'

In her childhood Minnie had had enough experience of washing in a tin tub, and was not put off by the prospect. It was starting to sound like fun. At least she would have him to herself.

Their boots and jodhpurs were to be delivered by the end of the week. Meanwhile, they spent their time cycling and exploring the nearby beauty spots, Tiger's Leap and Wildflower Hall amongst them. He teased her about the number of photographs she took. They laughed a lot.

Back in their suite she put her arms round his waist and leaned against his shoulder, breathing in the smell of his body. 'Wouldn't it be nice to have dinner sent up here tonight. It's such a beautiful view and there's a full moon.'

'Not tonight, dearest,' Darius said. 'Didn't I tell you? I've asked a few friends to join us for dinner this evening. We've arranged two tables of bridge afterwards.'

Minnie dropped her arms from his waist, frowning. 'You never mentioned it. What people – do I know them?'

'Perhaps not. The Pandays – they are here to look at a school for their daughter. The Jacksons – he's about to retire from Grindlays Bank, and old Ashok Mehta – you know him from Bombay. Also, poor Mrs Hutton – she's here alone. I feel sorry for her, poor lady. Her husband was captured at the fall of Singapore.'

'But, darling, apart from Ashok I don't know any of these people. When did you meet them?'

'I met them while you were not feeling well. They are quite charming, I'm sure you'll like them.'

Minnie had her doubts about that. She was aware that Darius had a propensity for attracting hangers-on and sycophants.

During dinner that evening she felt on edge. Ashok Mehta, a neighbour from Bombay whom she knew quite well, was the first to join them, much to her relief. The Jacksons were a sweet couple from Delhi looking for a house to buy in Simla for their retirement. The Pandays from Banares talked mostly about their only daughter: 'The climate is much better here for Kiki – she's rather delicate, you know.' Minnie expected 'poor Mrs Hutton' to be a mousy, middle-aged woman anxiously awaiting news of her prisoner of war husband and was ready to show her every sympathy.

'Poor Mrs Hutton' turned out to be a thirty-year-old peroxide blonde. Minnie had seen her around the hotel in the company of different men and she seemed to be having a good time. Shapely and long-legged, she was partial to tight dresses and young men. Unfortunately, there were hardly any of the latter, so she directed her full attention to Darius. She fawned over him, hanging on to his every word as if he were the wittiest, most intelligent man in the room. Minnie watched with mounting irritation as Darius lapped up her flattery, filled with admiration for her plucky attitude over her husband's plight.

'These British with their stiff upper lip,' he remarked while they were undressing that night. 'One simply has to admire such conduct.'

Stiff upper lip, my foot, Minnie thought. Mrs Hutton was having the time of her life, and Darius was flirting with her. Tears pricked Minnie's eyes.

She said nothing, but they didn't make love that night.

Nor did they on the following two nights after their bridge games when Darius partnered poor Mrs Hutton. They lost consistently against Minnie and Ashok. On the third evening, he declined to play, pleading an early start the next day.

'I thought you'd be glad of a last round of bridge with Mrs Hutton, darling,' Minnie remarked with a straight face on returning to their suite.

'Actually, I wanted to get away from her.' Darius sounded peevish. 'I found her rather irritating, didn't you?'

'I thought you liked her. You felt sorry for her, what with her husband a POW.'

'Not at all, I don't know what gave you that impression. In any case, she's a perfectly lousy bridge player.'

Darius was a bad loser.

That night his love-making was wild, almost angry. Afterwards, he lay on his side next to her, his arm flung across her stomach. Listening to the rhythm of his breath puffing gently through half-open lips, she wondered about the physical aspect of their relationship.

Before their wedding, he couldn't get enough of her, perhaps because they acted discreetly. The occasions were fewer, never taking place at either of their homes, but rather at the Juhu beach house.

But to her surprise, since their marriage he often found it difficult to perform, as if he had lost his desire for her. Minnie was patient and tried to be understanding. The best times, the most passionate, were usually after something had frustrated him, made him angry or irritable. First, he became petulant and sulked, and then, as Minnie sought to calm his mood, his arousal was sudden and passionate. On her part, a certain look from him was enough to stir her senses. Sometimes he crept up behind her, cupped her breasts and pressed himself hard against her. It was like an electric shock and her body responded instantly with a quivering, liquefying heat that made her weak at the knees. Just thinking of those moments brought on her desire. She often wondered why Darius did not seem able to respond in the same way. It was almost as if he needed a catalyst to get him going.

They left the hotel at dawn on horseback together with the shikari and reached the campsite three hours later. The cook-porter and a couple of other porters, who had set up the tents and facilities, greeted them with mugs of hot sweet tea. The location was as Darius had described, unspoilt and pristine, a kaleidoscope of spring flowers growing profusely, some familiar but others that Minnie could not put a name to. It was also much as she thought it would be: remote and basic, silent except for the gurgling of the river and strange bird calls. In the late afternoon, Minnie watched Darius and the shikari fishing upstream for the mahseer that inhabited the waters.

It took nearly an hour for Darius to land his catch, a twelve-pounder, similar in size to salmon but with a black skin and mean-looking mouth. It was big enough to feed everyone around the campfire that evening. Though large and bony, the mahseer was full of flavour. The cook-porter smothered it with a paste made of coriander, coconut, lemon and chilli and grilled it over a wood fire. It gave off a mouth-watering aroma, the flesh was flaky and moist and had a delicious charred taste.

After eating, Minnie and Darius sat close to the burning logs with a hot drink. She leaned into his circling arms. They talked quietly about nothing much, flowers and fish, about stars and mountains, about poetry and love. Unfamiliar animal noises came from the dark beyond the area of light around the tents. The huge star-filled sky predicted a frost. A little distance away the porters squatted around their fire, wrapped tightly in woollen blankets pulled over their heads, resembling shadowy anthills in the flickering light. Minnie's hands and feet turned icy. With dread, she wondered how she would endure the night in the tent.

She survived it better than expected. The quilts on the camp cots were surprisingly warm and snug. In the morning they fished. Minnie was delighted to catch two large specimens, with the shikari's help. In the afternoon, drowsy from the heat and the morning's exertions, she napped in the tent. Darius was not to be seen when she awoke. She found him at last sitting on an outcrop of rocks near to the stretch he had fished the previous evening. She was about to call out when she noticed that he was not looking at the scenery. Deep in concentration, he was writing on a notepad propped against his knees. She watched him in silence for a while. It pleased her to see him writing again.

They had two days more of bliss, fishing and riding. On the last day they caught small fish similar to perch. Darius scraped clean a space on a rock overhanging the river, gutted and split the fish and placed them flat on the stone. Half an hour later, the sun's heat on the rock had cooked them through, ready to eat.

They broke camp in the afternoon and set off on the return journey. The sun had tanned Minnie's face and arms. Her cheeks were pink, her eyes bright. She ached a bit, and longed for a good hot soak, yet she felt exhilarated and happy. She was sure they had bonded in spirit more intimately than ever before and was certain that the on and off nature of Darius's desire for her would be resolved.

They arrived back at the hotel before dusk, tired and contented, a slight fishy odour trailing in their wake.

'Let's have a drink before we go up,' Darius suggested.

At the bar they ordered two whisky sodas and found a table in a corner near the fireplace.

'What's the plan for tomorrow, Darius?'

'We could have afternoon tea in The Mall and catch the early movie show, if you like.'

'Sounds good to me. Do you know what's on?'

'I think it's a Ronald Colman film called—'

'It is called *Random Harvest*,' a familiar voice interrupted Darius in mid-sentence. '*Mes chers amis,*' the voice boomed, 'I thoroughly recommend it to you. I have seen it twice, but I will happily come with you and enjoy it for a third time.'

Speechless with astonishment, Minnie looked up to see Albie, nattily dressed in plus fours, brogues and a flat cap. He had popped up from nowhere like a genie from a bottle, and stood before them, his face wreathed in smiles.

'*Ma chère Minnie,*' he said, planting a kiss on her surprised cheek. '*Mon cher Darius, comment vas-tu?*'

He drew up a chair nearest to the fire, sat down and beckoned a waiter. 'Bring me a whisky soda – make it a double, please. And you, *mes enfants*, you have been having a good time, *n'est-ce pas?* You must tell me all you have done.'

Minnie glanced at Darius for a reaction, but his head was under the table, retrieving the box of matches he had dropped on the floor.

'Albie,' Minnie found her voice at last, 'what on earth are you doing here? Where are you staying?'

'But, *ma chère*, where else am I staying but here!' He paused, beaming all over his face, eyes twinkling with childlike glee behind his glasses. He rubbed his hands in front of the fire. 'Did Darius not tell you? He knew I had never been to Simla, and he kindly invited me to come and stay. *Quelle chance, n'est-ce pas?* Yes, I am here for the whole week. We shall have such fun, won't we?'

The rest of the honeymoon passed in blur. It seemed to Minnie that Darius spent more time with his friend than with her. Albie suggested all kinds of physically exhausting things to do, hill climbing and horse trekking amongst them, which she couldn't keep up with. It left her feeling excluded. Darius was affectionate enough with her after these excursions, but she felt she had become a non-participant at a glorified Boy Scouts camp. She could not decide if Albie arranged this on purpose, or if he was simply being unthinking and selfish. She acted the good sport, pretending she didn't mind. She did not want it to be said of her at a later stage that she cramped Darius's style by prohibiting him doing the kind of strenuous activities he enjoyed.

She pondered about this after their return to Bombay. Perhaps, she thought, after four weeks of honeymoon, Darius had become bored and needed different stimulation.

In the end she accepted that to keep him she would have to let him have his freedom. Or at any rate let him feel he had it.

*

At dawn on their first anniversary, Darius entered Minnie's bedroom from the concealed passage that connected his room to hers. The quiet click of the door brought her awake, but she didn't stir, watching him through her lashes. His chest was bare, as were his feet, and he wore a cotton lungi – a sarong-type garment – knotted at the hip. He held a square red box and placed it on the bedside table. She lay still, feigning sleep.

Dawn light filtered through thin bamboo blinds. He drew up the blind on the French door, opened it and peered out on to the lawn. From her bed, Minnie saw the sea was hidden by mist. She heard the distant murmur of waves indicating a turning tide. A pair of hoopoe birds called, predicting a hot day ahead. The air was filled with the damp, early morning scent of jasmine and frangipani. The incipient whiff of charcoal, and a faint sound of throats clearing, hawking and spitting carried on the still air as life stirred in the servants' quarters.

Darius seemed to be waiting for something. Then Minnie heard it. The harsh shriek, a wail of agony. A pause and then again, and again. Raising her head, she made out two peacocks emerging through the early morning mist, ambling towards a banyan tree, the male's tail spreading fully, then subsiding and once more unfurling into a huge blue-green circle, the black-eye feather tips quivering as he strutted forward.

Minnie turned on her back and stretched, the thin sheet falling away to reveal one bare arm and a full, rounded breast. Darius came away from the open door and sat on the edge of the bed.

'You look luscious like that, my darling, all smooth and gleaming with your hair spread out like ink stains on the pillow. I wish I could paint you like this.' He bent his head and gently licked her nipple. Minnie felt it harden into a point.

She moaned and smiled. One hand reached into his hair, stroking it, pulling his head further on to her. She shifted over to make room for him, then ran her other hand over his arm, stroked his back, his thigh, then trailed her fingers towards the heat of his groin. Her eyes opened fully, dark with desire. Neither spoke. She felt his fingers stroking her, sending tremors of pleasure through her body as they searched and found. Then she was filled with mounting desire until her uncontrollable cry of release was echoed by the screech of the peacock.

Later they lay back, languid with contentment, quietly listening to the noises of their wakening household. Minnie stretched luxuriously. It had been so good this time. It hadn't always been like this, she remembered, but quickly pushed aside the fleeting thought. Darius leaned over to the bedside table and picked up the red box and a small envelope.

'Happy anniversary, my darling.' His smile was tender, loving, intimate. 'I hope you like it.'

She returned his smile. *God, he is gorgeous – his smile, his eyes…* She caught her breath, her heart melting with love for this beautiful, complex man. She slit the envelope, extracted the card and read the words he had written. The shortest of poems addressed 'To my Heartsflame'. Her eyes moistened, she kissed the card. Then she lifted the lid of the red box. Two rows of fat, glistening pearls glowed against a black velvet background. An initial flicker of alarm was quickly covered by a gasp of delight.

'Darius darling, they are absolutely gorgeous.'

'I'm glad you like them.'

'I'm speechless – I love them.'

'Here,' he said, taking them from the box, 'let me put them on you.'

She sat up and felt him draping them across her chest, moving them up and down over her velvety skin. They felt cool, smooth and heavy.

'I knew they would suit you – they come alive on your skin. You should always wear pearls. You'll wear them to the dinner party tonight, won't you?' He leaned on an elbow and looked at her approvingly.

'Of course. I can't wait.'

She turned her head and pressed her lips to his, but he drew away after a moment.

'I have to get ready, my darling. Jimmy wants to see me at his office. After that I'm going to the printers.'

He left the bed, blew her a kiss and slipped through to his room. Minnie rose and went to the dressing table. She was glad he was taking his new job seriously. Jimmy had at last realised where Darius's interests lay and had decided to let him produce a quality arts-based magazine called *Heritage*. It was just the thing he'd be good at, she was sure.

The day was going to be a scorcher. Already this early in the morning droplets of sweat formed above her lips. She sat in front of the mirror, fingering the necklace and looking at her reflection. He was right, pearls did suit her. She stroked the lustrous beads again and again. Cool to the touch, they glowed against her damp skin.

She knew she ought to feel happier. But the flicker of alarm she had first felt returned. She recalled an old saying from long ago: 'A gift of pearls brings tears and sorrow.'

She stared at the woman in the mirror, frowning, then unclipped the necklace, placed it on the table and quickly made the sign of the cross.

31

Friday, 14 April 1944

Minnie arrived early at her atelier for the eleven o'clock appointment with Mrs Dastur. Her girls had been working for weeks on a large order for a forthcoming Dastur wedding.

Despite news of the war raging elsewhere in the world, Bombay still felt a relatively safe haven. Although there was a feeling of austerity evidenced in the lack of goods available in shops, there was a thriving black market and almost anything was available for a price. The lavishness of the coming Dastur wedding was a case in point.

Minnie had been away from work for the past two days and knew that Mrs Dastur liked to deal with her personally.

'My dear Minnie,' Mrs Dastur said, hugging Minnie to her wobbly bosom, 'I just came to check how you were getting on with the order. The wedding is looming, you know, just around the corner. Nerves are jangling, tempers are fraying, there is hustle and bustle, toing and froing all over the house. I don't know if I'm coming or going and I am surrounded by incompetents. I need to supervise each and every single little thing myself. You wouldn't believe it!' she said, flopping on to the sofa.

She drew a tiny hanky from the depths of her cleavage and mopped the perspiration trickling from her two chins into the folds of flesh circling her neck. Minnie handed her a straw fan.

'Let me get you a cool drink, Freny my dear,' she said.

'Thank you, sweetie. It is so hot these days, I am literally melting away. At this rate there will be nothing left of me for my darling Dodo's wedding. And then there is the worry about the order. Will it be ready in time, I asked myself. Surely my dear friend Minnie will not let me down. But you see, I telephoned yesterday and the day before, and I was told you hadn't been in. Where is she? I asked. When is she expected? But nobody could tell me. Of course, I became burdened with yet another worry.' The effort of restraining her curiosity about the unusual absence was almost too much for her. Pursing her scarlet lips, she cast a hurt but questioning look at Minnie.

'Freny, my dear, it's quite simple. I do voluntary work at St George's Hospital.'

'Gracious me! Are you a nurse?'

'No, but I help out. Clara, my sister-in-law, got me into it. She is qualified, you know. They called me in once to help with some wounded Italian prisoners of war who didn't speak English. After that, it became a regular thing, twice a week.'

'But what about the work here, I mean to say…?'

'I promised you it would be ready in time, Freny, and it will be. Come and have a look at the tablecloth. It's nearly finished, and it looks great.' She got one of the girls to bring the work in. 'What do you think?'

Mrs Dastur's eyes disappeared behind plump, smiling cheeks, like currants in a bun.

'Such a clever lady, you are, Minnie. All this shadow embroidery…the colours…so soft… Oh look, these little butterflies, such sweetness. What are these flowers? Daffodils and forget-me-nots, you say. So dainty. All European flowers, isn't it? My Dodo's table will be the envy of her friends.' Mrs Dastur fanned herself vigorously. 'I'll collect it on Wednesday, if you say it will be finished by then. So nice to see you, Minnie, my dear.' Mrs Dastur gathered her bag and heaved herself off the sofa. 'Keep up the good work at the hospital. You're very brave to work there. I couldn't do it myself, of course. All those injuries, blood and bedpans and whatnot.' She clutched at her heart. 'My God – my constitution is so delicate, you know. I would simply faint. Besides, I'm too busy just now with the wedding and all.'

Shortly after she left, Claudia was dropped off from school. She came skipping into the workshop, her black braids flapping against her back, and threw herself at Minnie.

'Can I help you, Mummy?'

'In a minute. What did you do today at school?'

'We played hopscotch at break time. We drew the squares with chalk. Deena took it from the blackboard and the teacher got cross. Said we shouldn't be wasting her chalk. Then we did Geography.'

'How exciting! What did you learn?'

'We learnt all about the River Thames in England. Big ships can sail up all the way to London. That's the capital of England, did you know? The same ships come here. There was this huge map on the wall. Teacher showed us the countries in Europe where they are having the war. They look ever so small. I thought

England would be much bigger, but it's really tiny. All the countries in the world are coloured differently, but most are pink. England is pink, too. So is India. Teacher said all the pink countries belong to England.'

'You have learnt a lot today, my darling. I'm so proud of you. Now, it's time to fetch Bobby from playschool and then we'll go home for lunch.'

Minnie took the afternoon off to prepare for a dinner party Darius had arranged at the Taj Mahal Hotel to celebrate their second anniversary. Wearing only a thin cotton housecoat, she dozed on the cherry-pink chaise longue in her bedroom. She was woken with a start by a cacophony of cawing nearby. Glancing out of the open window she saw a large flock of crows surge up from the grass where they had been feeding, flapping their wings in wild agitation. In the same instant there was a tremendous boom, a sound like a colossal thunderclap that hurt her eardrums. She jumped up in fright, heart thumping. *It's a bomb*, she thought. The sound had come from the direction of town. She glanced at her watch. It was six minutes past four.

She rushed into the kitchen calling for the bearer. He and the other servants and their families were milling around the courtyard in alarm, having also heard the deafening noise. The women and children were wailing. Two windows had shattered; glass lay in shards in the flowerbeds.

'What is it?' she asked. 'Does anyone know what's happened?'

'Nobody knows, memsahib,' the bearer replied. 'Look, look…' He pointed to the back of the house. In the distance, she saw a thick black column of smoke rising above the tree line.

'Oh my God! Where are the children?' She became frantic. 'Karsan, go and fetch them and ayah, quickly. They're at Mrs Smith's house down the road.'

She hastened back to the drawing room to phone Darius, but his number was engaged. She tried several times, then replaced the receiver. It rang immediately. She snatched it from the cradle.

'Hello, Darius?'

'No, not Darius. This is Clara. Have you heard?'

'I heard a tremendous noise. What's happened, Clara?'

'There's been a huge explosion downtown. Victoria Dock has blown up. An ammunition ship caught fire. It's terrible…terrible.' Clara's voice faded and crackled over the line. 'Complete devastation, I'm told. The whole area is ablaze. I'm going to the hospital. The matron phoned me and Barbara. She asked us to round up as many helpers as we can. Will you come?'

'Yes, of course.'

'I guess you haven't managed to contact Darius. The area around his office has been severely damaged apparently.'

'I couldn't get through to him.'

'Try again. He must know what's happened. Come here as quickly as you can. Bring the kids, they can stay with Dolly. You won't get home tonight.'

She hung up.

Minnie tried Darius's number again. This time there was no answer. Oh, dear God, where was he?

Another huge explosion boomed from the city. The house rocked. The tinkle of splintering glass broke the ensuing silence.

The time was twenty to five.

32

The car carrying Minnie, the children and the ayah screeched to a halt in front of the entrance to Clara's apartment block.

Minnie entered the building with the bewildered children gripping her hands in fear. They squashed into the small lift and she pressed the button for the third floor. The apartment door was open. Clara and Dolly stood on the balcony. Clara was already dressed in her nurse's uniform. Dolly was looking through binoculars in the direction of the port. Silently, Minnie took the glasses from her, and twisted the dial to focus on the black mushroom darkening the sky, higher and wider than the one from the first explosion. Above it, circling on the rising air, she made out a dense flock of seagulls, like silver arrows against the swirling anthracite cloud. She shivered.

The three of them returned to the four excited children gathered in the drawing room.

'Listen to me carefully, children,' Clara said, taking charge. 'You are all going off to stay with Aunty Dolly for a day or two. There's been an accident in town and lots of people are hurt. Aunty Minnie and I are going to help at the hospital.'

'There'll be lots of blood and stuff, won't there?' Joey asked. 'I'm the oldest so can't I come and see what's happened, Mummy?'

'No, you can't, you little ghoul. Now please, all of you, be good and do whatever Aunty Dolly tells you. Is that clear?'

'Yes, Mum. Yes, Aunty,' they chorused. 'When will you be back?'

'Tomorrow, or the day after. Off you go and fetch whatever toys you want to take with you.'

'Have you heard from Franco?' Minnie whispered to Clara as the children left the room with the ayah.

'He phoned to say the hotel is okay,' Clara replied. 'They are far enough away so no major damage, luckily. Shattered windows mainly. He's setting up a first-aid centre and a canteen for the emergency services. What about Jimmy? Have *you* heard, Dolly?'

'Jimmy is not hurt, but the building has been damaged.' Dolly looked anxious. 'He said a piece of metal the size of a bus landed on the roof. They think it is part of a ship. Lucky nobody in the office was killed. Masses of broken glass simply everywhere – all the windows are smashed. There are a lot of dead and badly wounded people lying in the streets.'

'What about you, Minnie, did you hear from Darius?' Clara asked.

'Not a word.' Her voice was close to breaking. 'I left a message at home if he phones. I told the bearer to keep trying the printers' number.'

The phone rang. It was Jimmy for Dolly. Minnie and Clara waited anxiously. 'Yes…' they could hear her saying. 'Yes…yes…go on…' Finally, she hung up.

'He says the roads are being cordoned off. The damage is colossal. Victoria Dock has been virtually wiped out. Several fires have started caused by burning bales of cotton in the cargoes.'

'What else?' Clara enquired, handing Minnie a uniform to put on.

'Two companies of the East Yorkshire Regiment, other army and RAF units are reporting to the dock area. All available ambulances and fire engines have been called out. Even the officers and men in the transit camp at Colaba are on standby. That's all he knows.'

Clara attached a starched white triangular veil to her hair with bobby clips and did the same for Minnie. She picked up a canvas holdall containing spare uniforms. 'Come along, Minnie, we've got to get moving.'

Downstairs, Minnie jumped into Clara's Hillman.

'How will we get through the police cordons?' she asked.

'Don't worry. They'll let us pass when they see the red cross on the veil.'

Clara was right. The uniform let them through all the roadblocks, many of them set up to prevent the curious coming to have a look at the disaster. By five thirty they arrived at the hospital, less than two miles from the explosion area. There was hardly room to park. The place was jammed with every conceivable kind of vehicle carrying injured men, women and even children. A man was pulling a handcart with two people on it: a woman with bleeding, mangled feet, a man with skin peeling off his burnt arms and torso. A bullock cart rolled up carrying four wounded, its owner leading the frightened bullock by its halter. An ambulance clanged to get by, unloading three stretchers bearing severely burnt sailors.

Inside the hospital, the corridors were crammed with the injured lying on mattresses on the floor. The place reeked of blood, urine and sweat. Footsteps clanged on the stone floors as stretcher-bearers carried in their loads. The moans, cries and screams of pain from the injured merged into a steady background din.

Reporting to the matron, Minnie and Clara found her clearly deluged with work. 'The operating theatre is full,' she told them, bustling back and forth to a cupboard full of packets of bandages. 'They are dealing with the most severe cases.' She handed an armful of bandages to an orderly and made notes on a pad. 'Clara, Dr Advani asked for you to scrub and assist. Minnie, we have a stream of volunteers. I want you to sort them out. Give them tasks to do according to their ability. Do the rounds of the corridors and wards. Assess the priorities and report to the staff nurse.'

Volunteers arrived from all over the city, rich and poor, Indians, Europeans, Eurasians, all wanting to assist wherever they could. Minnie directed them to the various areas where help was needed. Even those with no particular skill were sent round wheeling trolleys with tea, water or cigarettes for the wounded. A trivial task, perhaps, in face of the enormity of the injuries involved, but she knew that a simple drink of water could save a life in these stifling April temperatures.

She turned her hand to anything that needed doing. She had no awareness of time passing. It was as if they were all working in a vacuum. While emptying a bedpan she was called to Matron's office. It was nine thirty by her watch. The injured were still pouring in, with no let-up. Her feet were swollen and throbbed. Her damp, stained uniform clung to her back. The humidity made her hair frizz and curly wisps stuck to her forehead. She wiped the sweat out of her eyes with the back of her hand.

'Where's Clara?' she asked Matron, whose uniform and cap even now managed to look crisp and clean.

'Still in theatre.'

'There was a message you wanted to see me.'

'Yes, madam, I do indeed.' Matron's tongue seemed ready to lash out a reprimand. 'Let me say that just because you are a society lady doesn't mean you can bend the rules.'

Minnie bristled. 'What do you mean? What rules have I bent?'

'The one about visitors.'

'I never have visitors.'

'You have one now. You know it's not allowed while on duty.' She paused. 'He said it was a special day.'

Minnie's heart lurched. She looked up. Matron was trying to hide a smile.

'Go on. He's in the waiting room. I'll give you fifteen minutes, that's all.'

Minnie rushed across the hall and flung open the door marked Visitors. There he stood. Her beautiful, darling man, half turned towards the window, with a cigarette holder between his lips. He looked utterly normal against the turmoil around her. He stubbed the cigarette in an ashtray. She walked into his arms and he held her close.

'I've been terribly worried. What happened?' she sniffled. Her lips moved against his shirt, muffling her voice. She breathed in the familiar scent of his warm body. She felt his mouth against her damp hair.

'I left the printers early,' he said. 'Jeevan was driving back to the office along Frere Road when we saw the first explosion. We were more than a mile away, but it blew the car across the street. It was terrifying. Stuff came hurtling through the air like giant fireworks. A lump of burning something fell in front of us just missing the car. Jeevan was terrific. He kept his head, slammed the car into reverse and backed down the road for two or three hundred yards.'

He stroked her hair, tightening his arms round her. 'We made our way through secondary streets and little lanes keeping north. Then we heard the second explosion. It took us a couple of hours to get to the west of town. The roads were jammed. Fire engines were racing in from all directions. Army trucks all over the place. By the time I found a phone that worked, Dolly told me you and Clara had reported to St George's.'

'Thank God you are safe, darling. But it was dangerous for you to come down here. You should have phoned the hospital.'

'I know, but I needed to see you. It's our special day.'

She smiled through her tiredness, happy to have his arms round her, relieved that he was safe. Darius lit a cigarette, handed it to her and lit another for himself. They smoked contentedly for a few minutes. Her weariness slipped away, and she felt a renewed burst of energy. She put out the cigarette and moved out of his embrace.

'I can't stay, darling. There's too much to do. Maybeline – that's the matron – will slay me if I don't get back.'

'Sure, I understand. By the way, I brought you a change of uniform. Thought you might need it. Is there anything else I can do for you?'

'I don't think so. Except…you could help here, you know.'

'How?'

'You could carry stretchers. Or push beds to the operating theatre.' She took his hand and pulled him towards the door. 'Come along, let's ask Matron.' She was not about to give him a chance to protest.

They entered the office. 'This is my husband,' Minnie said. 'He'd like to help. He could push trolleys or something.'

The matron looked at the handsome, immaculately dressed man standing in front of her. 'Looks as if he's never pushed anything heavier than a pen,' she muttered.

'Oh, Matron…' Minnie protested.

'Well all right, I'm sure we can find something for him to do. Show him where to go for the trolleys.'

At two in the morning, Minnie took a break in the waiting room where several of the volunteers and nurses were resting or asleep. She was exhausted. Clara came in to join her. She walked across the room stiffly and looked in pain.

'What's the matter?' Minnie asked anxiously.

'I've been standing for over ten hours – and I can't bend my knees. They seem to have locked solid.'

Minnie helped Clara to stretch out on a sofa and gently massaged her swollen knees and in a few moments, she was fast asleep. Minnie gathered a couple of cushions from an armchair, placed them on the floor and lay down. She was too tired to worry about cockroaches, mosquitoes or other creepy crawlies. Neither the heat nor the noise kept her from sleeping soundly.

It seemed it was only five minutes later that she felt a hand shaking her awake. Peering from under leaden eyelids she saw a bleary-eyed but bandbox starched and pressed Matron standing over her.

'Sorry to disturb your beauty sleep,' Matron said gently. 'It's six o'clock, time to get going, I'm afraid. Have a bite to eat at the canteen and report back to me.'

Minnie looked for Clara, but the sofa was empty. She stretched her arms and yawned. Every bone in her body ached and her eyes felt gritty and sore. What she wouldn't give for a cool shower or a glass full of ice. She rose and stumbled to the holdall Darius had brought with her fresh uniform. He had left a note. *Decided to go to Dolly's. Thought you'd like me to look in on the kids.* Guilt swamped her. She hadn't given the children a thought since her arrival hours earlier. She picked up the clean uniform and took it to the ladies' room.

Ten minutes later she emerged feeling better able to face another gruelling day. She hadn't realised until she reached the canteen just how hungry she was. Her last food had been at lunch the previous day, and this morning she did justice to an altogether heartier breakfast than she normally had at home. Afterwards, she entered Matron's office where a gaggle of assorted volunteers were gathered.

Matron was dishing out orders, signing bits of paper, answering the phone and checking lists all at the same time.

'Minnie, here are the new helpers. Carry on like yesterday with the corridors and the ground-floor wards. How long can you stay?'

'As long as you need me.'

'Good girl,' came the brisk answer. 'In that case, you can go off at noon. But I'd like you to be back at eight o'clock. I want to put you upstairs in D Ward for the night shift. We're short-staffed up there.'

'Isn't that the Services ward?'

'That's right.'

'Why aren't they at the military hospital in Colaba?'

'No spare beds there. These patients were admitted before the explosion.'

'I'll be here at eight,' Minnie said. After the gore and blood and ghastly injuries she had witnessed among the casualties in the crowded passages, it would be a relief to work for a few hours in a ward of soldiers who were not explosion victims.

Minnie returned to the hospital that evening clean and refreshed. A cold shower, a good sleep and an early dinner with the children had done wonders for her. Night shift on D Ward would be less strenuous than the previous day's work. She reported to the duty sister at eight o'clock.

'You shouldn't have much to do. They've had their meal and the doctors have been round. From time to time you can walk up and down between the beds to check on them. I'll be back by ten to give their medication. I am glad of the break – not eaten a thing since noon. If there's any trouble, ring through to the common room.'

Minnie watched the sister hurrying towards the stairs, her rubber heels squeaking on the tiled floor, then she settled down in the glass cubicle from where she had a clear view to the end of the ward. There were two rows of twelve beds. Most of the men were asleep or dozing, others were leafing through magazines with their reading lights on. A couple were in traction with a bandaged leg hoisted in the air. It was unbearably hot. Four ancient ceiling fans creaked sluggishly trying to provide relief, but sweat trickled down Minnie's back. She fanned herself with a sheet of paper.

After a while she left the cubicle to make her first round. She walked silently down the passage between the rows of beds, reading the names on the medical charts hooked on to the end bedrails. Esposito, Giovanni. Bonomini, Carlo.

Morelli, Enrico. Palazzi, Luigi. It dawned on her that these patients were Italian prisoners of war. Bonomini, Carlo was awake and looking at her curiously.

'Good evening,' she whispered in Italian.

A look of pleasure passed over his face. 'Good evening, Signora,' he replied eagerly.

She stood at the foot of his bed and they talked in low tones so as not to disturb Esposito, Giovanni asleep next to him. He confirmed that the twelve Italians in the ward were naval officers prisoners of war. They were captured in Alexandria in 1942, sent to a Prisoner of War camp in Karachi and four months ago were transferred to the camp in Colaba on the southernmost tip of Bombay. Minnie felt a pang of pity listening to his story. He spoke no English and was delighted to be able to talk to a nurse, as he called her, in his mother tongue.

A low voice called from two beds away. 'Signorina Marapodi!'

Minnie was astounded to hear her maiden name. She approached the bed from where the voice had spoken. A man lay flat on his back under a kind of cage from the waist down. He was bearded and thin, with sunken cheeks and deep blue eyes. He looked vaguely familiar, but she couldn't place him.

'Signorina Marapodi, I am not mistaken. It really is you, isn't it?'

'My name was Marapodi, yes, but how…?'

'Do you not recognise me? I expect I've changed a bit. We met many years ago.'

'I'm afraid I don't remember,' she apologised.

'Surely you must remember?' He smiled, holding out his hand. 'You were travelling to India with two ladies. On the *Galileo*?'

Minnie's eyes widened and her mouth gaped. He gripped her hand in both of his.

'I was the first officer. I'm Paolo Della Croce.'

33

'Paolo Della Croce! Good heavens! Of course, I remember. I did not recognise you at first, what with the beard and all.'

Paolo smiled. 'But you, Signorina Minnie, I would have recognised you anywhere.'

'It was such a long time ago. What – seventeen years, is it?' She fell silent for a moment, not knowing how to bridge the awkward gap. 'I see you are a *comandante*. You must have joined the regular navy. How did you get to India?'

'I joined up at the outbreak of the war and was taken prisoner in Alexandria in forty-two.'

'What's wrong with you?' she asked.

'I have a cracked pelvis.'

'How did that happen?'

'Very foolishly, I'm afraid to say. We do gymnastics in the camp to keep fit. I was trying to be clever with the vaulting horse. I made a mistake and took a heavy fall on the concrete – missing the mat completely.' His tone was self-mocking. 'It doesn't pay to show off.'

'I didn't know you were in the camp,' Minnie said. 'I visit some of the prisoners occasionally – and I regularly invite six or seven officers for lunch on Sundays, now that they are allowed out of the camp during the day. It's strange we haven't met before now.'

'Not surprising. There are several hundred men in the camp, and you can't know them all. I was transferred to the Colaba camp about a month ago and I've been here in hospital most of the time.'

Minnie felt self-conscious. It was difficult to know what more to say to him. The unexpectedness of coming face to face with the past made her tongue-tied. 'I'd better go and check up on the others. I'll be back soon,' she said, touching his hand briefly.

She continued the round, glad of the excuse to play for time. She remembered thinking about Paolo Della Croce for a while after her arrival in Bombay. They had kept in touch sporadically for some time, but her replies to him had fizzled out as she became more involved with Edoardo.

The rubber soles of her shoes squeaked on the wooden floor. The mosquito-proof mesh and blackout blinds across the wide windows obstructed any chance of a fresh breeze. The four ancient ceiling fans clicked in unison, their flat blades slowly pushing the heavy air round, creating the illusion of a cool draught. She paused briefly at each bed. One man asked for fresh water, another wanted his pillows adjusted. Most were glad to have a damp cloth passed over a clammy forehead. Two officers were in conversation. Those who weren't asleep were delighted to have a few words with her in their native tongue. They wanted to know the latest news about the explosion.

'When it happened yesterday,' one of them said, 'we were sure it was a Japanese air raid. But we hadn't heard any planes or sirens. Then we thought it might be sabotage.'

'No, it was an explosion in the docks,' Minnie said. 'A ship blew up.'

She returned to the ward sister's cubicle to make her notes. Tapping a pencil against a pile of books she looked out at the dimly lit room full of beds with a growing awareness of the incongruity of her situation. Until six months ago when Italy surrendered to the Allies, these wounded Italian officers were considered the enemy. Being segregated to this ward, she wondered if they were still thought of as enemies, since eventually they would need to return to the camp in Colaba? She regarded them simply as injured men, no different from the civilian casualties in the wards and corridors downstairs. So, what did that make her? In the eyes of the British, had she, too, appeared to be the enemy, and a collaborator in the eyes of her countrymen? Where *did* she belong and to whom were her loyalties due?

She rubbed her temples, feeling the start of a headache behind her eyes. She thought she had found her haven in the Dubash family. In truth she felt completely comfortable amongst the Parsi and Indian community, greatly thanks to Clara and Dolly who had always treated her like a sister. For that reason, she was wholeheartedly accepted by their friends. Roshan was the only one who made her feel like an outsider.

She sighed and glanced at the clock: it was time to do her rounds again. Paolo was awake when she got to his bed. She drew up a stool and sat beside him.

'Tell me about yourself. What did you do after we last met? You never came back to Bombay, did you?' she asked.

'I came back once and tried to look you up, but you had gone away for

Christmas. And then, well, I got married. My wife didn't like me being away for such long periods.'

'How long have you been married?'

'Nearly ten years.'

'Have you any children?'

'Two little boys. Michele is nearly seven, and Luigi is four. I haven't seen him since he was six months old.' He tried reaching the drawer in his bedside table. Minnie stood up and opened it for him. 'I have a photo in my wallet. It is quite old of course, but you can see they are nice-looking boys.'

He handed her a dog-eared photo showing a round-faced woman with thick dark eyebrows and an incipient moustache staring stiffly ahead. On her lap sat a chubby baby with dark hair like hers, and by her side a little boy in short pants stood to attention, smiling broadly at the camera. With his lighter hair, he resembled his father.

'They are fine-looking children,' she said, handing back the photo, 'Your wife has…great presence.'

Paolo sighed, taking back the photo and smoothing it with the palm of his hand. 'I imagine how they have grown, and what they are doing now, and…' his voice trailed off. 'I received a letter from my wife before Christmas, through the Red Cross. It took four months to reach me. I don't know if she received my reply. I have heard nothing since. She wrote that she was thinking of going back to her folks in the provinces, near Anzio. I hope they didn't go there after all. I can only pray that they are safe.'

It was plain that he had heard about the Allied invasion at Anzio in January 1944. Minnie didn't know how to ease his anxiety. She reached out and squeezed his hand.

'The lines of communication must be terrible, and it's probably not possible for her to send you a letter. I haven't heard from my family in Rome for over a year.'

'You are right, I'm sure.' Clearly, he was troubled by the subject and tried to bring himself under control. 'But now tell me about yourself. I see from the ring on your finger that you are married, in which case I can hardly go on calling you Signorina.'

'Yes, I am married, in fact, remarried. I have two children – a girl and a boy – from my first marriage. They are my pride and joy. My surname now is Dubash.'

He looked puzzled. 'It doesn't sound an Italian name. English, perhaps?'

Minnie explained and by the time the ward sister came back at ten o'clock, she and Paolo had caught up with the main events in their lives over the past years.

'I shall come again tomorrow. Would you like me to bring you anything?' she enquired before going off duty. 'A bit of fruit, perhaps, or magazines or books?'

'There is one thing you could do for me,' he replied, rasping a hand across his chin. 'It's far too hot for a beard. I would give anything for a packet of decent razor blades.'

In the following fortnight, as the immediate crisis subsided, Minnie was called on less frequently by the hospital. Her duties were not always on D Ward, but before going home she always dropped in on the prisoner of war patients for a quick chat and to see if they needed anything.

She bumped into Father Alessi a couple of times who hinted broadly that as she was good enough to bring fruit and goodies to the patients in D Ward, she might think of doing the same for the boys in his orphanage. Since Father Alessi came to Minnie for lunch on the third Thursday of each month and left with a large parcel of clothes and foodstuffs, plus a cash donation, she felt she was already doing her bit for the mission.

'Next time I come for lunch, may I bring one or two of the Italian officers with me?' Father Alessi asked with a smile and his usual bluntness. 'They would enjoy home cooking for a change.'

'With pleasure, Father. But it will have to wait until my return.'

'Are you going away?'

'I'm taking the children to the hills for a few weeks during the hot weather. But tell me, Father, I didn't think POWs would be allowed to leave the camp.'

'My child, there are ways of wangling things.' Father Alessi tapped the side of his nose with a knowing look. 'In exceptional cases, of course.'

The gesture he made was incongruous and yet familiar. Minnie hid a smile. If he hadn't been a priest, he would surely have been a *mafioso*.

Paolo Della Croce made good progress, she noted on her visits. He was undergoing physiotherapy and was being made to walk a little each day. It would not be long before he went back to the camp. Certainly, before she returned from the summer break. She wondered if she could ask Father Alessi to bring him to lunch at her house but thought better of it. The good father had strongly disapproved of her divorce and remarriage. He considered her to be in a perpetual state of sin and she was still unable to receive the sacraments in church. This did not prevent him, however, from accepting her hospitality and her largesse.

As the hot weather became intolerable, schools broke up for the summer holidays and it was time to make for cooler climes. To escape the heat Dolly had taken a house for the three families in Mahabaleshwar, a favourite hill station in the Western Ghats, less than a day's journey by train and bus. Although not as cool and refreshing as Simla would have been, it had the advantage of being close enough to Bombay for the menfolk to travel up for a week or two without having to endure a three-day trip each way.

Shortly before leaving for Mahabaleshwar, Minnie took the children swimming at the Willingdon Club one afternoon. Her friend, Barbara Davidson, was seated on the lawn under an umbrella, watching her own older children having a diving lesson.

'Hello, Minnie,' she called, waving. 'Come and join me for tea after your swim.'

Minnie waved back. She liked Barbara, who had a tremendous sense of humour, and had proved to be a loyal friend. After their swim, having deposited Claudia and Bobby with the supervisor in the adjoining playground, Minnie sat with Barbara. They ordered a pot of tea for themselves and chips and ketchup for the children. Barbara was chairman of the British Women's Association that year and spoke about her recent involvement in raising a disaster fund for the families of the explosion victims.

'It's been hard work,' she said, lighting a cigarette. 'We've raised a hundred thousand rupees in two weeks, which is pretty good going. But that's enough of my news. Tell me what you've been up to. I hear St George's think you're doing useful work with some of the POWs.'

'It's the least I could do; I suppose simply translating when necessary is useful enough. Do you know, one of the POWs in D Ward was a man I met seventeen years ago? He was the first officer on the ship that brought me out to India. I couldn't believe it.'

'What a coincidence. Did you recognise him?'

'No, he recognised me. I expect he'll be back in Colaba camp by the time I return.'

A waiter approached carrying a tray with the tea, a plate of biscuits, two large portions of chips and a bottle of ketchup. He set it down on the table and poured the tea, handing the cups to the two ladies.

The two friends chatted happily. Minnie told her how delighted she was that Darius had been given the job of producing and editing a new arts magazine. It was exactly what Darius wanted and he was full of enthusiasm for the project. He wanted it to be a record of the rich artistic heritage his country had to offer as well as a vehicle for contemporary art and poetry.

'The first edition is expected to come out in July,' she said. 'He's very excited about it. He's got together some excellent features, though he's had a few problems with the printers.'

Barbara poured herself more tea. 'Oh dear, Minnie! Look who's coming across the lawn. I'm afraid she's spotted us. Never mind, she can join us for tea.' She raised her voice and waved. 'Hello there, Roshan, how are you?'

'Hel-lo, Babs dear, how delightful to see you,' Roshan gushed. 'May I join you – hope you don't mind?' Not waiting for an answer, she sat down. 'No, no, my dear, no tea for me. All that tannin is not good for the skin. I'll have a fresh lime juice with ice. Oh, Minnie, I didn't see you sitting there. Haven't seen you for ages. You're well, are you?'

'I'm extremely well, thanks, Roshan.'

Barbara held out a plate of chips.

'No thanks, Babs dear, chips are so bad for the digestion.'

Minnie knew her friend hated being called Babs.

'You don't know what you're missing – they're delicious,' Barbara said, popping one into her mouth. 'We've just been talking about Darius and the magazine.'

'Oh indeed, the magazine. His little baby. He is simply besotted with it, just like a small boy with a new toy.' She shook her head indulgently. 'Let's hope he doesn't get bored with it. Isn't that so, Minnie?'

'I assure you, Roshan,' Minnie said, her hackles rising, 'he is dead serious about this undertaking, and he's determined to make it a success.'

'But there have been too many delays for the launch,' Roshan insisted. 'It's almost as if he doesn't quite know how to handle such a large project.'

'You're quite wrong there, Roshan.' Minnie was not going to let her get away with these disparaging remarks. 'He knows exactly how to handle it. The delays have been entirely caused by the printers.' She reached for her teacup. 'You know what a perfectionist Darius is. He won't accept a sloppy job. He's down at the press in Parel every other day looking at proofs and heaven knows what to try and get it right.'

'That's not what I've heard,' Roshan sniggered. 'He's not there all that often.'

'Nonsense,' Minnie snapped. 'He was even down there at the time of the dock explosion. That's how dedicated he is.'

'No, he wasn't at the printers at all that day.' Roshan sipped her lime juice calmly.

Minnie stiffened. 'Of course he was, he told me so. Where else could he have been?'

'I was reliably informed he was having tea with Shireen Cambata. At her house.' Roshan paused. She looked as if she were savouring the moment. 'I thought you knew about it, Minnie.'

The tension in the air crackled. Barbara looked embarrassed. Minnie felt as if she would explode. Slowly she reached forward, picked up a fat chip, dipped it into the ketchup and put it in her mouth.

'Certainly, I knew about it, Roshan,' she lied. 'He met her for lunch, not for tea. He went on to the printers afterwards.' She licked her fingers long after the saltiness had dispersed.

Who the hell was Shireen Cambata?

34

'Darius, who is Shireen Cambata?' Minnie asked with a casualness that disguised her seething anger. As a rule, she did not take Roshan's spiteful digs seriously. But this time the niggling thought persisted, sore as the first sign of toothache, that the wretched woman might have a point.

'Who did you say, dear?' Darius took his time helping himself to grilled pomfret from the platter held out by the bearer, then dismissed the servant with a wave of the hand.

'Shireen Cambata. Do you know her?' Minnie was still outwardly calm.

'The name doesn't ring a bell. Why do you ask?'

'Roshan told me you spent the afternoon at her house in Worli on the day of the dock explosion.'

'Oh, that Shireen! I remember now.' He busied himself dissecting the fish. 'Ashok Mehta introduced her to me while I had lunch with him at the club. She invited us to her place for coffee.'

Minnie waited for him to go on.

'Apparently she wanted a job on the magazine. But she has no experience. I said there were no openings. At present.'

'Might there be later?'

He shrugged his shoulders, looking vague. 'Who knows? Possibly.'

'You told me you were at the printers in Parel all that day – that's a long way from the club. You know how anxious I was.'

'I got in touch with you, didn't I?'

'Hours later, Darius!' she burst out. 'Hours during which I was sick with worry.'

Darius shoved his plate aside. 'Take this back to the cook,' he said petulantly to the bearer. 'It's too salty.' He threw his napkin on to the table. 'What does it matter what time I got in touch – I came looking for you, didn't I? You saw I was alright.'

He pushed his chair back, avoiding her gaze, and started to chew the nail of his little finger, a habit of his when agitated.

'That's not the point,' she insisted. He ignored her. She recognised the danger signal but carried on even though she knew she was on tricky ground.

'You didn't go to the printers at all that day, did you, Darius?' she asked quietly.

This time he looked straight at her, unsmiling. 'So, what if I didn't? Are you checking up on me, my dear?'

'I've never had to do so before. Do I need to now?'

He sat back and lit a cigarette. 'It would be most unwise.' A plume of smoke drifted from his nostrils. There was a hint of menace in his tone.

Minnie drew a deep breath, struggling for composure. 'I am anything but unwise, my darling, as you know.' Her response was light, breaking the tension between them. She reached across the table to touch his hand.

'But please remember, Darius, I will *not* be made a fool of.'

He held her gaze steadily for a moment or two, still unsmiling, then rose from his chair. 'No, my dear, you will not be made a fool of.'

Minnie and the children spent a harmonious five weeks in Mahabaleshwar with Clara and her brood as Dolly's guests. The war and its anxieties seemed remote and were pushed into the background. But Minnie was glad to arrive back at her own home in Bombay in time to establish a routine before the onslaught of the monsoon rains.

With Darius at the office and the children at school again, she sat on the veranda in her dressing gown, waiting for her breakfast to be brought, savouring the moment of peace in the empty house. Even this early it was a sultry, breathless morning, and she dabbed at the sweat trickling down her neck and between her breasts. The sun filtered weakly through the grey layers of moisture-laden clouds, which pressed down towards the horizon ready at any moment to release the weight of water they could barely hold. The sea was the colour of milky coffee, with silent, oily swells lifting, rolling, crashing angrily on the shore. A rumble of thunder sounded. Minnie sighed and stretched her arms above her head, longing for the relief the first rains would bring. Presently the bearer brought in her tray with a copy of *The Times of India*. She unfolded the paper and read the banner headlines:

    ALLIED TROOPS LAND IN NORMANDY
    HEAVY CASUALTIES FEARED

The next few weeks passed in a blur of activity. The more Minnie heard about the war in Europe, the more she felt the need to keep busy, to blot out her anxieties. Rome had fallen to the Allies early in the month, and King Vittorio Emanuele had abdicated in favour of his son, King Umberto II. She avidly followed the reports about the landings in Normandy. There was no doubt it marked a turning point, giving rise to a glimmer of hope in Europe. Hope for what? Hope that it might soon be over? Hope that there wouldn't be too many casualties? Hope that the battles would stop and return to what it was before the war started?

She found herself increasingly apprehensive about the Allied advance in Italy. Her thoughts were for her parents and brothers. With no news from them for more than two years, she wondered, as she did almost daily, what they were doing, how they were, how they had managed during this time. She simply refused to consider they might be dead, or injured, or bombed out. She guessed that Neddy and Donna Rachele would have been smart enough to make the right connections with the authorities. But the political and military tide had turned, and she wondered how they would fare now that the Allies were pushing through. The more she read about the Allied successes – Perugia taken in June, Livorno and Ancona in July, the fall of Florence in August – the more she wanted to fill her days with anything that would take her mind off these, and other thoughts.

Business was doing surprisingly well, and orders kept flowing. She served on a committee to raise funds for Sister Serafina's convent, and she continued to help at St George's. She and some of her friends continued inviting a few Italian officers from Colaba camp every Sunday for lunches at home.

'Not another one of your Italian feasts!' Darius puffed with irritation when told Minnie was holding a lunch party for them.

'Darling, poor things. They do appreciate home cooking and the company of the other ladies and kids. Please try and join us this time, won't you?'

Darius wrinkled his nose. 'Darling, do I have to? I find them quite boring. I'd really promised my friend Dinsoo a round of golf.'

Just another excuse, thought Minnie. She knew he felt awkward in their company. At times she believed that because he hadn't joined up, he thought the officers felt contempt for him for sitting out the war in safety and comfort.

Claudia and Bobby, on the other hand, enjoyed these gatherings and the great fuss and attention paid to them by the officers, many of whom saw in these two a reminder of their own children back home. Paolo Della Croce of course became a regular and because of his and Minnie's past acquaintance, a strong rapport of understanding and friendship grew between them. At times Minnie felt he could almost read her mind, particularly when she tried to mask underlying worries.

'I think there is something troubling you, my dear Minnie,' he said as they strolled in the garden one Sunday after lunch. All the children were playing tag and the officers were sitting in the shade of a banyan tree in conversation with Minnie's friends.

'Of course, the news about the war troubles me,' she replied vaguely. 'I think about my family in Rome.' She turned to him. 'You must understand what it's like. It is so much worse for you.'

'That's not what I mean, *cara signora*. It is something else, more elusive, that you are anxious about. I can sense it.'

'Perhaps you can sense more than I can, Paolo,' she said with a laugh, trying to put him off. 'These are worrying times for us all.'

'That's true enough. But yours is a difficult situation.' He paused, and she looked up at him but remained silent, sensing that he did not want to overstep the line between interest and prying. They reached the sea wall and watched the foam cresting on the lazy blue waves before flopping on to the rocks a hundred yards away. The tide was almost in. Paolo took her hand.

'Often it is easier to talk to a person from the same background, the same country. You know how much I admire what you do, Minnie. You have been incredibly kind to me – to all of us. It has made a big difference. If there is anything I can do to help, you need only say.'

'Oh, Paolo, you are imagining things. I am perfectly alright, I assure you.' She squeezed his hand. 'But I appreciate what you've said…and I will remember it.'

They turned and walked towards the group under the banyan tree.

Paolo was right, of course, but until she heard him say it, she had not wanted to admit it to herself. Her relations with Darius were like a seesaw: up in the clouds one minute, flying, soaring, face to the sun, heart bursting with love and tenderness for this man, her man, this passionate, sensitive, creative person, whose exquisite poetry must one day become known to the wider world. The next moment her emotions hit the ground with a spine-jolting bump, her heart squeezed by alarm, uncertainty and mistrust towards this other man, not hers, but whose? This was a stranger, with an often-uncontrollable temper; one who was cold and withdrawn, cruel even, and seemed to enjoy inflicting physical and mental pain. Who, on seeing her brought to tears of anger or misery, would in a flash become contrite and turn again into her tender, loving man, her passionate lover, wanting, persuading, getting immediate fulfilment for his sudden desire and fulfilling her own, in a way that Edoardo never had.

One afternoon she woke from a nap and prepared to take tea on the veranda, when she heard a murmur of voices coming from the direction of Darius's study. In his absence no one was allowed in his study except herself and the servants. Even when he was working there, she tried never to disturb him. Curious, she went to investigate and opened the door without knocking. A laughing Darius was seated on the sofa between Roshan and another woman, an arm around each. A handsome, slim young man was taking a photo of them. Minnie felt a flush rising to her cheeks.

'Darius, darling, you said you were going to be home late today,' she exclaimed in surprise.

'I changed my mind, darling,' he said, looking slightly put out. The two women moved away from him as he withdrew his arms.

'You should have called me if you were bringing guests.'

'I thought you were lunching at Dolly's.'

'It got cancelled.' She turned to her sister-in-law with a tight smile. 'Roshan, the servants didn't tell me you were here. I would have come earlier if I'd known.'

'Actually, I came to see Darius,' Roshan drawled. 'I didn't think it was necessary to bother you.'

Minnie felt her temper rise. 'You never bother me, Roshan,' she replied evenly. Her gaze moved to the two strangers. 'Aren't you going to introduce me, Darius?'

'Sorry, I thought you knew each other. This is Satish Desai,' he said, pointing at the graceful young man who had stopped taking photos and put his Rolleiflex down. 'He's the photographer for the magazine.' Minnie acknowledged his joined-hands greeting as Darius continued. 'And this is Shireen Cambata.' He turned towards the beautiful girl on his left. 'Shireen, this is my wife, Minnie.'

Minnie's stomach lurched, but she managed to flash a smile. 'Ah, Shireen Cambata. I'm glad we meet at last. I've heard a lot about you. From Roshan, of course.'

Shireen flicked her silky black hair behind her shoulder. 'Likewise, Minnie,' she replied, heavy-lidded eyes glancing briefly at Darius before fixing on Minnie. 'I thought Darius must have told you about me,' she said in a girlish, sing-song voice.

'What should you have told me, Darius darling?'

She watched Shireen throw a melting look at Darius. Minnie felt like slapping the little tart's face and wiping the smirk off her thick lips. She noticed a sparkle of enjoyment in Roshan's eyes.

Darius shifted uncomfortably then rose to his feet to light a cigarette. 'I was sure I had mentioned it. It must have slipped my mind. I've appointed Shireen as sub-editor of the magazine.'

'Have you indeed? How interesting.' Minnie suppressed her anger with an effort. 'You must be pleased, Shireen. I suppose you've had lots of previous experience. With magazines, I mean?'

'No, it's my first job, actually. The magazine and I are both in our infancy, so to speak, but I'm sure I'll learn as I go along.' She giggled loudly.

'I don't doubt it.' Minnie's irony was lost on her. 'And how did you meet?'

'Oh, Roshan introduced us ages ago, you know.' Shireen's high-pitched voice grated on Minnie's ears.

'I might have guessed,' Minnie murmured with a grim look at her sister-in-law, who merely raised an eyebrow and gave a slight shrug.

'She's been such a good friend to me, haven't you, Roshan?' Shireen prattled on. 'As soon as she heard that I was looking for a job, she said assistant editor would be just the ticket, suit me down to the ground, didn't you, Roshan?' She flashed a smile at Roshan, then looked coyly at Darius. 'Straight away she introduced me to Darius. He thought with my qualifications I could work my way up from sub-editor to assistant editor in no time.'

'I see, and what qualifications are those?'

'I have a BA Second Class failed in History of Art from Elphinstone College,' Shireen replied with a prim smile.

'Ah, how appropriate.' Minnie nodded her head. 'And I'm sure you have other qualities that will take you far.'

Obviously sensing the build-up of tension in Minnie, Darius came across to her and slipped his arm round her waist. 'Sweetheart,' he said, a warning note in his voice, 'we've nearly finished taking photos. Let's have one of all of us together.'

Minnie shook her head and moved away from him. She would bide her time. 'Not this time, darling, I have things to do.' She addressed the others. 'It's been most interesting meeting you, but I must go now. I shall leave you all to…your sub-editing tasks.'

She walked out of the room, leaving the door open.

35

1944–45

After returning from the club that evening, Minnie went to Darius's study. He was working at his desk, a cigarette held in his left hand, its smoke drifting upwards with a sickly smell. He put down his pen after a moment or two and gazed at her in silence. She knew it was not the right moment to question him, but her anger had not subsided, and she wanted an explanation for his inviting people she didn't know into her home without consulting her.

'But I didn't invite them.' He looked at her coolly through a haze of smoke. 'Roshan brought them here.'

'She wouldn't have done that without telling you first.'

'Okay, so she did tell me first, what of it?'

'That's just the point, Darius. She didn't *ask* you – she told you. You always do whatever Roshan tells you. She simply snaps her fingers and you jump. Can you never say no to her?'

'Don't talk such rot, Minnie.' Darius ground the cigarette into an ashtray. 'She's my sister, after all. She knows she can do certain things without asking.'

'And she takes full advantage of it. You should have let me know. This is not Roshan's house to do as she pleases, this is my home.'

'And mine.'

'As your wife, I am mistress of this house. Roshan is not.' She walked to the open window and stood facing him, her back catching the slight breeze coming in with the tide. 'I put up with your friends, Darius, and heaven knows some of them are hardly friends. I entertain them, I ignore their bad manners, I laugh at their crude jokes, I overlook the fact that often they act as if I am not their hostess but simply part of the furniture.' She paused and took a deep breath. 'But I will not put up with Roshan bringing that woman into my home when gossip about you and her is flying about town. Gossip that until now I have been able to disregard, but not if the subject of it is shoved under my nose.'

Darius pushed back his chair.

'What nonsense, Minnie, nothing is going on between Shireen and me.'

He would not meet Minnie's gaze, and started chewing on his left thumb.

Minnie could not stop herself from going on. 'I wish I could believe you,' she said. 'But rumours don't start for no reason.'

'You're imagining the rumours, dear girl.'

'Don't patronise me, Darius. If that's true, then why haven't you told me about her before now? Why the secrecy? Why didn't you tell me about her appointment as sub-editor? You've talked to me about everything else connected with the magazine. Why do I have to find out like this?'

Darius stood up and began pacing the room. 'You're making a big fuss about nothing, Minnie. She's going to be working with me and that's that. Roshan thinks she'll make a good sub-editor.'

'So what Roshan thinks carries more weight than my feelings?' Minnie felt her voice becoming unsteady. 'Darius, I'm not going to stand for it. You will just have to un-appoint her. Please. It will end the gossip.' She turned to leave the room.

'Shireen Cambata stays.' His words cracked like a whip, stopping her in her tracks.

'Darius!'

'Listen, Minnie. I appointed her. I made the decision and you will have to lump it.' His eyes were bright with anger. 'She's coming to our party on Saturday and I expect you to treat her nicely.'

Minnie breathed heavily, backing away as he advanced. 'How could you invite her without asking me first?' She felt panicky, as if she were losing control, and took a deep breath. 'If Shireen comes, I won't be there.'

'Yes you will.' Darius's voice was hard. He stood close, looking down at her. A muscle twitched at the side of his mouth. 'You will act the gracious hostess and carry out your duties.'

'Absolutely not!'

The palm of his hand cracked across her cheek, the force of it making her stagger against a side table. A vase of zinnias crashed to the floor. Eyes stinging, Minnie gasped and clutched her smarting cheek. She turned and stumbled towards the door, but Darius moved fast. His hand reached past her and slammed it shut. Grasping her shoulders, he pinned her against the wall, holding her so that she couldn't move. Minnie panted, waiting for him to release her. What was happening? Was this the end? How could he have hit her?

Tears streamed down her cheeks and her shoulders heaved. He no longer loved her. The thought was almost more than she could bear. She turned her face away from him while trying to control her weeping, but felt his taut body pressing against hers. Disconnected words pierced the fog in her mind.

'Minnie, Minnie, my darling. I'm so sorry…I didn't mean it… Look at me, sweetheart. I'm sorry… Please forgive me.'

He forced her to turn towards him, but she shuddered, pulling away.

'Don't,' she mumbled thickly, covering her face with her hands. 'Don't touch me.'

She was aware of him tugging her hands from her face as she resisted.

'Please, darling, look at me,' Darius pleaded, stroking her arms. 'I'm so sorry. I love you. You're the only one for me…you know that.'

Through swollen eyes she saw the look of desperate contrition on his face as he took out a handkerchief, dabbed her wet cheeks and wiped her streaming nose.

'You're my Heartsflame, my life, I'm lost without you,' he whispered.

Cupping her head between his hands, he fluttered light, butterfly kisses on her eyes, cheeks, forehead, chin. He gathered her to him, murmuring endearments between kisses which grew ever more passionate.

At first Minnie remained rigid, her emotions in conflict with her senses, but gradually felt herself melting. His touch never failed to arouse her and now his mouth on her throat and a hand on her breast set her on a slow burn. She felt his arms tighten around her; his lips pressed on hers and her body softened, moulding itself to his. She responded despite herself, her flesh tingling under his fingers, her breath coming in short bursts as he strained against her. Her body dissolved into him, her limbs fusing with his until at last a shuddering white light engulfed her.

Later, lying in his arms on the sofa, she felt as soft and plump as a ripe mango. The bitterness had been flushed from her mind like dust washed from leaves after a rainstorm. She shivered as Darius's fingers stroked her hip, his lips against her hair. Breathing quietly, she asked herself if this was to be the pattern of their future. The happiness, the physical rapture that she felt with Darius came at a cost.

She wondered how long she would be prepared to pay the price.

Shireen lasted a mere three months as sub-editor for the magazine. Even Darius had to admit she was more incompetent than the picture Roshan had painted of her. Minnie learned that Darius, with considerable tact, had suggested that Shireen's talents might be better suited to be a model for a fashion magazine where her voluptuous figure and languid looks would be an asset. There would also be a good chance, Darius had hinted, of being discovered by some film producer, perhaps leading her to greater fame than she would achieve as a sub-editor.

Roshan was indignant when she found out that her protégée had been dismissed. 'I suppose you put Darius up to this,' she said to Minnie over the phone.

'Of course not,' Minnie replied with irritation. 'There was no need. Anyone could see she wasn't suited for the job. We both know the reason why you persuaded Darius to employ her. But it didn't work, Roshan, and I advise you not to try that stunt again.'

'I don't know what you mean.'

Minnie took a deep breath. 'Come on. Don't take me for a complete fool. You know perfectly well what I'm talking about.' She twisted the telephone cord around a finger. 'You think that throwing a sexy piece like Shireen at him is going to make him start a sordid little affair. That's what you would like to happen.'

'What rubbish! You are quite paranoid, Minnie. Why should I want that?'

'Because you are always trying to create trouble between Darius and me. And you would love him to come running back to you if things went wrong.' There was no answer. She untwisted the phone cord. 'He's married now, Roshan. You can't expect to influence him at every turn. You treat him as if he hasn't left home. He's a grown man, not a little boy. He can make his own decisions.'

A bitter laugh came over the line. 'And some have been disastrous ones.'

'Maybe that's because he tries to escape your domination, and any decision he makes for himself is preferable to you making it for him.' She picked up a pencil and began doodling on the sketchpad.

'You can't be expected to understand us, Minnie. You're a foreigner, you don't know our customs. I've looked after Darius since he was six. Naturally, he takes my advice.'

'Nobody denies how much you care for him, Roshan. But I love him, too.'

'Maybe so. But you don't understand him like I do. He needs me. You don't realise how close we are.'

'No doubt you are. But not as close as he and I are. After all, I sleep with him.'

There was a long pause before Roshan replied. 'That may not be for much longer. And then he'll come back to me. He always does.'

'What are you trying to say?' The pencil point snapped under Minnie's tightened grip.

'You'll see. Mark my words.'

'Don't sound so cryptic, Roshan. If you have anything to say, then do so.

Otherwise shut up, keep out of our business and stop making trouble. I really don't want to listen to any more.'

She slammed the phone into its cradle.

Try as she might for the rest of the day, she could not put Roshan's insinuation out of mind.

36

Late in 1944, Minnie was in her atelier one morning reading *The Times of India*. She was going through the article about Franklin D Roosevelt's re-election as president of the United States, when to her surprise Franco entered her office.

'Why are you here?' she asked in alarm.

Franco gave her a strange look and took her hand. 'Come and sit down,' he said, drawing her to the sofa. He handed her an envelope. 'I got it today. It's from Neddy.' His voice was thick with emotion.

Minnie gasped, her eyes filling with tears. She put on her glasses and drew out the first of three tightly handwritten pages on flimsy paper. It was uncensored and dated the previous August.

'How did you get it?' she whispered.

'Through the Swiss consulate general,' Franco replied.

It was the first news from home in nearly three years. Minnie read on. Neddy didn't mention any names, but from what he wrote it appeared the family had been relatively safe during the worst times thanks to their friends in high places and to other factors.

'Do you know what other factors?' Minnie asked.

'I suppose he means his dealings in the black market,' Franco murmured.

Recently, however, Neddy wrote, they had kept a low profile and were distancing themselves from their previous connections. Donna Rachele was suffering from kidney problems, and Don Peppino's eyesight was affected by cataracts.

'Poor Mamma and poor old Papa. I wish there was something we could do for them. And listen to this! Neddy got *married* two years ago to someone called Luisa. Did you know her, Franco?'

'Don't you remember? Her family lived on the first floor of our apartment block. They now have a little girl called Anna.'

The letter went on with other news. Salvatore had joined a group of partisans in the Abruzzi mountains. The family had heard nothing from him for almost a year and feared for his safety.

Minnie read on. After the third reading she gave it back to Franco. Her eyes brimmed with tears of relief. 'Neddy has seen Edoardo's family,' she said. 'I must phone him and pass on the news.'

'I'm sending a letter back to them,' Franco said. 'The Swiss consul said he would be able to help. Tell Edoardo to send me a letter, I'll include it in with mine.'

Christmas that year was spent in Ootacamund in the Nilgiri Hills of South India, again with Dolly, Jimmy, Clara et al. The children rode in the mornings, they went for endless picnics, and there was a proper Christmas tree. It was decked with silver and gold garlands and tinsel and coloured glass bells; angels dangled from the branches and cotton wool lay on the branches as make-believe snow.

Minnie had bought the children new outfits. What Claudia liked best was that they were proper winter clothes: wool skirt, Viyella blouse, Chilprufe vest, woollen knee socks and jumpers and cardigans that Minnie had knitted. She complained to Minnie that the wool itched, but admitted it made her feel grown up. Bobby's favourite thing was that the house was blessed with lots of wide staircases. He hadn't ever been able to slide down banisters before and did so at every opportunity.

The children could stay up until ten o'clock on Christmas Eve and Minnie stood at the door with them to hear carols sung in the garden by a group of people carrying lanterns and wearing gloves and mufflers against the freezing air. Claudia didn't want the fire lit in their bedroom for fear that Santa Claus would get burnt if he tried to come down their chimney. There were arguments as to which chimney Santa would choose to come down. Joey reckoned his bedroom because he was the oldest. It irritated Claudia that Joey always trotted out his being the oldest in order to be first at everything.

'But, Mummy,' she complained, 'I'm the oldest girl, why shouldn't he come down *my* chimney?' She appealed to Clara: 'It's not fair, Aunty Clara.'

Clara put a stop to that argument by stating that it was to be the drawing room chimney, because it was the widest one and Santa was rather too large to come down any of the others.

A few weeks after their return to Bombay in the New Year, Bobby came rushing into Minnie's bedroom one afternoon. 'Mummy, Karsan says there's a man in the drawing room for you.'

'Who is it, poppet?'

'Don't know.'

'Well, let's go and see who it is.'

Edoardo was waiting for her in the drawing room.

'*Carissimo* Edoardo,' Minnie said as she embraced him. 'When did you get here? Where are you staying?'

'Got out yesterday and I'm staying at my friend Noshir's. Hello, Bobby, my boy. You *have* grown a lot. Won't you give Papa a hug?'

Bobby became bashful and buried his head against Minnie's hip. It was nearly a year since Minnie had taken the children to see Edoardo in Satara, although they had spoken on the phone every month, so she was not surprised at Bobby's sudden shyness. 'Come on, darling, say hello to Papa.'

'Don't you remember me, Bobby?'

Bobby peered at Edoardo. 'A bit. You look different.'

'That's because I'm not wearing khaki shorts, and I shaved my moustache,' Edoardo said kneeling in front of the little boy. 'Don't you remember how I used to take you piggy-back?'

For a few weeks Bobby was bashful whenever Edoardo came to see them at the house. It was only after Edoardo took the children to the zoo one day and let them ride on an elephant that the ice broke.

Meanwhile Darius continued his frequent trips away on business. He was preparing a special edition of the magazine on the Ellora and Ajanta cave carvings and murals and would go up-country for a few days at a time with his photographer, Satish Desai, and sometimes with Albie. *Heritage* was going from strength to strength, largely due to superb photography, good reproductions and specialist articles. In the months since its launch it had gained a select but devoted readership. Even Jimmy was pleasantly surprised by the success his brother had achieved against all expectations and felt relieved that Darius seemed at long last to have found a sense of direction in his life. 'Due mostly to your encouragement and faith in him, Minnie darling,' Jimmy remarked.

Minnie scoured *The Times of India* daily for news from Europe. March saw great advances by the Allies in the war in Europe. April was filled with momentous events, starting with the unexpected death of President Roosevelt from a brain haemorrhage, followed by revelations of Nazi death camps and Hitler's suicide. On 28 April Mussolini and Clara Petacci, his mistress, were shot by Italian partisans and strung up by their heels from the façade of a petrol station in central Milan. On the 29th the rest of the German divisions in Italy capitulated to Field Marshall Alexander and a week later Germany signed the instrument of unconditional surrender at General Eisenhower's HQ in Rheims.

The war in Europe was over. Now the military focus was on the war with Japan.

The next few months found Minnie joining in the city's state of euphoric activity, which reached the highest pitch of elation with the news of the Japanese surrender in August. She noticed a lot of changes, some small, others more significant. Mail from and to home was received and sent with more ease. While waiting repatriation in troop ships, the now ex-prisoners of war moved freely within the city. Partly due to heavy monsoon seas and partly to the lack of adequate transport, it would be several months before they could be sent back home. The same applied to British civilians wanting to return to England who were also delayed due to a lack of transport.

It seemed as if the entire city was an immense waiting room for people arriving from some far-flung place or leaving for an indeterminate destination. Refugees from Europe held in transit camps in other parts of India descended by the trainload on Bombay waiting for visas, for quotas, that would allow them to be shipped out to other countries. Poles, Czechs, Hungarians, Jews and Russians formed a large melting pot of displaced and uprooted humanity. Many homes took in parentless children or teenagers while they waited for the Red Cross to allocate them to a destination country.

Amongst all this turmoil, in the more populous areas of the city the first signs of strife between the Hindu and Muslim inhabitants became evident, as if predicting the future countrywide disorders. Minnie's Muslim driver became afraid of taking the car downtown to her suppliers and so she took to driving there herself. There were other signs of turbulence in the bazaars where nationalist demonstrations took place. While visiting her bead merchant in the market one day, Minnie witnessed, for the first time, a crowd of angry marchers holding banners blazoned with the slogans *Jai Hind, Jai Hind* or *Quit India*. She returned home, thoroughly shaken by the episode, aware with sudden clarity that she would be facing great changes. This feeling was reinforced after VE Day and more so after VJ Day following the terrible atomic explosions of Hiroshima and Nagasaki. Although she knew Jimmy and Darius actively supported the move for independence, she wondered what the future would hold for Europeans like herself in the aftermath of the British pulling out of India.

Despite these unsettling times, Minnie and her circle of friends continued entertaining former prisoners of war. It was as if the civilians, having escaped the real hardships of war, were trying in some measure to thank those far from their homelands who had seen active duty.

Among the Italian officers many formed firm friendships with their hosts and hostesses that were to last long after they were repatriated.

Paolo Della Croce had become a great favourite not only with Minnie but also with Dolly and Clara. He was intelligent and well read and spoke good English and French. He was astute and had an enquiring mind that appealed to Jimmy, who at one time offered him a job in Bombay if he chose to stay on.

One evening while strolling in the garden before dinner, Minnie asked Paolo about Jimmy's offer.

'He's offered me a job. But I need to get home and sort out things there before thinking of jobs abroad.'

They wandered towards the sea wall arm in arm and she pointed at the setting sun.

'You must watch carefully, Paolo. Look out for the green light.'

'What green light?'

'At the moment the last bit of sun disappears behind the horizon, there is a green flash. It's supposed to be lucky and you can make a wish on it.'

They watched the huge orange globe sink slowly behind the grey edge of the horizon, diminishing from circle to half-circle to a quarter, and at the moment it vanished they saw the tiny green spark and presently the sea and sky melded into a single wash of amethyst.

'What was your wish?' Minnie asked.

'It won't come true if I tell,' he laughed.

'Perhaps you wished to take up Jimmy's offer?'

'I'm not saying. But I will certainly keep in touch with him.'

'And with me, I hope,' Minnie said.

He took her hand. 'But of course with you, Minnie. You know I'll never forget you.' His smile was wistful. 'I'll be gone shortly, and there are one or two things I wanted to say. You must have guessed what my feelings are for you.'

'Shhh, Paolo. Don't say anything you might regret.'

'I would never regret it.'

'But I might, Paolo.' She sighed. 'I love my husband.'

'I know you do. But you and I...there *is* something special between us.'

Minnie looked at his handsome, kind face as if seeing him for the first time. The denial she was about to voice stopped short in her throat. She didn't know what to say. She felt his arm about her, slowly bringing her close, his lips warm and gentle on hers. This was a goodbye kiss, a thank-you kiss, a remember-me kiss, a silent I-love-you kiss.

'You feel it, too, don't you, Minnie?' he said, drawing back.

She gazed into his eyes without replying, then leaned her face into his shoulder to hide the rush of tears.

37

1945

Paolo was due to be repatriated to Italy in September 1945. As the date of his departure grew closer, Minnie wanted to spend more time with him, but was conscious this might give off the wrong signals, both to him and to gossipmongers. She contented herself with meeting him while in the company of others.

Many of the officers prepared farewell gifts for the families who had befriended them in token of their appreciation for the hospitality and kindness shown. Paolo made her a beautifully crafted rosewood document box with a secret compartment and her initials inlaid in silver on the lid. She often stroked the smooth lid, tracing the initials with her finger, and thought with pleasure of the love that had gone into producing this beautiful object.

The day of their departure was dull and muggy, though a cooling breeze coming off the sea kept the temperature within bearable limits. A crowd of well-wishers, including Minnie, Clara and Dolly, gathered on the dock saying their farewells to the group of Italian officers. Last-minute gifts were showered on them, mostly items obtained on the black market: tins of Craven A or Senior Service cigarettes, packets of razor blades, biscuits, jars of humbugs, half-bottles of brandy, tins of Gibbs dentifrice, Hamam soap, Brylcreem, chewing gum.

Clara busied herself taking photos. 'Just look at them, Minnie, don't they look gorgeous!'

Minnie had to admit they did. Their crisp white uniforms showed off the deep tan on their faces and arms. She marvelled at how the Italians always managed to look as if they had stepped out of a fashion magazine, even in uniform.

'Come on, chaps, let's have a smile,' Clara called. 'Honestly, Minnie, they look as if they've come from a seaside holiday, not two years in a camp. What will their families think!'

Some of them may not have families to go back to, Minnie thought sombrely.

The ship's siren sounded. One by one the men said their last goodbyes. Cries of 'Don't forget to write', 'Give my love to Italy', *'Arrivederci, belle signore'*,

'Good luck, boys', '*Grazie di tutto* – thanks for everything' wafted to and from the gangway as they slowly boarded the ship. Paolo embraced Clara first, then Dolly, whose tears were flowing freely. Then he turned to Minnie and drew her aside.

She swallowed hard to release the lump in her throat and leaned into his arms where he held her for a long moment.

'*Carissima* Minnie, my beautiful friend.' She heard his voice as if it were coming through a fog. 'Words can't express what I feel. This is not farewell. We *shall* meet again. I know it. I will it.'

'Who knows what the future holds,' she murmured. 'Go with God, Paolo. I wish you luck. I wish you happiness.'

'Remember me, *carissima*, if you ever need a friend.'

He kissed her on both cheeks and then gently on the mouth. At last he drew away and stood before her, and she could see the sadness in his eyes. He straightened and raised her hand to his lips, murmuring the formal words of respect: '*bacio la mano*.'

The gangway was lowered. The siren gave a long blast, sending scavenging crows and seagulls flapping and squawking into the sky. As the tugs began pulling the ship away from the quay, the strumming of a mandolin wafted towards the waving crowd below. In the hush that followed a clear tenor voice rang out with the liquid notes of the Neapolitan song 'Torna a Surriento'.

The lovely melody with its poignant words filled Minnie with unbearable sadness. Tears held at bay until now spilled over and rolled unchecked down her cheeks. She felt a pang of longing, of homesickness so intense for her beautiful, wounded country that it left her breathless. The yearning to be back – to see the familiar sights, to see her parents, to hear the beloved language of her youth – overwhelmed her. Through the blur of tears, she made out Paolo's figure standing apart from the crowd at the prow of the ship, an arm raised high to her. Now she too raised her arm, biting her lips to stem the tears, until at last the song faded with the increasing distance, and the slowly turning ship slid Paolo away from sight. Lowering her arm, she stood still until the tears stopped and dried on her face. She watched long after the tugs released the ship and it boomed its final siren blast.

She had never felt so alone.

A few weeks later, Minnie detected a change in Darius's behaviour for the first time. She couldn't put her finger on exactly what was causing it. He appeared to be restless since returning from a journey with Satish Desai to photograph

Persian miniatures at the maharaja of Mysore's palace. Satish was a regular visitor at the house, frequently dropping in after office hours. He had a lively personality and developed a bantering, easy relationship with Darius, though he was more restrained with Minnie. She was used to seeing him around but often felt that his bouts of teasing went rather too far and wondered at Darius's tolerance.

They were still in the hall sorting out the baggage when Minnie greeted them. 'Will you stay for dinner?' she asked Satish.

'No, Minnie,' Darius interrupted before Satish could say anything. 'He's not staying for dinner.' He sounded grumpy. 'He's got to get on with the photo layouts. We can't waste any more time.' He turned to Satish. 'You don't mind, old boy, do you? I'll see you in the office in a couple of days,' he said and went through to his study.

Minnie was embarrassed at her husband's churlishness. 'Sorry, Satish, but do have a drink before you go.'

'It's okay, Minnie. He's right. We're both tired. I need to get home.'

At dinner Minnie asked Darius about his trip but he barely talked, saying only that it had been boring, and that he had been under the weather. After their meal they sat reading in the drawing room. He took up the newspaper, but a few moments later Minnie saw it drop to his lap while he stared vacantly into space.

'Darling, what's upsetting you. Is it Satish?'

Darius gave her a searching look. 'What do you mean?' he snapped.

'I was only asking, darling. I wondered if his photos hadn't come up to scratch. He seems rather inexperienced. No need to bite my head off.'

'Nothing like that, the photos were fine,' he said grumpily.

Minnie was taken aback by his abrupt reaction and made no reply. They sat in silence for a few minutes until Darius rose and said he wanted an early night.

He left the room, leaving Minnie to wonder what it was that had made him so moody.

He stayed in his bedroom for three days, saying he felt unwell. He wrote a bit, smoked a lot, played loud music on the gramophone, hardly ate. One morning he emerged dressed for the office, fresh and smiling, ordered the driver to bring the car round, had breakfast with Minnie and acted as if nothing had happened.

'Are you feeling well enough to go in to work today?' Minnie asked.

'Sure, darling. I'm fine. I was just tired, felt rather low, you know.' He shot a glance at her and smiled. 'It happens from time to time. I get low. You mustn't worry about it.'

But she did worry, because his dark moods became more frequent and lasted for longer periods each time. At last he was persuaded to see a doctor who diagnosed him as suffering from depression.

Dr Parmekar was a dapper little figure, bald and with a smooth, round face. Even in the hottest weather, he always wore a white Nehru jacket, its brass buttons embossed with an anchor, a reminder of his years in the navy.

'I've written out a prescription for a medication that has a calming effect,' Dr Parmekar said, handing it to Minnie when he joined her in the drawing room. 'Make sure he takes it regularly, particularly last thing at night. Also, he should avoid coffee and alcohol.' He hesitated before going on. 'He appears to be under considerable strain, dear lady. Is there anything I should know about, anything that might contribute to his state of mind?'

'Nothing special I can think of...' Minnie paused. 'He was upset at being turned down when he went to enlist, but that was years ago. Surely it couldn't be that?'

'One never knows with these things, dear lady. It may have undermined his confidence and he's brooded on it for too long. He needs to get away for a while.'

'But that's just it, Doctor. It is nearly always after he's been away on a business trip that he gets into one of these dark moods.'

'I see. He is a rather nervous type. I've known him a long time, you know. Perhaps these trips are putting him under too much pressure.' The doctor made some notes on a pad and slipped it into his case. 'See how he gets on, dear lady. If there is no improvement, he may need to see a psychiatrist.'

Minnie was horrified at the suggestion. It couldn't possibly come to that. She needed to confide in someone, like her lovely friend Barbara Davidson. But recently Barbara had her own worries on her mind.

Turmoil grew in the city week by week. In February 1946 sixty people were killed in Bombay when demonstrators set fire to grain warehouses, banks and shops. Then came news that the Indian Navy mutinied. The mood between the Hindus and Muslims in downtown areas became ugly and violent with bloody rioting occurring in cities all over India. There was talk of civil war.

The British began leaving India. It didn't strike Minnie how much more rapidly things were changing than she had expected until she and Barbara were talking about it over their weekly lunch meeting.

'I didn't want you to hear this from others, Minnie,' Barbara said over the meal. 'But the children and I will be going back to England soon.'

Minnie was stunned. 'Oh, Barbara, I can't believe it! But you will come back, won't you?'

'No, my dear, this will be for good. The children have to go to boarding school, and I need to sort things out for my parents.'

Minnie's eyes filled with tears. 'How soon?'

'As soon as we can get passage.'

'What about Tom? You can't leave him here alone for long. Too many women would throw themselves at him.'

They laughed.

'Don't I know it, so you'd better keep an eye on him for me, Minnie.' Barbara smiled. 'Don't mention this to anyone, because nothing is certain. But the chances are that Tom will be recalled to head office in London. He may be offered a seat on the board.'

'That's wonderful news.'

'Not a word, Minnie, mind you. It may not happen at all.'

'I wish you weren't leaving,' Minnie said with a sigh.

'Me too. I've loved India. But honestly, I think our time is up here. I'm not only suggesting Tom's time and mine. I mean the British. It's the end of an era, Minnie.'

With lunch over, they moved to the veranda for their coffee. 'You know what's been happening ever since Gandhi was in discussion with the British cabinet delegation in March.'

'You mean about forming a Federation of States?'

'That's right,' Barbara replied. 'But of course, it won't come off because that dreadful trouble-maker from the Muslim League, Mr Jinnah, wants complete separation from India.'

'I've met Jinnah,' Minnie said. 'I thought he was rather sweet.'

'He certainly has an eye for a pretty lady,' Barbara said. 'But sweet he is not. Tom says he is a real hard nut, quite intransigent. Tom thinks that as soon as there is independence the old British hands will be made to feel unwelcome. He reckons there will be a blood bath before then.' Barbara called the bearer to take the coffee tray away. 'I don't suppose you've thought of leaving, Minnie, have you?'

'No, of course not. How can I? Besides I don't think it will be as bad as you predict.'

'I suppose it's different for you. You're married to Darius, you'll be okay, though it will still be dangerous for a while. But what about the children?'

'What do you mean?'

'I mean their education. Have you thought about schools? Standards here are bound to drop. What about university studies further down the line?'

'I've not given it much thought. I'd supposed they would continue their studies here.'

'Well, do think about it. If there is any trouble or danger, you can always send them to me in England.'

'Oh, Barbara, what a wonderful thing to say.'

'I mean it, Minnie.'

'Yes, I know you do. Thank you. I may take you up on it.'

In the three months that followed Barbara's departure, Minnie missed her friend dreadfully. Life at home was not easy when Darius was unwell.

The children were made to keep quiet, they were prevented from doing things in the house, roller-skating on the veranda was stopped, they were sent to their friends' houses to play, and could only use the garden after five o'clock.

One afternoon, Minnie took the tea tray herself to Darius's room. He lay back in an armchair with eyes half closed as Minnie poured the tea.

'Here you are, darling,' she said, handing him a cup.

'There's no need for you to bring the tea, Minnie. It's the bearer's job to do that.'

'It's no trouble, sweetheart,' Minnie said, feeling a bit put out. 'There have been two phone calls for you,' she went on. 'I told them to call back after six.'

Darius did not respond, but Minnie ignored his silence. 'The children want to know if you'd like to come into their wigwam. They've built it near the *gul mohur* trees. You can see it from the window.'

Darius turned his head towards the trees with their mass of flame-coloured flowers. 'Pretty pathetic little effort that is. It's just a tablecloth and two poles!'

'Darius, how unkind! They tried their best without your help.'

Darius glanced at her and shrugged his shoulders.

He was often unkind to her at these times, saying things that hurt her feelings and made her feel rejected, although she was sure he did not mean them.

A few nights later a short poem appeared on her pillow. She knew from experience this was a signal that he was emerging from under the black cloud and had begun writing again. Similar poems had appeared in the past on her dressing table or her desk. They were always addressed to 'My Heartsflame' and consisted of anything from two lines to half a dozen verses. She treasured them all and hid them in the secret compartment of her rosewood box. Some of the poems moved her to tears, others made her smile, but a few made her feel uneasy.

Each time she forgave him the unhappiness and worry he had caused, so relieved was she to see him getting back to his normal self. She understood this was his way of telling her he was on the mend, that they could resume their relations as if nothing had happened. Yet each time it became more difficult for her to be easy and spontaneous with him. She feared she might say or do something that could trigger a flare-up of temper followed by yet more depression. She became guarded in what she said and how she behaved. But the emotional seesaw was wearing her down and gradually she felt a hardening of feelings towards him.

In August 1946, three days of bloody rioting in Calcutta followed a violent clash between Hindus and Muslims, with Hindus suffering the heaviest casualties. Thousands died after a demonstration during a day of action organised by the Muslim League calling for their own separate state of Pakistan.

Dolly phoned while Minnie was washing her hair. She wrapped her head in a towelling turban and held the receiver to her ear.

'Have you heard about Hirji Khan?' Dolly's voice sounded muffled against the thickness of Minnie's towel. *What on earth is Dolly phoning about at this time of the morning?* Minnie wondered with irritation.

'What about Hirji? He's supposed to partner Darius tomorrow,' she said. Hirji was a pleasant, jolly businessman of about fifty, a heavy cigar smoker and an excellent card player who often partnered Darius at bridge.

'Well, he won't. He's dead.' Dolly's subdued voice came to her as through a fog.

Minnie gasped. 'What happened?'

Dolly sounded close to tears. 'He was on the train from Calcutta to Delhi. It was stopped and set upon by Hindus.'

Minnie listened with growing horror as Dolly recounted the events. The Hindus acted with unspeakable savagery. They surrounded three Muslim carriages including one carrying women in purdah and children and slaughtered the lot. Hirji was in the next carriage and tried to escape but was hacked to death and his head cut off.'

Minnie shuddered with fear. 'But he wasn't even Muslim – he was a Parsi! How could they do such a dreadful thing?'

'They didn't care,' Dolly replied. 'He was in the wrong carriage at the wrong time, and he wore a beard. To them, that meant he was a Muslim.'

The news of this horrible, senseless killing chilled Minnie to the bone and for the first time she feared for her children's safety.

She remembered Barbara's offer and wrote to her.

38

1947

The S.S. *President Monroe* steamed slowly into the port of Naples on a glorious day in July 1947. Minnie and the children were positioned at the rails on the top deck. A pale wedge-shaped smudge tumbled away from the cindery roots of Mount Vesuvius towards the turquoise sea, widening steadily as the ship edged into the embracing arms of the dock. The smudge defined itself as buildings and houses, and soon they could make out streets, roofs and small matchstick figures. Claudia and Bobby hopped from foot to foot with excitement.

'Look at Mount Vesuvius, children,' Minnie said.

'Why is smoke coming out of the top?' Claudia asked.

'It's because it is a volcano.'

'What is a volcano?' Bobby asked.

'It's a mountain with a hole in the top,' Minnie answered. 'Sometimes it explodes and shoots out fire and flames high into the sky. Like a giant firework.'

'Is that going to happen today?' Bobby asked in alarm.

'I hope not. We don't want to be covered in ash, do we? You just watch the mountain carefully. Look, there's a bit of smoke coming out of the top like it does in a chimney. Can you see it?'

Bobby moved closer to Minnie and squinted into the sun looking for puffs rising from the mountain.

Claudia slipped her hand into Minnie's. 'Is Uncle Neddy going to meet us, Mum?'

'That's what he said, darling. Keep a sharp watch out for him.'

'But I don't know what he looks like.'

'He'll look a bit like your Uncle Franco.'

'And will your mamma and papa be with him?'

'I don't know. It's a long way for them to come. Remember to call your granny Nonna and your grandpa Nonno because they don't understand Grandma and Grandpa and try to say the phrases I've taught you in Italian.'

'How long since you've seen them, Mum?' Claudia asked.

'A long time, darling. Long before you were born.'

Minnie sighed, a lump forming in her throat. *This poor, beautiful city. What a pounding it took. Look at it – full of holes and gaps like a sock waiting to be darned. Will it ever be the same again?* Cutting across her thoughts came the first sounds of Neapolitan dialect from the stevedores on the quayside. Her eyes misted, and she blew into her hanky.

'There's a man waving to us, Mum,' Claudia said, tugging at her blouse.

Minnie looked down at the dock and saw the dapper figure of a man dressed in a light fawn suit waving a Panama hat. A lady stood next to him in a short-sleeved blue and white dress, a large straw bag hooked over her arm. *I don't remember him being so short.* She waved back, and the children copied her.

'That's your Uncle Neddy, and that must be Aunty Luisa standing next to him.'

'He doesn't look a bit like Uncle Franco,' Claudia observed. 'He's quite fat.'

The reunion on the dockside an hour later was highly emotional. Everyone kissed and hugged each other several times over. The children got their cheeks pinched and their faces and hair caressed, while incomprehensible compliments were showered over their heads. The grown-ups blew their noses a lot while Claudia and Bobby watched Minnie almost disappearing into the embrace of a funny little man with a big nose, smoky blue eyes and wavy black hair. 'Minnie *cara*,' he called in between planting noisy kisses on both cheeks. Minnie returned his kisses, wiped her eyes and laughed all at the same time.

Minnie couldn't remember later how they got away from the docks. The next thing she knew Neddy was herding them on to an ancient-looking coach with their many pieces of luggage piled on the roof. Every seat was taken, and all the passengers were talking at once. Many carried baskets of foodstuffs. One lady had a cage with two hens on her lap. The smell of garlic and salamis, tomatoes, grapes and sweaty bodies filled the coach. Minnie shut her eyes, remembering the familiar odours of her youth. *The country may have changed but the pungent aromas had not*, she thought, and slid open a couple of windows to let in some fresh air.

A great grinding of gears set the bus in motion. The skinny driver sat with a foul-smelling cigarette glued to his lip and his left hand welded to the horn. His right hand passed rapidly between steering wheel and gearshift as he manoeuvred the vehicle, stuttering and weaving, through crowded, potholed streets, past bombed-out houses, piles of rubble and into the chaotic and roaring stream of traffic. On reaching the outskirts of Naples, he finally unglued his hand from the horn, shifted down a gear, grasped the steering wheel with both hands and started the long, winding climb on the crowded highway to Rome.

Neddy had rented a large apartment for them in the same building he and Luisa lived in with his parents. Donna Rachele and Don Peppino were waiting on the pavement outside the entrance.

Minnie hugged Don Peppino, who clutched her closely as if he would never let her go. 'Minnie, Minnie *amore mio, che bello rivederti* – how wonderful to see you again,' he murmured again and again, while tears streamed into his grey moustache. 'How I've prayed for this moment.'

Then Minnie turned to her mother. The embrace they exchanged was the warmest that Minnie ever recalled. They were both crying. Donna Rachele kissed her daughter over and over. 'Minnie *quanto sei diventata bella* – how beautiful you have become,' she said.

'Mamma, you have remained the same,' Minnie said, caressing her face. 'Except for your hair. It suits you short, looks quite fashionable.' She stroked her mother's white hair, remembering when it had been honey blonde. Minnie felt a pull at her skirt. Claudia and Bobby looked up at her.

'Children, say hello to your grandmother like I taught you.'

'*Buon giorno, Nonna, come stai* – good day, Nonna, how are you,' they both chimed.

'*Ma come! Parlate italiano, che bravi,*' Donna Rachele said.

The children looked at Minnie. 'What did she say, Mummy?'

'She said how clever you were to talk Italian.'

'But that's all we know, except to say goodnight and goodbye and how'd-you-do!'

'Never mind, children, Nonna knows you'll soon pick up more words.'

As the days went by, it was obvious that Donna Rachele was not well, but age and illness had mellowed her. She was delighted to get to know her grandchildren, but this did not prevent her from criticising the familiarity they showed to their own mother.

'You have not taught them how to respect their elders,' she remarked to Minnie.

'Times have changed, Mamma,' Minnie replied gently. 'Other countries have different habits. It does not mean they do not respect me.'

'Now, now, Rachele, no criticising,' Don Peppino added. 'Remember your promise.'

Minnie heard his remarks with amazement. She had never known him to admonish her mother, however mildly. He seemed to be more animated than she remembered, less downtrodden.

'Tell me, Minnie *carissima*, what are the children saying?' he asked her. 'They keep asking me things, but I don't understand what they want.'

'They want to know if you can play cards with them. I told them you were good at *briscola* and *rumino*.'

'Now that *is* something I can teach them,' he said, and went to fetch the cards and gather the children about him.

It was a good time for catching up with family news. All past bitterness was put aside, and Minnie enjoyed getting to know Neddy's wife, Luisa, and their little girl, Anna.

'What news of Salvatore?' she asked her father the next day over lunch. 'When is he coming to visit?'

There was a brief silence as she observed her parents exchange glances. Donna Rachele pursed her lips and went to the kitchen to fetch the next course.

'He's well, I think,' Don Peppino said without enthusiasm. 'Your mother doesn't like to talk about him. After he joined the *partigiani* during the war he drifted away. He seldom sees or calls us. It's a shame, but that's how it is. And you heard that Aldo died?'

'Of course, Papa,' she replied gently. 'He died before Edoardo and I married.'

Don Peppino nodded. 'Was it that long ago?' he murmured.

Minnie stayed in Rome for six weeks through the heat of July and August. Although the children enjoyed most things about living in this city, there were certain aspects they found strange. Everywhere buildings, shop fronts and pavements seemed to be falling to pieces. At the market, while shopping for vegetables and fruit, Claudia couldn't take her eyes off a young girl about her own age dragging a wooden crate mounted on two tiny wheels. Inside the crate was a wailing baby.

'Look at that girl, Mum,' Claudia said, digging her elbow into Minnie's side. 'Why can't the baby be in a proper pram – no wonder it's bawling. Look at her dress, there are patches all over and they don't even match up.'

'Claudia, I won't have you making such remarks,' Minnie snapped, grabbing Claudia's arm. Her daughter gaped in astonishment. 'You have to understand, darling. People here are still terribly poor. There's been a dreadful war. They couldn't buy things like thread or material. Not even food sometimes.' They walked away from the little girl. 'You don't think they *want* to go around with crates for prams and patched dresses, do you? They haven't anything better.' She dragged Claudia by the hand. 'Don't stare.'

'But Nonna and Uncle Neddy don't wear patched clothes,' Claudia replied. 'And they have plenty to eat and have lovely things in their apartment, silver and paintings and carpets and all sorts.'

Minnie tightened her lips. 'Well, we won't go into how they managed to get all that now.' *There are always those who can do well out of others' misfortunes*, she thought.

Transport was difficult. There were no buses or trams near the apartment, and to get to the centre of town they needed to queue for a *camionetta*. This rather exotic name described the rickety, canvas-covered army surplus trucks used as buses, where passengers were shoved on like cattle – standing room only, of course – to endure a bumpy, smelly, stifling journey to their destination. It was terribly crowded, and one time Claudia whispered to Minnie that the man squashed up close behind her was pressing a hard lump into the small of her back and it quivered and twitched and made her feel funny. Minnie turned around and let loose a volley of furious words at the man who quickly edged away and got off at the next stop.

Despite all Minnie's stories about hardships in Italy none of them was prepared for the reality of the post-war situation. They had not expected to see so many beggars in the streets. Somehow it seemed worse than the beggars in India. Minnie understood her children's shock especially when they watched kids of their own age coming to blows over a fallen tomato or apple at the street market or seeing a woman in rags sitting on the pavement suckling a baby. Worse still was to watch grown men scramble and fight with these same children to retrieve a cigarette butt tossed into the gutter. Minnie herself was on the verge of tears to see a decently dressed man politely ask Neddy, when they were seated at a café, if he could have the contents of the ashtray on the table. Later, she noticed the same man selling five cigarettes made from the tobacco retrieved from the fag ends.

Sometimes Minnie caught Claudia and Bobby silently watching boys younger than themselves squatting to polish shoes for a customer seated at a café table. She saw how upset they were to witness children outside a butcher's shop fighting like dogs for scraps of meat set aside for them; how uncomfortable they felt to look at grown men going through rubbish bins, picking out tins or bottles, even retrieving bits of food; to see men in threadbare clothes sleeping on park benches; to see women and children gathered at kitchen doors of restaurants, waiting to be given leftovers.

What Minnie and the children did enjoy was going to the parks where they nearly always found a cart selling the most stupendously delicious ice creams. They watched puppet shows and went for donkey rides in Villa Borghese or swam at the huge open-air pool at the Foro Italico. They loved going to the cinema when Uncle Neddy got them free tickets. They enjoyed learning the card game *briscola* from Nonno or having a chocolate cake at Giolitti's.

'This is where I used to work,' Minnie told them. They loved eating out at restaurants at night, where men in colourful costumes strummed guitars and sang lovely songs. They were thrilled with their visit to St Peter's and insisted on going right up to the top of the cupola where they scared themselves silly by looking down at the ant-like figures far below.

The summer that year ended all too soon and the time came for Claudia and Bobby to say farewell to Nonna Rachele and Nonno Peppino.

It was time to pack their suitcases. To go to England.

It was time for boarding school.

39

They left from Rome Stazione Termini, which was still undergoing renovations, and changed trains at Milan, boarding the Thomas Cook Wagons-Lits bound for Calais. The children were thrilled to be able to walk up and down corridors from coach to coach, which they could never do on Indian trains. Minnie was glad they were keeping themselves amused, as she was feeling under the weather. She had not been quite herself since leaving the ship at Naples, having suffered considerable seasickness during the journey. In Rome, despite her mother's marvellous cooking, she often felt ill when presented with certain dishes, and looked forward to the plainer food she hoped to find in England.

And find it she did, but the plainer food in post-war England turned out to be, in some cases, awful. Her abiding impression of London was of being surrounded by the odour of stale boiled cabbage and fried sausages, which made her want to throw up. It pervaded their small family-run hotel off Sloane Square. Even when she tried to get away from it, the smell followed her down every street turning, every doorway they passed. Things improved later when they travelled down to Nettlebed in Oxfordshire to stay with Barbara Davidson. Here the countrified aromas of horses and hay were more tolerable.

Barbara, as usual, proved to be the best of friends. She accompanied Minnie and the children to visit their boarding school to meet the headmaster. Minnie wanted both children to be together, hoping they would feel less homesick than if they were at separate schools. Heathdown, near Reading, seemed to be the best suited. It was similar in its progressive outlook to Millfield, it was one of the few co-educational schools in the area and was located close to Barbara's home. The children were impressed with the grounds and facilities.

'Mum, it's even got a swimming pool,' Claudia said, full of enthusiasm. 'And when I get to senior school, I'll have a room all to myself.'

Bobby kicked a stone on to the velvet lawn as they walked back towards the car. 'But we aren't allowed to climb any of the trees,' he said with a sigh. 'And I'll be in a dorm with twelve beds, and I won't know *anyone*, Mum.' He scowled and slithered along the gravel path.

The next few days were spent buying all the unending necessities listed by the school. Minnie noticed that Claudia and Bobby did not appear quite as thrilled at the prospect of boarding as they had been at first. She guessed they were distressed because she was about to leave them in unknown territory. They quickly understood it was one thing to have English friends at school in India, but quite another to deal with the English on their home ground. They voiced their fears to Minnie.

'Well, it'll be strange for the first few days. But remember, you won't be the only new ones. The other children will be in the same boat. You will all be first-timers together.'

They were sitting on Minnie's bed, the children in their pyjamas, while Minnie was shortening the sleeves on Bobby's jacket. 'The other children will have to get used to the new surroundings, too, the same as you. You'll make friends in no time and then things will seem much easier, I promise you.'

Despite her assurances, there were tearful scenes between them, which left Minnie feeling wretched. She could not understand how English mothers managed to keep the famed stiff upper lip when parting with their sons and daughters, when she felt her heart breaking at the prospect. She promised to write once a week and to visit them as soon as she could.

'Remember, darlings, I love you more than anything. Even if I'm far away, I shall be thinking of you all the time. And I'm terribly proud you are being so brave about this.'

There were moments when she was filled with misgiving about her decision. She had chosen the boarding route with great reluctance. She admired many things about the British – their manners, their sense of fair play, and their civic responsibilities – and had complete faith in the English education system. That wasn't what concerned her. Her worry was how Claudia and Bobby would fit in, or not fit in. How would they be treated, she wondered, with an Italian surname and the war still fresh in people's minds? Children could be horribly cruel to those they considered outsiders. The knowledge that Barbara was close by and would have them stay for half-terms and the Christmas and Easter vacations was her one comforting thought.

Her depression and doubts were not helped by the fact she was not feeling well. Much of the English food was stodgy. She had put on weight and her clothes felt uncomfortable. *I must go on a diet as soon as I get back home.*

One day she felt so ill, she couldn't get out of bed. Barbara called the doctor.

'Well, Mrs Dubash,' he said after examining her, 'you have not got food poisoning, nor are you anaemic. You do not have any tropical illness. In fact, I congratulate you on being very healthy. I must also congratulate you,' he added with a smile, 'on being pregnant.'

'Pregnant?' Minnie was shocked. 'You must be joking, Doctor!'

'Indeed, I'm not, but the tests will confirm it, I'm sure.'

'I'm forty-three years old, Doctor. I cannot possibly be pregnant!'

But the results of the tests confirmed his diagnosis. At first, she could not get used to the idea. To be pregnant at her age, she felt, was unseemly. Besides, did she want another child? But she knew she did and hugged her happiness close to herself. She would wait to tell Darius the good news in person on her return. He had often said that he loved Claudia and Bobby as if they were his, but she was sure when he heard about his own child he was bound to be as delighted as she was.

The day came at last when she had to say goodbye to the children. First to Bobby, in his junior school dormitory where she helped him unpack. The dorm looked stark and clinical with pale green walls and two rows of six beds arranged on either side of the room. His narrow bed had a white cotton counterpane tautly drawn over a hard mattress and a thin pillow. 'Isn't this nice,' Minnie said with a bright smile, but in her heart, she couldn't help thinking how different this was from his bouncy, cosy bed at home. She helped him stow his possessions in a small bedside cabinet and hung his clothes in one of the tall metal lockers at the end of the room.

Other new boys were doing the same thing with their mothers, but at one point, for a few precious moments, the dormitory emptied, and Minnie found herself alone with Bobby. He pressed himself against her, his arms tight round her waist, his shoulders shaking with sobs.

'I don't want you to go, Mum. Please don't leave me.'

'My sweetest darling, I don't want to leave you. You know I must, though.' Her voice cracked with emotion as she held him close. 'But all the love in my heart will stay with you, right there,' she said, placing her hand over his heart. 'And every night before you fall asleep, you must imagine my arms hugging you tight, because that is what *I* shall imagine doing at the very same time. Our thoughts will be like two fingers touching on either side of a window pane.' She held a hanky out for him. 'Now dry your eyes, my darling, before the others come back – don't let them see you cry.'

Matron appeared shortly after to take the new boys to the refectory for tea. 'Don't worry, Mrs Farinelli, he'll soon settle in. But it might be best for you to leave while they are at tea.' Minnie wanted to correct her about the name, but let it slide.

Her last glimpse of Bobby was of his small figure in grey shorts and jacket, standing at the top of the stairs. He looked so different to most of his fair-haired companions, with his black hair, big dark eyes and tanned legs. He turned to wave, his face pale and solemn, his lower lip trembling. She blew him a kiss, watched him follow the other boys down the stairs until he was out of sight, then sat on his bed in the silent, empty dorm, and wept.

It was less traumatic parting from Claudia, who had made friends already with a couple of girls from abroad and was taking the goodbyes more in her stride.

'If there's anything you need, darling, or if you feel unhappy, write and tell me,' Minnie said while helping to unpack her trunk. 'I've given you Barbara's phone number for emergencies, and Matron has it as well.'

Claudia shed a few tears as they parted, and Minnie wiped her eyes. 'I'm proud of you, my pet, for being so brave,' Minnie said, hugging her close. 'Please keep an eye on Bobby for me; he was very upset when I left him.'

'Don't worry, Mummy, I'll look after him,' Claudia replied, pleased to be entrusted with this responsibility.

Minnie felt drained after the two farewells. Even now, as the boat train clacked its way past the oast houses and hop fields of the Kentish countryside, she felt blank and exhausted, unable to keep back the tears, unbelieving of how hard it was to leave her children behind.

She would miss braiding Claudia's long hair, feeling its silkiness through her fingers. She would miss slicking down Bobby's unruly mop with a wet comb, looking into his clear brown eyes with their long lashes, miss his gappy smile. A year seemed such a long time. It might even be longer with the new baby due. How would they react to the news of a brother or sister? These thoughts tumbled in her mind, like a dog chasing its tail. By the time she reached Rome, all she wanted was to get back home to Bombay as soon as possible.

She spent the remaining time with her mother and father. There was no doubt Donna Rachele was very ill, and she was admitted to hospital for kidney treatment. She was expected to stay for several weeks according to the doctor.

Minnie prepared for her departure with a heavy heart, knowing she was leaving her father in a state of high anxiety. She had not expected him to miss Donna Rachele as much as he did. He seemed bereft without her presence in the house, almost physically shrunken. Only when at her bedside did he appear to be his old self again, happy when his wife chided or bossed him, which she now did in such a restrained and gentle way that Minnie hardly recognised her mother for the hard, strong woman of the past.

On the last day they said their goodbyes. Sitting on the edge of her mother's bed, Minnie was overcome by how tender and affectionate Donna Rachele was with her.

'You have brought up your children very well, *cara* Minnie,' Donna Rachele said, patting her knee. 'They are a real credit to you. And you have done wonders with your looks, very attractive. Your hair is much nicer than I remember it.' They laughed, recalling how often Donna Rachele had criticised her daughter's wild hair. 'I know you will miss the children, but I'm sure this next one will make you very happy.'

Minnie flushed. 'How did you know, Mamma? I haven't told a soul.'

'After five children, I know all the signs, my dear. Does your husband know?'

'Not yet. I wanted to wait until we were alone. Don't tell Neddy or Luisa. I want Darius to know first.'

'I won't mention a thing. But please tell your father, it will cheer him up.' She caught Minnie's hand and held it. 'Tell Neddy to look after Papa for me, he looks so miserable.'

'Mamma, nobody can do it like you. You can look after him yourself when you get home.'

'Who knows when that will be. We shall see.' Donna Rachele sighed, shrugging her shoulders. For a moment her eyes swam. 'Have a good journey, *cara*, and take care of yourself. Write to us when you arrive.' She wiped her eyes. 'Now plump up the pillows for me, they've become lumpy. And on your way out tell the young duty nurse that the pasta at lunchtime was overcooked – quite inedible.'

As she left the ward, Minnie looked back at her mother lying against her pillows, her face lined with pain. They held each other's gaze. She wondered how this small innocuous-looking woman with her cropped white hair could have put so much fear into her and her brothers all those years ago.

Minnie blew a kiss and tears welled in her eyes as she realised with sudden clarity this would be the last time she would see her mother.

40

A couple of days after leaving Naples, Minnie's despondent mood changed, and she let the joy of the pregnancy take over. The journey through the Suez Canal was uneventful and the Arabian Sea calm; Minnie slept a lot, read a lot and relaxed. Ten days later, on a steamy October afternoon, the ship docked at Ballard Pier and Darius came bounding on board to meet her with his arms full of roses. Happiness overwhelmed her as they kissed, and she wanted to tell him the good news straight away. But that could wait until they were alone, and meanwhile she recounted what she had done and seen on her trip.

'Darling, it's awfully good to have you back home,' Darius said, putting his arms around her when they reached the privacy of their bedroom. He nuzzled her neck. 'I think you've put on a bit of weight, my love. All the good food on the ship, no doubt. Never mind, it'll soon come off in this heat.'

Had he guessed? Should she tell him now? No, the moment wasn't right; she would wait for the following day.

Darius released her and lit a cigarette. 'I know you must be exhausted by this heat. Why don't you have a relaxing bath? I'll get cook to make you a light supper and afterwards you should get an early night.'

'That sounds marvellous – just what I need. Will you eat with me?'

'No, I'll have dinner later. Satish is dropping in.'

'Darling, did you have to ask him here on my first night back? I thought we'd have a bit of time alone together.'

'He's coming with me to Kolhapur to photograph a temple. We have an early start in the morning.'

'Oh, Darius, don't tell me you're going off tomorrow,' Minnie wailed.

'Sorry, darling, it cropped up at the last minute. I tried phoning you on board but couldn't get through. It's only for three or four days, and then we can catch up on all our news.'

Minnie hid her disappointment; she knew better than to argue when he was in one of his stubborn moods. After all, three or four days would speed by, and she could unpack at leisure and wait for a more relaxed atmosphere to tell him about the baby. But after Darius's departure early next morning, Minnie felt let down and restless. She missed the children more than ever, and the house seemed empty without them. She couldn't settle to anything, and the sultry heat was getting her down. She longed to float in cool water but didn't want to swim at the club's pool where her pregnancy might be noticed. The beach seemed the perfect solution; just what she needed to unwind until Darius's return.

Years earlier Darius had bought a plot of land at Juhu, in a coconut grove by the sea with a decrepit-looking shack on it. Over the years he had improved the shack until it was comfortable, though still rather primitive. They often used it for Sunday lunch parties. The children adored going there for long weekends and half-terms. Apart from the attraction of trying to climb the coconut trees, another magnet of interest for them was to see if the on-site caretaker's black pigs had produced any more piglets.

For Minnie, the best part of all was to wake up before sunrise and walk along the almost deserted beach; to feel the newly washed sand cold under her bare feet; to observe the fishermen from the nearby village rhythmically heave in their net and tip its gleaming, silvery catch into the baskets held by the waiting womenfolk, then watch as each one trotted off towards the village, balancing the heavy basket on her head.

She left in the late afternoon the next day, driving the twenty miles slowly to avoid potholes in the roads, and thinking she would need to have some maternity clothes made soon as everything was now too tight around the waist and her breasts were swollen and sore. She must make an appointment with the gynaecologist as soon as possible, she thought, as she swung the car along the rutted path snaking through the coconut grove towards the beach house. It was blissfully peaceful. The wind sighing through the palm leaves echoed the distant swish of waves from the outgoing tide. The sun was starting to dip below the horizon and in no time at all it would be dark.

As she parked the car, she thought it strange the caretaker was not around. She frowned, noticing that the windows and the back door leading to the kitchen were open, but no lights showed and there was no sign of life. She entered the kitchen and walked through to the front terrace. The cane furniture was laid out, which meant somebody was using the place. A rustling sound came from one of the bedrooms. Feeling a little frightened, she tiptoed to the room and edged the door open.

Silhouetted against the window, in the waning purple dusk, she made out two tall, naked figures tightly entwined. There were glimpses of long, muscular limbs moving and rippling. Large hands gripping firm buttocks. Flat chests, broad shoulders. Then one of the figures slid down to kneel in front of the other. The last shreds of twilight fell on their faces as they turned their heads this way and that, breathing heavily, eyes glazed, blind to their surroundings.

Recognition and shock hit Minnie like a fist in the stomach. She staggered backwards, clasping her hand to her mouth, turned and lurched from the room, through the kitchen and out of the house. Her eyes would not focus. A drumming filled her head, deafening her ears; her legs felt like jelly. She stumbled towards the car and leaned her forehead against the cool metal, then bent over and retched on to the sand. Her clammy hands slipped on the door handle before she could tug it open and get behind the wheel. Taking deep, rasping breaths, she sat for several moments trying to regain control of her emotions. She felt unreal, as if her mind were floating on a different plane to her body.

When the pounding in her heart slowed, a numbing disbelief took over. Her hands shook as she twisted the ignition key and pushed the starter button. The engine turned over on the first try and she switched on the headlights. The brief Indian twilight had given way to inky night. Turning the car round, she grazed the rear bumper against a tree trunk, and then jolted down the sandy path twisting between the palms until she reached the tarmac road two hundred yards away. Her actions were automatic. Changing gear, she stepped on the accelerator and sped down the empty road towards the highway a mile away.

The scene she had witnessed seemed to be imprinted like a photograph at the back of her eyes: Satish and Darius – her beautiful Darius – entwined, oblivious to anything but each other.

She blinked rapidly. When her eyes cleared, she made out a large, stationary shape looming in the headlights in the middle of the road, chewing cud and staring at her. She jerked the wheel round, slamming on the brakes. The car skidded side on into the cow with a horrible thud, swerved across the road on to the verge and crashed into a culvert. The impact threw Minnie forward. The top of her head cracked on to the rear-view mirror, her body slammed into the steering wheel. A searing pain shot through her arm.

Then the world blacked out.

Later, Minnie thought she heard the distant sound of bells ringing and muffled voices; felt herself being lifted. Later still, she sensed the smoothness of a sheet under her right hand, a leaden weight on her left arm; she heard the rhythmic drone of a fan. She tried to open her glued-down eyelids, heard a voice say, 'Can you hear me, Mrs Dubash? You're alright, dear, take it easy.' Her legs felt heavy. The side of her head throbbed and ached.

Yet later, there was another voice. Somebody sat on the bed, taking her wrist in two fingers. She half opened her eyes and saw a two-headed man with two mouths, two noses, two pairs of spectacles and several eyes. He was talking to her. His faraway voice was kind, but the sound of his words came and went like waves crashing and ebbing on sand.

'You had a nasty accident, Mrs Dubash. Fortunately, there are no serious injuries. It could have been a lot worse. We've put a few stitches in your head. And you have a dislocated shoulder.' He paused and stroked her hand. 'But I'm afraid you lost the baby.'

Minnie stared at his two wavering heads for a long moment, then slowly shut her eyes and turned her face into the pillow.

The vision of Darius and Satish together flashed inescapably across the screen of her mind.

41

1947–48

The slowly turning overhead fan was the first thing Minnie saw when she woke the next day. She felt dizzy and her head ached. Her left arm hurt, and her stomach was sore. The room was completely white, with bamboo blinds shading the windows. A strong smell of Dettol pervaded the air. She could hear children in a playground outside, chattering in Hindi. Hindi was also being spoken in the corridor outside her room. Her eyelids drooped. A hand touched hers. Opening her eyes, she saw Dolly sitting beside the bed.

'How long have you been here, Dolly?' Minnie's words were slurred.

'A while, sweetie.' Dolly stroked Minnie's hand. 'Are you in pain?'

Minnie nodded. 'My head hurts.' She could feel it was bandaged.

'What happened? Do you want to tell me?'

'It was dark. I hit something. I don't know what.' Minnie shut her eyes. 'Where am I?'

'This is Santacruz hospital. What were you doing in this area?' Dolly asked.

'I wanted…to get away,' she whispered, 'to have a few days on my own. I went to the beach house at Juhu. I couldn't get in.' The lie came automatically.

'Darling, you should have told me, I'd have come with you,' Dolly said. 'Anyway, it was dangerous to drive back in the dark on those rough roads. See what happened!'

Minnie ignored the reprimand. She tried to move her left arm and winced with pain. Licking her dry lips, she turned her head towards the water jug. Dolly poured a glass and helped her to drink.

'Have you spoken to the doctor, Dolly?'

'Yes. He described your injuries. I tried to get in touch with Darius right away but was told he was in Kolhapur. I phoned the hotel there, but they said he wasn't booked in.' Dolly took out a hanky from her bag and mopped little trickles of sweat from Minnie's neck. 'I've told Jeevan, the driver, to find Darius and tell him to come as soon as he can.'

'No, Dolly. Please. I don't want Darius here!' Minnie gripped Dolly's hand, anxiety filling her.

'Why ever not, darling?'

'I don't want to see him. He mustn't come here.' Minnie struggled to sit upright, her eyes wide with alarm. The effort sent stabbing pains through her head. She lay back, breathless.

'Very well,' said a surprised Dolly. 'If that's what you want, you'll see him at home after you get discharged.'

Minnie started to weep. 'I don't want to go home,' her voice rose. 'I can't go home. *Please*, Dolly, can't I come and stay with you?' she pleaded in desperation.

Dolly sat on the edge of the bed and put her arm round Minnie. 'Sure you can, darling,' Dolly said. 'Why didn't I think of it. What with your shoulder and your poor old head, how on earth would you manage!' She prattled on with placating words as Minnie wiped her eyes. 'Let me phone the house to prepare the guest room for you.'

A doctor entered before Dolly could leave. He stood at Minnie's bedside and looked at her chart. 'Good morning, I am Dr Mehta. How are you feeling now, Mrs Dubash? Did you get any rest?' he asked in a singsong voice, coming around the bed to take her pulse.

Minnie nodded.

'I am advising sleep is best for you. Kindly limit your visitors until evening time,' he continued, then looked pointedly at Dolly. 'Has her husband been told?'

'Doctor, her husband is away,' Dolly replied. 'I am her sister-in-law and she will be coming to stay with me when she is discharged.'

'I'm most happy to hear that, madam.' He put a thermometer under Minnie's tongue. 'She will need plenty of care. Poor lady had a terrible shock. She will be much distraught at losing the baby.'

'Baby? Wh…wh…what baby?' Surprise made Dolly sound uncomprehending. 'She wasn't expecting a baby. Was she?'

'Indeed to goodness, she was. Beg pardon, I was not aware you did not know of her condition. As you are related, I was simply assuming…' His voice trailed off. 'Well, in truth, she was more than four months gone. Her husband should be informed.'

Dolly shook her head. 'Yes, yes, of course. I wonder why he didn't tell us. None of us knew she was pregnant. How dreadful, poor thing.'

'Yes, indeed.' The doctor seemed uncomfortable. He removed the thermometer and read it, before shaking it down. 'Please excuse me now, I have rounds to make.' He patted Minnie's hand, smiling. 'Get plenty of rest, Mrs Dubash. I will come again this evening, never fear. If you are needing anything at all, dear lady, simply ring for the nurse just outside.'

He waggled his head at Dolly and left the room. Dolly turned to face Minnie. They gazed at each other in silence. A drop trickled down Minnie's cheek. Dolly put her arms round Minnie, gently rocking her to and fro.

Minnie wept, her shoulders heaving with sobs. She tried to blank out the flashes of Darius's face she saw through the tears. She might have been able to forgive Darius's infidelity with another woman. She could have defended herself in that situation. But not this – not this rejection of her as a woman; this betrayal of the most vulnerable part of herself; the unconditional love she had given him. She felt cheated. Above all she wept for the baby she had lost. She would never know if it had been a boy or a girl. She would never feel it in her arms, at her breast, its cheek against hers, its tiny hand grasping her finger.

Sadness engulfed her like a wave, and she wondered if it were possible to die of such aching grief.

She became aware of Dolly's murmurings as they clung together. 'I'm so, so sorry, my darling girl. I had no idea. No idea at all. Darius never told us a thing.'

'Darius didn't know,' Minnie snuffled. 'You mustn't tell him, Dolly. Please promise me you won't tell him.'

'Why not?' Dolly asked, puzzled. 'Why don't you want to see him?'

Minnie shook her head, brushed away her tears and wiped her nose with the back of her hand. Dolly handed her another hanky. 'I can't tell you,' Minnie said. 'Not now, please. Just keep him away. But I'd like to see Sister Serafina. Could you arrange that?'

'Of course – I'll call her when you're back at my place.'

Two days later, Minnie was comfortably settled in the guest suite at Dolly and Jimmy's house. It consisted of a bedroom and a sitting room with high raftered ceilings. The furnishings were green and white chintz on covers and curtains. White louvred shutters kept the rooms shaded from the fierce outside glare. A dressing room and a large white tiled bathroom completed the suite.

Minnie slept a lot and ate little. She was grateful for Dolly's help in getting dressed. Certain things were hard to do with her left arm strapped to her chest.

'Darius is back, darling,' Dolly told Minnie a day or two later while buttoning the back of her pink cotton blouse. 'He wants to see you.'

'No, I'm not ready for that,' Minnie replied firmly.

'But, sweetie, people are starting to talk. Why don't you want to see him?' Dolly paused. 'Tell me, dear, did you meet someone else in Italy? Is that it?'

'Oh, Dolly, don't be ridiculous.' Minnie gave a bitter laugh and picked up a hairbrush to put through her hair.

'What am I to tell Darius? I've made umpteen excuses, but he doesn't understand why he can't see you.'

Minnie frowned, putting down the brush. Unhappiness dulled her eyes. 'I can't face him just yet,' she sighed. 'I want to talk to Jimmy first. Alone, if you don't mind, Dolly.'

Jimmy came to see her before lunch. Minnie started by stating point blank that she wanted a divorce from Darius. She noticed his astonishment at this announcement. Little by little she told him the whole story. She spoke of Darius's violent mood changes, his physical treatment of her in the past, how she had tolerated and forgiven time and again because of her love for him.

With elbow leaning on the arm of the sofa and chin cupped in his hand, Jimmy listened to her in sombre silence until she had finished.

'Minnie dear, I am so sorry to hear all this,' he said at last. 'But all marriages go through troubled times. Surely you can patch things up. Would you like me to have a word with him?'

'Absolutely not,' Minnie said vehemently. 'It's gone beyond patching up.'

'What then? Has he been having an affair with another woman?'

Minnie said nothing. If only it were that simple.

Reluctantly, she told him how she had found Darius and Satish together. Jimmy's raised eyebrows in an otherwise expressionless face led Minnie to think that he already knew.

'Did you know about them?' she asked bluntly.

'No, I did not.' His denial was hesitant.

'But you suspected it, I feel.'

'Not with Satish,' Jimmy admitted. He seemed to be searching for the right words. 'Darius was involved in a similar situation once before. Many years ago. It occurred in Cambridge, and he was sent down because of it.'

'Oh my God!' Minnie groaned. 'Now I understand. But why didn't you tell me this before? You had no right to keep it from me.' She was deeply angry now.

'It was a one-off incident. He swore he was not homosexual – it was simply one experience while under the influence of drinks or drugs. He said it would never happen again.'

'Did Dolly and Clara know? Oh God!' Minnie went cold as a thought occurred to her. 'Did Roshan know? Am I the only one who didn't?'

'Not at all,' Jimmy reassured her. 'I promise you. No one knows. It had to be kept quiet. *They* think he was sent down for gambling and drinking.'

'All the same, Jimmy, you should have told me,' Minnie said bitterly.

Jimmy looked at her with compassion before replying. 'Would you have believed me, darling?' His voice was gentle. 'He loves you,' Jimmy continued. 'I know he loves you deeply, but…'

'But he's attracted to men too. Is that what you mean?' Minnie added.

Jimmy gave a silent nod. 'Do you love him still?' he asked.

Minnie's eyes moistened. 'I've loved him more than anything. I don't know what I feel now. You can't turn love on and off like a tap. But honestly, I don't think I can handle this. I can't bear the thought of what he has done, of what he is. I feel so betrayed. I don't see a way out of it except divorce.'

Jimmy stood up and poured himself a Scotch and soda from the tray the bearer had left on the side table. 'Darling, don't start down that road if you can avoid it. Not yet. Divorce would be a huge scandal, for you and for the family. All the dirty linen being washed in public. Too many repercussions.'

Minnie's temper flared. 'Is that *all* that concerns you? How it would affect the Dubash family?'

'Not only us, dear girl,' Jimmy replied, looking at her with a steady gaze. 'It will affect you as well. Most particularly you.'

'What do you mean?'

Jimmy took a sip of the Scotch and drew a chair up in front of Minnie. 'First of all, how could you prove the allegation? You'd need to employ somebody to report on his movements, interview servants and all that. Rather sordid, don't you think? Do you want that?'

Minnie remained silent.

'Besides, he would deny it all. It would be your word against his and people would be bound to believe *him* and not you.'

'Why would they do that?' Minnie asked, surprised.

'Because of who he is. Because he has powerful family connections.'

'But I have friends who would be supportive. They'd believe me.'

'Would they?' Jimmy rose and walked to the window.

Minnie followed him with her eyes. A thought occurred to her. 'You would support me, wouldn't you?'

Jimmy sighed and walked back to the chair. 'Darling, much as I love you, I'd prefer to sit this one out. I really don't want to take sides. I'm sure you understand.'

His words jolted her. She had not expected this reaction. She said nothing, waiting for him to go on.

'I'm trying to play devil's advocate,' he continued, 'so that you are aware of difficulties that could arise. You would need good legal advice, but I'm sure what I say will be confirmed. At present, all doors, socially speaking, are open to you because you're married to Darius. That would not be the case if you divorced. Besides, he could, in all probability, contest allegations and imply the baby you lost was not his. After all, you didn't tell anyone you were pregnant, and you *were* away for a long time in Europe. If he did, it would have serious financial implications for you.'

Minnie looked shocked. 'But that's not true and it's terribly unfair!'

Jimmy rose and went to sit next to Minnie. 'Yes, it is unfair, but unfortunately that's how things are.' He took her hand. 'My advice is to be cautious, talk things through with Darius. Calmly. Perhaps see if you can come to terms with the situation. Suggest an amicable trial separation. But don't be intransigent and do not do anything in haste.'

After he left, Minnie tried to evaluate the situation dispassionately but found she couldn't be impartial enough. Her hurt bled like an open wound and anger glowed like a furnace. She wanted to scream and cry, revile Satish and rage at the injustice of the whole business. Her world had been turned upside down. She felt robbed and cheated of something precious and she wanted vengeance.

She wanted to hurt Darius as much as he had hurt her. The only way she could think of achieving this – in spite of Jimmy's practical advice – was to create an almighty scandal, shaming Darius in the eyes of Bombay society.

Sister Serafina came to visit her again that afternoon. She sat silently, hands folded under her grey tabard, listening to Minnie's outpourings of grief and anger. Twice Minnie saw her make the sign of the cross, her lips moving in silent prayer. She knew this good woman was praying for Darius and the soul of her lost child.

'I don't know what to do, Serafina,' Minnie said. 'I want to go to sleep and wake up and find that none of this has happened. But I cannot sleep, I am too full of anger and sadness.'

'*Carissima* Maria Erminia, my dearest friend,' Sister Serafina said, removing her hands from under the tabard and touching the black cross that hung round her neck. 'What has happened to you is terrible. You have been deeply wounded, and it is only natural you should feel such anger. But anger will not do you any good, it is a destructive force.'

Sister Serafina leaned forward and gently touched Minnie's face.

'God is with you and with His help you must learn to forgive. Through the power of prayer, you will be able to put the past behind you. I imagine you want vengeance. But Darius is still your husband, and remember that you loved him deeply once, perhaps still do. For the memory of that love, even though he has wronged you, you should try to forgive him. If you seek to destroy him, you will only destroy yourself. With God's help you will find the strength to overcome this. I will pray for you, my dearest friend.'

She rose to take her leave and embraced Minnie.

'Tomorrow we will say a mass for the soul of the little lost one,' she said gently before leaving the room.

Minnie spent a sleepless night, lying down, getting up, pacing the length of the room, unable to settle. The bedside light cast long shadows in the corners of the room. A gecko scurried up a wall. She lit an incense stick to keep away the moths that were attracted by the light. Her thoughts rattled around in her head like dice in a shaker. She mulled over the words of advice she had heard that day. Her friend in troubled times, the inner voice of caution and wisdom, prodded her like an insistent finger: *Slow down*, it said. *Clear your head. Think of your children. Think without anger.*

Pragmatism came as the night sky lightened to pearl grey. Leaning out of the window she gazed at the waking city far below, at the hazy twinkle of lights curving along the Queen's Necklace. The night scent of jasmine filled the room.

The screech of a peacock drew her attention. She waited, watched it emerge on to the lawn below, strutting slowly from the shadow of the trees and out of the dawn mist.

She rubbed her tired eyes. Jimmy was right: she had more to lose than to gain by creating a scandal.

Drawing a deep breath, she realised she would have to meet Darius.

Darius came to see her that afternoon. It was a meeting full of tension, both acting like boxers circling each other in a ring. Despite her resolve to be objective, Minnie was outwardly stiff and cold. *How can he not have changed?* she thought, looking at him. She felt herself to be a different person to the one she had been four days earlier. He, on the other hand, seemed the same, not a single line more on his forehead or a grey hair on his head, with the same sweet smile, the same intense, melting eyes. If she wasn't careful, she could let herself be seduced again by his charm.

And yet this time something had altered in her. The steel strand of her love had not quite ruptured, but it was severely weakened.

Darius was nervous and seemed not to know how to start the conversation. He was upset to see her arm strapped up, and tried to touch it in sympathy, but she flinched away from him. He sat in the armchair opposite hers, leaning forward.

'Oh, Minnie, sweetheart, what have you done? You're hurt – how did it happen? Why have you kept me waiting for two days?'

'I think you know why, Darius,' her voice was even but distant.

'I don't understand you at all, Minnie. Tell me what has happened to you? What is happening to *us*?'

She couldn't believe what she was hearing. He appeared genuinely not to know. She couldn't tell if he was pretending or not. Jimmy would not have betrayed her confidence to him. This made it more difficult for her to tell him.

'I had an accident. I crashed the car.'

'When? How did it happen?'

'Dolly told me, but when?'

'It was in the evening after you left for Kolhapur with…Satish.' She could barely bring herself to utter the name she hated. 'I had some good news for you. I'd been trying to tell you it ever since I got back from Italy but didn't have a chance.'

'What good news?'

'That I was expecting a baby.'

'Oh, Minnie.' His eyes lit up. He looked at her hopefully, but she continued sharply before he could say anything else.

'I wanted time to myself, to think. I thought I'd go to the beach house at Juhu for a day or two.'

Darius sank back heavily, the blood draining from his face. 'And did you go?'

'Yes, Darius. I went. I thought Dolly and Jimmy were there. But it was you I saw. You with Satish. I thought he saw me. Didn't he tell you?' She shut her eyes. 'I don't much remember the accident. I'm told I hit something. A cow, I think.'

'Oh, Minnie!' Putting his elbows on his knees, Darius buried his head in his hands. 'I never meant this to happen. Never meant to hurt you.'

His muffled voice reached her but she barely paid attention to his words.

'I lost the baby, Darius.' Her voice was expressionless.

'Dear God!' He lifted his head to look at her, his eyes glistening, misery etching deep lines around his mouth. 'I am so, so sorry.'

They fell silent, withdrawing into their protective shells, strangers to each other. At last, Darius rose. Walking to the window, he looked out across the rooftops for a few moments.

'There is nothing I can say that will make you feel better,' he said quietly, turning to face her. 'I can only tell you how things are. What I am. A long time ago, in my late teens, I discovered that I am attracted – physically attracted – to particular types of people. Usually to women, but occasionally also to young men. It has nothing to do with emotions or love. My first sexual experience was with a girl who seemed a real tomboy, slim and wiry, with hardly any breasts, no hips, smooth long legs and neat, firm buttocks. She looked, and most often acted, like a boy. There was no emotion involved,' he repeated. 'It was purely sexual. Since then that type has attracted me. There were many young men like that at Cambridge. Did Jimmy never mention what happened there, the reason I was sent down?'

He fell silent, turning to stare out of the window before facing her again, hands clasped behind his back. 'All that changed when I met you. You were the complete opposite physically and yet the desire I felt for you was more powerful because my feelings, my heart, my emotions were totally involved. You bewitched my senses. What I felt for you, and what I still feel, is stronger than anything I've experienced for anyone else.' He paused, moved away from the window and paced the room. 'You bring out the best in me. You give me confidence. You make me believe in myself. You stir my imagination. Through you my creativity flourishes. The thought of losing you makes me panic. You are the stability in my life, my anchor, my inspiration, the flame that keeps my heart warm.' He stopped and looked steadily into her eyes. 'I know that I have hurt you deeply, for which I am sorry beyond the expression of words.' He paused, looking sad. 'I also know that I might do it again.'

He drew up a chair next to Minnie and sat, looking at her for a sign, a reaction, but she remained as still as a statue, her eyes firmly fixed on him.

'I cannot promise a similar situation will not occur in the future,' Darius continued. 'I don't seem able to control it. I do not love Satish, but I am attracted to him. If not to him, it may well be somebody like him in the future. I should have told you ages ago, but I took a chance it would not be necessary.'

Once again, he paused and leaned forward before continuing. 'I've put my cards on the table, Minnie. I am trying to be as honest as I can with you. I am deeply, deeply sorry for what has happened, and for how you found out. I don't want to lose you. I love you with all my heart and always will. But it is up to you. The question is: can you forgive me? Can you accept the situation? Can you live with it?'

She did not answer immediately. He tried again to touch her injured arm, but she drew back.

He seemed genuinely contrite, she thought. Since she had loved him so passionately, she knew she ought to feel more forgiving, and rise above this shocking discovery. She appreciated his honesty, knowing how much it must have cost him to speak this frankly.

But it was too late now. Things had changed irrevocably. The thread of trust had snapped. A numbing sadness and anger pervaded her soul. It was difficult to think clearly. Her head throbbed. His closeness confused her, almost repelled her. The grief she felt for the loss of her baby prevented rational thought. What she wanted more than anything was for Darius to leave her alone, so she could think things through. She began to cry.

'I don't believe I *can* forgive you, Darius. I can hardly think straight. You are asking me to accept the situation, to live with it. No, I cannot. It is too much for me to bear. I feel the only solution is a divorce.'

She lifted her head and wiped her nose with a hanky. She saw the fear in his eyes.

'No, please, my Minnie, not a divorce. I beg you. Can't we work something out? Talk things through?'

Minnie did not reply straight away. 'I am in no condition to talk this through at present,' she said at last, meeting his anxious look. 'You must understand that. I need time. I want us to live separately for a trial period. At the end of that time we can talk again. That's the best I can do.'

'How long a period?'

'I'd say a year. Perhaps more.'

Darius came and put his arms around her gently. Minnie kept herself rigid.

'As you wish,' he whispered with a choking voice. He bent to kiss her on the forehead. 'I'll make the necessary arrangements.'

42

1949

The year's trial separation did not bring about their reconciliation. Minnie realised Darius did not want a divorce, and that he was prepared to go to considerable lengths to prevent a complete break. Minnie did not press for one and they agreed to a formal, legal separation.

She continued to live in their house while Darius went to live with his sister. The amount of alimony Darius settled on her was adequate rather than generous. Minnie recognised too late that the solicitor acting for her was not prepared to get on the wrong side of the powerful Dubash clan. As a result, he had not pushed for the best deal. But her pride would not let her fight for more. She determined that her business would provide her with a living and threw herself wholeheartedly into making a go of it.

Because of the children, she was in regular correspondence with Edoardo, who had established a business in Calcutta. His latest letter contained a surprise.

Calcutta, 12 February 1949

Dear Minnie,

Thanks for your letter and the photos of the children.

I was sorry to hear about the difficulties between you and Darius. I cannot say it came as a complete surprise. Darius is the most charming chap, but he has a wild and unstable streak in him, which must be difficult to handle. I hope for your sake that a reconciliation will occur, if that is what you desire.

Let me tell you the latest from this end. City life has been tense here since Mahatma Gandhi's assassination a year or so ago. Street riots occur in all areas and at times it is unsafe to drive into the city. The rioters do not discriminate whether one is a Muslim or Hindu or a European, and one does not go out at all at night.

However, the good news is that I have opened a new office here. And secondly, the reason I am writing is to let you know that I am engaged to be married. My fiancée is a Hungarian refugee called Floriana Sándor. She and her husband had a dreadful time escaping from Hungary during the war, finally ending up in India at a camp in Dehra Dun where her husband died of dysentery. I have known her for several months and we plan to marry in May.

That's all my news. I'm sorry I can't send you the maintenance this month for the children, but things are tight here at present. I will send it as soon as I can and meanwhile enclose a postal order for twenty rupees. Please put ten each into Claudia's and Roberto's piggy banks. I hope matters will improve by next month.

So long for now.

Affectionately,
Edoardo

Minnie's relationship with Darius improved insofar as it was a polite and civilised one. He seemed pleased to see her if they bumped into each other on social occasions and acted with his usual courtesy. Occasionally he would drop in on Minnie at home, or invite her for coffee at Bombelli's or the Taj.

Her social life began to change, as Jimmy had predicted. She was grateful that her closeness to Dolly and Jimmy gave her some protection. Doors were still open to her because of the Dubash connection and there was no doubt it helped in her business dealings. However, it soon became apparent she was no longer invited to certain parties and functions, to which previously she would have had an automatic entrée. Many of her and Darius's friends took his side after their split and dropped her socially. One or two openly ostracised her. She became more discerning in choosing her friends, but at the same time she learnt to become diplomatic and pragmatic.

The children were Minnie's greatest pleasure and she looked forward to them flying out for the summer holidays that year. They would stay with her for a month before going on to visit Edoardo and Floriana in Calcutta.

On their return from Calcutta in mid-August, it was time for Minnie to take them back to school in England. They stopped off in Rome for three weeks to visit Neddy and his wife, who had moved in with Don Peppino after the death of Donna Rachele in 1947, just after Minnie's last visit. They also visited Edoardo's family as Minnie wanted the children to keep up contact with them.

Early one evening Minnie took Claudia and Bobby to Giolitti's for their favourite ice creams. As she searched for a free outside table, she thought she recognised a man seated with a group of people. She looked again. Could it be?

'Paolo Della Croce!' she exclaimed. She was sure it was Paolo.

The man looked up in surprise and stared at her. Shoving back his chair, he rose and extended both his hands to take hers. 'Oh, Minnie, *che bella sorpresa*, what a lovely surprise!' he said, smiling with delight. 'What are you doing here?'

'We're here visiting my father and now I'm about to take the children back to boarding school in England. You remember Claudia and Bobby, don't you?'

'Most certainly I do.' How are you both? Claudia, you've become a beautiful young lady, I hardly recognise you.' Claudia smiled and tossed her fourteen-year-old head with pleasure at the compliment. 'And, Bobby, do you remember me?'

'Yes, I remember,' Bobby said after a pause, a grin spreading across his face. 'You taught me to fly a kite.'

'You've grown a lot – you'll soon be taller than your mother. How old are you now?'

'Nearly twelve.'

'How long are you staying?' Paolo asked Minnie.

'Only another few days.'

A voice from the table behind called to Paolo.

'Where are my manners?' Paolo said. 'Minnie, allow me to present you to my wife, Tina.' He turned to the table, where several people were seated.

Minnie saw a smartly dressed woman in a grey silk dress rise from the table, and vaguely recognised her from the photograph Paolo had shown her years earlier, when he was in hospital. Her small pebble-grey eyes stared unsmiling from under bushy black eyebrows, and there was still the suggestion of a moustache on the upper lip. With a double chin that sank into a short neck, and a prominent bosom, she reminded Minnie of a well-fed pouter pigeon.

'Tina, my dear,' Paolo said jovially. 'Let me introduce you to Signora Dubash. She is the lady who was so kind to me in India.'

'Pleased to meet you, I'm sure,' Signora Della Croce said with a strained smile. She rose from her chair, offering Minnie four limp fingers to shake. 'Paolo has often spoken about you, Signora, and your kindness to him. When I think of the hardships my beloved suffered in that heathen country, I am simply grateful he returned safe and sound to the bosom of his loving family.' She linked her arm through Paolo's.

Minnie suppressed a smile. 'We did what we could for all the prisoners of war,' she murmured. She could feel Tina's eyes watching her expression, sizing her up.

Paolo introduced his two sons, Michele and Luigi, and his in-laws, who sat next to them stiff as a pair of guardian crows protecting their nestlings. The boys fidgeted. Michele pulled Paolo's shirt and whispered in his ear.

'They want to watch the jugglers' show at the end of the square,' Paolo said. 'Minnie, would Claudia and Bobby like to go with Michele and Luigi to watch it? And perhaps you could join our table?'

Claudia nudged her mother. 'I'd like to go, Mummy.'

Minnie hesitated, glancing across the cobbled square to where a crowd was gathered waiting for the show to start. She nodded, and the four youngsters went off together.

Tina turned to her husband. 'Paolo, your ice cream is melting. We mustn't impose on Signora Dubash, she must be very busy.'

Minnie put on her brightest smile. 'I won't stay. I want to watch the jugglers myself. I shall get some ice cream and join the kids,' she replied.

'Allow me to get it for you,' Paolo said, pulling out a chair. 'Do sit down meanwhile.'

Tina sighed. 'Signora Dubash, you can't imagine what a relief it is to have him home safe and sound. We are fortunate that he has settled well here. Papa has offered him the job of manager at his tomato cannery.'

'How nice. And has he accepted?' Minnie asked.

Paolo returned carrying four large tubs of ice cream.

'I was telling the Signora that we might move to Latina if you take up Papa's offer. After all, what could be better than to live quietly in the countryside surrounded by those who love you?' She flicked a speck of lint off Paolo's sleeve before glancing at Minnie. 'Don't you think so, Signora?' she asked pointedly.

'I'm sure your husband will do whatever he thinks best, Signora,' Minnie replied, noticing Paolo's face tauten with irritation. The message to Minnie was quite clear. Tina was reclaiming her territory.

Minnie pushed back her chair and rose from the table.

'Let me carry the ice cream for you,' Paolo offered.

Minnie and Tina shook hands, both murmuring that perhaps they could meet on another occasion. She and Paolo walked slowly across the square towards the puppet show. She felt a familiar tingling shock when his arm brushed against hers.

'Can we meet alone before you go?' Paolo asked, slipping his fingers through hers once they were hidden among the crowd of spectators.

'Oh, Paolo, if there were more time…' Minnie sighed. The meeting with Tina had made her feel uncomfortable. 'It's too rushed, Paolo. I'm leaving at the end of the week.'

'Tomorrow. Please,' he pleaded.

They met at a smart little café in Piazza Bologna. Conversation between them was a little stilted, both feeling somewhat tongue-tied. They spoke about their children, their work, their different lives until this moment. When it was time to leave he took her hand in both his. He looked deep into her eyes. 'Shall we meet again before you go?'

She held his gaze for a long moment before slowly withdrawing her hand, then stretched up to kiss his cheek.

'It's best we leave things as they are.'

43

1951–53

Minnie never did get to meet Edoardo's wife, Floriana. She regretted it most when, two years later, she received news from a devastated Edoardo of his wife's sudden death.

Calcutta, 2 February 1951

'…I can't begin to tell you what I feel, cara Minnie. In fact, I can't feel. I am numb, dazed, as if my entire body and brain were under the effects of a Novocain injection. It happened incredibly quickly; within a week she was dead. Typhoid, the doctor said. She was only thirty-two.

I know what people used to say about her. That she was frivolous. Yes, she was. That she was shallow. That too, I admit. That she had no concept of the value of money, except how to spend it. That was quite true; it used to drive me crazy. That she was not clever. True, she was hardly an intellectual. That she was a flirt. Indeed, was she ever a flirt! That I was too old for her. Yes, I was, but she never made me feel old. I know people wondered what she saw in me and I often wondered myself. But she saw something, because it was not I who swept her off her feet. It was she who swept me off mine.

What people did not say, what they could not see, were the other things about her that I saw. She was warm and alive; she was tender and teasing. She was humorous and light-hearted. She made me laugh until the tears rolled down my cheeks. She brought light into my day. She filled my emptiness. She was graceful in mind as well as in body. And she gave me a daughter who even now at twelve months looks just like her. Graziella, with the same green eyes and golden hair.

I don't know how to cope with this little mite. I can't even change a nappy properly. With Claudia and Bobby, it was always you who did that. I don't want to rely on the nanny. I don't want Graziella growing up only among the servants, good as they may be. This is the only solid thought emerging from my frozen brain. But the solution eludes me.

Please keep in touch.

Most affectionately,
Edoardo

Later that year Edoardo wrote again before Minnie accompanied the children back to boarding school at the end of the summer holidays.

Calcutta, 20 August 1951

Dear Minnie,

Just a quick note I am sending through Claudia and Bobby together with photos of them with Graziella. I thoroughly enjoyed their visit and think they did too. I took a few days off and we went up to Shillong in Assam to visit a tea estate. It was a super trip. They have been a great help with Graziella and went several times to the Montessori school to drop or fetch her. They met Clara's friend, Amrita, the lady who runs the school and who very kindly admitted Graziella at Clara's request, even though she was too young. Amrita and I have become firm friends and I can't imagine how I could ever have managed without her assistance.

I don't know if you allow Claudia to wear quite as much make-up as she does, but I suspect not. She has become very pretty. I'm not sure her mind is on her studies, it seems to be too full of thoughts of boys!

Why don't you come up with Clara next time she visits?

With much affection,
Edoardo

Returning from accompanying the children back to school in England, Minnie stopped in Rome to visit her family, before flying back to Bombay. After her visit to shops in London, and now in Rome, she was full of new ideas for her business. With Christmas looming she anticipated a flood of orders and was glad these would keep her too busy to brood about the children's absence. She received another invitation from Edoardo to visit and took him up on his offer.

Calcutta, 20 November 1951

Dear Minnie,

I'm glad you were able to come up with Clara this time. It was good to see you again. Thank you for the presents you brought for Graziella, which I will keep for Christmas, and many thanks, too, for bringing the parcel from my family in Italy and all their news.

I was pleased that you liked Amrita when you met her. I see a great deal of her, as you know, and am hugely grateful for her support and help with Graziella, who has become quite close to her.

Amrita has invited us to spend the Christmas break at her family holiday home in Darjeeling. I expect it will be quite cold, and have bought some Chilprufe vests, wool socks and a wool coat for Graziella.

I hope you have a happy Christmas and a prosperous New Year on the business front. Bobby has written, but I haven't heard from Claudia for a few weeks. Tweak her ears for me and tell her she owes me a letter!

With love,
Edoardo

Express Delivery

Calcutta, 10 January 1952

My dear Minnie,

I am writing to let you know that Amrita and I are getting married on the 31st of this month. It will be a quiet wedding with only about a dozen guests between members of her family, and friends of mine. I know people may think it is an indecently short time since Floriana's death to remarry, hardly a year. Of course, I have not forgotten Floriana, but Amrita and I get along extremely well and are good friends. Graziella is devoted to her and I know how much the little one needs a mother. This is paramount to me, although I am genuinely fond of Amrita as I believe she is of me. I am certain that this will be a good partnership. We have many interests in common and she is an able and self-sufficient person. I know you will be happy for me, dear Minnie.

I have cabled Bobby and Claudia and plan to phone them at the weekend. Amrita joins me in sending our love.

Edoardo

A year later, early in 1953, the owner of Pompadour, Bombay's leading couture designer, placed an order with Minnie to supply the handbags for each creation at her annual fashion show.

Minnie was delighted with this important order and gave it top priority to meet the deadline. One afternoon she was immersed in work in the atelier of her smart new premises on Warden Road, humming a tune as she sketched fresh designs for the show. Life was a far cry from the period of the incident five years ago that destroyed her marriage and left her on the edge of despair, she reflected. She was forty-eight years old, in good health, still active and creative. She had reached a contented acceptance of her situation, her business was flourishing and, though her circle of friends had changed, she enjoyed a good social life.

A quiet knock interrupted her thoughts.

'Please, madam, there is a gentleman in the shop wants to speak to you,' her shop assistant Ruby said, poking her head round the door.

Minnie sighed. She didn't want to be distracted at this time. 'Who is it, Ruby?'

'I don't know, madam, he didn't give a name.'

'What does he want? Tell him I'm busy. Can he call back later?'

Ruby returned after a moment. 'No, madam, he can't call back. He wants to see you now. He said he will wait until you are free.'

Minnie removed her glasses in exasperation. 'Is he selling anything, Ruby?'

'No, not at all, madam,' Ruby replied, raising her hands. 'He is a pukka sahib, Madam. Only, well…he talks funny.'

Minnie peered at Ruby, pursing her lips in irritation. Talks funny? Whatever did this gormless girl mean? Did she mean funny ha-ha, or funny peculiar? There was nothing for it: she would have to deal with this person herself. Brushing the hair back from her sticky forehead, she entered the front of the shop.

'Yes,' she said. 'What can I do for you?'

All she could see against the light was a bulky shape bending over the window display. It straightened up and turned around. A smiling, bearded face appeared before her, vaguely familiar.

'How are you, dear lady?'

With his back to the window and his face in shadow, Minnie could not make out the man's features. Although the voice sounded muffled, she seemed to recognise its deep timbre. 'Excuse me, do I know you?'

'I should hope so,' came the reply, loud and clear this time. 'I've come a long way to see you.' He stepped forward into the light and Minnie saw a strong nose, deep blue smiling eyes and a flap of blonde hair falling over one eyebrow.

Minnie's breath caught in her throat. She raised a hand to her lips. 'Paolo! Is it you?'

'None other, *cara signora*.'

'I don't believe it!'

She clasped his outstretched hands.

'It's incredible,' she stammered. 'I never thought we'd meet again. When did you arrive? Tell me everything. Wait. Ruby!' she called. 'I don't want to be disturbed. No phone calls.'

'Very well, madam.'

'Oh, and bring us some coffee, dear, will you?'

She took Paolo's arm. 'Come, let's talk in my office.' She laughed with excitement.

The office, part of her workroom, was small, with two easy chairs placed in front of the open French window. The breeze scattered a bunch of sketches and fabric samples across a desk against the wall.

They sat by the French window, looking at each other, tongue-tied but all smiles.

Minnie brushed down her skirt, pushed her unruly curls behind her ears and wished she had visited the hairdresser. She glanced sideways at Paolo. There were touches of grey in his beard and a scattering in his blonde hair. He was wearing dark blue linen trousers and a checked cotton bush shirt. He wore no socks but highly polished brown loafers and looked cool and stylish.

'Now, what brings you here?' Minnie asked while pouring the coffee Ruby brought in. Paolo took a sip and leaned back.

'You are looking at the new shipping agent for the Lloyd Triestino line. I'm here on a four-year contract. I arrived yesterday.'

'Oh, Paolo, that's wonderful news. How exciting. Is that a promotion for you? How did it happen?'

'It's a great opportunity, and it all happened quickly. The chap they had originally appointed suffered a massive stroke.'

Paolo took out a silver cigarette case, opened it and offered it to Minnie, who shook her head. She watched him choose a cigarette, tap it on the back of the case and light it with a match held in the cup of his hand.

'After our last meeting I didn't think...' Minnie let the sentence trail off.

'Neither did I, to tell the truth.'

They drank their coffee in silence.

It's best we leave things as they are. Those were the last words they had exchanged then, Minnie recalled, looking at him over the rim of her cup.

'Will your family join you here?' she asked, pouring more coffee.

'The boys will come out to visit. But Tina will not.'

'What changed to allow you to come here?'

Paolo laughed. 'It was too good an offer to refuse. For the last couple of years Tina and I have lived apart. We meet from time to time for the boys' sake. But she prefers to stay in Latina near her parents. Mind you, she would have preferred me to be posted to Rio, which I was also offered.'

'Why didn't you take it?'

Paolo set down the cup. His eyes never left Minnie's.

'You know why, *carissima*,' he said.

Minnie smiled with sheer pleasure, as if a weight had lifted from her shoulders.

A few weeks' later, Darius phoned Minnie at home. 'I'm coming over now,' he announced without ceremony. 'I need to clear up something with you.' He rang off before the astonished Minnie had a chance to ask what it was about.

He arrived half an hour later, striding into the air-conditioned study, looking tense and drawn. She had heard his behaviour in public was becoming increasingly eccentric, and judging by what he was wearing now, she could well believe the rumour. He was dressed in the Hindu style, with thin white pyjama-like trousers, a knee-length muslin kameez, simple brown leather chappals on his feet like those worn by peasants, and an elephant-hair bracelet around his wrist. His well-oiled hair touched his shoulders. Despite the bizarre manner of dressing, he still oozed a magnetic sex appeal.

She stood up behind her desk. 'What can I do for you?'

'I hear you are seeing your old lover again,' he said icily. 'I'm telling you now, I won't put up with it. I will not have you make me lose face.'

Minnie's hackles rose. 'What are you talking about?'

'That Italian chap. The POW who was always hanging around you in forty-four. Della Cosa, something like that.'

'You mean Paolo Della Croce?'

'That's the fellow,' he said, pointing a finger at Minnie.

Minnie put a hand on the desk to steady herself. 'You are completely mad, Darius. Paolo has been nothing but a good friend to me.' Her voice rose in anger.

Darius placed both hands on the desk and leaned towards her, his eyes glittering. 'Where there is smoke, there is fire. I hear on good authority you've been carrying on with him.'

Minnie stepped back. 'What good authority would that be? Your sister?'

Darius did not reply.

Minnie paced the room. 'I might have guessed!'

'He's back, though, isn't he?' Darius said, following her. 'And you have been seeing him!'

Minnie tapped a pencil on her desk. 'I see a lot of people, including him. It doesn't mean he is my lover. Why pick on him and not somebody else?'

Darius looked sullen. 'Because I know he was special to you. You can't deny that.'

She came back to her desk. 'I don't deny he's a special friend. But it's a friendship, that's all.' She looked at him, her eyes glinting with anger. 'Until this moment, I have never been unfaithful to you, Darius. You *know* that.'

'Does that mean you might be in the future? I couldn't bear it, Minnie.'

'But we're not married any more, Darius. What I do now is *my* business. You have no right to pressurise me like this and make demands. Not after what you did.'

Darius bowed his head. 'I know, it's irrational. But I can't help it.' He cast a pleading look at her. 'Whatever's happened in the past, I still love you. I still need you.'

'Only when it suits you, it seems,' she snapped.

He sank into the armchair. 'You don't understand, Minnie. I need to know that you still care for me, that you are on my side. You know what I mean.' He clutched his head as if he had a headache. 'When I imagine you and him together, it drives me crazy. I want to punch his face.'

'Don't be so foolish, Darius.' Minnie sighed in exasperation. 'You're behaving like a jealous child.'

He jumped to his feet, an intense, dark expression clouding his eyes. 'I'm warning you, Minnie, I won't put up with it.'

A shudder of fear ran down her spine.

Without another word, Darius turned on his heel and stormed from the room.

*

What happened between Minnie and Paolo over the next two years was as inevitable as it was gradual. They dined out together, went to concerts and the cinema, and he was the perfect escort when invited to the same dinner parties and dances. They played bridge as partners at the Willingdon Club. Paolo joined the Royal Bombay Yacht Club and taught Minnie to sail.

There was no clap of thunder, no sudden revelation, no blinding flash to mark the turning point in their relationship. Love crept up on them unawares, silently and stealthily. Like a cat on padded paws that slides its body against one's legs, waiting to be caressed, so love entwined itself around them until it became comfortably lodged in their hearts.

When at last Minnie recognised the strength of their feelings, it was almost as if it had always existed between them. For the first time in years she felt safe and protected. Not since Uncle Harry had she experienced a similar sensation of calm and perfect trust. Perhaps this was what a lasting love should be, she thought. She knew she could rely utterly on Paolo's quiet strength and support, so different to the rollercoaster of passion and turmoil she had experienced with Darius, and the delusions and disappointments of her marriage with Edoardo.

Minnie was contented as never before in her personal life. She gained a new confidence in herself, a fresh sense of her own value. In spite of this, she was cautious in relation to Darius, afraid he might take vindictive action against Paolo if he suspected the true nature of her feelings. She continued to be discreet and careful in public with Paolo, apparently good friends, even flirtatious at times, but no more than that. Only two close friends besides Clara and Dolly knew of their relationship. At regular intervals they managed to sneak away for a weekend at Marve, a more remote beach hideaway than Juhu. A good friend lent them her house for their meetings that guaranteed them privacy.

Throughout this period, Minnie became aware that Darius was starting to attract the attention of the literary world, even as his personal conduct grew more bizarre. His magazine *Heritage* was sought after as a reference source for many of the great artistic treasures to be found in private hands. He gave her two books of his poems when they were published, and she read favourable reviews of them in literary journals. She congratulated him when he was invited both to the United States to read his poetry at the Tanglewood Festival, and to the Prix Femina in Paris. On the occasions when he visited her, he seemed eager to keep her abreast of his work. He told her how he had been deeply affected by T.S. Eliot's 'The Waste Land', which had inspired him to start his latest work.

This was to be an epic poem about the growing conflict countrywide between the need to clear and cultivate virgin land to feed the masses and the need to preserve the ecology of that same terrain.

'It is not a fashionable concept, I know,' he said to her. 'But I absolutely believe it to be true. Although I seem to be a lone voice on this issue,' he added with a touch of regret.

Minnie began to hope that Darius's success would mellow him and make him more amenable to the idea of divorce. She was tired of the furtiveness she and Paolo needed to exercise in their relationship, constantly watching their behaviour.

She went to see him one day with high hopes of reaching an agreement.

'Why would you want a divorce now?' Darius asked, becoming agitated and chewing on a fingernail. 'There's no particular reason, is there?' he barked.

'Things change, Darius,' Minnie replied gently. 'Life does not stand still, you know. We need to move on.'

But he wanted none of it. He did not want a divorce, as he had no intentions of remarrying. What was wrong with the status quo, he enquired. It suited them both.

Not so, she replied. She wanted her freedom.

'Freedom from what?' he asked. 'You have pretty much all the freedom you want now. Surely *you* don't intend to remarry, do you?'

She tried to reassure him she had no plans to remarry. Darius on the other hand became suspicious of her motives and pleaded with her, insisting she should drop the notion of divorce for the reasons he had stated years earlier. He knew she would not use his relationship with Satish against him. She acknowledged this tacitly, regretting their agreement, but knowing she would not go back on her word.

She left in despair feeling she would never be free of Darius, but knew she wasn't tough enough to play dirty and force his hand on the issue. She realised that at some deep level Darius was still emotionally dependent on her. In an undefined way, she understood that her presence in his life acted as a defence against the fears and insecurities that bedevilled him.

44

1954–57

Minnie and Paolo met at Marve at the weekend, arriving separately. Minnie loved this secluded spot and the beauty of its pristine beach. There were only a few other holiday homes here, which ensured their total privacy. For her, this fact, and being able to escape from the bustle, filth and chaos of the city, made the tiring journey worthwhile.

Paolo had already arrived ahead of her and helped to unload the car. In the late afternoon they went for a long walk on the almost deserted beach, then swam in the sea that was as tepid as a bath. Afterwards they sat close together on their towels on sand that still retained the day's heat. They hailed a passing *nariyal-wallah* carrying a basket of coconuts on his head. He squatted before them and deftly trimmed and sliced open a couple of fresh young nuts. Minnie and Paolo drank the cool milk and watched the fiery sun sink into the indigo sea.

After showering and changing, Minnie cooked a light meal, which they ate on the open veranda. The mellow light from a couple of kerosene lamps shed a golden circle on the table and cast flickering shadows beyond.

Paolo enquired how her meeting with Darius had gone.

'Not well, I'm afraid,' Minnie sighed. 'He's being totally irrational. He still will not agree to a divorce.'

Paolo squeezed her hand. 'I have news too. Tina is coming out at Easter. She wants to see if we can effect a reconciliation.'

Minnie frowned. 'Is that likely?'

'No, but for legal reasons there must be a last attempt before a binding separation agreement can be reached.'

'How long does she intend to stay?'

'Six months, probably.'

'Oh, Paolo!' Minnie gripped his hand. 'Where does that leave us?'

'Much the same as now, I suppose.'

She shook her head. 'We shall have to see much less of each other. If not, she's bound to guess and will make life difficult for you. For both of us. What about the boys? Will they come out too?'

'They come at the end of June when term ends. It will be a good break for them both. Especially Michele. He starts university in Milan in October.'

'How time flies. I forget he's not much younger than Claudia. I'm sure she will be delighted to show him around.'

'Are Claudia and Bobby coming out again for the holidays?'

'Yes, although they'll go to Edoardo in Calcutta for part of the time.'

She handed Paolo an ashtray and went to the kitchen to make coffee and brought it out to a small table under a coconut tree. They sat drinking the hot brew in comfortable silence, gazing at the bright scattering of stars in the inky sky. The long palm leaves rustled and sighed in the light breeze. Snatches of local dialect and laughter carried through the dark from pinpoints of light bobbing along the beach towards the fishing village a mile away. A cat jumped over the boundary wall and disappeared into a bush.

'I hope Claudia isn't going to be a problem as she has been in the last year or two.' Minnie lit a cigarette and watched its tip glow in the dark.

'What was the problem?' Paolo asked.

Minnie inhaled deeply. 'She kept changing her mind about what subject she wanted to do at university. Modern Languages one minute, English Lit the next. She even thought of going into acting.' Minnie chuckled. 'That would have been natural for her – she is such a drama queen.' She flicked ash on to the grass. 'She never understood I couldn't afford to keep her at university for three years. I wanted her to do something practical, like a secretarial course.'

'Rather dull, don't you think? What did she choose eventually?'

Minnie smiled. 'My good friend Barbara Davidson suggested she should go to Paris and do the Cordon Bleu cookery course.'

'Did she?'

'She did indeed and loved it. Terribly useful to her when she marries and has to entertain.' She took a last puff and stubbed out the butt. 'I must try to get her to stay on in Bombay,' she murmured, following her train of thought. 'She might meet the right man, make a good marriage.'

'Minnie, Claudia is over twenty-one. You must stop trying to organise her life,' Paolo said with a note of warning.

'I'm not. I simply think she'd have more opportunities here.'

Paolo settled back in the chair, clasping his hands behind his head. 'Darling girl, I think you will find that young people these days don't follow their parents' advice, as *we* used to. They want the freedom to choose for themselves. You know what happened with Michele. Against all family advice, he insisted he wanted to study Law at the Istituto Bocconi in Milan. In the end he won.'

'I understand, but it is different for a boy. It's important he has a degree. That's why I'm keen for Bobby to get a place at Oxford or Cambridge. But for a girl it's not always necessary. After all, she doesn't need a career; it's better that she should marry well.'

'I don't agree at all, *carissima*!' Paolo sounded astonished. 'The world has changed a lot since the war. We're in 1957 after all and people think differently these days.'

'Perhaps, but despite India's independence and all that, life continues pretty much the same,' Minnie replied hesitantly, almost as if she needed to reassure herself that life would go on as before.

'You're quite wrong there, Minnie.' Paolo leaned forward, arms on knees, sounding solemn. 'I've only been here three years, but even I've noticed the change. Mark my words, it won't be long before all the foreign businesses will become Indianised, some even nationalised. The British will leave in droves. They are already leaving.'

Minnie looked at him with a puzzled frown. Even in the faint light, she could make out his serious expression. Of course, she was aware that attitudes towards the British had changed after independence and would continue to do so. Barbara had intimated as much, but could it be so drastic?

'Surely that can't be,' she stammered. 'They've been here for centuries. I know the Indians want their freedom, but how would they manage without British knowhow?'

'Probably very well in the long run, but in any case, even in the short term they want to do it *their* way. It's only natural. After all, just look at the example of our own children. They don't want to do things our way. They want to make their own decisions, and we must let them. On a larger scale, it's much the same with a new nation.'

'Yes, but I can't imagine the British not being an important presence in this country.'

'Those days are counted, darling. Not just for the British, but for the Europeans in general. Look at the new arrivals. None of them are the type that will live in India for decades, make their lives here like the old timers – like you, for instance.'

Minnie sighed. In her heart of hearts, she knew he was right. Most of the newcomers, British and European, were on short-term contracts, eighteen months to two years, and for the most part were technicians or mechanical engineers. Indian management was replacing the old company bosses and managers of traditional foreign firms. Many of the new ex-pats did not bother to bring their families out with them for such short periods. They seemed less interested in integrating with the old India hands, socialising mainly within their company's group. Minnie had noticed that often there was hardly time to get to know them properly before they were transferred elsewhere. Social life was becoming more transient. There was no longer the sense of community there once was: the comfortable feeling of shared experiences, of having weathered storms as well as high points together, of having lived through the turbulent period of transition and change.

'It looks as if we shall both be busy with family commitments this summer,' Paolo said, smiling at Minnie's crestfallen expression. 'It will only be a short while. It won't change anything for us really, will it, darling?'

Minnie put aside her worries and enjoyed the rest of the weekend. Not for the first time she thought how much she relied on Paolo's quiet strength and guidance, how much she loved this man with his steadfast devotion and honesty. But during the long drive back to town on the Sunday evening, she thought back to their conversation. A sense of foreboding came over her for the rest of the journey.

Arriving home, she parked the car in front of the long flight of steps leading to the front door. She took in the familiar building, the pot plants on each row of steps, the patch of peeling yellow plaster on the wall near the top (*must get that repaired before the rains start*), the night watchman's seat, neatly folded, with his knitting in a paper bag beside it. So familiar, so much part of her world. But it was as if she were seeing them for the first time.

She sat in the car, intensely aware that something far-reaching was going to happen. She knew at that moment – as if a curtain had drawn aside revealing a hidden window – that her life was about to undergo a drastic sea change.

On a sweltering day in May Minnie made the tedious drive to Santacruz airport to meet Claudia's plane. At arrivals she was told the flight was delayed by two hours.

'Why didn't you let me know before I left home,' she asked, irritated.

'Many apologies, madam. We tried, but you know what the phone lines are like these days,' came the bland reply from the desk officer who escorted her to the air-conditioned VIP lounge. 'However, madam, we will take you straight into the Customs hall to meet your daughter after the plane lands. You will have more privacy.'

The Dubash name still carried its magic, Minnie thought, as she resigned herself to a long wait. A small group of people was standing expectantly by the arrivals door carrying garlands of marigolds and tuberoses in readiness for the traditional Indian greeting to a VIP or returning relative. She lit a cigarette, inhaled deeply and let the smoke trickle through her nostrils.

Minnie knew it wasn't the state of the potholed roads or the chauffeur's erratic driving through the crowded slums that had made her feel irritable. It was the thought of seeing her daughter that put her on edge. She must try to remember Paolo's advice about seeming to control Claudia's life.

Minnie almost missed her daughter entering the Customs hall amongst the crowd of passengers.

Her heart sank. *Good heavens just look at what she is wearing!*

Claudia was dressed from head to toe in black. Her middle-parted dark hair hung like limp curtains framing her pasty face. Heavy kohl outlined her topaz eyes, giving her the air of a panda. She wore large hoop earrings, and her flight-swollen feet were squeezed into pointed shoes with four-inch stiletto heels. She looked ill and unhealthy, as if she had not seen the light of day for a long time. But all was forgotten when Claudia spotted her, rushed over, dropped the duty-free bags she was carrying and threw her arms round Minnie.

'Darling, how lovely to see you at last,' Minnie said, embracing her daughter. 'Did you have a good flight? Are you tired? How much luggage have you got?'

'Not much, but let's get through Customs quickly, it's so hot,' Claudia laughed.

They picked up the dropped bags, linked arms and walked to a counter to wait for the luggage.

'Darling, why on earth are you dressed like that? You look like a cross between a gypsy and a funeral mourner,' Minnie asked lightly, but immediately regretted her words. She felt Claudia bristle.

'Don't you like it, Mum?'

'Well, it's not… It is simply…just, well, a bit strange. Not quite what I imagined to be Parisian chic.'

Claudia tossed her head and sniffed. 'It's the existentialist style. Everybody dresses like this on the Rive Gauche. Juliette Gréco, Édith Piaf – most celebrities. It's the sort of thing I wear all the time.'

Minnie squeezed her daughter's arm. *We shall soon change that, my girl, wait and see.* 'Never mind that now, darling, tell me all your news. All about Paris and what you've learned on the Cordon Bleu course.'

Minnie was pleased that right from the start of the long summer vacation, Claudia slipped into the social life of Bombay with ease and quickly settled into a routine of swimming, golf and tennis. When the monsoon broke and the rains became too heavy, she took up squash, and after Bobby's arrival from England he too joined in the activities.

Although Minnie was glad to see her children having a good time, the increasingly hectic round of parties Claudia attended disturbed her. She tried to lay down some ground rules, such as not staying out after one in the morning and going out in a group rather than with a single man, but Claudia often flouted these restrictions and angry scenes followed between them.

Minnie's tension increased with the imminent arrival of Paolo's family, even more so when Paolo asked her to be a friend to Tina for the duration of her visit.

'But, Paolo, how can you expect me to pretend like that?'

'You met her in Rome after all, and you are the only contact she has here outside the family. She might think it strange if you avoid her.'

He was right, of course, and Minnie took Tina under her wing, going out of her way to put her at ease in her new surroundings. After one of their shopping trips during a lull between heavy cloudbursts, the grateful Tina insisted on asking her back to the house for tea. Minnie listened to Tina talking about her father's business, and how she hoped Paolo would change his mind and join the firm even at this late stage. But if he did not, then Michele would be groomed to take it over. There was an unusual tenderness in her voice when Tina spoke of her eldest son.

'I thought Michele wanted to be a lawyer,' Minnie said.

'Yes, so he says. But once he's graduated, I'm sure he'll see the sense of taking over the family business.' She talked about her life in Italy, her father's successful cannery south of Rome, her hopes and ambitions for her two sons. Minnie listened with mounting disquiet. Tina spoke as if taking for granted that Paolo would form part of her future expectations.

Paolo joined them on his return from work, followed by Michele, both brushing spatters of rain from their clothes. Minnie had hoped he would come home early and the sheer pleasure of seeing him outweighed the uneasiness of having to act casually in his presence, exchanging pleasantries and small talk.

While Tina poured a cup of tea for her husband, Minnie and Paolo exchanged glances. His intense blue eyes and the slight smile on his lips made her heart leap. Her hand trembled with a sudden surge of desire, rattling the cup and spilling tea into the saucer.

'Michele, get Signora Minnie another cup from the dining room,' Tina asked her son.

'No, Tina, please don't bother. I have to go, I'm out for dinner this evening.'

'What a shame you can't stay longer, but thank you for taking me around today. Perhaps we can do it again another time?'

'With pleasure,' Minnie replied. 'Just phone me when you want to go.'

'Paolo dearest,' Tina said, resting her hand on Paolo's arm. 'Will you see Minnie to her car? There's an umbrella by the door. Ciao, ciao, Minnie.'

Minnie did not like the assured tone and possessive gesture Tina used in addressing her husband. After all, weren't they supposed to be as good as divorced? The sharp horn of jealousy prodded her. Surely there was no intimacy between them?

Paolo and Minnie walked quickly down the front steps and on to the paved path overhung by sodden hibiscus bushes to the parking area at the side of the house. It was dark, and the sky was throwing down its load of water in heavy sheets, too wet even for the night watchman to be out. Hidden by the enormous black umbrella, Paolo linked his arm through Minnie's and immediately she felt comforted by the closeness of his body. The path was unlit, and they barely managed to see enough from the small flashlight Paolo held to pick their way among the muddy puddles.

'Paolo, it's so dark; you really ought to have lights on this path. It's dangerous.'

Paolo laughed. 'Surely not!'

'It could be. You know, snakes and things…'

'I know, darling. The electrician keeps promising to come, but the bad weather holds him up. All the fittings need changing, but we manage okay with torches.'

Minnie shivered and clung to his arm. She wanted him so much it made her feel quite weak. Safe in the knowledge they wouldn't be seen under the umbrella, she responded eagerly as he pushed her against the car door and kissed her, pressing her close with one arm until she could barely breathe.

'Can we meet somewhere?' he asked breathlessly.

'Yes. A friend is letting me use her studio apartment,' she whispered. The rain on the car door had soaked the back of her dress, but she did not mind. She licked her swollen lips, savouring the familiar taste of him, willing this moment to last. 'It's free for us on Thursday afternoon from two until six.' She gave him the address.

'I'll be there. Until then, remember I love you.' He kissed her hard once more, his hand on her breast sending a shaft of heat through her body.

The drive home was slow in the beating rain and by the time she parked the car and went indoors, depression settled on her once again. She ran her bath and while waiting creamed her face and wiped it clean with tissues. Peering at her reflection in the mirror she noted with silent satisfaction that her skin was pretty good for her age, smooth and wrinkle free with just a touch of looseness under the jawbone. Her hair was still black and glossy although recently the hairdresser had begun to use 'a little something' to cover the incipient grey above the temples.

Reviewing the day, she concluded that although Tina was pleasant enough, it was her narrow, provincial outlook that Minnie found hard to take. She felt uncomfortable with the situation and the strain was starting to tell. The more she longed to feel Paolo's body against hers, the guiltier she felt. Did Paolo find Tina attractive? Was she trying to win him back? Worse still, was he sleeping with her? The very idea filled Minnie with dread and unreasonable anger. Surely, he would not! But…it was something she needed to know.

She slipped on her housecoat, went to the drawing room and poured herself a stiff Scotch.

45

1957

As weeks passed, Minnie and Paolo only used the flat two or three times, feeling it to be too risky to meet more frequently. But one afternoon Paolo dropped by her house on the pretext of finding Tina with her.

'You didn't warn me you were coming, Paolo. Is it wise?' She was overjoyed to see him and ordered tea to be brought to the air-conditioned study.

'I couldn't stay away any longer. I know you don't go to the shop on a Wednesday, so I took a chance. I've missed you so much, my love,' he murmured into her hair.

He held her close and they talked, catching up on news. He was finding life with Tina difficult, he told Minnie. There were frequent quarrels; she wanted him to return to Italy, saying it was the only chance of salvaging their marriage. He tried to make her understand matters had gone beyond that point and an amicable separation would be in everyone's interest. Tina accused him of having an affair, saying she had heard rumours to that effect.

'I denied it, of course,' he said, kissing her ear.

There was a knock at the door, and they moved quickly apart.

'Sahib is here to see you, memsahib,' the houseboy announced, and to Minnie's horror, Darius strode into the room.

'Minnie, my dear, I have just brought these riding boots for Bobby, do tell him—' He stopped in mid-sentence on seeing Paolo. His face drained of colour, his eyes looked black and cold as marble.

'It seems I have interrupted something,' he said icily. 'What are you doing in my wife's house, may I ask?'

'Good afternoon, Darius, how are you?' Paolo replied calmly, ignoring Darius's hostility. 'I thought Tina was having tea with Minnie and came here to fetch her. But I seem to have got the day wrong.'

'A convenient lapse of memory,' Darius remarked sarcastically. He held out a pair of highly polished riding boots, waving them at the houseboy. 'Boy, take these to Bobby sahib's room.' Then he turned back to Paolo. 'I'm sure you won't mind leaving now. I have things to discuss with my wife.'

'Darius!' Minnie exclaimed with exasperation. 'This is not your home. You can't barge in here without warning. You have no right to order my visitors around as you please. What did you come for?' She turned to Paolo. 'There's no need for you to go, Paolo, I'm sure Darius will not stay long.'

'Don't worry, Minnie, I was about to go anyway. Thank you for the tea.' He shook her hand. 'I'll speak to you soon,' he added in a low voice.

He turned and beamed a smile at Darius. 'Goodbye, Darius, I'll leave you to your chat. Perhaps you and I could have a round of golf sometime.'

For several weeks afterwards, Darius dropped in more frequently to see Minnie on various pretexts, often unannounced. He made suggestions for her business, advising her to branch out into interior décor and to get more exposure to the tourist market by renting premises in the city centre.

Although Minnie appreciated his ideas and offers of help, she wondered why he was taking this belated interest in her and couldn't help thinking he was trying to keep tabs on her movements.

'Darius why do you come here so often?' she asked impatiently during yet another unannounced visit. She raised her voice to make herself heard over the roar of the heavy rain thumping against the canvas monsoon blinds.

'Does it bother you?' He sounded aggrieved. In fact, he had been anxious and jittery ever since arriving. She recognised the signs: he was back to his ganja-taking habits.

'It is rather strange, isn't it?'

She watched him chew his lower lip and frown while his left knee jiggled nervously. After a pause he gave a deep sigh and a forlorn expression crossed his face.

'You know, my dear, it's so comfortable here, and peaceful. It relaxes me.'

'Well, you are hardly acting relaxed today. Look at you! A bundle of nerves, I'd say, it's enough to make anyone jumpy! I'm sorry, Darius, but your visit is not convenient. You'll have to go. I'm expecting people for tea. You'll make everyone uneasy.'

Darius rose abruptly, shoving his hands into the pockets of his linen trousers. 'You want to get rid of me because you are entertaining that Paolo chap again,' he said sulkily.

Minnie stood up. His swings of mood this afternoon made her

uncomfortable, and she felt her temper rising. 'I've told you before, Darius. It is none of your business who I entertain. You must stop badgering me and respect my privacy. We are legally separated and no longer bound to each other. Please remember that.'

Darius chewed his lower lip furiously, glaring at her. 'You will always be bound to me, Minnie,' he replied harshly and stormed out of the room.

Minnie stood at the window and watched in alarm as he revved the car engine furiously before roaring off. What *was* the matter with him? He'd never been this bad. Something had to be done. She would have to speak to Jimmy about him.

The monsoon that year was particularly heavy. Minnie's mood was one of irritability. When it wasn't steaming hot, the leaden skies threw down lashings of rain. The humidity was unbearable, and everything smelled of mildew. Her ancient Studebaker was giving her trouble, and she couldn't find her favourite cigarettes on the black market. Tired and lethargic, she was snappy with the children and frequently on the verge of tears.

It was a huge relief when Claudia and Bobby finally flew to Calcutta to stay with Edoardo and his family. At the back of her mind she knew her prickliness was connected to her being unable to meet Paolo as much as she wanted. At last she made a doctor's appointment hoping he would prescribe a tonic for her tiredness.

'My dear Minnie,' the doctor said, peering at her over the top of his glasses. 'Your symptoms are perfectly normal for a woman of your age. It's only the change of life.'

Damned menopause. Damned old age creeping up on top of everything else. That's all I bloody need.

By August she had settled into a sketchy routine. She longed for the end of September when Tina and the boys were due to return to Italy. Meanwhile, she began looking for a suitable location in the downtown city to open a shop for the expanding business. At the same time, she was kept busier than ever at work with orders for the forthcoming Ganpati festival in mid-August.

Heavy rain had prevented Minnie taking Tina on another shopping trip and they were chatting in the sitting room. Minnie handed Tina a cup of tea while explaining the significance of the Ganpati celebrations.

'It's supposed to mark the end of the monsoon. Of course, the rains continue for a while, but the worst is over. It's when the fisher folk can take their boats out again.'

'How do they celebrate it?'

Minnie was about to explain when the bearer knocked and announced Darius's arrival. Although he appeared jittery and restless, for once Minnie was pleased to see him.

'I've been telling Tina about the Ganpati festival, but you can describe it to her much better than I can,' she said, ordering a fresh lime juice for him.

'It is a wonderful feast day,' Darius said, his nerviness replaced by genuine fervour. 'You cannot imagine what the crowds are like and what a colourful occasion it is. It takes place on Chowpatty Beach, you know, quite close to here. You must not miss seeing it.'

'I don't know that I could go on my own,' Tina began. 'Would you come with me?' she asked Minnie.

'No, allow me,' Darius interrupted. 'Minnie doesn't enjoy that kind of thing. I would be delighted to take you and the boys, dear lady. It would be my pleasure. And your husband too, if he is free to come.'

Minnie was taken aback by this unexpected suggestion. Perhaps it was his way of trying to make up for past churlishness towards Paolo. Although it was out of character for him, she was relieved that she would not have to accompany them. Darius suggested they should go on the day of the final ceremony, which was the most spectacular. Tina was thrilled and accepted with pleasure.

The day before they were to visit Chowpatty, Darius phoned Minnie to say there was a small change of plan. He asked her to apologise to Tina and explain that he had been unavoidably called away on business but had made provision for a member of his staff to accompany them to the festivities and act as their guide.

The rain kept off for most of the day, making it steamy and humid, but in the late afternoon clouds thickened. Minnie wondered if Paolo and the family were enjoying the festival ceremonies and remembered the first time she had witnessed them.

In her mind's eye she saw scenes as clearly as if they had occurred the previous week. Families carrying decorated clay statues of their beloved elephant god Ganesha/Ganpati across the sandy beach to the edge of the sea. The menfolk performing puja with offerings of marigolds, jasmine, rice, betel nuts, turmeric and red powder, before immersing the deity in the waters. She remembered the processions, the singing and dancing, the attractions on offer: musical events, jugglers, acrobats and magicians, wrestling bouts and games of skill. The air filled with the pungent odour of spices, charcoal grills, burning incense sticks, coconut juice, roasted chickpeas and jasmine hair oil. It was a kaleidoscope of colour, noise and smells.

She was reading in the air-conditioned study before dinner when the phone rang.

'Memsahib, memsahib Minnie,' an agitated voice spoke at the end of the line.

'Who is it?' she asked sharply.

'Memsahib, is Jeevan speaking – please, memsahib, you come quick, quick.'

'Jeevan, what's the matter? Has anything happened to Darius sahib?'

'No, no, Darius sahib gone Poona. I be in Della Croce sahib house.'

'Why are you at Della Croce sahib's house?'

'My wife living in next-door compound. Please, memsahib, big accident here.' He sounded panicky. 'You come now now please before police. They must be come soon.'

'What's happened?' Fear gripped her throat.

'Some *goonda* peoples try to rob Della Croce memsahib. She hurt. Also, Della Croce sahib very bad hurt, I think maybe die.'

'Oh my God,' Minnie gasped, feeling the blood drain from her face. 'Paolo!' She thought she would pass out.

'Not Paolo sahib, memsahib. Is small sahib, Mikey, very bad hurt.'

'Michele!' Her relief was followed by guilt. 'I'll come right away and bring the doctor. Who told you about it?'

'Chowkidar hears *tamasha*, much noise, and finded memsahib lying in garden. He is know me well, he call me.'

'Did you call the police?'

'No, memsahib, I think is more better you call.'

'Don't touch anything. I'll be round in five minutes.'

She phoned her family doctor, Dr Banaji, before flying out of the house.

It had been raining heavily on and off for the last couple of hours. Making her way up the path in the dark to the front door of Paolo's house, she noticed the hibiscus bushes looked as if they had been trampled. Whatever had occurred, all traces of footsteps and evidence would be washed away, she thought. The chowkidar, the night watchman, and members of his family were cowering under an umbrella near the front steps. He held a torch to light her way to the door. She stopped.

'*Kya hogaya?* What happened?' she asked him. But he replied in a torrent of Marathi she could not understand.

She entered the drawing room. A distraught Paolo was bent over his incoherent wife lying on the sofa, pressing a blood-soaked towel to her forehead. There were deep scratch marks round her throat, the top of her sodden dress was ripped, her left hand badly grazed where her wristwatch had once been fastened. Paolo's clothes were covered in blood, as were Jeevan's standing next to him. Behind him stood an ashen-faced, dazed-looking Luigi, staring speechlessly at his mother.

Michele lay on the floor. The hair on top of his head was matted and blood was seeping into the yellow Tabriz rug under him. A ribbon of dark brown matter trickled from the corner of his mouth. His chest barely rose.

Minnie stood still with shock taking in the horrifying scene. 'How did this happen, Paolo?' she whispered.

He looked up, only now aware of her presence, and shook his head unable to speak. Minnie crossed the floor to Luigi and put her arm round his shaking shoulders.

'Luigi, help Papa. He must attend to Michele, so you need to look after your mother. Keep the towel pressed hard on her wound and talk to her.' She squeezed his shoulder. 'She'll be all right, dear, the doctor will be here any minute.'

Luigi took Paolo's place. Minnie handed him a clean towel and Luigi pressed it against the wound with one hand while the other gently stroked his mother's hair. 'It'll be all right, Mammina,' he murmured, 'the doctor is on his way.'

Paolo and Minnie knelt beside Michele's prone body. 'I hear a car,' Minnie said, lifting her head.

In fact, it was the sound of several cars. Dr Banaji strode into the room followed by a man in uniform.

'Minnie, I had to call the police,' he said, taking in the situation at a glance. He examined Tina, looked at the wound and asked Jeevan to bring in plenty of hot water. Then he turned his attention to Michele, put on his stethoscope and examined him.

'Mr Della Croce, I've called for an ambulance. Your wife and son will both need to go to hospital. Your wife's injuries are not serious, but she may have concussion. I'm afraid though your son is in bad condition. He has a critical head injury. I believe he also has a ruptured spleen. He is deeply unconscious and needs immediate attention.'

'Doctor, please do everything you can.' Paolo sounded desperate.

'Officer,' the doctor called to the CID officer, 'whatever statements you want to take, please do it later. I need to get these people to the hospital with the utmost urgency.'

The ambulance arrived. Two orderlies carefully laid Michele on a stretcher and carried him to the ambulance where a nurse took over. They returned for Tina.

'Sir, you can come in the ambulance with your wife and son,' an orderly said.

Paolo turned to Minnie. 'Would you look after—'

'Of course, I'll look after Luigi,' she interrupted. 'I'll bring him to the hospital. Which one is it, Doctor?'

Breach Candy Hospital was the nearest with the most up-to-date equipment. By the time she and Luigi arrived, they found Paolo pacing up and down in a private room off the main ward.

'Tina's in surgery,' he said. 'But they're still examining Michele. They've called in a neurosurgeon. They won't let me see him yet. Outlook is not good.'

Paolo looked old and haggard. Minnie took him by the arm and made him sit with Luigi on the bench beside her. Paolo reached out with his free arm and circled his son's shoulders, drawing him closer.

'Paolo, can you tell me what happened,' Minnie said.

'We were returning from the ceremony at Chowpatty,' he began. 'We left the beach and walked to Marine Drive to catch a cab. It had started to rain a bit. Then I remembered I had to pick up a report from the office, so we hailed two taxis. Luigi came with me to the office downtown while Tina and Michele drove home.'

He paused, rubbing his eyes and forehead. 'When we arrived at the house – it can't have been more than an hour later – we found this terrible hubbub. The chowkidar was shouting all over the place, and people from the servants' quarters were huddled around a shape on the path. Jeevan was there – said he'd been called by the watchman – telling me something dreadful had happened.' Paolo stood up and paced the room restlessly. 'Tina and Michele were lying on the ground, in the rain. The chowkidar was flashing his torch and I could see all this blood running over the flagstones. Tina was moaning dreadfully. Jeevan said the chowkidar told him he had heard a taxi drawing up and the doors slamming but had left his shelter to fetch his dinner and didn't actually see Tina and Michele. He only heard them talking as they walked up the path. It was dark and raining. He doesn't know exactly what happened next, but he heard shouting and screaming. He hurried back. He saw two men running away and found Tina and Michele on the ground.' Paolo paused and rubbed his forehead.

'I can't believe this is happening,' he added.

Luigi clutched his father's arm. 'Papa, what's happening to Michele? He won't die, will he?'

Paolo held him close. 'Oh, son, I don't know. Let's pray he gets through.'

A nurse opened the door. 'The surgeon would like to see you now, Mr Della Croce.'

He returned twenty minutes later looking grim. Michele's head injury was severe, causing swelling on the brain. He had sustained considerable internal injuries as well. The prognosis was not good; the surgeons could not operate until the swelling subsided. The next twenty-four hours would be crucial. They advised Paolo to stay by his son's bedside. Luigi insisted on staying as well.

Meanwhile, the CID officer wanted a statement from Paolo.

Minnie thought it best to leave them. 'I'll go home now,' she said. 'But phone me the minute you have any news. I'll be back in the morning.'

She left the room as the CID officer entered.

The next evening, returning from her third visit of the day to the hospital, Minnie had just parked when she saw Darius's car turn into the drive. He followed her into the house, looking dreadful. Pale, drawn, unshaven, he was still wearing his khaki travelling clothes.

'Have you eaten, Darius? You can join me in a bowl of soup if you want. I'm exhausted and want to get to bed soon.'

'No soup, thanks. But I'll have a Scotch.' He sounded weary.

'Help yourself, you know where it is. Why have you come at this hour, Darius? I'm too tired for an argument tonight.'

Darius lit a cigarette and sucked in the smoke. 'I've only just heard the terrible news of what happened last night. I can't imagine what you must be going through. I only came around to offer you my sympathy.'

'What for?'

'Oh, Minnie, I know how brave and strong you can be, and I admire you for it. Still, although personally I didn't like the fellow, I know you were fond of that Paolo chap.' Darius seated himself next to her on the settee. He attempted to put his arm round her, but she pulled away. 'I'm told he's not expected to live. I'm truly sorry for you, my dear.'

'You've got it all wrong, Darius,' Minnie said, frowning. 'It wasn't Paolo who was attacked. It was his son, Michele. Poor young man, he's on the critical list.'

Darius sprang up from the settee. 'What did you say?' he almost shouted.

Minnie looked up in amazement. Darius's face had drained of colour; his cheek twitched wildly.

'Do you mean to say it was his son who was attacked, not Paolo?'

'That's right. Paolo wasn't even there when it happened.'

'Oh, good heavens. Poor, poor boy. What a dreadful mess. How could...? What hap...' His voice tailed off. He drained his glass, got up and stumbled to the drinks cabinet. He poured himself another stiff measure and downed it in one gulp. His hands trembled. He appeared confused, his eyes darting around the room. Drops of perspiration trickled from his forehead along his jawline.

'This is dreadful news. I'm truly shocked.' He shook his head. 'Poor boy,' he murmured again. 'Look, I have to go, Minnie. I'm really exhausted. Long journey and all that. Let me know about, you know, what happens.'

Without another word and still clutching the whisky glass he staggered from the room.

46

1957-58

Paolo phoned Minnie to say Michele was hanging on by a thread.

The critical twenty-four hours turned into thirty-six. Minnie visited the hospital and did what she could. Paolo did not move from his son's bedside except to see Tina, who was concussed and in shock. He looked worn out and smelled sweaty and stale. Minnie brought a change of clothes for him and Luigi. After a shave, shower and a cup of strong black coffee, he seemed refreshed.

Forty hours passed. Minnie crossed her fingers and looked into Paolo's tired eyes. They spoke little, having exhausted everything there was to say. The unthinkable fears were left unsaid. The hours crawled. Towards evening the surgeon came to examine Michele while they waited outside.

'Mr Della Croce, you have a very determined son,' he said, entering the room. 'He has not regained consciousness, but he is fighting. The swelling on the brain is decreasing. That's a good sign. If it continues, we should be able to operate tomorrow.'

Paolo's eyes brimmed. The surgeon continued, 'Please be aware that he is not off the critical list, but he has a better chance now than twenty-four hours ago. Of course, we don't yet know how much damage there is to his other functions.'

'But he will live, won't he?' Paolo asked.

'The odds are better than they were. We will know more in the morning.'

Michele was still in hospital a month later. The injuries were severe. He had lost the use of his left arm and leg. His vision was blurred, and speech affected, as was his memory, although he recognised his family. He suffered with blinding headaches. Rehabilitation would be a long and arduous process. The specialised care he required, the doctors advised, would be more easily found in Europe or America.

Meanwhile, the police investigations into the assault revealed nothing. The perpetrators of the attack had melted away into the overcrowded bazaar areas. Tina's necklace was found later tangled in a bush in a nearby garden. The watch was never found.

Minnie was with Paolo and Tina, now back at home, when the CID officer called round with the retrieved items.

'We think it was a question of mistaken identity, Mr Della Croce, sir,' the CID officer explained. 'It was money they were after, not jewellery. Mrs Della Croce's distinctive necklace especially would have been too easy to trace. They kept your son's wallet, of course.'

'But he had hardly any money on him.'

The officer shrugged. 'For such people, even a little is enough to buy bhang. It is my guess they mistook your son for you – you would have made richer pickings for them.'

Weeks later, Paolo called on Minnie at her house. Ever since the accident, they had not met at the apartment. Minnie sensed he was depressed. Their relationship had changed.

'I feel guilty that Michele took the brunt of what was meant for me,' he said. 'I could have protected myself better against an attack.'

'At least he is on the mend now,' Minnie murmured.

'I worry about his future. Will he ever recover fully? It will be years before he can continue his studies.'

'Darling, try to be positive. He will be ready to travel back to Italy soon and Tina's parents will be a great help. How is she coping with him now?' Minnie had not seen Tina recently.

'Not at all well. She has gone to pieces. She doesn't want to leave the house or see visitors. She thinks it's only a matter of weeks before Michele is back to normal.'

He stood up and crossed the room to the French doors. A breeze was coming off the sea, billowing the voile curtains. Raucous caws announced the dusk gathering of crows.

'She wants to go back to Rome as soon as possible,' he said with his back to Minnie.

'Has she decided when?' Minnie didn't like talking to Paolo's back.

'Next month. We're booked on the next sailing, providing the doctors give Michele the go-ahead.'

'We?' Minnie queried in alarm.

Paolo came to sit beside her. 'Yes, my darling. We.' He clasped her hand. 'I have to go with them,' he said softly.

'Oh, Paolo!' Minnie wailed.

'I'm sorry. You must understand why – she can't cope with him at all. I've got to think of him. His future, and Luigi's too. I can't abandon them now.'

Minnie felt as if a fist were squeezing her heart. 'How long will you be gone?' she asked in a daze. 'You will be back, won't you?'

The immense sadness on his face gave her the answer she dreaded. She snatched her hand away. 'You've resigned from the company, haven't you?'

'Not resigned. I've requested to be called back.'

'So you won't return here at all?'

'It's unlikely.' He tried to put his arms round her, but she pulled away.

'What about us?' Her voice choked.

'For the present we'll have to put "us" to one side.' He took out his handkerchief and wiped away the tears trickling down her cheek. 'We *will* find a way, I promise you.'

Minnie's head was in chaos. She wanted to blame him, but what for? For choosing his family over her? *Damn his sense of duty.* But she knew that had the positions been reversed she would have done the same.

'But after all our plans… Paolo, this is the second time you're leaving me!' her voice rose. She wanted him to feel guilty.

He took both her hands and forced her to look into his eyes. 'But I came back as I promised. We had a second chance.'

'Yes, but life doesn't give one a third chance.'

'Don't think that way. Believe me, in life we must make our own chances. Maybe next time you will have to come to me.'

She didn't follow his meaning. Her immediate thought was that once back in Italy and taken up with all the problems confronting him there, he might forget her. Out of sight, out of mind. She shut her eyes. She must banish these childish notions.

'I will never stop loving you,' he said, as if she had spoken her thoughts aloud, 'but he is my son and I love him too. He needs me now. I have to do this. You know that, don't you?'

She nodded dumbly. A physical pain shot through her chest leaving her breathless with despair as her world shattered about her. This time she did not pull away from his arms but clung to him fiercely as if the power of her embrace were enough to prevent him leaving.

*

Minnie spent the days following Paolo's visit in a vacuum of deadened feeling. A phone call from Dolly jolted her from her frozen state of mind.

'Sweetie, the reason I'm phoning is that Jimmy and I need to discuss something with you. Can you come over?'

Minnie wondered listlessly what it could be. 'Sure I can come. When would suit you? Tomorrow? Friday?'

'No. Now, Minnie.'

'Now? You mean after dinner?'

'No, I mean in the next half hour.'

Dolly met Minnie at the top of the stairs and ushered her into Jimmy's study. She was surprised to see the Dubash company doctor, Dr Parmekar, was present.

'What's so urgent? Am I to make up a fourth for bridge?' she joked.

'No, darling, this is serious,' Jimmy said. 'It's about Darius.'

Alarm bells started ringing in Minnie's head. 'What's happened?'

'When did you last see Darius?'

When *had* she last seen him? 'Not for several weeks. Why? Where is he?'

Jimmy and Dr Parmekar exchanged glances. 'He's in hospital.'

Minnie sat down. 'Oh dear, what's the matter with him? Is it serious?'

'Yes, Minnie my dear, it is.' Dr Parmekar took over. 'Darius's behaviour has been extremely erratic for the past weeks.'

He pulled up a chair in front of Minnie and leaned forward, arms resting on his knees. 'A few days ago, he was found curled up in bed in the foetal position and utterly incoherent. That is when I was called in. He hadn't eaten for days and in my opinion was in the throes of a severe nervous breakdown. I admitted him the same day to the psychiatric ward at the JBM Hospital.'

Minnie was appalled. 'What will happen to him?'

'He is still being assessed. But we need to know what led up to this. Did anything happen to trigger it? Can you shed any light? How was he when you last saw him?'

Minnie frowned. When had it been? 'It was soon after the Ganpati Festival. He had been away for a few days and on his return learnt about the dreadful attack on Mrs Della Croce. You remember the attack, don't you?'

'Of course,' Dr Parmekar replied, taking off his spectacles and rubbing the lenses with a pristine hanky.

Minnie got up and paced in front of the sofa. 'Let me think. It was a day or two after that. He came to my place to say how sorry he was, knowing they were my good friends. It struck me at the time he was very agitated.'

She sat down again. 'I remember he drank a lot of whisky. News of the incident had really upset him. Especially when he heard how badly injured young Michele was. He kept muttering "poor boy, poor boy".' She looked up at the doctor. 'He was still clutching the whisky tumbler in his hand when he left. It was most odd.' Just as odd, Minnie thought, as the shifty looks she noticed Jimmy and Dolly exchanging with each other.

'What do you think, Doctor?' Jimmy asked.

'I'll pass this on to the psychiatrist tomorrow.' Dr Parmekar turned to Jimmy. 'I'll also mention your proposal to him. I'm sure he will agree to it.'

'What proposal is that?' asked Minnie.

Jimmy cleared his throat and glanced again at Dolly before replying. 'The psychiatrist has indicated that Darius will need to be admitted for a longish period.'

'How long?' Minnie sounded shocked.

'I don't know. Six months at least. Probably more. We propose to send him to a clinic I know of near Baden-Baden in Germany. It has a first-rate reputation.'

Minnie felt a lump in her throat. 'I'd like to see him before he leaves.'

She saw Darius at the hospital the day before his departure, to say goodbye. Never a heavy man, he was now skin and bone, with sunken cheeks and dull eyes. He sat by the window in his room, with a light shawl draped over his lap. He was sedated, and conversation was stilted.

'I'm terribly tired all the time, Minnie.' His speech was slow and slurred. 'But I can't sleep well. There are such terrible dreams. I'm sure it's the medication.' He paused. 'How are you? How's that poor boy, Mikey?'

'He's out of danger, but the family are taking him back to Italy for treatment.'

'They're sending me away too for treatment, you know. I'm not well.'

'I know. Near Baden-Baden. I'm sure you will feel better there.'

'It will be a change. Good mountain air. Meadows and a lake…' his voice trailed off.

When it was time for her to go, Darius gripped her hand with a strength that surprised her. '*Heartsflame*,' he whispered. 'Do you remember? Can I write to you? Will you write back?'

She squeezed his hand. Her eyes brimmed. Bending down she kissed him gently on the cheek. His skin felt dry and he smelt stale. 'Of course, I remember. I promise I'll write.'

*

Minnie was too troubled to sleep that night. The bedroom was humid and airless, and the air-conditioning did little to cool her clammy limbs as she tossed and turned in bed. When the first gleam of dawn lightened the sky, she got out of bed, threw open the French doors and went out on to the veranda. Leaning against the damp wooden railing she yawned and stretched. Her sleep-heavy eyes peered at the trees. A milky haze veiled the casuarinas at the bottom of the garden. All the most important people in her life were leaving. Abandoning her. Paolo back to Italy. Darius to Germany. Bobby to Oxford. Even Franco and Clara talked about leaving India.

Minnie waited. Presently she heard the plaintive screech of the peacocks as they slid ghostlike out of the grey mist.

She shivered. A sense of loneliness enveloped her.

She felt as if she were being cast adrift.

It was several months before Minnie started receiving the occasional letter from Darius. The cramped and tortured handwriting reflected his state of mind, Minnie observed sadly, as she tried to decipher his often-illegible scrawl.

To her surprise, Satish Desai rang up one day out of the blue.

'I've just come back from Germany,' he said.

Minnie did not know he had been away. She had little contact with him and was always guarded and uncomfortable in his presence. She could not find it in herself to forgive him for the way her love for Darius had been betrayed because of him, but with her newfound love in Paolo, her attitude towards Satish mellowed when she realised that he was genuinely devoted to Darius, who frequently treated him with cruel contempt. Despite this, she knew he had stuck patiently and loyally to Darius through all his tantrums and irrational behaviour.

'I went to see Darius,' Satish continued.

'Did you indeed?' she said icily. 'He didn't write to me about your visit.' She wanted to show that she was still on reasonably good terms with her estranged husband, that the bond between them transcended his relationship with Satish.

'He is in quite a bad way,' Satish said diffidently. 'He is not responding to the treatment as quickly as the doctors hoped.' There was a degree of anxiety in his voice. 'To tell you the truth, I was shocked at his appearance. He seemed so…I don't know how to put it exactly – diminished, is the best I can describe. Like a gas light turned down low.'

'I understood he was making progress.'

'Sure, there is some improvement, but it will take longer than we think,

I fear. He has ups and downs and doesn't want to see people – I mean people from home.'

There was a pause as if neither of them had anything further to say.

'Satish, why have you phoned?' Minnie knew she sounded testy and unfriendly.

'Actually, he talked about you a lot in a kind of rambling way. That's why I'm calling. He kept saying how he would like to see you.'

'Did *he* ask you to ask me?' she said sharply.

'Not at all. But I know that is what he wants.' Satish paused. 'Would you consider it?' he added quietly.

Minnie hesitated before replying. 'I'll give it some thought.'

She arrived in Baden-Baden on a glorious day at the end of September. The leaves had put on their rich autumn shades and the smell of wood fires lingered in the air. She booked in at a comfortable *gasthaus* within walking distance of the clinic.

Darius seemed pleased to see her, but Minnie was taken aback by his appearance. Pale and thin, he looked old, his face shrunken, eyes dark-circled and dull. As he took her arm to guide her to the visitors' lounge, she noticed the tremor in his fleshless hand. Her heart twisted with pity for him.

'Would you like to see the grounds, my dear?' he asked after lunch. 'It's a lovely day.'

'That would be nice,' she replied with a cheery smile.

'I'll go to my room for my jacket. Be back shortly.'

Twenty minutes later he returned wearing a heavy winter jacket, a woollen scarf, cap and leather gloves.

'It's not *that* cold outside, is it, Darius?' Minnie asked.

He glanced out of the window with a surprised expression 'Well, I don't want to catch a chill,' he mumbled as they set off.

She looked at him surreptitiously. He appeared strange in his winter outfit, almost as if he felt protected only when swaddled in layers of heavy clothing.

The next day they went for a longer walk. Again, it was mild, with a light autumn mist.

'Next week I shall go collecting mushrooms in the woods with Werner the gardener,' he announced as they strolled along a leaf-strewn path.

'Do you like collecting mushrooms?'

'Yes, but you have to know the right ones to pick.'

'What else do you like doing?'

'I like raking the leaves. Werner lets me help him. When I'm better he says

I can help him mow the grass. And...' his voice tailed off.

She looked up at his face. He was watching a squirrel burying a nut. She tugged at his arm. He glanced at her in surprise.

'Oh, there you are, Minnie. We're having a musical soirée on Friday,' he said. 'You can come if you want.'

'I'd like that.'

He looked up at the trees. 'I want a hot chocolate. I like hot chocolate, you know.'

'Do you mean now?'

'No, they're closed now. When I go to the bank tomorrow. They do a good hot chocolate there.'

'Where? At the bank?'

Darius grinned. 'No, silly. Next door. At Boubelina's café.'

Dusk was falling. Conversation continued to be erratic and disjointed as they wandered back to the main building.

Minnie left him before dinner and returned to the *gasthaus* feeling incredibly sad. She had the odd sensation that she had been talking to an empty shell.

When a day or two later Minnie boarded the overnight train to Rome, not even the rhythmic rocking of the carriage could get her off to sleep in the narrow couchette. She was going to see Paolo for the first time in over a year, and she was afraid. Would things be different between them? Did he still love her? She was filled with misgivings.

Between Milan and Rome, she must have gone to the toilet half a dozen times. She applied fresh make-up, then took it off and started all over again. She pressed a damp cloth to her tired face. Peering into the mirror she wondered if Paolo would notice the new lines around her eyes. She patted on more face powder, redrew lipstick over her lips with a shaking hand and put another dab of rouge on to pale cheeks. It was too much, so off it came. *I shall look like a clown if I don't stop this*, she thought, and returned to her seat. Taking out a magazine, she read the same article four times before grasping what it was about.

At last the train drew into Stazione Termini. She pulled down the window but there was no sign of Paolo. A gentleman carried her two suitcases on to the platform where she stood looking about her with a sinking feeling.

'Minnie, your train was early,' a voice said behind her.

She whipped round almost tripping over the luggage at her feet and looked straight into Paolo's smiling blue eyes. He was just as tall as she remembered.

Greying blonde hair, smooth-shaven, broad shoulders under a crisp grey linen jacket.

'Paolo,' she whispered, her voice sticking in her throat.

They were silent for a moment. Then he reached forward and pulled her into his arms. For what seemed like an eternity they held each other close. Minnie heard nothing: not the hustle and bustle around them, not the sound of trains pulling out, not the whistles, not the cacophony of voices. Only the thumping of his heart, the smell of his aftershave, the feel of his skin on her cheek, the movement of his lips against her ear.

The next four weeks were amongst the happiest she could remember. They saw each other every couple of days at a serviced apartment Paolo had rented for the duration of her stay.

Michele and Luigi came with Paolo to dinner at Il Piccolo Mondo, a fashionable restaurant where she had booked a table. Tina was unwell and could not come. Minnie was relieved to learn this. Her eyes grew moist as she saw Paolo pushing Michele's wheelchair. Luigi hugged her enthusiastically, and Minnie bent to kiss Michele. Paolo did not offer to help his son as he struggled out of the wheelchair and hobbled a few steps to the table.

'I am im-improving with each day, Signora Minnie,' he stammered. 'Come on, Papa, don't stand there, I can't do everything myself. Help me pull out the table.' He spoke with dogged effort.

'You mean pull out the chair.'

Michele grinned. 'You know what I mean.' He looked at Minnie. 'Some words are difficult for me, but Papa makes me practise a new one daily. He's a real bully, Signora Minnie. He won't be satisfied until I'm top of the class.'

Minnie noticed the pride tinged with sadness in Paolo's eyes as he folded the wheelchair.

'What class?' Minnie asked.

'We go twice a week to a speech therapy group,' Paolo explained.

Michele flopped heavily on to the chair Paolo had pulled out. 'And physiotherapy too, don't forget. Soon I'll be able to get rid of that thing,' he said, pointing his chin towards the wheelchair.

Minnie glanced at Paolo who shrugged imperceptibly.

'Where's my nursemaid?' Michele called jokingly, banging his right hand on the table.

Minnie looked puzzled. 'Your nursemaid?'

'Luigi is my nursemaid. He must cut my food for me. It's just like being a child again. But at least I can wipe my own—'

'Michele,' Paolo interrupted sharply, 'please, we are in polite company.'

'Signora Minnie won't be shocked, will you, Signora?'

Minnie smiled, shaking her head. She was amazed at how cheerful and resilient he was. He cracked jokes mostly at himself throughout the meal, but underneath it all she detected a fierce determination to overcome his disabilities. She had no doubt he would succeed. But when she enquired about Tina, both boys clammed up and made non-committal remarks.

'She's not well, poor Mammina,' Michele said. 'She gets low now and then.'

That remark turned out to be a gross understatement, Minnie discovered as the conversation continued. She gathered Tina was no help to Michele, who had become prone to occasional epileptic fits following the trauma he had undergone. Nor could Tina accept that Michele's left side would be permanently impaired.

'She got a lot worse after I had my first *petit mal* attack,' Michele said in a matter-of-fact tone. 'It's not easy when she has her bouts of depression.'

Over the next weeks, Minnie's fears melted away: time and distance had not diminished Paolo's love for her. By the end of her stay she knew their feelings for each other had weathered the difficulties. They would never change.

Nevertheless, Minnie tacitly accepted that Paolo would not, and indeed could not, start proceedings for separation from Tina in the present circumstances. She wondered if sooner or later those circumstances might alter. What would it be like for her to live in Rome to be near Paolo? Would she be content to be his mistress, seeing him only when he could spare the time away from his sick wife? She thought not. Better to be content with meeting him in a year's time.

And what if the situation does not change? She sighed. *Don't cross that bridge until you need to.*

47

1959

Back home in India, Minnie immersed herself in her rapidly expanding business. Nineteen fifty-nine brought a new worry for Minnie with Clara's announcement that she and Franco had decided to leave India to return to Italy.

'Why now, Clara?' Minnie asked over lunch at the Willingdon Club.

'We've been thinking about it for quite a while,' Clara said, pushing away her plate. 'Things have changed for us.' The hotel group Franco worked for had been sold to an Indian consortium, she explained. The new owners wanted to 'Indianise' the management and had appointed their own man to the board of directors, the position Franco had expected for himself. He became disillusioned with what he considered to be an unfair appointment.

'He's right, you know, Minnie. Life is changing for the Europeans here.' Clara beckoned to a waiter and ordered coffee to be brought to the lounge. 'Franco put out feelers in Italy. The upshot is he's been offered a really good job in Florence.'

They left the table and moved to comfortable armchairs in the lounge overlooking the eighteenth hole. The overhead fan stirred the air above them, offering a cool respite from the sticky afternoon. They talked more about the proposed departure, Franco to leave in March and Clara to follow on in June. Minnie grew more downhearted by the minute. It was clear this was no spur-of-the-moment decision. Franco and Clara had been planning this for some time. Her expressions of pleasure for Clara's obvious joy about the prospective move masked her own unhappiness at the thought that another of her vital supports was leaving her behind.

A phone message from Edoardo awaited her at home.

'Sahib phoning from Calcutta,' the bearer announced. 'Him say arriving airport day after tomorrow with memsahib. Him call again today evening time.'

She would be glad to see Edoardo, glad they had remained on good terms after the divorce and their respective remarriages, and usually saw each other whenever he flew in from Calcutta for business. She wondered why he was bringing Amrita. Did that mean he was bringing the children as well? Graziella must be about eight now and Sunita, his daughter with Amrita, would be five or six, both old enough to travel. Minnie cheered up. She liked Edoardo's third wife and looked forward to seeing her.

Claudia had gone out for the evening yet again, so Minnie dined alone that night. She worried about her daughter's constant partying and the rather frivolous and superficial company she kept. She wished the girl would settle down with a suitable partner, but Minnie knew she could only influence her to a point. She realised times had changed since the days her mother had tried to force suitors on her. Nevertheless, Minnie did not want any of the airy-fairy bohemian types Claudia seemed to favour. A man of substance with property and means is what she should aim for, Minnie felt; somebody like Sorab Manecklal, the son of Minnie's good friend Avi Manecklal. He was handsome and sporty, a nice young man, a bit older than Claudia. She was glad that Claudia was seeing a lot of him.

The phone rang, interrupting her daydreams. Over the bad connection Edoardo's tinny voice crackled into the earpiece.

'We're coming down for a wedding on Thursday,' he said. 'I wanted to take Claudia with us.'

'She's out tonight, but I'll tell her. Where will you be staying?'

'With Franco and Clara.'

'Then you must have heard their news?'

'What news is that, Minnie?'

Minnie hesitated. Had she put her foot in it? 'Perhaps you'd better hear it from them.'

'Come on, Minnie, out with it. It's not a secret, is it?'

Briefly she told him what she had learned from Clara.

'Good for Franco,' Edoardo said after a pause.

'You don't sound surprised. I don't think it's the right decision, do you?'

'I'm not surprised, but yes, I think it *is* the right decision. I've been thinking along those lines myself.'

'Edoardo! Leave India?' Minnie was shocked. 'You can't mean that, surely?'

She heard him sigh. 'I'm seriously considering it. Life in this country is changing fast. Listen, I must hang up. Tell Claudia I'll call her from Franco's place. Ciao, ciao.'

The line went dead.

Minnie sat immobile for several minutes holding the receiver in her hand, frowning and staring into space as if she could see something there she hadn't noticed before.

Minnie rang the shop next morning to say she would be late. She wanted a chance to talk to Claudia who had come home from her dinner date in the early hours. She waited at the breakfast table, eating her fruit and turning the pages of *The Times of India*. Already this early in the day the outside temperature was in the high eighties. Beads of sweat formed on her forehead. Her cotton housecoat stuck to a moist patch between her shoulder blades, and her fingers left damp traces on the page she held. At this rate she would need to shower again before going to work.

Pushing aside the paper, she glanced at her wristwatch. Claudia was running late for work. Minnie let out a deep sigh. Why was it that, love each other as they might, there was always a measure of tension between Claudia and herself? Were her expectations of her lovely daughter too high? What had happened to the promise she had shown? Claudia's one-time potential seemed to have been frittered away. The only thing she ever saw through to the end was her cookery course in Paris.

She wondered where Claudia had been the night before and with whom but knew better than to ask. Her daughter could be as stubborn as a mule when she chose, but Minnie knew that if she did not press too hard, Claudia would eventually talk about it.

'Good morning, Mum, why aren't you at work?' Claudia breezed into the dining room.

'Morning, sweetie.' Minnie put down her glasses. Her daughter looked as if she had slept for ten hours instead of barely four. 'I don't have to go in early today. I thought I'd have breakfast with you. Your father phoned last night.'

'What did he want?' Claudia asked, spooning yogurt into a bowl.

'He wanted to have a word with you. He's come down to attend a friend's wedding. He was a little tetchy that you were out yet again.'

Claudia lips tightened and she gave a shrug, saying nothing.

'It must have been a great party considering the time you got back.' Minnie couldn't help making a dig.

'It wasn't a party, Mother, it was just dinner.' Claudia sounded fed up.

Being called Mother was a signal to Minnie that irritation was building up. She poured a cup of coffee and pushed it towards Claudia.

'Anyone I know?' she asked as casually as she could.

'You're fishing, Mother. I wish you wouldn't.'

It was not what she wanted to hear. She feared Claudia was going out with too many unsuitable men, mostly much older than her, but she controlled her irritation. 'Will you return your father's call today?'

Claudia gulped the coffee and got up. 'Sure, I will, later. Have to dash now.' She planted a kiss on top of Minnie's head, grabbed a banana and swirled out of the room.

Two days later Minnie watched Claudia get ready for the wedding reception she was attending with Edoardo and Amrita. She gazed with pride at her daughter, thinking how pretty she was with her Audrey Hepburn gamine looks. Her newly cut black hair fell in jagged licks on her forehead, curled neatly behind her ears and tapered into the V of her long neck. Thank heavens she had abandoned her previous austere existentialist look, Minnie thought as she helped Claudia to slip on her dress, a shell-pink silk moiré A-line with short cap sleeves. It had a demure high neck in the front but was deeply cut away at the back, exposing a surprising expanse of velvety skin.

'Darling, this colour suits you wonderfully, you look lovely,' Minnie said with a smile, while Claudia fixed a string of pearls round her neck. 'Will you be going out with Papa and Amrita tomorrow night too?'

'No. I'm going to a party tomorrow.'

'With Sorab?'

Minnie knew she was flying a kite here. She had noticed that Claudia had gone off Sorab recently and wondered why.

'No, Mother, not with Sorab.' Claudia sighed with impatience, unscrewed a lipstick and applied it to her lips.

Minnie frowned. 'Darling, I don't like you going out with men who are so much older than you. Like that chap you were out with the other night. He's had a string of girlfriends.'

Claudia rubbed her lips together. 'So what?'

'I'm simply telling you that it doesn't look good. You're a young girl and he has a reputation. People will gossip about you. Besides it reflects badly on me that I'm seen to be allowing you to go out with types like that.'

'Well, actually it is *your* reputation you are worrying about, Mother, not mine,' Claudia replied sharply.

'That's not what I mean at all. I'm warning you, though, he'll never marry you. All he wants is a good time.'

'I don't want to marry him, for heaven's sake, Mother, all I want is a good time as well,' Claudia snapped.

Minnie was startled. 'Don't be crude, Claudia. You must think of the future. You can't go gallivanting about with all and sundry and with no sense of propriety. You'll get yourself a reputation and then where will you be?'

'Mum, we've argued like this before.' She tossed the lipstick on to the dressing table with a clatter. 'I'm sick and tired of it. Besides, who are you to talk?'

Minnie ignored the jibe. 'But honestly, sweetheart, why can't you patch things up with Sorab? Is it wrong of me to want to see you settled? He is a lovely man and seems so in love with you.'

Claudia puffed in frustration. 'Sometimes, Mother dear, you are not at all clued up, are you?'

'What do you mean?'

'Sorab's not at all in love with me.' Claudia looked at her mother as if she were a child. 'We're just friends. He's involved with someone, but it's all hush-hush. I act as cover for him. That's the only reason he likes going out with me.'

Minnie's little pipe dream crumbled to dust, but immediately curiosity got the better of her.

'Who is he involved with?'

'I've no idea. He's very secretive about it, so I guess it's someone prominent. Nobody knows.'

'Not even his mother?'

'Especially not his mother!' Claudia exclaimed.

Oh dear, poor Avi, thought Minnie. *It's bound to be someone she doesn't approve of.* She wondered if her friend knew who it was.

For the next few months, much to Minnie's irritation, Claudia continued to play the field. It was only after she heard that Claudia was being seen regularly in the company of Hamish Stuart that Minnie's alarm bells rang long and loud. He had a reputation for being a heavy drinker and a womaniser.

Hamish was Assistant Managing Director at Guthrie, Henderson & Co. A fun-loving Scot not long separated from his flighty wife, he was a popular member of the Bombay Gymkhana Club. A good sport and a keen supporter of the amateur dramatic society, he was liked by everyone. But Minnie did not take to him because he was not the sort of man she wanted for Claudia. Having met him socially several times, Minnie found him to be self-confident and charming, yet behind his considerable appeal she detected a hard and strong-willed core. She was determined that his charm offensive would have no effect on her, though she realised he refused to be intimidated by her cold resistance to him.

Matters came to a head one Sunday at the breakfast table. Claudia had sneaked home just before dawn. Minnie was inwardly seething and exasperated. She cut a papaya in half, scooped out the seeds and squeezed the juice from a lime over the orange flesh. The smell of freshly brewed coffee wafted through from the kitchen.

'Claudia, I will not have you coming home at five in the morning like a little tramp,' she said firmly. 'You're only twenty-two. Hamish is thirty-eight, he's much too old for you.'

'Age doesn't matter these days, Mum,' Claudia responded quietly, buttering her toast with no trace of aggression or defensiveness. Her calm manner only confirmed Minnie's misgivings that this was not a passing flirtation.

'Leaving that aside now,' Minnie went on, 'the thing is, he is married.'

'Yes, but he and his wife are separated.' Claudia spooned marmalade on the toast.

Minnie raised her eyebrows. 'For goodness' sake, Claudia, surely you know they parted once before and got reconciled. Who is to say it won't happen again?'

'I don't think it will. She's been having affairs all over town.'

'And I suppose you think he has not?'

'Not any more.' She took a bite of toast. 'In any case, they have filed for divorce.'

'I didn't know that. Still, I'm not happy about it, Claudia. Let's hope you come to your senses before you get yourself named as co-respondent in a messy divorce case.' Minnie dropped her napkin, pushed back her chair and left the table.

The divorce proceedings *were* messy with accusations flying from both parties. At one time it looked as if Claudia would be dragged into it, to Minnie's great distress. By Christmas 1959 Guthrie, Henderson's head office stepped in to distance Hamish from scandal by transferring him to their New Delhi office. Claudia wanted to go with him. At home there was a furious row.

'You can't go, I forbid it,' Minnie threatened in desperation.

'You can't forbid me anything. I'm almost twenty-three now, for heaven's sake!'

'If you go, I won't talk to you again.'

'Oh, Mother!' Claudia looked stricken. 'Can't you understand that I love him?'

Early in the New Year of 1960 Hamish left for New Delhi. Claudia was miserable but stayed on with Minnie. For a few tense weeks Minnie thought she had won the battle of wills. Her attitude softened. One evening she returned home from the shop to be handed a note by the bearer. 'From Claudia Missy,' he said.

> *Hamish has found a house for us. I've gone to join him. This is the address if you want to contact me. I love him, Mum, and I love you too. I didn't want to be forced to choose between the two of you, but you are making me do it.*

Minnie rushed to Claudia's bedroom. The wardrobe and chest of drawers were empty. Minnie's heart felt like a lump of lead. Her throat ached, and she longed to cry.

It was clear that Claudia would not be coming back.

48

1960–62

In her hurt and anger, Minnie did not contact Claudia. She did not return Claudia's phone calls, nor did she open her letters. She did not speak to her for almost eighteen months, although she kept abreast with her news through third parties. In 1961 when she heard that Claudia was pregnant, she sent her a brief note. *I hope your child will bring you as much joy and happiness as my children brought me.* Two months before the baby was due, Minnie got a phone call from Hamish. He was coming to Bombay to see Minnie.

Unsmiling, she received him in the drawing room, offered him a whisky and soda and sat in her favourite armchair while waving him towards the sofa. He had not changed much since she last saw him. His slim figure and erect bearing, perhaps indicating a military background, made him appear taller than he was. His face was broad with a receding hairline, deep-set mid-brown eyes, and a firm mouth that could, and often did, break into an engaging smile. He wore a gold signet ring on the little finger of his left hand. He looked fit and healthy and Minnie had to admit that there was something appealing about his rugged looks.

After the minimum of polite exchanges, he came to the point without preamble.

'Somebody has to bring you both to your senses, Minnie, and I am not about to wait until hell freezes over before you or Claudia take the first step. The decree absolute for my divorce came through last week.'

Minnie stared at his highly polished brogues.

Hamish got up to put more ice cubes in his glass. 'Our baby is going to be born in wedlock, not out of it,' he continued, and took a mouthful of whisky.

Minnie noticed the deeply tanned skin of his arms and neck, bearing evidence of the many hours he spent on the golf course, and waited for him to go on.

'I know you don't much care for me,' Hamish said, 'but I love your daughter. I am not prepared to see her being hurt and miserable because of what's happened between you and her. She wants her mother around for the birth. You need to put your pride and differences aside, Minnie. This nonsense has gone on long enough.' He ran a hand over his hair. 'We are getting married in ten days' time at the Scots Kirk in New Delhi. Both of us would like you to be present. I have booked a room in your name at the Grand Hotel. Please be there.' He drained his drink and placed the empty glass on the side table next to Minnie. His eyes bored into hers.

It was the last thing Minnie had expected to hear and her eyes pricked with tears of relief. This was the gesture of a generous and caring man. Perhaps she had been wrong about him all this time. This was not the time for false pride.

She returned his steady look. 'Thank you, Hamish. You are quite right,' Minnie said after a long pause and smiled with genuine warmth. 'I will certainly be there. Please stay and have another drink and tell me about Claudia.'

Minnie flew into New Delhi three days before Claudia's wedding. There was an emotional reunion at the airport. Claudia wore a green-checked maternity dress and flat sandals. Her face had lost the gaunt look that Minnie remembered, her high cheekbones softened by newly rounded cheeks.

Minnie's stiffness evaporated as they hugged closely. The hard sphere of Claudia's belly pressed against her own, and after a moment she felt another sensation, a small undulating wobble that tickled her. She pulled back.

'Darling, I felt it move,' she whispered in amazement.

'Yes, he moves a lot. Look.' Claudia smoothed the dress over her stomach and pointed to small surges pushing up the material, like yeast bubbles breaking through batter. She placed Minnie's hand on her tummy.

'I'm *so* glad to see you, Mum.'

Minnie nodded. 'I am, too, my darling.' They looked at each other in silence, smiling and full of tenderness, their intimacy renewed by the touch of their hands and the magical movement under them. The rift was mended and for the next three days they never stopped talking, as if making up for lost time.

In the circumstances, the marriage ceremony was kept simple and low key. Edoardo and Amrita had come from Calcutta, with Graziella and Sunita acting as flower girls. Edoardo stood proudly by his daughter as witness, from time to time wiping his fogged-up glasses with a handkerchief. As they repeated the words after the minister, it was plain to Minnie that her radiant Claudia and Hamish seemed oblivious to everything except each other.

Later, a reception was held at the golf club followed by an informal dinner for the few family members and close friends. After the ceremonials ended and the happy couple were sent on their way to the hills and lake of Nainital for their honeymoon, Minnie returned to her hotel with Edoardo and Amrita. They went to the bar for a nightcap. The décor with its tartan upholstery would have made a Scottish Highland chief feel at home. A wealth of stags' heads on the panelled walls stared at each other from dusty glass eyes. The Britishness of the setting was in direct contrast to the Indianness of the waiting staff with their turbans, long white tunics and red cummerbunds. Edoardo found a corner with comfy wing-backed armchairs, ordered coffees and cognacs and settled into the seat with a sigh of relief.

'I'm glad to see you here, Minnie,' he said. 'Until a week ago I did not think you would attend the wedding.'

'Until ten days ago, I didn't know they were getting married,' Minnie replied. 'If it hadn't been for Hamish I would not be here.' She told them about Hamish's visit.

'We shouldn't dwell on the past.' Edoardo sniffed his cognac. 'It's good that you've made your peace because we have something to tell you, and I wanted to say it in person, not by letter.'

'What is it?'

'I've sold the business. We are leaving India.'

Minnie caught her breath. 'Oh, Edoardo, not you too!' She turned to Amrita. 'Tell me it's not true, Amrita.'

'It is true enough, Minnie,' Amrita replied gently.

'Why is everyone leaving India after all this time?' Minnie burst out angrily.

There was an awkward silence. A waft of pungent cigar smoke drifted over their table. She coughed, drained the coffee in a couple of gulps and put the cup down. A waiter appeared from nowhere and silently filled it again. At the next table, the clink of ice dropping into a glass cut across the uncomfortable stillness.

'Will you live in Italy or England?' she continued more calmly. 'Are you happy to go, Amrita?'

'We'll go to Italy, of course,' Amrita replied. 'Yes, I'm happy about it and I think it will be best for the children.'

Minnie slumped back in her seat, thoroughly dejected. 'Everyone's leaving me,' she muttered miserably.

'You have Claudia, and the baby to come,' Edoardo said. 'Besides, I understand Darius might be coming back shortly. That's a good thing. He seems to be completely over his illness now.'

'I'm glad he is better,' Minnie said. 'But what has Darius got to do with it? He is hardly going to be a support to me when all my friends have gone.'

Edoardo and Amrita exchanged a look. 'That's not the point,' Edoardo hesitated.

'What are you driving at, Edoardo?'

'It's time you too thought about leaving India, Minnie. You need to talk to Darius and clarify your position. You must think about your future, my dear. You need a settlement. A divorce and a settlement.'

Minnie knew that Edoardo was right. 'He's never wanted to consider divorce before now. I've asked him enough times.'

'Maybe it will be different if he knows you want to leave Bombay.'

Minnie thought about Paolo. She did not want to see him only once a year for the indefinite future. Would he ever leave his wife for her? Minnie knew that Paolo's sense of duty would not allow him to make a clean break with Tina. These semi-clandestine meetings once a year were not enough for her, but so far, she had not forced the issue. Ultimately, she knew that her desire to be with Paolo was becoming more important than other considerations.

Edoardo's words jolted her into a sense of reality. It was not simply a question of a settlement from Darius. All kinds of problems darted into her mind: most importantly, she would have to find a buyer for her business.

She sighed. 'You're probably right, Edoardo. I will speak to Darius when he returns.'

Six weeks after the wedding, in January 1962, Claudia gave birth to a baby son, Andrew. Banished by the obstetrician to the anteroom outside the labour ward, Minnie and Hamish waited anxiously, each with their own thoughts, listening to the muffled instructions and sounds that came from behind the heavy swing doors. At last a little Goanese nurse stuck her head round the door and with a broad smile announced it was a boy. Hamish's face turned ashen and he sank on to the bench. Minnie gripped his hand. Euphoria set in as Hamish was called in to see the baby and after a few minutes Minnie too was ushered in. Claudia looked exhausted but happy and bursting with pride.

'Look, Mum, isn't he beautiful?' she asked, holding up the little bundle cradled in her arms.

Minnie gazed with wonder at the puckered puce face with its crop of ginger hair, its wrinkled skin, tightly shut slitty eyes and tiny snub nose. She laid a finger against his petal-soft cheek.

'He is absolutely gorgeous,' she murmured and fell instantly in love with her new grandson.

49

1962–64

At the start of the hot weather season, Minnie heard through friends that Darius had returned to Bombay and was staying with Roshan. She got a call from him one day to ask if he could come over to her place.

'Minnie, my dear, it is good to see you again,' he greeted her, slowly following the bearer through the French doors of the sitting room on to the veranda. 'I can hardly believe you are a grandmother – you are much too young and still as beautiful as ever.'

She rose to meet him, and they exchanged an affectionate embrace.

'I'm glad you're back, Darius, and I hear you have not lost your silvery tongue. Come and sit down and tell me what you've been doing.'

They settled on the wide cane sofa overlooking the garden and the sea. A slight breeze came off the incoming tide, rustling through the casuarina trees and wafting the sweet scent of frangipani flowers in full bloom. The bearer placed an ashtray on the cane peg table beside Darius. He looked enquiringly at Minnie, waiting for an order.

'Will you have a whisky, Darius?'

'No, dear, it's too strong. It's the medication, you know. I'll have a small beer,' he said, lighting a cigarette.

The bearer beamed, waggled his head and scurried off to fetch the drinks and tell the other servants that the sahib was back.

Minnie observed Darius as they chatted. He was gaunt, clean-shaven and his uncut black hair was heavily streaked with silver. But the anxious, angry look of a few years ago was gone. Although he had not broken his smoking habit, she noticed that his fingernails were no longer bitten to the quick.

'Are you glad to be back?'

'It's nice in a way, but…' he sighed '…I really don't know. I liked it in Baden-Baden in the end. It was peaceful. Life seemed more real there than it does here.' He tapped ash into the ashtray.

'But you have your friends here. You'll get back into the swing of things in no time.'

'That's just it. I don't want all that. Roshan's already trying to organise my life for me.'

'Will you continue to stay with her?'

Darius threw his hands into the air and looked upwards as if imploring divine help. 'Not if I can help it. She's completely impossible.' He ground the cigarette stub into the ashtray until it was pulverised. 'She still rescues animals. Do you know she has seventeen dogs and twelve cats? And keeps a couple of goats in the garden. None of them are trained, of course. She allows them to sit on all the furniture – not the goats, of course – and at least a dozen of them sleep in her bedroom. There is cat and dog hair everywhere you go. I'm continuously sneezing. And she talks baby talk to them!' He rolled his eyes at Minnie. 'You cannot imagine how irritating it is. I can't move around the house without tripping over the damn creatures.'

Minnie laughed. 'I heard she had become a bit eccentric.'

'Well, I've decided to move out to Juhu. I sold the old shack and bought a large plot of land a mile away. I'm having a new house built with a swimming pool. When it's ready I shall live there permanently.'

'It's a long way to commute every day, Darius.'

'I don't intend to commute. I want to write. If the office needs me, they can bring the work to me out there.'

From the accounts that Minnie heard several months later, Darius had commissioned a luxurious modern home fitted with every comfort and decorated with magnificent artefacts and antiques. Although she was invited several times, Minnie never went there. Darius occasionally came into town and would drop in to see her. She noticed the change in him. His hair was down to his shoulders now, and he had grown a beard. He had reverted once again to dressing Indian-style, all in white, with a flowing knee-length kameez and baggy cotton trousers. He told her he went swimming daily and walked for miles on the beach. He received a steady stream of visitors, when he chose to, both social and work related. He seemed perfectly contented to lead this reclusive life. It allowed him ample time and the right ambiance for his writing. Minnie heard that in literary circles he was being compared to Allen Ginsberg. He said he hoped to complete the lengthy narrative poem he had started before his illness, in time to submit it for the Emily Dickinson Prize.

*

John F Kennedy's assassination in Dallas on 22 November 1963 had a profound effect on Minnie. She was still shaken and shocked by the news when she went to spend Christmas in New Delhi with Claudia, who now had a second child, a two-month-old baby girl, Francesca.

By the spring of the New Year, Minnie found her business was growing too demanding for her flagging energies. Her sixtieth birthday at the end of May was fast approaching and she was tired. Her heart was no longer in it. If it had not been for her business partner, Myrtle Pereira, she would have packed it in twelve months ago. Ever since Edoardo's departure from India, she had begun to plan for her own leave-taking from the country that had been home to her for almost forty years.

It no longer felt like home.

She spoke to Myrtle of her decision to sell the business.

Minnie drove to Dolly's house and parked the car in the drive in the shade of a banyan tree. She trudged up the long flight of steps to the huge marble-floored hall. On the landing the day watchman on duty stood up and salaamed her.

'Salaam, Abdul, how are you?'

The watchman waggled his head and smiled broadly. '*Theek hai*, mem.'

'Children alright?' she asked.

'*Haiji*, memsahib. All okay. New baby is come.'

'Another one? How many is that, Abdul?'

He held up the fingers of one hand and the thumb of the other.

'My goodness me, Abdul, you really must stop. Was it a boy?'

Abdul shook his head, the smile sliding off his face to be replaced by a look of forlorn resignation.

'Oh dear, another girl. Never mind. She will be pretty like her mother.' Minnie fished out a ten-rupee note from her handbag. 'This is for the new baby. I'll bring some clothes for her when I come next time.'

She walked up the long, covered passageway that separated the reception areas from the sprawling bedroom suites and verandas. She paused to look at the magnificent bird's-eye views over the city and the distant harbour. Gone were the palm trees that bordered the sandy beach when she had first arrived forty years ago. In their place was a busy road bordered by a sea wall on one side and six-storey mansions on the other.

The sound of clipping in the garden reached her ears as she started up the last set of steps to Dolly's suite of rooms. Sure enough, the mali – the gardener

– was squatting on his haunches, bony knees poking out of baggy khaki shorts, snipping at a low box hedge with a pair of old shears. His tiny wife stood behind him. Tucked under her arm she held a wide straw basket into which she placed the cuttings picked off the ground. The garden was immaculate, each bed with a different variety of flowers: one with red and orange cannas, tall and straight as pokers; another with a mass of marigolds in every shade of yellow, their acrid, sour scent overpowering in the hot sun. In a shadier spot, a bed of pink begonias formed a cool contrast to the other fiery colours. Bougainvilleas twined round the pillars of the walkway, their heavy bracts of magenta, lemon or white bowing to the ground. From the servants' quarters near the garages came the mouth-watering smell of roasting chapattis. The keening cry of a red kite hovering high in the sky set up alarm caws from crows in the banyan tree. Minnie stood for several minutes taking everything in: the colours, the smells and the sounds.

It was as if she needed to imprint the entire scene indelibly on her memory.

Dolly was recovering from pneumonia and Minnie had visited her daily during her illness. 'Hello, Dolly darling, how are you feeling today?' Minnie asked, bending to kiss her cheek.

They discussed Dolly's plans to throw a large party to celebrate Minnie's approaching sixtieth birthday.

'Did I tell you Clara is arriving next week for a couple of months?' Dolly said. 'She didn't want to miss the celebration.'

'I'm so glad,' Minnie said. 'It will be wonderful to see her.'

They chatted for a while, making up menus for the party. 'Don't forget to give me your guest list soon,' Dolly reminded her as Minnie took her leave.

After showering that evening, Minnie put on a housecoat, switched on the air-conditioning in the bedroom and sat at the desk to make up the guest list. It saddened her to think how few of her old friends and family would be around to celebrate with her. Most of her friends had left Bombay in the past seven years, retired or transferred elsewhere. As for family, there wouldn't be many of them. Edoardo and Amrita, happily settled in Italy, would not come. Bobby could not come. Neither could Franco. Thank goodness Clara would be around.

She glanced at her watch wondering if it was too late to phone Claudia in Delhi. Eight forty-five. Claudia would still be up. She would have finished feeding the new baby. Minnie gazed at the silver frame on her desk showing the latest photo of the little one. She picked up the phone and asked the operator to connect the number.

'Hello, darling,' she said on hearing Claudia's voice. 'How are you? How are the children? Good. How much does Francesca weigh now? That's wonderful, and I'm glad to hear the colic has stopped. Now, darling, the reason I'm phoning is that the birthday celebration is back on again. Dolly is quite recovered now. Anyway, I take it you will be coming with the children? That's marvellous. What about Hamish? No? I thought perhaps not. Have you any news about his promotion?'

Minnie listened to Claudia's explanations while doodling on the writing pad. 'What did you say? You're moving to the UK in August? Darling, isn't that a lot earlier than you expected? Yes, of course I'll come up and help with the packing. No, I'm not sure who else will be coming to the party. Aunty Clara will be here, as you know. No, I haven't invited Darius yet.' Minnie sighed. 'I'll think about it. I'd better hang up now, darling. I just wanted to let you know the party is on again. Bye, sweetie, sleep tight.'

She placed the phone back in its cradle. The air-conditioner hummed loudly as it blew out a stream of cool air, making a windowpane rattle. She scribbled a reminder to have the machine serviced. Deep in thought, she sat on, tapping her pen from time to time on the notepad. How strange that a casual phone call could result in a watershed being reached. Were there any ties remaining to keep her in India once Claudia and her family left the country?

Tiredness swept over her. It was clear that she would have to arrange a meeting with Darius.

The time had come.

50

1964

Minnie phoned Darius the next day to arrange a meeting. His secretary informed her that he had gone with a group of young French tourists to an ashram in Mysore and would not be back for a few weeks.

She put down the phone. *Bloody typical, taking a bunch of long-haired layabouts to some obscure guru. All they'll do is sit around talking about the search for inner peace or eternal truth or some such fashionable nonsense. I'll have to wait a month before I can talk to him.*

She had little patience with the new breed of tourist that had begun filtering into India recently. None of them had much money and they would lodge in areas of the city that no self-respecting European would dream of frequenting. She had seen them in the bazaars, trying to dress and act like the poorer Indians who only took advantage of them. The men went around unshaven, often barefoot, with unkempt hair and wearing torn and mended hand-me-down jeans. The girls wore ankle-length skirts or tatty jeans and a singlet, their frizzy dull hair tied back with scraps of cloth. They carried their meagre possessions in a rucksack or rolled up in a bedding roll on their back. All looked in need of a good scrub, although secretly she had to admit that she liked their music. This change in her musical tastes was due to Bobby. Recently he had sent her a couple of LP records of a group called The Beatles. It was a far cry from Ella Fitzgerald or the Rat Pack, but the new music grew on her.

Minnie was appalled to see these young people casually eating directly from street stalls or in the cheapest Irani shops, places where cleanliness was doubtful and which long-term residents like herself knew to avoid. It amazed her that more of them were not struck down with food poisoning, dysentery or typhoid.

She heard rumours that they got high on bhang, ganja and other drugs, but overall were a peaceful lot. Their aim appeared to be to embrace some of the precepts of tolerance, meditation, peace and harmony with nature and all living creatures as set out in the teachings of Hinduism and Buddhism. Peace and free love was what they were in search of and what they practised – particularly the free love.

It surprised Minnie that many of them gravitated towards Darius. Maybe it was because the sentiments expressed in his poetry, chiefly those of a protest nature, appealed to their sense of rebellion against the establishment. Not for nothing was he referred to as the Indian Ginsberg. In any case she knew that Darius liked to be surrounded by small groups of eager young disciples.

'I think you do it because it flatters your ego,' she once said to him.

'Not at all, my dear, they genuinely appreciate my work. We discuss serious matters. I feel in tune with their views, or rather they with mine.'

'If you ask me,' Minnie said bluntly, 'they are nothing but a bunch of lazy spongers. Word must have got around that you are a soft touch. I heard you had eight of them living at your place recently. And apparently when they left, your collection of Moghul snuff boxes went with them.'

But Darius would hear no wrong about his hippie friends and became sullen as he usually did when in the wrong. Minnie knew when to stop and she changed the subject.

Darius returned her call the week before her birthday in May. 'What did you want to see me about, Minnie?' he asked.

'I need to talk to you about my future, Darius, but not over the phone.'

There was a long silence at the other end of the line. 'I understand,' he said at length. 'Shall we wait until after your birthday party?'

'I'd prefer to do it before,' Minnie replied.

'In that case, why don't you come out to my place on Wednesday evening? We can have dinner by the pool.'

Minnie's instinctive reaction was to suggest he come to her house instead. Juhu held bad memories for her and she didn't fancy bumping into Satish. Pragmatic as usual, she decided it would not do to antagonise him at this stage. There was too much at stake.

'Will you be on your own?'

'Yes,' he laughed. 'No Satish, no house guests, no hippies.'

She smiled into the phone, relieved. 'That's fine, Darius. I'll turn up at six thirty, if that's alright.'

Minnie told no one that she was to meet Darius. She dressed carefully for the occasion, choosing a pair of plain dove-grey linen slacks and a matching shirt patterned with cream tulips. She hesitated over jewellery, but in the end decided on a single yellow topaz dress ring with matching ear-clips, an early gift from Darius. She decided to drive the car herself, dispensing with the chauffeur, and felt slightly foolish for the secrecy, as if she were going on a first clandestine assignation.

The short Indian twilight had turned to inky dark by the time she arrived at Darius's house. She drove through the open gates, the tyres crunching on the sandy driveway illuminated by a few dim garden lights. She parked near the front entrance rather than at the side of the building by the garages, which was an unlit area. She had never been able to shake her fear of the dark. She rang the bell, and as she waited she caught an imperceptible flutter of movement from a downstairs window. She peered into the gloom but saw nothing. The leaves of the palm trees scraped and rustled in the warm breeze. She heard the gentle whoosh and suck of the receding tide and from the distance came the tinny sound of Indian songs playing in the village far down the beach. From inside the house came the strains of Debussy's 'Clair de Lune'. She pressed the bell again.

The music stopped, and a moment later Darius opened the door. He was barefoot and dressed in his habitual Indian style. His thick grey-streaked hair was slicked behind his neat ears and curled outwards falling to his shoulders. His almost white beard, newly trimmed, hugged his narrow jaw. He held a large tumbler of whisky and soda in one hand.

'So sorry to keep you waiting, my dear. I forgot I had to answer the door myself,' he said, taking her elbow and drawing her into the house. 'I gave the servants the night off. There's some shindig on in the village they wanted to go to. I didn't think you would mind.'

'No, I don't mind. I've left the gate open. Is that alright?'

'Perfectly fine. Jeevan will shut it later.'

'Dear old Jeevan. You know that he comes to see me now and then? Isn't it about time you retired him?' she asked.

'Not a bit. I don't know what I'd do without him.'

Minnie looked around the exquisitely furnished room.

'You've done this place up beautifully, Darius,' she said, passing her hand over the colourfully painted Rajasthani furniture of the kind found only in maharajas' palaces. The walls bore several paintings by the most notable contemporary Indian artists and several wooden temple carvings. Rare bronze statues of Indian deities and delicate Moghul miniatures were displayed around the room. A collection of fine Chinese jade and ivory figures stood on glass shelves in a niche. 'It is like a Hollywood film set!' she said looking around her.

'Well, I'm quite happy with the result,' Darius said with pride. 'Come, let us go outside. I'll fix you a drink and we can sit by the pool. It's much too warm in here.'

He opened the door of an ebony bar cabinet while Minnie wandered outside. Her gaze travelled over the terrace. Set into an immaculate lawn surround was a twenty-five-yard stretch of limpid aquamarine water illuminated by six porthole lights, its surface barely creased by the mild breeze. It was magical. She stepped off the terrace on to a clearly lit paved area with comfortable cane chairs and a table laid out for a meal. She pulled out a chair and sat down. Something at the side of the house caught her eye. Had she noticed another movement? For a moment she had the odd sensation of being watched.

Darius joined her carrying a bottle of Scotch. He replenished his glass and handed her a gin and tonic. 'We can eat whenever you want. I told cook to make a cold meal because he too is off tonight. It's in the fridge by the barbecue. Grapefruit cocktail, lobster mayonnaise and mango fool.'

'How delicious,' Minnie murmured. Truth to tell, her stomach was churning with nerves and she had no appetite. She got up, picked up her G and T and strolled to the sea wall at the end of the lawn with Darius following. She peered at the pale sandy beach twenty feet below and listened to the soft murmur of the waves. They sat side by side on the wide ledge of the wall sipping their drinks, making desultory conversation.

'What's the news of your friend Albie?' Minnie asked.

Darius threw back his head and laughed. 'You won't believe it. Albie has become very staid. He bought a boarding house in Earls Court in London and rents out rooms to young tourists and students. He has become fat and calls himself Professor Kuczynski!'

Minnie smiled, recollecting what a charming rogue he was.

'What a lovely setting this place is, Darius, I can well understand you wanting to live out here.' She looked back at the house which, from this angle, appeared its best with the ground floor rooms all lit. A single dim light shone from one of the upstairs windows. Darius's bedroom, she imagined.

'What did you want to talk about, Minnie?' Darius asked, lighting a cigarette.

She hesitated, not quite knowing the best way to start. 'I'm thinking of leaving India. For good.'

'Minnie, you astonish me. You simply can't do that!'

'I think I have to.'

'But why? You've lived here for such a long time. All your friends are here, your family, Claudia and the children, your business. This is your home.'

Minnie felt herself beginning to choke. 'Many of my friends have left or died. If you haven't noticed, most of my family have left, too. Claudia and her lot will be going for good in August.'

'I'm sorry to hear that. I didn't know.' He turned his head to blow out a stream of smoke. 'But that doesn't mean you shouldn't stay on.'

'What's there to stay on for?'

'For God's sake, Minnie. You have a good life here. You are one of us.'

'That's just it. I'm not one of you any more. When we were still married, I really did feel "one of you". And for a long time afterwards too. But everything is changing, now, and it saddens and unsettles me.'

'Minnie, this is your home,' Darius insisted.

Why is he trying to dissuade me? 'It doesn't feel like home any longer, Darius.' Her voice cracked, and she felt tears hovering. 'Please excuse me, I need to use the bathroom.'

'It's upstairs, second door left on the landing,' he said, pointing towards the first floor. She glanced up. All the upper windows were in darkness. How odd, she thought, as she fled towards the house.

She turned the landing light on before mounting the stairs. By mistake she opened the first door on the left. It was a bedroom. A towel lay on the floor. Light from outside filtered through the window. She crept towards it and peered out. It overlooked the side of the house above the garages. A silver Jag stood on the forecourt, sidelights on, engine gently idling. She thought she recognised it. Somewhere a door creaked, and a silent figure emerged from the shadows, carefully opened the driver's door and looked up towards the house. Minnie jerked back from the window. Her hands felt clammy; her breath came in gasps. The car door clicked. She heard the motor engage and reverse quietly out of the forecourt.

She recognised the man. It was Sorab Manecklal.

The implication of seeing Sorab was like a slap in the face. She stumbled into the bathroom, switched on the light and stared at herself in the mirror. A red tide of anger crept up her neck and cheeks. Tell-tale pieces of mystery fell into place. *How could Darius carry on with the son of my friend? How could he? Oh Lord, and here I was trying to match-make between Claudia and him.* Minnie splashed water on her flushed face and patted it dry, then dabbed eau-de-cologne liberally around her neck and arms. She needed to keep her cool.

'You were up there a long time,' Darius said, his speech slurred. He stood swaying slightly near the edge of the pool, dabbling a foot in the water.

Minnie glanced at the table and noticed with dismay the bottle of Scotch was now half empty.

'I went into the wrong room.'

He seemed a little startled. 'Have another drink. I've just mixed a fresh one.'

She shook her head and leaned against the table.

'Would you like to eat, then?' Darius asked.

'Not just now,' she replied briskly. 'I'll come to the point, Darius. I would like a divorce.'

'Ah! I thought that might be what you had come to ask.'

'It's time this thing was settled, don't you think?' She picked at a small bowl of nuts from the table. Darius lit a cigarette and inhaled deeply. He paced along the edge of the pool. Minnie pulled aside a chair and sat down.

'Darius, do stop walking up and down. You're making me dizzy.'

He stopped in front of her. 'There's something else, isn't there, Minnie?'

'Yes. I would like a reasonable settlement.'

'I see. And what do you call reasonable?' His tone became cold and guarded.

'That would be for our lawyers to negotiate. I would prefer it to be an amicable settlement. I don't want to have to bring up in court the reason for our initial separation.'

Brooding eyes stared at her through the smoke drifting from his nostrils. 'And what would you do with your settlement?'

'I want to go back to Rome.'

'You mean you want to go and live with your lover, Paolo.' He resumed his nervous pacing. 'I can just see it now. A sweet little nest for the two lovebirds.' There was a hard edge to his voice now. He paused in front of her again and brought his face close to hers. His eyes glittered.

'I certainly don't want you to have *my* money so that you can live with him.'

Minnie moved away from him, frightened by Darius's change of mood. His manner had become mean and querulous.

'Don't be ridiculous, Darius. Of course, I'm not going to live with Paolo.'

'But I know that you see him every year.'

'That doesn't mean I'm going to live with him. He won't ever leave his wife or son.'

'Why not? I would have thought he'd do it for you.'

'His wife has never recovered from the tragic accident that happened here. She's physically and mentally ill. And his son is crippled. He'd never abandon them.'

Darius rocked unsteadily on his feet. He took a last drag of the cigarette and flicked the butt into a bush.

'Ah yes, the son. Poor chap. It wasn't meant for him, of course,' Darius mumbled. 'They bungled it, got the wrong man.'

Minnie straightened up sharply. 'They got the wrong man? What on earth do you mean?'

Darius's eyes seemed unfocused and he began to splutter. 'It was the father they were supposed to get, not the son.'

'Supposed to get? What makes you say that? How do you know?'

Darius shrugged and wobbled on shaky legs.

Minnie grabbed his arm. 'How do you know?' She raised her voice. 'Did *you* have anything to do with it?'

Darius tried to smile. He put a hand on her shoulder to steady himself. ''Twas only meant to scare 'em a bit.'

'Oh my God,' Minnie whispered. 'You knew. You arranged it. You set it up. How *could* you?' A crescendo of rage engulfed her. 'You bastard. You fucking bastard.' She made a fist of her right hand and punched him across the face with all her strength. The huge ring on her finger gashed into the side of his nose. Blood spurted out of his nostril and sprayed the front of Minnie's shirt. Darius yelled in surprise and staggered backwards. Minnie raised both hands and shoved him as hard as she could. He teetered, tried to regain his balance, and fell heavily into the pool. Minnie turned and ran to the house. Blind with fury, she rushed into the drawing room, grabbed her handbag off the sofa and dashed out of the front door.

She reversed her car and swung on to the driveway. As she did so, the headlights beamed on to a black car parked almost behind the garage. She had not noticed it from the upstairs window and didn't recognise it. Sweeping out of the gateway on to the road she was gripped by the memory of a similar incident at Juhu all those years ago. It sobered her up and she drove home with care.

Her house was in darkness on arrival. A single light shone over the front door. Nobody was about. Without a sound, she let herself into the hall where she left a note for the driver to get the car washed first thing in the morning. In her bathroom she removed her shirt and tried rinsing off the splatters of blood in the hand basin. Seeing her tired face in the mirror, she noticed one ear-clip was missing. 'Damn it,' she said to her reflection. 'Damn, damn, damn the bloody man!'

She'd look for it in the car the next day. If it wasn't there, she'd have to phone the house. She didn't want to talk to that swine Darius, so she'd have to ask Jeevan to look for it. She was too drained to worry about it now. She took a sleeping pill and went to bed.

She was woken the next morning by a loud knocking. It was ten o'clock.

'What is it, Karsan?'

'Please, memsahib, washerwoman is here for laundry.'

'She's supposed to come tomorrow. What day is it today?'

'Today Thursday, memsahib.'

So it was. Somewhere she had lost track of time. The following Sunday was her birthday. She felt in no mood for celebrations. The rage and frustration from the previous evening glowed like a dull ember in a grate. She arrived late at the shop and told Myrtle she wanted to work undisturbed in the office.

At twelve thirty Myrtle knocked to say Clara was on the phone and needed to speak with her urgently.

'Put her through,' Minnie said, turning off the radio.

'Minnie, have you heard the news yet?' Clara's voice was high with anxiety.

'Yes, you mean Jawaharlal Nehru's death. Isn't it tragic? I've just heard about it on All India radio. It's terrible news. I don't know how this country—'

'No, Minnie, not Nehru,' Clara interrupted. 'The news about Darius.'

Minnie felt anger engulfing her at the mention of his name. 'What about him?' she snapped.

Clara hesitated. 'I don't know how to tell you. It's too awful.'

Fear quickly displaced the anger. 'What is it?'

'Darius is dead. He was killed last night.'

Minnie gasped. Her hands and face turned to ice and she felt light-headed. The voice on the line faded as a loud buzzing filled her ears, and she heard no more. The phone dropped from her hand as she fell forward. Her head hit the desk with a thud.

51

Minnie's first frantic thought when she revived was that she had killed Darius. By the time Clara drove round to be with her, Minnie, though numb with shock, gladly agreed to Clara's insistence to take her to stay at Dolly's for a few days. Minnie sat in stunned silence sharing the grief with her two friends, barely able to control her weeping. She let them talk, but was unable to take anything in.

Overcome with emotion and feeling desperately guilty, she wanted to blurt out to Dolly and Clara what had taken place between her and Darius. But instinct warned her to exercise caution and to keep silent. The sound of anxious comments from the two sisters droned over her like a swarm of bees while she tried to focus clearly on her movements the previous night.

She had driven to Juhu alone. This was not unusual. She often took the car without the driver if she was going short distances to the club or a friend's, or even to the cinema as she had done a couple of evenings earlier. She was certain nobody had seen her at Darius's house. The servants were all out.

She tried to remember what had happened with Darius. It was true there had been a lot of blood from his nose when she hit him, but the blow hadn't been hard enough to cause him a serious injury. True, she *had* pushed him, and he *had* fallen heavily into the pool. It was just possible he could have hit his head on the concrete edge as he fell and drowned. She had not waited to see him surface, but instead had rushed off in a fury.

She worried that Darius might have told someone that she was due to be there. Perhaps the cook, asking him to prepare a meal for two. But hadn't he let the cook and the other servants off for the evening? And although she had caught a glimpse of Sorab Manecklal earlier on, she was sure he had not spotted her. *The chances are he won't have seen my car. Besides, he certainly wouldn't want it known that he was at the scene of the crime. Though, if it came to it, I could vouch that Darius was still alive when he drove away. No, of course not – I'd have to admit to being there myself. Can't do that. Nobody saw what time I got home so I think I'm safe enough*. Minnie rubbed her ring finger, which felt sore, and looked at it. It was bruised and swollen. She sucked in her breath, remembering. *The missing ear-clip – please God, don't let it be found!*

'Minnie dear, here you are,' Clara's voice penetrated the morass churning in her head. She placed a glass of icy gin and tonic on the side table. 'You haven't heard a word of what we've been saying, have you?'

'Forgive me,' Minnie replied, taking out a hanky and dabbing her tears. 'I can't seem to take the news in. I know you've told me, but how was he killed? Could it have been an accident?'

Clara exchanged a look with Dolly. 'No accident. Somebody killed him. The CID inspector said he received severe head injuries and had been punched in the face.'

Minnie's stomach churned. Her hands felt clammy. 'Do they have a suspect?'

'Not yet, but they say it was somebody he knew.'

'How do they know that?'

'There were signs he was expecting a guest. The table by the pool was laid for two, though they only found one glass. He'd been drinking while waiting.'

Minnie frowned and twisted a hanky round and round her finger. 'Where… was the body found? Was it by the pool?' And what had happened to *her* glass?

'They wouldn't say,' Dolly said. 'But they want to take statements from us. From you too, Minnie dear.'

'A statement from me?' Minnie stammered, taking a large gulp from her drink.

'Yes dear, it's routine, you understand. They want to know when we last saw him, what he was like at the time…do we know names of his regular visitors, that kind of thing.'

Minnie swallowed another mouthful. The alcohol steadied her nerves, giving her a measure of calm she badly needed.

'When should I speak to the CID?'

'The inspector will be back here at three to take our statements.' Dolly looked at her watch. 'It's nearly one now, I think we should have lunch.'

Minnie's first impression of Detective Chief Inspector Kulkarni was of a polite and seemingly understanding man. He was portly but unimposing, more like a well-fed merchant than a police officer. He was nearly bald, had unusually bushy eyebrows, and pixie-pointed ears with fleshy lobes. His ready smile showed a marked gap between the two front teeth that gave him a benign appearance. He waved his assistant to an upright chair while he settled himself in the armchair opposite Minnie. Her initial heartening feeling was dispelled as soon as he took out a pair of rimless spectacles and hooked them behind his protruding ears. He removed a sheaf of papers from his briefcase, lifted his head and addressed her. His eyes were unwavering, intelligent, alert, his expression now serious. She wondered why he looked vaguely familiar.

'Madam, when did you last see Mr Dubash?'

Instinctively, Minnie felt she could not underestimate this man as he began his questioning. 'About a month ago, before his visit to Mysore.'

'Not more recently?'

'No, not since his return.'

'When did he return?'

'I don't know. He didn't tell me when.'

'Then you did have contact with him recently?'

'Oh yes, we spoke on the phone at the weekend.'

'I see. What did you talk about?'

'He described his trip.' Minnie crossed her legs. 'We talked about the party my sister-in-law was throwing for my birthday this Sunday. That will be cancelled now, of course.'

The DCI tugged the lobe of his left ear. 'Why did you phone Mr Dubash's secretary a couple of weeks ago saying you needed to speak to him urgently? What was so urgent?'

Minnie was taken aback. How on earth did he know? She had not anticipated this question. Best to tell him part of the truth, she decided. 'I had wanted to speak to him urgently at the time, about a decision concerning my business. On later reflection I thought the matter could wait a while.'

'Would you care to explain?'

Minnie sighed. 'Inspector I have lived here for forty years. As you know, I have a commercial business, but I have recently decided to sell up and return to my home country. I wanted Mr Dubash's advice about possible purchasers before it became public knowledge. He has good contacts.'

'Did you not discuss the matter over the phone when he called?'

'No, it is hardly a subject to discuss over the phone.'

'Presumably, then, you will have arranged to meet?'

'I invited Mr Dubash to my birthday party. We arranged to have a private talk then.'

DCI Kulkarni removed his spectacles and beckoned to his assistant who had been taking notes. He addressed him in a low voice in Hindi, which Minnie couldn't make out. The assistant nodded and resumed his seat.

'Now, Mrs Dubash,' the DCI continued, again pinching his earlobe. 'Can you account for your movements yesterday evening?'

Minnie was prepared for this question and had rehearsed what she was going to say.

'Usually I play cards at the Willingdon Club on Wednesday evenings, but I cancelled it in the morning.' Her voice was steady, and she held his gaze.

'Why was that?'

'I went to the cinema.'

'Which movie did you see?'

'It was *Zorba the Greek* playing at the Eros cinema. It ends today and I didn't want to miss it.'

'Who did you go with?'

'I went alone.'

The DCI looked puzzled. 'Surely it is unusual for a lady to go alone?'

'I often go alone. I love the cinema. My brother in Italy is a film producer and I like to keep up.'

'Indeed, I understand he co-produced Federico Fellini's latest film.'

Minnie tried to hide her astonishment. She straightened her back. *What more does he know about me?* 'How did you know that, Chief Inspector? Few people do.'

'I also am a movie buff, Madam, and your maiden name is quite unusual – it was not difficult to put the two together,' he murmured with a smile. 'But to return to the business in hand, what time did it end?'

'It finished around nine thirty.'

'I will need to check with your driver.'

'He had the night off. I frequently drive myself in the evenings.'

The DCI's lips tightened, the smile quite gone. 'Where did you go after that?'

She explained she had not gone straight home. She had driven to the Willingdon Club to see if she could play a last few rubbers of bridge, but in the event had not actually gone into the clubhouse.

'Why not, madam?'

'There were no parking spaces left near the entrance, only in the overspill car park which has no lighting. I was nervous of walking all the way to the clubhouse and back in the dark, so I drove home.'

'I see.' The DCI tugged his ear again. 'Can anyone verify that you were at the club?'

Minnie shrugged, feeling a bit anxious. 'I don't know. It was late. I didn't see anyone.'

'What time did you reach home?'

'It must have been around ten forty-five, not later. I was in bed by eleven thirty.'

The DCI looked at his sheaf of papers, shuffled a few pages around and replaced them in his briefcase.

'Thank you, Mrs Dubash,' he said, rising to his feet. 'That will be all. You may join the other ladies now. I believe the funeral has been arranged for the day after tomorrow at the Tower of Silence.'

Minnie felt tears smarting her eyes. 'That's correct,' she replied, getting up from the sofa. 'Have you any thoughts who might have killed Mr Dubash?'

'Not yet, Madam, but we know he was expecting a visitor. There will be an inquest, of course. We may need to ask you more questions.'

'Before you go, Mr Kulkarni, may I ask something? Have we met before?'

The DCI gave a small smile. 'Briefly, many years ago, Madam.'

'Really, I don't recall. When was that?'

'In circumstances you may not wish to remember. You were visiting…the "cages" in Grant Road.'

Minnie stared at him in amazement.

'I was working undercover at the time, as a chowkidar, a watchman.'

The memory of that episode flashed up and Minnie realised she needed to tread warily in her dealings with him.

'It's a small world, Mr Kulkarni,' she said with a forced smile.

At the door he turned to her again. 'I trust you are not planning to go out of Bombay at any time, Mrs Dubash?'

The veiled command in the DCI's voice sent a shiver down her spine. She sensed that this insignificant-looking man was like a terrier dog. He would not let go. The matter was far from closed.

'No, of course not, I shall be available whenever you wish.'

Minnie was left feeling like a piece of chewed string. She was certain DCI Kulkarni saw through the story she had decided to give, but she had stuck to it. Now she had to keep her nerve and hope for the best.

She was trembling by the time she got back to Dolly and Clara in the sitting room where tea was waiting for her. She felt more strongly than ever that she needed to tell somebody what had happened. She couldn't bear to keep the knowledge to herself.

'Dolly, if dinner is not until eight, I'd like to pop round to Mother Serafina at the convent.'

*

It all spilled out with Serafina – now promoted to the position of Mother Superior of the convent. Minnie left out nothing. She told her how angry she had been with Darius; how frightened she was when she heard the news; how she believed herself to be responsible for his death; how she lied to the CID about seeing him the night he was killed.

'I don't know what to do now, Serafina,' she said. 'I don't think they believed me. If I tell them the truth, they will certainly think I did it. How could I prove I did not? I'm sure they must have found the ear-clip I lost. That's why they are playing a cat-and-mouse game with me. I know it. I feel it.'

'My dear Maria Erminia, dear child, don't get yourself in such a state.' Mother Serafina patted Minnie's arm. Her voice was soothing and comforting. 'You are being a bit paranoid. All right, perhaps it was not the wisest thing to lie to the CID, particularly if they find your ear-clip. But what is done is done. Don't anticipate anything that may not happen.'

'What am I to do?'

'My dear, don't do anything. If your conscience is clear you don't have to worry. Pray, my dear. Pray to the Lord to see you through this hard time. I too will pray for you. Remember, I am always here if you need me.'

Minnie returned to Dolly's house in a calmer state.

Dinner was a sombre affair. Jimmy's day had been turned upside down trying to deal with Roshan, the police, the post-mortem and the funeral arrangements. He did not talk much and took two phone calls during the meal. Above all he was deeply saddened. More than once tears came to his eyes. Dolly could not control herself and kept bursting into sobs. Minnie found she too had to struggle hard to overcome her tears. Only Clara remained relatively collected.

'We've postponed the birthday party in the circumstances, Minnie,' she said.

'Of course, that is absolutely right. I'd quite forgotten about the party.'

The funeral took place two days after DCI Kulkarni's visit, following the post-mortem. Minnie caught sight of Satish among the mourners dressed in white, as they walked in pairs thirty yards behind the corpse-bearers up the hill to the Tower of Silence. He looked utterly wretched and bereft. She felt sorry for him, realising his loss and sense of anguish were every bit as painful as hers and Jimmy's and Roshan's.

Minnie returned to her own house the day after the funeral. She felt she would be better off alone in familiar surroundings and spent the time dealing with messages of sympathy. On impulse, recalling Satish's grief-stricken face, she sat at her desk and wrote him a letter of condolence and told the bearer to deliver it by hand.

On Sunday she received a cable wishing her a happy birthday and a huge bunch of red roses from Paolo. She had not had time to tell him the news about Darius. She would have to phone him that evening. There were greetings telegrams, cards and flowers from other friends abroad who also had not heard.

She took a phone call from the CID. Her heart sank as she spoke to DCI Kulkarni. He wished to interview her again and arranged to call on her the following day.

One more delivery arrived in mid-morning. It was from the florist at the Taj Mahal Hotel. A cellophane-wrapped spray tied with white satin ribbon enclosed a single long-stemmed orchid with a profusion of orange-yellow flowers along its stalk. Each perfect waxy petal glowed like an ember against a bed of white tissue paper. Minnie felt faint, the blood draining from her face as she stroked the familiar bloom and her vision blurred. A tear ran to the corner of her mouth and she licked it away, tasting its saltiness. A note was tucked in the folds of the tissue with her name scratched on a heavy cream envelope in the broad black strokes of Darius's handwriting. She slit it open and pulled out his monogrammed card.

Dearest Minnie,

Do you remember this? The Dendrobium Burana Fancy – 'Heartsflame'.

I send this on your sixtieth birthday to say how sorry I am that things did not work out between us; sorry for what happened, for the harm I caused you, for the deep hurt you suffered. I want you to know that despite the choices I made, you are the only woman I have ever truly loved. You believed in me when no one else did. You were and are always important to me, always my inspiration and forever a part of my life. It was an honour and a privilege to have had your love and it means a great deal to me that we are still friends. I wish you many years of health and happiness.

With the greatest affection, ever yours,
Darius

Minnie broke down completely and wept from the depths of her heart.

*

By early evening she felt calm enough to get ready for dinner at Dolly's house. While she was running the bath, the bearer knocked on the bedroom door.

'Please to come in, memsahib?'

'Yes, Karsan, come in. What is it?' she asked.

'Please, memsahib,' he said. 'Small packet come for you.'

That would be from Bobby, Minnie smiled. He had remembered after all. She came out of the bathroom and took the packet from the bearer's hand. She turned it round and around. It was hard, the size of a cigarette packet and wrapped in brown paper. There was no name, no postage stamp.

'Where's the letter?' she asked, puzzled.

'No letter, mem. Only packet.'

It was not from Bobby after all. 'Who brought it? Did they leave a message?'

'Satish sahib driver brought. No message. Only say please give to memsahib *ekdum* quick,' he said, leaving the room and shutting the door behind him.

Slowly Minnie unwrapped the package, more mystified than ever. It was a small green cardboard box. She opened the lid.

In the centre, nestling on white tissue paper, lay her missing ear-clip.

52

Within a few days, Darius's solicitors got in touch with her about his will. All the family had been summoned to his office. Jimmy, Dolly, Roshan, Clara and, to Minnie's surprise, Satish Desai. When they were settled round the table, the solicitor began reading out the will.

There were no surprises. Jimmy was left a collection of first edition books. He was made literary executor of Darius's work, along with Satish. Dolly got paintings, as did Clara; Roshan was bequeathed the house she and Darius had shared, plus a substantial sum for her charitable trust for stray animals. Minnie was moved to learn that Darius had remembered Claudia and Bobby with a bequest of fifty thousand rupees each. She herself was left the house she lived in, plus a continuance of alimony payments, so long as she remained domiciled in Bombay.

A one-million-rupee fund was left to start a foundation to help new writers, artists and poets, to be administered jointly by Jimmy and Satish.

There was a pause before the solicitor continued. All eyes turned to him.

'Lastly, my house at Juhu and its contents, and the residue of my estate in its entirety, to my dear friend and companion Satish Desai.'

There was a gasp from Clara. Everyone turned to look at Satish. His face was drained of colour and he looked in shock. Satish would be exceedingly wealthy now.

Clara leaned forward to look at the lawyer. 'It's not fair!' She turned to Minnie. 'Surely you will contest the will, Minnie, won't you?' she asked point blank.

Minnie knew that as Darius's long separated – but not divorced – spouse, she could contest the will. But to what good? Fleetingly she weighed up the consequences of such an action. Despite what many thought of her motives at the time, it was never for his money that she had married Darius. Why would she want it now? Money could not replace the rapture and excitement of their early days, nor make right the heartache and misery she had endured later with him. There was no fight left in her for a contestation. She had other worries on her plate now.

Minnie glanced at Satish sitting across the table from her and held his look for a long moment. He appeared lost and troubled, and in as much a state of shock as she was. She wondered if he was thinking about the missing ear-clip. He need not have returned it to her.

She took a deep breath. It was time to draw a line in the sand.

'No, Clara, I will not contest the will,' she replied firmly.

The enquiry into Darius's murder continued for six months. DCI Kulkarni kept returning to the house for more talks. Minnie was aware that with his careful, clever questions he was trying to find a chink in her account of events that would connect her to the scene of the crime. She knew that *he* knew she had been there that evening. Even now that her missing ear-clip was back in her possession she still lived in fear that he might find other evidence to place her at the beach house. She stuck to her story, but as time went on, she thought she sounded less convincing.

During this time, Minnie seriously set about trying to dispose of her business. It proved not to be as difficult as she had first imagined. By a stroke of luck her partner, Myrtle Pereira, decided to buy her out, although not for the asking price. Minnie knew that Myrtle had got a bargain, but she no longer had the will or energy to hold out for more. Darius's death had profoundly affected her and the cat-and-mouse game she sensed the inspector was playing kept her in a state of constant tension. There were days when she felt at the end of her tether and all she longed for was to leave everything behind and escape to somewhere, anywhere. She was no longer in love with Bombay or its life. Maybe it was her imagination, but she thought that even her relations with Dolly and Jimmy were under strain. She felt lonely and frightened.

The enquiry seemed to Minnie to be unending. She was harassed most days by reporters wanting a story, and photographers followed her everywhere. The police seemed no further forward in finding the perpetrator of the murder and as time went on Minnie's sense of disquiet increased.

Then one day it all stopped.

DCI Kulkarni came to visit her yet again. Minnie ordered tea to be brought to them on the veranda.

'I understand you have sold your business, Mrs Dubash,' he said.

'How do you know that, Chief Inspector? I have told nobody.' She was afraid he would reiterate that she should not think of leaving the country.

His eyes gleamed with intelligence. 'It is my business to know many things, madam. But that is not what I came to say.' He picked up his cup and slurped the tea noisily. 'An excellent tea, if I may say. Moodi's Nilgiri blend, I believe?'

'You certainly know your teas, Mr Kulkarni.' Minnie marvelled again at his knowledge.

'Amongst other things, madam. We all have our specialities, isn't that so?' He tilted his head and looked at her for a moment, sucked up the last of the tea and put the cup back on the saucer.

'Now for the reason I have come. It is about the case of Mr Dubash, deceased.'

Minnie stiffened.

'The enquiry is to be wound up.'

'Wound up? What do you mean?'

'The case is closed. My superiors have concluded that we have come to the end of our searches. There will be an open verdict of death caused by person or persons unknown.'

'But, but…I don't understand.' Minnie was taken back. 'Last time we spoke I thought you seemed fairly sure you would be making an arrest shortly.'

The inspector lowered his eyes and flicked at a speck on his trousers. 'It seems it was a false trail. No, my superiors are satisfied that the case is concluded.' He paused. 'It is my opinion the murderer was an itinerant person, a gipsy, a Hijra perhaps, high on bhang, asking for money. Mr Dubash was known to be generous, but he often associated with undesirables. As you are no doubt aware, madam.' He gave her a meaningful look. 'Also, he was rather authoritarian. Perhaps the man insisted on more than Mr Dubash was prepared to give, he was dismissive, a fight ensued…who knows?' The inspector shrugged his shoulders. 'Nobody heard, nobody saw, anything. No witness has come forward. The killer would have slipped away in the dark and disappeared into the shanty towns. It is like looking for one particular blade of grass in a cricket field.'

'But why, Chief Inspector? Considering all your effort. It doesn't make sense to me.'

'Madam, we all have to take orders from our superiors. Some matters are best left…what is the expression? "Let sleeping dogs lie."' He cleared his throat. 'Mr Dubash had powerful connections,' he murmured.

Minnie folded her hands. *So that is it: the family has intervened.*

The DCI rose from his seat and picked up his cap. 'I am to retire soon, madam, so I shall not see you again. I am sorry, I realise it is distressing for you – and the rest of the family of course – not to find a culprit. But as things stand, I can safely say that you are free to leave the country at any time, if you so wish.'

'Thank you, Chief Inspector,' Minnie replied in a daze, getting up.

'I wish you a safe journey, madam.'

DCI Kulkarni joined the palms of his hands together and raised them to his forehead in a deep *namaste*, the traditional Hindu gesture of farewell.

Book Three

53

1994

Minnie did not know what snapped her out of the nightmare, gasping for breath, heart pounding with fear. Was it the screech of peacocks? Or the crash of monsoon thunder? She listened. Not a sound pierced the black, velvety silence. Then the clang of a church bell tolling the half hour brought her back to the present. To her room, at the convent, in Rome.

The bed sheet was twisted tightly around one leg. She tried untangling it, but the effort sent pain shooting into her swollen knees. She turned slowly on to her back and stared into the dark, waiting for the spasm to subside. The luminous dial of the alarm clock gave out a green glow. Half past three. Her eyelids drooped but she forced them to stay open. It had been a long time since she had had that same nightmare.

'Go away,' she whispered into the dark. 'Stop tormenting me, Darius. You know I didn't do it.'

She had dreamt about him again. She saw him lying at the bottom of the swimming pool, his handsome face looking at her from under the surface. The water was clear aquamarine except for pale red swirls around his floating hair. He was smiling and his lips moved. She saw herself shaking her head and backing away from the edge, but his hand shot out and grabbed her leg. That was when she woke up, panting. The dream was so vivid she could sense his presence in the room.

'Darius, please,' she murmured, 'after all this time, can't you let go? I'm sorry for what happened. You didn't deserve to go like that. But I've told you repeatedly I only pushed you that night, nothing more. You know who it was, and it wasn't me. I'm so tired, Darius. Why don't you leave me alone?'

There had been too much excitement in the previous couple of days, what with the family gathering to celebrate her nineteenth birthday and her interview for the BBC with Francesca. She was emotionally and physically exhausted. Her granddaughter's questions had churned up memories best forgotten and now they danced and leapt about in her mind like swifts swooping and rising in the sky. *Maybe I shouldn't have given Francesca all those letters to read. Though strictly speaking I didn't give all of them. No, she must not read* that *one.*

Her leg felt as if it were gripped in a vice. Minnie sighed. It was hard to believe those last months in Bombay following Darius's death happened thirty years ago. The events still seemed so vivid to her. She shifted position in bed, trying to ease her aching joints. It was exceptionally warm for this time of year and the heat always seemed to make her arthritis worse. The church bell struck four times. Without her hearing aid in, it sounded muffled and far away, barely audible. She was wide awake now. Soon she would put on the bedside light, take a Voltarol for the pain and try to read a bit.

She couldn't concentrate on reading. She tried to make order of the jumbled thoughts crowding her mind. She would have to tell Francesca about the poems. It had been a secret for too long.

It was Paolo's suggestion that had made her decide to have them published when her finances became depleted. She would not have thought of it herself. And Michele had made all the arrangements so that she would remain anonymous. She was terribly proud of Michele, as if he were her own son. He had fought against his handicap, taken a law degree at Rome University, gone to Harvard to do a Masters, and was now one of the most sought-after lawyers specialising in international law. He had not been able to attend her birthday celebration but phoned to say he would come to see her soon. He looked so much like his father. Her Paolo. Her beloved, darling Paolo.

'Thank you, dear Lord, for having given me Paolo,' she whispered. How lucky she had been to have loved and been loved by that wonderful, steadfast, honourable man. After Tina died, they spent fourteen of the happiest years together on his smallholding in Fara Sabina outside Rome. Not that far from this convent.

'Who would have thought you would make a farmer's wife?' she remembered Paolo teasing her as they sat sipping wine in the shade of the olive trees overlooking rows of tomatoes that would need picking the next day.

'You mean a farmer's concubine more like?' Minnie laughed.

'Whose fault is that? It's not as if I haven't asked you to marry me.'

'I know, sweetheart. But you know my reasons.'

'Michele would be delighted.'

'But Luigi wouldn't. He would probably say I was marrying you for your tomatoes!'

'Think about it, Minnie my darling. Apart from anything, I want you to have the security.'

Minnie smiled, but said nothing.

'Your finances are pretty dire,' Paolo said gently. 'After you lost all that money from the sale of your business and—'

'Please, my love, don't remind me,' Minnie cut in with a touch of bitterness. 'One of the more foolish things of my life was to trust Dadaji to get the money out from India through the black market.'

Paolo patted her hand and she laced her mud-stained fingers through his. 'I should have done it officially, through the Reserve Bank. When he died so unexpectedly, I couldn't believe the money simply vanished with him!' She sighed. 'It's no good crying over spilt milk. I don't want to talk about it again, Paolo.'

'*Tesoro mio*, you have to face facts,' Paolo said. 'You don't even own a house or an apartment. If we marry, and anything happens to me, you *must* have a property in your name.'

'I can sell my jewellery.'

Paolo leaned towards her. 'Your jewellery wouldn't be enough, my love.' He took her chin in his hand, turning her face towards him. 'You have to sell those poems.'

'Darius's poems? Never, I couldn't do that,' Minnie replied in a shocked voice.

'You must. Please listen to me. It's essential. I believe they may be worth a lot.'

They *were* worth a great deal of money, she found out; more than enough to buy her a lovely little apartment. When Paolo became ill, they sold the apartment and the farm and moved to the convent. And after Paolo died, Michele had advised her on sound investments, which had allowed her to live on here in comfort and style. She had a lot to be grateful for.

Minnie spent most of the next morning with Francesca and the rest of the interview. She had dressed carefully, put on her make-up, and looked elegant and alert. After it was over, they celebrated with a glass of sherry.

'I think I could get used to being a TV star,' she said to her granddaughter. 'How much do they pay?'

Francesca laughed. 'The BBC are notoriously stingy, don't count on it.'

'Listen, darling, I have to tell you something. Strictly off the record.'

'You sound serious, Nonna.'

'Have you ever wondered how I managed to afford living in a place like this? It's not cheap, I can tell you.'

'Of course, we've all wondered. We assumed Paolo had made adequate provisions.'

'It's not like that. I never took anything from Paolo, except his love. It's something else. I know you've read most of Darius's poems. Have you read the letters I gave you?'

'A few. There hasn't been time to go through them all.'

'There's one I didn't give you.' She blinked and wiped her glasses. 'Hand me that dictionary.'

Francesca fetched a brown leather-bound dictionary from the desk. It was worn and the pages were yellow with age.

Minnie laughed at her mystified expression. 'I know, you think I should throw this away. But my father gave it to me the day that I left Italy for India. It has never left me. Here.' She drew out an envelope from the back, it too rather yellow. She extracted a card from it and a sheet of paper with broad handwriting in ink that was bronzed with age. 'Read these.'

Francesca took the papers. A faded yellow orchid, tissue thin, was stuck to the card.

Minnie,

Roses are traditional for rose-like women. But you are no rose. You are this orchid: rare, exquisite, dazzling, mysterious, unique: the Dendrobium Burana Fancy called 'Heartsflame'.

Darius

Next, she unfolded the piece of brittle paper.

To my beautiful Minnie, my deepest love, my inspiration, my muse, my true Heartsflame, I dedicate this poem.

There followed a poem that Francesca read and reread. At length she looked at her grandmother in awe and handed them back.

'So, you were Heartsflame. That series of poems published posthumously were yours, weren't they? You were the anonymous donor, Nonna?'

Minnie nodded, smiling quietly.

'Why did you never say so?' Francesca handed the papers back to Minnie.

Minnie sighed. 'It was a private matter, darling. The poems were personal. I didn't want the exposure. The public's curiosity would have focused on me. I didn't want to rake up the way he died. This was how I wanted to remember him, not what he became later.'

She returned the papers to the envelope and slipped it in the back of the dictionary. 'I'll keep it for now. When I'm gone, you can have the letter. But promise to keep it safe.'

After lunch Francesca said goodbye. She was due to fly back to London the next morning and would not have time to return to the convent in the evening.

'I'll see you in a month or two, Nonna. Be good until then. And thanks for the letters. What are you going to do this afternoon?'

'I'll take a little walk after five, go and visit Paolo and tell him all that's happened. In the evening I'm playing bridge.'

Francesca laughed and bent to kiss Minnie's cheek. 'You still talk to him as if he were alive. Mind how you go and do take the walking stick with you, Nonna, don't forget.'

Minnie laughed. 'Go on, darling. Drive carefully. Let's have more interviews when you come back. I really enjoy them, and there's lots more to tell.' She went to the balcony and watched Francesca climb into the car. How she loved her granddaughter – so clever, so beautiful, so kind. She waved goodbye. *I must introduce her to Michele's son next time. Such a handsome, clever young man. Just right for her.* Minnie smiled at the prospect. *Ah well! Time now for my siesta.*

Francesca went shopping before returning to her parents' apartment in the early evening. They had flown back to their home in Geneva the previous day and it was wonderful to have the place to herself. She made a few phone calls, poured herself a drink, took it through to the bathroom and enjoyed a long, perfumed soak in the bath. She was towelling her hair dry when the phone rang.

'Signora Claudia?' a man's hesitant voice said at the end of the line.

'No, the Signora is not here. I am her daughter, Francesca. Who is calling?'

'This is Dr Morelli speaking from the Convento Santa Teresa. I must speak to Signora Claudia. It is about her mother, Signora Minnie.'

'Signora Claudia is abroad. If it's about my grandmother, can I help?'

'Signorina Francesca, you must come to the convent straight away. There has been an accident.'

Francesca's heart contracted with fear. 'What's happened, Doctor? Is my grandmother ill?'

'She is in a serious condition. I cannot explain on the phone. Please come straight away.'

'I'll be there in half an hour.'

Francesca threw on her clothes, rushed out of the building and drove like a demon through the early evening traffic. She arrived to find the convent in turmoil. Sister Serafina was in tears and seemed to have shrunk to half her already tiny size. The Mother Superior was ashen-faced and two of the nuns were shaking and sobbing. Thoroughly alarmed by now, Francesca accompanied the Mother Superior to her parlour where she was introduced to Dr Morelli.

'Doctor, please tell me what's going on. I left my grandmother a few hours ago and she was perfectly alright.'

'Signorina, I am very sorry to tell you that – that your grandmother was in an accident this afternoon. You must prepare yourself.' He looked troubled. 'We did all we could, but her injuries were too great. We could not save her.'

'Is she…dead?'

'I'm very, very sorry.'

Francesca felt her throat tighten and tears filled her eyes. 'But she cannot be dead. What injuries? What happened? Please tell me.'

The doctor remained silent. Mother Superior spoke.

'Signora Minnie was walking back from the cemetery around five o'clock. She often went there to visit, to put flowers, to see…'

'Yes, Mother, I know about her visits to Signor Della Croce's grave.'

'She was walking back on the gravel avenue. Her hearing aid was not switched on. She didn't hear…'

'What didn't she hear?'

'The car.'

'But cars are not allowed to use the avenue after five.'

'That's true. No public cars. But the sisters use it for their driving lessons.'

Francesca's eyes widened. She sat quite still, hands clasped in her lap.

'Sister Clotilda was having a driving practice. Your grandmother did not hear the car. Clotilda was driving slowly, but she didn't see Signora Minnie until the last moment.' Mother Superior drew a deep breath and shut her eyes. 'She pressed the accelerator instead of the brake.'

Francesca's hands flew to her mouth.

'Your grandmother died shortly after.'

Francesca's breathing came short and fast. She rocked back and forth in the chair.

'What happened to Sister Clotilda?'

'She was taken to hospital in a state of collapse. She has been heavily sedated. The police will question her when she can talk.'

Francesca nodded, tears trickling down her cheeks.

'The funeral arrangements… Who will…?'

Mother Superior interrupted gently. 'I took the liberty of phoning the funeral director we use. I said you would speak to him about your wishes. Signora Minnie expressed to me her desire to be buried next to Signor Della Croce. They had adjoining plots.'

'Thank you, Mother. I will speak to the funeral director after I inform my family.' She wiped her eyes with the back of her hand. 'First I would like to see my grandmother.'

Sometime later she found herself in the room, looking at Minnie lying on the bed seemingly asleep. There was not a blemish on her. Two nuns were praying at the bedside but rose and left the room when she entered. Francesca sat by the bed, tears rolling down her cheeks, but it was not until she touched Minnie's thin, icy fingers that she realised fully that Minnie was gone. She looked for a tissue. A small photo of Paolo stood on the bedside table. The brown leather dictionary lay beside it. She picked it up and read the copperplate writing on the flyleaf. *To my dearest daughter, Minnie, at the start of her big adventure, from her loving papa. Remember us always.* Turning to the back she found the first 'Heartsflame' poem she had read that very morning. But there was another envelope with a letter folded inside. She drew it out.

The handwriting was not Darius's. It was dated 27 May 1970.

My dear Minnie,

By the time you receive this letter, you will have heard the news. I cannot leave without putting a few matters straight. Do you know, when my world crashed, you were the only person outside my few friends who sent me a letter of condolence? You and I both loved Darius and he loved both of us, each differently. You knew what he was like: charming and kind, tortured and cruel, weak but resilient, a dichotomy, passionate, but all too often insensitive to others. And he was so charismatic and talented. Without him my life is nothing, nothing at all. I cannot bear the emptiness any longer.

After your ear-clip was returned, you must have wondered, and perhaps guessed, what happened that night. Yet you said nothing, you hinted nothing.

> *You kept silent. Even after the will was read out, in which you were left so little. You could have contested it like the others suggested. It was your right to do so; you were not divorced, after all. You could have gained a lot more if you had. But you did not.*
>
> *I was there at Juhu that night, of course. You saw my car. I was watching. I saw him with Sorab. I saw Sorab leave; saw him getting into his car. I saw you. I saw you hit Darius. He was all right, not badly hurt; he simply got a bloody nose, a soaking and a bruised ego.*
>
> *Do you know what he was going to do? After all our years together! He said they meant nothing to him. He was going to leave me for Sorab. It was more than I could bear. I couldn't let him do that. I loved him too much.*
>
> *In the end I didn't let him do it.*
>
> *I feel that my inheritance should have been yours by right. I also know you will not accept it now. And so, I have put it into a trust for Claudia and Bobby and their heirs. Darius truly loved them and so it will seem to have been left to them by him.*
>
> *Yours,*
> *Satish Desai*

A small newspaper cutting, sepia with age, was attached to the back of the letter. It was from *The Times of India*, dated 30 May 1970.

> *Mr Satish Desai, the energetic and talented editor of* Heritage *magazine, was found dead in his home today. Death was self-inflicted from a gunshot wound to the head. He had been suffering from depression for some time.*

Francesca slipped the papers into the envelope, placed it back in the dictionary, and put the dictionary under Minnie's hand. She took a last look around the room and made for the door but stopped, frowning. Supposing the nuns or the undertaker threw the dictionary away, she thought. It was a battered old thing. Worse still, supposing they read the letters. She couldn't allow that to happen. She had promised her grandmother. She returned to the bed, picked up the dictionary, scooped Paolo's photo from the bedside table and put both into her handbag.

Her eyes brimmed with tears as she took a last look at her grandmother's serene face. Then she left the room.

Acknowledgements

This book would never have seen the light of day had it not been for the encouragement and help I received from several people. Firstly, thanks to David Almond, my tutor at two Arvon Foundation courses I attended. His kind observations made me feel I could be a writer. Next, thanks to Louise Green, my excellent creative writing tutor and friend; to Helen Hart for her friendship and sound advice given long before she started SilverWood; to Ali Reynolds who got me to cut out unnecessary waffle and characters – my big failing; to Catherine Blom-Smith for her help and guidance; to my two writing groups in Bristol and Johannesburg from whose members I learnt much. And to Anthony, for giving me a much-needed push to get the work published.

Lightning Source UK Ltd.
Milton Keynes UK
UKHW010142050121
376396UK00006B/1445